Praise for Valerie Hansen and her novels

"Her Brother's Keeper is a fascinating look at long-buried secrets."
—*RT Book Reviews*

"Valerie Hansen's story offers a heartwarming romance with enough suspense to keep the pages turning."
—*RT Book Reviews* on *Out of the Depths*

"Kudos to Valerie Hansen for writing an exceptional story with a puzzle that's nearly impossible to solve."
—*RT Book Reviews* on *Hidden in the Wall*

"Interesting characters and plenty of action and suspense."
—*RT Book Reviews* on *Nightwatch*

VALERIE HANSEN
Her Brother's Keeper

Out of the Depths

Love Inspired

LOVE INSPIRED BOOKS

Recycling programs
for this product may
not exist in your area.

ISBN-13: 978-0-373-65154-2

HER BROTHER'S KEEPER AND OUT OF THE DEPTHS
Copyright © 2012 by Harlequin Books S.A.

The publisher acknowledges the copyright holder
of the individual works as follows:

HER BROTHER'S KEEPER
Copyright © 2005 by Valerie Whisenand

OUT OF THE DEPTHS
Copyright © 2006 by Valerie Whisenand

www.LoveInspiredBooks.com

Printed in U.S.A.

CONTENTS

Books by Valerie Hansen

Love Inspired Suspense

*Her Brother's Keeper
*Out of the Depths
Deadly Payoff
*Shadow of Turning
Hidden in the Wall
*Nowhere to Run
*No Alibi
*My Deadly Valentine
   "Dangerous Admirer"
Face of Danger
†Nightwatch
The Rookie's Assignment
†Threat of Darkness

Love Inspired

*The Perfect Couple
*Second Chances
*Love One Another
*Blessings of the Heart
*Samantha's Gift
*Everlasting Love
The Hamilton Heir
*A Treasure of the Heart
Healing the Boss's Heart

*Serenity, Arkansas
†The Defenders

Love Inspired Historical

Frontier Courtship
Wilderness Courtship
High Plains Bride
The Doctor's Newfound Family
Rescuing the Heiress

VALERIE HANSEN

was thirty when she awoke to the presence of the Lord in her life and turned to Jesus. In the years that followed, she worked with young children, both in church and secular environments. She also raised a family of her own and played foster mother to a wide assortment of furred and feathered critters.

Married to her high school sweetheart since age seventeen, she now lives in an old farmhouse she and her husband renovated with their own hands. She loves to hike the wooded hills behind the house and reflect on the marvelous turn her life has taken. Not only is she privileged to reside among the loving, accepting folks in the breathtakingly beautiful Ozark mountains of Arkansas, she also gets to share her personal faith by telling the stories of her heart for all of the Love Inspired Books lines.

Life doesn't get much better than that!

HER BROTHER'S KEEPER

For we walk by faith, not by sight.
Therefore, if any man be in Christ,
he is a new creature: old things are passed away;
behold, all things are become new.
—*2 Corinthians* 5:7, 17

To Franci—your kindness, forbearance and selfless love during tremendously difficult circumstances showed all of us God's love in action.
Bless you for being you.

Prologue

Rebecca Tate leaned against the edge of the phone booth outside Serenity's only grocery store and dialed the last of the four numbers on her list. Thankfully, the name scrawled on the back of the old photograph had been very unusual. If it had been something like Jones, instead of Keringhoven, she would have been overwhelmed with choices.

Ringing began. Becky's throat tightened. She'd told herself it was silly to get so excited, yet she couldn't help anticipating success with every call.

From the time she'd been old enough to ask questions, she'd wondered about her origins, about the family she'd never known. Aunt Effie had done a wonderful job of raising her. But that didn't stop her curiosity. All Becky wanted was the truth. Effie had told her so many wild, fanciful stories about her parents, especially lately, that she couldn't tell what to believe.

She was subconsciously counting the third ring when a gruff male voice interrupted with "Hello?"

His irate tone put Becky off so much she completely forgot the polite introductory speech she'd used when she'd made her earlier calls. Instead, she launched right into her story. "Mr. Keringhoven? You don't know me, but maybe you can help. I found an old photograph. It's of a family, standing by a Christmas tree. The woman looks like me and I thought…"

"What are you calling me for?"

"Be-because there was a last name on the back of the picture. Your name. And my birthday is right before Christmas, so I thought maybe—"

The man cursed. "Who are you?"

If he'd sounded even slightly amiable she'd have told him. It was the rancor sizzling through the line that kept her from speaking frankly.

"It doesn't matter. I'm sorry to have bothered you."

"Wait!"

Becky slammed the receiver down to silence his expletives. She was trembling. If that awful person was any example of what her real family was like, she was glad Aunt Effie had been the one to take her in after she was orphaned.

The list of phone numbers she'd gleaned from a search on the Internet fluttered to the ground. Becky snatched up the paper and crumpled it into a tight ball before tossing it into the trash can next to the soda pop machine. She was done looking for relatives, distant or otherwise. If Effie wasn't going to tell her the whole truth about her parents, then she'd be satisfied with what little she did know.

Besides, if the Good Lord had wanted her to make contact with her extended family, as she'd thought when she'd first stumbled across the old photograph, she'd have succeeded. Clearly, such a reunion wasn't in God's plans. The sooner she accepted that, the better off everyone would be.

Chapter One

"**S**he's what? Oh, dear. Hold on."

Becky covered the telephone receiver with her free hand and swiveled the desk chair to face her boss. "It's Aunt Effie, again. She's dragging a ladder out of the garage and the neighbors are worried."

Brother Fleming arched his bushy gray eyebrows and rolled his eyes. "Knowing Effie, I can certainly understand why."

"So can I. I'm sorry. I know you wanted me here to meet your friend this afternoon but I'd better run home. I'll get Effie calmed down and hurry back as soon as I can, I promise."

The portly preacher nodded. "Don't worry about it. Brother Malloy will understand. There'll be plenty of time for you two to get acquainted before I actually retire."

Grabbing her purse, Becky gave him a parting smile. "I'm going to miss you, you old softy. Who else would put up with a secretary who's always taking time off in the middle of the day?"

"Logan Malloy will," Fleming said. "I've already told him a little about your home situation. He's a good man. He'll support you—at least for the short time he's going to be here helping us out."

She'd reached the office door. "You really don't think he'll want to stay permanently? I don't see why he wouldn't."

Fred Fleming shrugged. "Brother Logan is more suited to city life. After Chicago, Serenity's bound to be too dull for him."

"Dull? This place? Not with Aunt Effie around." She patted her ample shoulder bag. "If you need me for anything, call me on my cell phone. I've got it right here."

"Better leave me the number then."

"It's on the Rolodex on your desk. Remember?" No wonder she was so good at coping with her forgetful aunt, Becky mused. In the last couple of years she'd gotten plenty of practice by looking after her absentminded boss.

He nodded sagely. "Of course, of course. Well, get going, young lady. Don't worry. I'll find it."

Becky wasn't so sure. She delayed just long enough to flip through the file and tag her number with a sticky note, then hurried to the door and flung it open.

It didn't swing smoothly. There was a thud and a hesitation, followed by "Ow!"

She would have lost her balance if she hadn't had a hold on the doorknob. She saw a man's fingers curl around the outer edge of the solid oak door. Moments later, half his face peered past it, revealing one deep brown eye.

She gasped. "Oh, I'm *so* sorry."

The man stepped fully into the doorway and blocked her path. He was covering his nose with his hand but even so, she could tell this was one good-looking accident victim.

She tried to dodge past him and failed. "Please excuse me. I'm really in a hurry."

"Obviously. I'd hate to think it's always this dangerous to visit Fred."

Behind her, Becky heard her boss's exclamation of joy. "Logan! Welcome. Come in, come in. You're early, my boy."

Boy? Where? Becky's gaze traveled swiftly across the man's broad chest, checked out the shoulders of his sport coat, and sped back to his face. So, this was the Logan Malloy she'd heard so much about. Well, well! The singles classes at Serenity Chapel were sure going to fill up when the women in town got an eyeful of him.

"I'm Rebecca Tate," she said, grabbing Logan's hand and shaking it very briefly. "Pleased to meet you. I really do have to hurry. Family emergency. Fred will explain everything. Excuse me?"

Wondering how the doorway had shrunk since the

last time she'd passed through, she sidled by him and hurried down the hallway.

Logan chuckled as he watched her disappear around a corner, then sobered and turned to Fred. "Was that the one? She has the right reddish hair and blue eyes."

"Yes, that's her," the older man said. "She and her aunt are the only ones I know who fit the profile you gave me."

"Does she know what we suspect?"

Brother Fleming crossed the room and quietly closed the door before he answered. "No. And I want you to promise me you'll keep it that way until you're absolutely positive. I wouldn't have gotten involved if I didn't care what happens to her."

"I told you I'd do my best."

"Do better than your best," Fred said. "She's a very special person. I don't want to see her hurt."

Logan's voice was firm. "Neither do I."

Until recently, Becky had thought her job as church secretary was perfect. She loved working for gray-haired, disorganized, gentle Brother Fleming. Except for her aunt's failing mental health, her biggest worry in life had been correcting spelling errors in the pastor's monthly newsletter, or making sure his necktie wasn't decorated with the remnants of his latest meal. There were times when the sweet old guy drove her crazy but she loved him like a father. Unfortunately, Fred had decided to retire and had invited an interim pastor to stand in for him until the church pulpit committee could find a permanent replacement.

Though she'd only seen Logan Malloy for a brief moment after smacking him in the nose with the door, there was something about him that gave her pause. He was far younger than Brother Fred. And much better looking. But it was more than that—a jittery feeling she couldn't quite explain. But one thing she *was* certain of: any woman in town under the age of ninety-nine was going to be beating down the church doors to meet the new temporary preacher.

She pulled up and parked in front of the old stone house she shared with Effie. It was small but adequate for the two of them, and the yard gave her aunt plenty of opportunity to garden. Effie's spring peonies were in full bloom, their heavy blossoms weighing down the branches till they almost touched the ground. One good Arkansas storm and those petals would fall like floral confetti.

Mercy Cosgrove was waiting at the curb, wringing her thin, withered hands, while another elderly neighbor, Thelma McEntire, sported a halo of blue plastic hair curlers and clutched a poodle against her ample, flowered blouse.

Mercy hurried around the car, pink house slippers scuffing the pavement. "Oh, Becky. I'm so glad you came. I didn't know what to do. I was gonna call the fire department till I remembered how mad Effie got the last time."

"Everything'll be fine. I'll handle it. Where is she?"

The old woman pointed a bony finger. "On the roof. See? She shinnied up that there ladder like a dumb kid. No sense at all. And at her age, too."

"Oh, my. Now I *have* seen everything."

Heart pounding, Becky shaded her eyes, paused near the base of the ladder and tried to appear calm. "Hello, up there."

"Oh, praise God!" Effie hollered like she thought she was in the front row at a tent revival. "You made it! Hallelujah!"

"That's right. I'm here. You can come down now."

"Nope. Can't. Not done yet. You get your little self up here with me, missy. I need your help."

"Me?"

Becky didn't think it would help to remind Effie how frightened she'd always been of heights. While the other kids were scaling rock piles and climbing trees, she'd stood by and watched, accepting their ridicule rather than admit her fear.

"Why don't you just come down here so we can talk?" Becky asked.

"Not till I get this baby barn swallow settled back in his nest with his brothers and sisters. He fell all the way down the chimney. You should of heard the racket he was makin'."

Glad she hadn't worn a skirt to work that morning, Becky rubbed her sweaty palms on her slacks before grabbing the sides of the ladder. She lifted one foot, put it on the bottom rung, and froze—except for the uncontrollable trembling that shook her to the core.

She swallowed hard. Scared or not, she had to climb. It was sending that conclusion from her mind to her quivering muscles that was causing the delay. Finally, she forced herself to move by concentrating on the imminent danger Effie was in.

Don't look down. Don't look down. One step at a time, she told herself. *You can do it. Oh, Lord, help me!*

Knuckles white, face flushed, head swimming, Becky finally climbed high enough to peek over the eaves. Her gray-haired aunt was perched casually on the sloping side of the shingle roof, knees drawn up, gnarled fingers cupped around the small, dark body of the swallow fledgling. She looked as relaxed as someone sitting in an easy chair.

"Please come down," Becky begged. "We can call that wild bird rehabilitation guy and let him handle this. I know I've got his number."

"I couldn't find it. Looked all over a'fore I climbed up here. Nice view, though. You can see all the way to the church. How's Brother Fred doing?"

"He's fine, Effie. He sends his regards. But he needs me back at work and I can't go until you're safe."

"I'm safer up here than lots of the places I've been in my life." She gave a throaty chuckle. "Just can't get the rain cap off the chimney so's I can see the nest good. I can hear this little guy's family, though. They've gotta be right close to the edge here."

"Then they'll still be there later," Becky reasoned. "Why don't you bring the baby over here and show me?"

"Well…" Effie started to stand.

"That's right. Upsy-daisy. I'm right here for you." Becky had no clue how she was going to get her aunt turned around and backed safely down the ladder, but at least they were making progress.

Effie reached the edge of the overhang and stopped with the toes of her worn sneakers practically touching Becky's nose. She scowled at the yard below. "I see the busybodies are all gathered. What're they starin' at, anyway? Lots of people climb ladders. Happens all the time."

"Not to me, it doesn't," Becky said with a huff of self-disgust. "Would you please come down, Aunt Effie, before I faint dead away?"

"Land sakes, I forgot about your problem with heights. Don't you fret. You just go wait with my cheering section. I'll be down directly."

"I'm not leaving you up here all alone."

"I ain't alone. I got a new pet. Remember?"

"The baby bird doesn't count. He couldn't even take care of himself."

"Oh, all right. We'll do it your way. But only 'cause I love you."

"I love you, too. That's why I'm up here."

Becky had taken a step down, making room for

Effie's descent, when the old woman pointed. "Who's that?"

"Where?"

"Over there. In our driveway. Gettin' out of that fancy red car. He ain't from Serenity."

A leafy maple blocked Becky's view. "I don't have a clue. I can't see the drive from here. What difference does it make? Come on."

Instead of complying, Effie screeched, "No!" and scrambled up the roof all the way to the crest.

Becky was dumbfounded. She'd seen her aunt get upset over minor things before but she'd never seen such full-blown panic.

Forgetting her own fear, Becky was back up the ladder and had crawled out onto the roof before she had time to be scared. Staying on her knees, she followed the old woman all the way to the highest point and straddled the peak for balance.

Terror and confusion filled Effie's eyes. "Duck down behind the chimney. We don't want him to see us."

"Why not?" Becky's breathlessness was more from being up so high than from exertion.

"Don't know who he might be."

"What difference does it make? The yard is full of our friends. They'll look after us. You know that."

"Still, we'd best hide awhile."

"Why?"

"To be sure they ain't found us," the old woman

said. She lowered her voice to rasp, "Don't you trust nobody, you hear? Nobody."

Becky sighed. It was happening again. Poor Effie had been troubled with hallucinations for months. The episodes were not only becoming more frequent, but her illusions were apparently gaining strength. This was the most vivid, specific one Becky had witnessed.

"I think we'd be safer if we were both on the ground," she reasoned. "Then we could jump in my car and drive away if we wanted to."

"Wouldn't do no good. They're everywhere. I saw one of 'em in the bathroom again this mornin'. She was old and gray. Real mean lookin'. She made fun of me, too. Did everything I did."

Becky had heard that complaint before. Effie sometimes didn't recognize her own reflection. Becky hated to give up the last mirror in the house, but brushing her hair and putting on lipstick in the car on her way to work was a small price to pay for a loved one's peace of mind. As soon as she got the chance, she'd remove the door from the medicine cabinet and hide it away.

"I'll see she doesn't bother you again."

"You're a good girl." Effie patted her hand, then looked surprised. "Rebecca? What're you doing up here? Where's Flo?"

It wasn't the first time Becky had heard that name. When Effie was confused she often mentioned a Flo, or Florence.

"It's just me, Aunt Effie."

"Praise the Lord! I thought he'd got you."

"I'm fine. So are you. Nobody's going to get any-body."

Logan chose that moment to stick his head up over the edge of the roof and give a cheery "Hello."

Gasping, Effie toppled over backwards. She might have slid down the opposite side of the roof if Becky hadn't grabbed her.

"Whoa," Logan said, "I didn't mean to scare you."

"You could have fooled me." Becky pulled her frail aunt into a tight embrace and glowered at him. "What are you doing here?"

"I came to see if I could help. Fred told me where you lived and gave me the directions. I didn't think it would cause a problem."

Effie peeked at him. "Fred sent you?"

"Yes," Becky explained. "Aunt Effie, meet Brother Logan Malloy. He's the new preacher I told you about. He's going to be helping Brother Fred until the church can vote on a replacement."

"Nobody'll ever replace Fred," Effie said.

"Not in our hearts. But right now, I'll settle for let-ting Brother Logan help us down, won't you?"

The old woman's eyes widened. "I ain't goin' no-where with a stranger."

"He's not a stranger. He's an old friend of Fred's. Please? For my sake?" There were unshed tears in Becky's blue eyes.

"Well…okay," Effie said reluctantly. "But if he

tries anything funny, I'll teach him not to fool with decent folks."

"He's just going to guide you onto the ladder and then steady you while you climb down. Isn't that right, Brother Malloy?"

"That's right, Miss Rebecca," he drawled, obviously trying to imitate local speech inflections and failing miserably.

Becky giggled in spite of her precarious perch. "That is the *worst* southern accent I've ever heard."

"Sorry," Logan said, "I thought it might help. Okay. I'm set. The folks on the ground are steadying the ladder so it won't slip. Let's go."

Becky was glad Effie had decided to cooperate because there was no way she could have physically forced her to. She figured she'd be doing well to convince herself it was safe to crawl back across the shingles, not to mention stand up and walk to the ladder.

Thankfully, heights didn't bother Effie. She got to her feet and, tucking the baby bird in her apron pocket, proceeded as calmly as if she were on solid ground.

Dread of making the same trip brought a fluttering to Becky's chest, a lump to her throat. She'd been balanced astride the roof ridge like a rider on an immense horse. Before Logan returned, she intended to be waiting near the ladder rather than let him see her fear. All she had to do was swing one leg over and scoot that direction. All she had to was…move.

Hmm. Apparently, that was going to be harder to do than she'd thought. Just contemplating it made her shaking grow worse—if that were possible.

Totally disgusted with herself, Becky sighed. She was frozen to the spot like a deer mesmerized by the headlights of an oncoming car. Concern for Effie may have been enough to get her up on the roof, but she was going to need more than her own willpower to make the climb down.

She closed her eyes, intending to ask her Heavenly Father for help. Instead, she thought of the stale joke about the man sitting on his roof, praying for divine rescue from a flood. Waiting for a miracle, the man had turned away every boat that came to save him, so he eventually drowned. When he got to Heaven and questioned God about not sending help, he learned that the boats he'd rejected had been the answer to his prayers.

Becky smiled wryly. Okay. She got the picture. She was stuck on a roof, too. And Logan was her boat.

She guessed it wouldn't hurt to humor him and let him help her, just this once.

Chapter Two

Becky was still sitting in the same spot when Logan returned. He stopped at the top of the ladder, smiled and held out his hand. "Okay. Your aunt is safe. Now it's your turn."

"I, um, I have a confession to make," Becky said. "I'm scared of heights."

"No kidding. Is that why you're white as a sheet and about to shake the shingles loose?"

"You noticed."

Logan chuckled amiably. "It's pretty hard not to. What would you like me to do, sling you over my shoulder like a fireman and carry you down?"

"Only if you knock me out first," she quipped. "Being right-side-up is bad enough. I know I wouldn't like hanging upside down."

"How about a blindfold?"

She made a face. "You're just full of wonderful ideas, aren't you?"

"I try." Logan shrugged. "It's up to you. Do we do this the easy way or the hard way?"

"When it comes to heights, every way is the hard way for me. I can't budge."

"Sure you can. Instead of thinking about the whole descent at once, try focusing on one little movement. Wiggle your left foot."

"That's silly."

"So is spending the rest of your life on a roof. Humor me. Try it."

"Okay, okay," Becky said, flexing her ankle. "There. Satisfied?"

"It's a start. Now the foot on the far side of the roof. Done it? Good. Now bend your knee."

Becky could see how his method might work. Before he could give any more orders, she lifted her knee high enough to bring her leg over the crest and swung it around so she was sitting, facing him.

"You're a quick learner," Logan said, grinning. He held out his arms. "Can you scoot toward me or do I need to come up there and drag you?"

"Given those choices, I think I'd rather do it myself."

"Good for you. Okay. Come on. I'm ready."

She looked down at her formerly white, linen slacks. The knees were already ruined beyond what washing would repair. Scooting along on her rear would finish them for good. Oh, well. She could always buy more clothes. A person was given only one life to risk and if sliding was the best option then she'd slide. At least she couldn't lose her balance if she wasn't standing up.

Logan pointed to her feet. "You might want to ditch those slippery shoes first. I can't believe you came up here dressed like that."

"I wasn't planning on mountain climbing when I got ready for work this morning." She slipped her feet out of her low-heeled pumps. "There. Better?"

"Hopefully. Inch yourself over this way. Take it real slow and easy."

His warning pointed out the disparity in their relative positions. When she'd scurried onto the roof after Effie, she'd apparently traveled at an angle. Therefore, Logan and the ladder were not directly below her.

"Tell you what," Becky said. "Why don't you move over, instead?"

"I'd have to go all the way down and reposition the ladder. Are you sure that's what you want?"

"Yes."

"Okay. Don't go away."

She blew him a raspberry as his head disappeared below the level of the eaves. *Don't go away, indeed.* Brother Fred had forgotten to mention that his former seminary student had a satirical sense of humor. *Like mine,* she added, smiling slightly. Life held many funny moments if she merely looked for them and appreciated the chance to laugh.

"And this one is a dandy. Brother Fred is going to love hearing all about it." Her smile broadened.

Dear Fred. She was really going to miss him. Even though he was planning to retire to a small house on Lake Norfork and had promised to visit often, work wouldn't be the same without his fond greeting every morning.

Below her, she heard banging and shouting. Effie's shrill voice rose above them all. Becky gripped her shoes in her left hand and laid her right hand flat on the roof. The gravel coating on the old shingles was so loose that some of it actually stuck to her palm.

Logan had been right. If she'd had the nerve to try to walk the roof in her dress shoes, she'd probably have slipped and fallen. Given the choice of being frightened or breaking her neck, she decided she'd rather be scared silly than dead. She did, however, wish she'd made a little better impression on her new boss, even if his tenure was going to be brief.

Logan moved the ladder and headed back up as fast as he could. Becky hadn't looked very stable when he'd left her, and he could envision her exploding into hysterics at any moment. Instead, he found her smiling when he returned. Surprised, he decided it was best to proceed quickly, before she had a chance to refocus on her fright.

"Okay. I'm set," he said. His feet and legs remained braced on the ladder, his upper torso extending above the edge of the roof. He spread his arms wide. "Come on."

"Okay," Becky said lightly.

Amazed, Logan watched her start to push off. He'd expected her to inch along, slowly and cautiously. Instead, she sailed toward him like a kid racing down a snowy hill on a sled. Her feet were headed directly for his chest. At the last second, she screamed, twisted and smacked sideways into him like a gunnysack filled with potatoes.

Her momentum pushed them both backwards. Logan was sure they were going to fall. The ladder stopped almost straight up, teetered and then crashed forward into the metal guttering, bending it flat.

Breathing a heartfelt prayer, Logan held tight to Becky and waited for the next stage of the calamity, while below, her aunt was screeching words he hadn't heard since he'd left the military.

Becky wrapped her arms around his neck. Neither of them moved. Finally, she said, "You can put me down."

"No way. I'm not letting go of you till we're on the ground."

"I can manage the ladder. Really. If you try to carry me we could both fall."

"*Now,* you think of that." He rolled his eyes. "Okay. I'm going to sit you right here. I want you to bring your feet around *slowly*. Got that?"

"Of course."

"I'll believe it when I see it," Logan muttered.

As she turned, she looked into his eyes. "Are you sure you're a preacher?"

"Yes. Why?"

"You cursed."

"I did not. What gave you that idea?"

"Something you said while I was sliding. I'd rather not repeat it."

"That was a prayer for deliverance," he explained. "I suspect I'll need a lot more of them if I hang around you and your family for very long."

The lawn looked more inviting than ever before when they finally reached it. Becky did her best to appear unaffected by her ordeal as she gave everyone a hug, starting with Effie.

The older woman was blinking back tears when she excused herself and retreated into the house with Thelma and the poodle.

Becky thought about collapsing in a heap on the grass, rolling into a ball, hugging her knees to her chest and launching into happy hysterics. *Later,* she thought. *Later, I'll have a good, therapeutic, hissy fit.*

The idea of actually planning to fall apart struck her as comical. She was not the kind of person to look forward to periods of distress the way some people did. Sharing joy and celebrating life was more her style.

Logan grasped her shoulders and stared at her. "You okay? You look kind of funny."

"Me?" Becky blinked and started to grin. "If you think *I* look funny you should see yourself. You're a mess. There's almost as much dirt on you as there is on me."

Dusting off her hands, she reached out and began to groom Logan's thick hair with her fingers, meaning only to spruce him up in the same innocent way she would have Brother Fleming. Instead, she was caught by a sudden awareness that this was *not* the same as tending to her virtuous old boss. Traces of tenderness and awe flashed briefly in Logan's expression, surprising Becky, before he stepped away.

"I'm fine," he said gruffly. "Go take care of your aunt."

She looked around at her neighbors, then back to Logan. "Not before I thank you—all of you. If everybody hadn't worked together and kept that ladder from falling over, it could have been much worse."

Starting for the front porch, she paused. "Would you all like to come in? Maybe have a glass of iced tea or lemonade? I might even be able to find a few cookies."

The neighbors made excuses and left. But Logan gave Becky a lopsided smile. "A cookie, huh? You do know how to tempt me. I have a real weakness for cookies."

"Then we'd be glad to have you stay," Becky said amiably.

"You sure it's okay? I wouldn't want to give anybody the wrong impression." He thrust his hands into his pockets and struck a nonchalant pose.

"Thelma's still inside with Aunt Effie, right?"

"Far as I know."

"Then there's no chance of a misunderstanding. If those two aren't good enough chaperones to keep the gossips at bay, nobody is." She smiled knowingly. "Thanks for thinking of my reputation, though. Brother Fred said you were used to living in the city. I'm glad you realize how rumors can get out of hand in a little place like Serenity."

"The size of the town isn't the real problem," Logan said wisely. "We have small minds in big cities, too."

"I know what you mean."

"You lived in the city? Where? Little Rock?"

"No." Becky led the way inside. "I grew up in this house. But Aunt Effie didn't. She's told me what it was like in other places. Makes me even more determined to stay put, no matter what."

"Where's she from?"

"Oh, here and there. All over, I guess. She traveled a lot when she was younger."

Logan followed his hostess down the dimly lit hallway to the kitchen. "She must have mentioned some particular places."

About to answer, Becky noticed that the two older women were seated at the kitchen table, sipping mugs of tea, while the beige poodle sat at their feet. She was surprised when her aunt butted in to answer Logan.

"That's none of your business, young man. And I'll thank you to leave my niece alone."

"Aunt Effie! Mind your manners. Brother Malloy is going to be my boss, remember? He can't leave me alone. We'll be working together."

"I'd better go," Logan said quietly, nodding and backing away. "She's confused. I understand. We'll talk some other time, when my presence won't upset her."

Becky cast a questioning glance at her aunt, then escorted him to the front door. "I don't know what came over her just now. She's usually a real sweetheart. The doctor told me to expect mood swings. I apologize. I don't know why she was so antagonistic."

Smiling pleasantly, Logan stepped onto the porch. "Don't give it another thought. She's probably mad because she thinks I was too rough with you on the roof. I'm amazed everything turned out as well as it did."

"Me, too. Our guardian angels must have been working overtime." The agreement she'd expected wasn't forthcoming so she went on. "I love the verse that says, 'He shall give his angels charge over you.' It's in Luke, I think. Or is it in the book of Psalms?"

"Both," Logan said. "Well, I'd better hit the road. Still have an appointment to keep with Fred. He told me to tell you to take the rest of the afternoon off. Hope your aunt settles down soon."

Becky smiled as she watched him leave. Recalling what he'd said about being tempted by cookies, she broke into a broad grin. Cookies weren't the worst temptation she'd faced lately. Not by a long run.

Chapter Three

It had taken Becky longer than usual to dress for work the following morning.

The baby swallow had been turned over to the bird rehabilitation man and his phone number was posted on the refrigerator door, so she decided it was safe to wear a blouse and skirt instead of slacks. Even if another fledgling got crowded out of the mud nest plastered inside the chimney, Effie wouldn't have any reason to go back up on the roof. Then again, since when did Aunt Effie need plausible reasons for the crazy things she did?

Smiling, Becky pulled into the church parking lot. Two other cars were already there; Fred's familiar beige sedan was parked near the door and Logan's bright red convertible sat closer to the beautiful stained glass side windows. The sight of the second car made her pulse jump like a grasshopper on a sizzling summer sidewalk. She huffed. If the empty car did that to her, what was going to happen when she faced its owner?

She parked next to Fred's sedan, climbed out of her economy two-door, stood tall and paused to smooth her skirt, hoping she looked presentable.

It was silly to fuss over her appearance, she told herself. After all, Brother Logan had come here to work, not to admire her. Acknowledging that fact didn't negate her jitters one bit. As a matter of fact, the closer she got to the outer door at the rear of the church, the more nervous she became.

She paused, her hand on the knob, took a deep breath and walked in.

Her heels clicked on the tile by the door before being muted by the hall carpet. She'd heard male voices when she'd entered. Now, they were silent.

With a smile, she entered the office. Her grin broadened. Brother Fred and Logan stood side by side, smiling back at her. Fred was wearing his usual suit and tie, while Logan sported a black turtleneck beneath a brown sport jacket with leather patches at the elbows. The contrast was interesting to say the least.

"Good morning." Becky glanced at her watch. "Am I late?"

Fred was quick to reassure her. "No, no, my dear. Logan and I came in early to go over some of the duties he'll be taking on in my place."

Her brow knit. "Some? I thought he was going to sub for you all the time."

"Not exactly." Fred looked to Logan as if pleading for moral support.

"That's right," Logan said. "We'll be working together on church business for a few weeks, until I get used to the routine. Fred doesn't want his congregation to feel abandoned. You understand."

"I certainly do. No offense, but I'm going to miss him something awful." She turned away and busied herself rearranging piles of paperwork to hide the depth of her emotions.

Logan approached and perched on the edge of her desk. "How's your aunt this morning? Any more excitement?"

"Not since you saw her, but thanks for asking." Becky looked up at him with an apologetic smile. "A little prickly, wasn't she?"

"A little. Has she always been like that?"

"No. At least I don't think so. Brother Fred's known her ever since she came to Serenity. I'm sure he can tell you more about her early years. I was just a baby then."

"You've lived with her all your life? What about your parents?"

"I never knew them. They died when I was very young. Effie's the only family I have left."

"You don't say."

Becky toyed briefly with the idea of mentioning the old photograph she'd found, then decided against it. Logan wouldn't know anything about those people, and dredging up the past would only raise Effie's stress level. Someday, she might divulge her secret find to Fred, especially since the older man had always seemed so fond of her family, but she certainly wasn't going to do it with Logan present.

Looking past him, Becky smiled fondly at Brother Fred. "I left the updated list of hospitalizations and illnesses on your desk. The Landers boy went home yesterday so I crossed off his name. Other than that, I think everything is current. And you have two couples scheduled for counseling this afternoon, one at two and one at three-thirty. I'll go through the messages on the answering machine right now."

"Fine, fine."

She frowned at him. "Are you feeling all right? You look kind of peaked this morning."

"I'm just a little tired," Fred said. "Haven't been sleeping well these past few weeks. Probably nervous about retiring. I don't know what I'm going to do with all that free time."

"Knowing you, you'll find enough folks who need help to keep you occupied wherever you go," Becky said with clear affection. "You're a very special guy." Seeing Fred blush made her laugh softly. "Modest, too."

Logan was nodding. He stood. "Special doesn't even begin to describe our friend Fred. Anybody who's ever known him has been blessed beyond belief."

She looked from one man to the other and back. It was as if there was an unspoken brotherly bond between them; an invisible wall that was keeping her out. Fred had never acted withdrawn like this before. Even after his wife had passed away he'd been able to continue reaching out to others in need. So why was she suddenly getting the feeling he was hiding something from her? And what could Logan Malloy have to do with it?

Becky sat down at her desk and stared at her daily planner, focusing on nothing in particular, while her brain puzzled over the question. From their first contact she'd sensed something odd about Logan. It wasn't that he'd done or said anything wrong. It was far more subtle than that. She guessed it was partly because he lacked the same outward pastoral demeanor that was so much a part of Fred.

She knew she wasn't being fair to Logan, yet how could she help how she felt? There was definitely a reserve to him that was off-putting. Perhaps that was why Brother Fred hadn't recommended him as his permanent replacement.

Then again, maybe the real fault lay within her. She found Logan too attractive for her own good, so perhaps she was subconsciously prejudiced. That notion didn't sit well on her conscience.

She was reaching for the playback button on the answering machine when Logan covered her hand with his. "I'll take care of that for you."

"I always do it." Her skin was burning beneath his gentle touch. She pulled away. "It's no trouble, really."

"I insist." Cocking his head toward the pastor's private office he said, "I think Fred wants you to help him write a couple of letters."

"I can do that later."

Logan's hand remained on the answering machine. "Please? There isn't a whole lot I can do around here until Fred assigns me a job. I'd like to feel useful."

"Well, since you put it that way."

"Thanks." Looking satisfied, he stepped into her place behind the desk and usurped her chair as soon as she vacated it. Becky was entering Fred's office when Logan called, "And shut that door after you, will you?"

"But, we never…"

The elderly pastor met her, ushered her in, and took care of closing the door behind her.

Becky blinked in disbelief. Either something strange was going on here, or she'd been reading too many mystery novels. Maybe both.

Helping her boss with his correspondence wasn't nearly as difficult for Becky as keeping him focused on one subject at a time. Multitasking was one thing. Being addlebrained was quite another. She'd never seen poor Fred acting this bumfuzzled.

"Why don't we take a break and do some of this later?" she finally suggested.

Fred paced to the office door, opened it a crack and peeked out. He seemed to relax. "Fine idea. Looks like Logan's finished with the telephone. Why don't we see where he's gotten to? I think it's time you offered to drive him around town, don't you? Give him the grand tour? Show him Serenity the way we natives see it?"

She would have answered sooner if he'd given her a chance to squeeze a word in. When he paused long enough to take a breath, she quickly said, "I have an awful lot of work to do today, Brother Fred. The newsletter isn't ready for printing, and I still have to type Sunday's bulletin, and…"

"That can wait." Hustling her into the outer office he nervously clenched and unclenched his hands as if he were trying to decide whether to pray or dither.

Becky peered into the hallway. "I don't see Brother Malloy. I'm sure he'll be back in a minute."

"Fine, fine."

Her boss's building fretfulness was troubling. She put a steadying hand on his arm. "Look, you wait here in case he comes back before I do. I'll do a quick sweep of the church and grounds and see if I can find him. Okay?"

As she started off, Fred stopped her. "Becky?"

"Yes?"

His lips pressed into a thin line. The creases in his forehead deepened. "Never mind. Go ahead. Just hurry back."

"Are you feeling sick?"

"No. Of course not. Go on. I'll be fine."

Hesitating, she assessed the man she'd admired for so many years. Whatever was bothering him seemed less physical than mental. "Okay. Hang loose. I'll be back in a sec."

She circled the west Sunday School rooms first, checked the sanctuary proper, then swung around to the east side of the building. Through the clear border of the colorful tall glass windows she could see half of the parking lot. Logan was standing by his car with his back to her, apparently talking on a cellular phone. How silly. Fred must have forgotten to tell him he could use the office line for personal calls. They could always figure out any long-distance charges and settle up when the bill came.

Glad to have located him, she pushed the release bar on the outer door and swung it open. The clattery noise of the latch preceded her greeting by a split second. Smiling, she called, "Hey, Brother Malloy! We were looking for you."

Logan spun to face her. He muttered briefly into his cell phone and quickly flipped it closed. "I thought you were working with Fred?"

"I was. We're done. He sent me to find you." She sensed his displeasure and chose to elaborate. "I guess he was worried about you, although I can't imagine why. He's been acting kind of strange lately. I hope his health isn't failing."

"He seems fine to me," Logan said, joining her and holding the door open so she could precede him into the church, "but I'll keep a close eye on him if you want."

"Would you?" Her smile grew. "He's really special."

"To you, you mean?"

"To me and to everybody else in Serenity. You'd be surprised how many folks call him who aren't even members of this church. He's always willing to help."

"I know."

They entered the offices together. Fred was waiting. "There you are! I've asked Miss Rebecca to show you around while I hold the fort here." He sent a worried glance toward the answering machine. "Were there any messages?"

"A few," Logan said. He slipped a sheet of yellow paper from the bottom of the stack, folded it and tucked it into his jacket pocket. "Nothing important. I made a list for you. It's right there, by the phone."

"Wonderful, wonderful. I'll return those calls while you're gone. Have fun, you two."

"Wait a minute," Becky said, standing her ground and staring at her boss. "I said I'd go find him. I didn't promise to do anything else. Don't you think it would be best if *you* showed him around?"

Logan chuckled wryly. "You aren't afraid to be seen with me are you? If you have a jealous boyfriend, we can always invite your aunt to come along as a chaperone."

"That's the last thing I need. We'd have no peace at all if we included Effie. It'll be hard enough to explain why I was out with you, once word gets back to her."

"You could wear a disguise," Logan teased, smiling.

"What? Dark glasses and a mustache? Think that would work?"

"Not unless you tucked that beautiful red hair of yours inside a hat. I don't think I've ever seen hair quite that color."

"It's called strawberry blonde," Becky replied. "And I didn't get it out of a bottle. It's natural."

"I don't doubt it." Logan's smile faded. He reached for her arm. "Grab your purse and let's get out of here before your boss changes his mind and makes you slave over a computer all day."

"I can think of worse things," Becky muttered.

Yeah, like getting the shivers every time you touch me. And having my heart beat so hard you can probably hear it all the way across the room. And feeling scared and thrilled—all at the same time.

Logan insisted they take his car, with the top down, so he'd have a better view. "If you don't mind."

She shrugged. "Oh, no. Not at all. No sense trying to hide the fact that I'm doing the exact opposite of what my aunt asked. Might as well cruise around in a bright red convertible, make sure everybody gets a good look at us, and be done with it."

He held the passenger door for her. "Do I detect a touch of sarcasm?"

"More than a touch," Becky answered. "I know I'm a grown woman, but I owe Aunt Effie everything. I try not to upset her, especially lately."

Logan got behind the wheel, backed out of the parking spot and turned right onto Highway 62. "Do you think her condition is getting worse?"

"I don't know. It's hard to tell. Sometimes weeks will go by where she seems so normal I'll think she's well. And then some little thing will set her off again."

"There are new medications to combat senile dementia. They came along too late to help my mother but I've kept up with the research news. Just got into the habit of paying attention, I guess."

"Your mother isn't living?"

"No. Mom died while I was away. I came home for her funeral."

"I'm so sorry. What about your father?"

"Don't have a clue. Funny. All I remember about him is the smell of his cigars. And the way my mother cried after he left us."

"When did you decide to dedicate your life to the Lord?" Glancing over at him as she spoke, Becky saw the muscles in his jaw tense.

Instead of answering, Logan pointed. "Fred told me there's only one traffic signal in town. Is this it?"

"Yes. So far, at least. Make a right."

As soon as he had turned, Becky continued, "I heard there are long-range plans to widen the highway all the way from Memphis to Branson, so maybe someday we'll need more signals. Right now, though, one is more than enough." She chuckled. "Did Fred tell you what happened when they first installed this one?"

"No. What?"

"It caused lots of accidents. Some folks had driven through this intersection all their lives and never had to stop. They tended to overlook the red light. But that wasn't the funniest thing."

"Oh?" Logan slowed the car. They were approaching a town square, complete with a courthouse in the center and small businesses facing it from all four sides.

"No. Some of these people had never driven in the city. I know it's hard to believe, but they'd never seen a real traffic light, except in the movies or on TV."

"They understood red and green for stop and go, didn't they?"

"Oh, sure. The problem was making left turns. They'd see the green light, begin their turn, look up, and be faced with the red for the cross-traffic."

Logan stared at her. "They *stopped?*"

"Bingo. Right in the middle of the intersection. Just sat there till the light changed. I don't know how many of them got dented fenders from that little mistake but we solved the problem by sending out instructions in the utility bills."

"You're kidding!"

"Nope." She drew an imaginary X over her chest

with her index finger. "That's the truth. Cross my heart."

"Amazing. Looks like I have a lot to learn."

"Not really. These people are good, kind souls who would do anything for others. They have a lot of native intelligence, you know, old-fashioned common sense even if they haven't been exposed to outside influences as much as you have. Just accept them as they are and show them the same kind of respect you'd want in return, and you'll do fine."

"Do unto others, you mean."

"Exactly. We have some retirees and transplants living here, too. Some of them stay, some go back where they came from. I think a lot depends on their attitude. If they arrive feeling superior, they usually don't last long."

"But Effie stayed."

"Yes. And I'm thankful she did. Serenity is the kind of place where I want to spend the rest of my life. I wouldn't leave here for a million dollars."

"I'm glad you're happy," Logan said solemnly. He brightened. "So, I see the courthouse, and I made it through the tricky traffic light without getting hit. Where shall we go, next?"

Becky grinned. "Just park anywhere around here and we'll walk. My friend Belinda Randall works over at the chamber of commerce. We can start there and pick up a few brochures. Maybe even a local map, if we're lucky."

"If we're lucky?"

She laughed. "You have no idea. Up until a year or so ago, when we voted to start a 911 emergency service, most of the dirt roads around here didn't even have names. They didn't need to. Folks either gave directions in landmarks or counted mileage from the pavement. It made home visitations really interesting, especially if Brother Fred wasn't familiar with the family he was looking for and they couldn't tell us who had lived in their house generations ago. That's how we navigate half the time."

The astounded look on Logan's face made her laugh again. "You'll get used to it. Just think of us as one big happy clan. And always assume the person you're talking to is related to everybody. That way, you won't accidentally insult anybody's kin."

"Now you are kidding," he said with a raised eyebrow.

Grinning widely, Becky shook her head. She stepped out as he opened her door. "Nope. 'Fraid not. But don't worry, Brother Logan. Once you've preached a few good sermons you won't have a bit of trouble being accepted. I'm sure everyone will love you."

Becky made it as far as the curb before she realized that Logan wasn't following. She turned and stared at him. He was still standing beside his car, the color drained from his face as if he'd just seen a ghost. What could she possibly have said that would affect him so strongly?

She thought back over their conversation and wondered if it was her reference to kin, or sermons, or love that had left him so disconcerted.

Whatever the reason, she was beginning to agree with Fred's assessment of their interim preacher. Logan Malloy was too different, too citified, too out of his element, to successfully assume a pastor's role in Serenity.

Like Fred, she wanted what was best for their church members. And, like Fred, she found Logan to be good company, although she wouldn't go so far as to say they were buddies. Not yet. Nor would they ever have the chance to develop a lasting friendship if he left too soon.

Becky's breath caught. To her surprise and chagrin, she had to admit it was distressing to think about the day Logan would say his final goodbye.

She quickly cast about for logical reasons to explain those feelings and settled on gratitude. She owed the new preacher plenty. It wasn't every day a person got rescued from a slippery roof and practically carried down a ladder.

Aunt Effie would undoubtedly be thrilled to see Logan leave town ASAP, in spite of his good deed on their behalf.

Becky, on the other hand, already knew she was going to miss him. What she couldn't understand was how he'd become so important to her so quickly.

Chapter Four

Becky gave Logan her most amiable smile. "Come on. The chamber of commerce is right over there, next to the county library. You'll like Belinda. She and Paul, her husband, lived over in Cotter for awhile. I was sure glad when they decided to move back to Serenity. I missed her."

She sobered, then sighed. "I'm going to miss Brother Fred, too. He's a dear."

"He always speaks highly of you," Logan said, following.

"I love a boss who's prejudiced in my favor." Glancing back, Becky noted Logan's amused smile and felt warmth immediately flood her cheeks. "I mean, it's nice to be appreciated."

"You're lucky to have found a job where that happens."

"Luck had nothing to do with it."

"Oh?"

As Logan fell into step beside her, she wondered

why she'd never noticed how narrow and confining that section of sidewalk was. If she'd been wearing her sneakers instead of dress shoes, she'd have escaped into the grass alongside rather than be forced into such close proximity with such an enigmatic man.

Her *humph,* became a soft chuckle of self-derision. Talk about ridiculous. Logan Malloy had never done or said one single thing that should make her uneasy, yet she was feeling like a nervous, infatuated teenager on her first date. So she wasn't used to being around someone who acted so reserved. So what? Lots of people weren't as open and loving as the folks she'd grown up with. It was probably normal for him to be standoffish, given his background. But a southern "good ole boy" he certainly was not!

"Did I say something funny?" he asked.

"No, no." It took Becky a few moments to recall what they'd been discussing before her mind had taken off like a wild rabbit fleeing a hungry fox. "I, uh…I don't believe in luck. At least not the way most people think of it. Actually, I believe God got me my job."

"Like a heavenly employment agency?"

Becky grinned. "Something like that, yes. I was working at the ice-cream shop. Brother Fred came in for a sundae one day and we got to talking. When he mentioned an opening in the Serenity Chapel office, I knew that was the answer to my prayers."

"If you attended his church, wouldn't you have heard about the job anyway?"

"Not necessarily. And probably not in time to apply. That's another thing you'll have to get used to around here. Very few jobs have to be advertised before they're filled. And places for rent or for sale are usually spoken for before they're even vacant. Everything is by word of mouth. It's one way the local grapevine can be useful."

Becky chuckled at his confused expression. "We even have community-wide bridal and baby showers. Nobody sends out invitations. Folks just hear about it and show up with gifts. The same goes for fund-raisers like pie suppers and charity auctions."

Logan's puzzled look deepened. "Pie *what?*"

"Suppers. It's kind of an auction, except the money bid for the pies and other donated baked goods has nothing to do with their commercial value."

"Of course not," he said with a wry smile, "that would make too much sense."

Laughing, Becky nodded. "You're absolutely right. I remember a fund-raiser last year where one pecan pie sold for almost a hundred dollars."

"Whew! I've heard pecan is a rich pie but that's unreal. I hope the buyer enjoyed it."

"I think he did get to taste one little piece." Her companion's incredulous air spurred her to further explanation. "You see, after the bids are all in and the money's been collected for whatever the special need of the day is, we all stay and eat. Everything is shared. Even the expensive stuff. Makes it more enjoyable that way, and it's all for a good cause."

"Why don't you just ask for donations and skip the extra work?"

"Where's the fun in that?"

"It would sure be faster and a lot more efficient."

"Why be in a hurry when personally participating is so rewarding?" Becky smiled up at him. "The more I get to know you, the more I suspect that living in Serenity is going to give you a terrible case of culture shock. Just remember, if you get confused, ask me or Fred to explain what's going on before you get in too deep."

"I'm not as naive as you seem to think I am."

She couldn't help but laugh at his overconfidence. "You may have been at the head of your classes in school but around here you're liable to hear folks suggest you're not rowing with both oars in the water."

"I beg your pardon?"

"You know… That's like being a couple sandwiches short of a picnic. A few squares short of a quilt? Not the sharpest pencil in the box?"

"Ah. Where I come from, we say *dumber than dirt*."

Becky started across the street to the chamber of commerce office, noting that Logan had placed his hand on the small of her back to guide her safely through the intersection. His touch was barely there, yet it sent such an unexpected shiver of awareness zigzagging up her spine she figured she was lucky to remember what they were discussing, let alone come up with a lucid reply.

"Southerners are much kinder than that," she said. "We don't often resort to terms like *dumb* or *stupid*. Instead, we keep hinting at the problem till you get the idea."

"I'd much rather be told directly if I'm doing something wrong," Logan said.

She turned her head and settled her gaze on his face, trying to decide whether or not he was serious. A smile lifted one corner of her mouth. Her eyes twinkled. Her cheeks suddenly burned. "Well, if you insist. I think it would be best for both our reputations if you took your hand off my back."

Logan jumped away like a man who'd stuck his finger in an electrical socket and gotten a serious jolt. "Sorry. It was just a natural reaction. I didn't mean anything by it."

Becky's smile evened out and she nodded. "I was hoping you were trying to keep me from being run over—assuming there had been traffic in the street when we crossed."

"There was. There had to be." He looked sheepishly left and right. "There wasn't, was there?"

"Nope," Becky said with a giggle. "Nary a car. But don't worry. I'm sure not more than two or three gossips saw us. At that rate, it'll be hours before the news reaches Aunt Effie, so I'll have time to ask Brother Fred to explain everything to her."

Logan studied her expression. "You're not joking, are you?"

"Oh, no," Becky drawled, slowly shaking her head. "I wish I were."

Logan held the heavy glass door for Becky, then followed her inside. The Serenity chamber of commerce was so generic it was practically a caricature. Whoever had set up the office had obviously intended it to mirror big-city life, complete with austere chrome furnishings and a long, uninviting counter. The room looked as out of place in the quaint old town as he felt.

A young woman with dark hair greeted them warmly and came around the counter, her arms open. "Becky, hello. Who's your friend?"

Becky gave her a hug, then stepped back to say, "Belinda Randall, meet Logan Malloy. Brother Malloy is taking Brother Fred's place for the time being." Smiling, she gestured toward Logan. "I'm trying to explain small town life to Brother Malloy. I thought maybe you could give him some brochures? Maps of the area? You know, whatever you have handy."

"Gladly." The slightly older woman shook Logan's hand. "It's easy to see you're not from around here."

"Oh? Why?" One dark eyebrow arched and a smile began to quirk at the corners of his mouth. "Are you trying to tell me I'm missing a pizza—or something like that?"

Becky stared, first at him, then at her old friend, before she burst into laughter. "No, no. That was a picnic, not a pizza."

"Oh, right. I don't have enough food for the picnic. Now I remember." He knew he didn't have to explain that he was teasing. Her amusement was evident. Her friend, however, looked totally at a loss.

The chamber representative cleared her throat. "I was referring to your lack of a baseball cap. None of the local men would come to town without some kind of hat."

Logan looked to Becky. "Hey. You were supposed to help me fit in. How come you didn't tell me?"

That generated another nervous giggle. "Sorry."

"You should be. How can my mission here be taken seriously if I don't look the part? Am I supposed to wear this special headgear all the time or can I take it off to sleep?"

Chortling, Becky thumped him playfully in the shoulder. "Stop that. Poor Belinda is going to think you're as dumb as a box of rocks."

"Hey. I thought you gracious southerners didn't call people names."

"I'm ready to make an exception in your case," she told him, grinning broadly. "Grab some brochures to take with us and let's go. There's a lot more of Serenity to see."

Logan paused long enough to cause her to glance back at him. Feigning hurt feelings, he said, "Not till you get me the right kind of hat." It pleased him to see the sparkle of glee in her eyes, to hear her light-hearted laughter, to know he had been the reason for her joy.

That conclusion surprised and sobered him. He made it a rule to never become emotionally involved in his cases, especially those on the negative side. Rebecca Tate and her aunt were suspects, not clients. By the time his work in Serenity was finished, he might have brought her more sorrow than she'd ever felt before, made her hate the sight of him. If he let himself care what she thought, he'd be doing everyone a disservice.

Logan's jaw muscles clenched as the truth dawned. It was already too late. He'd started to like the very person whose quiet life he was probably going to destroy.

He steeled himself for the job ahead and forced a smile. "So, Mrs. Randall, how long have you known Rebecca? She tells me she's lived here since she was a baby. I suppose you could tell lots of interesting stories about her childhood."

"A few."

"That aunt of hers is quite a character, isn't she? Has she always been so odd?"

"Well…"

Becky interrupted. "I don't think it's right to put Aunt Effie down just because she's getting senile." She snatched up a tan baseball cap with "Spring River Country" printed on the front and smacked it into Logan's chest with more force than she'd intended.

All he said was "Ooof."

Grabbing his arm, she bid Belinda Randall goodbye as she hurried him out of the chamber office and back into the sunshine.

He resisted mildly. "What's the rush? I was just getting acquainted with your friend."

"I know. You sure like to ask a lot of personal questions, don't you?"

"I'm only trying to get my bearings. You know, develop a feel for the town."

"Then ask *me*." She started to scowl, squinting against the brightness of the clear day. "I don't know how they do it where you come from, but around here we don't make friends by grilling people. You were beginning to sound like a bad cop show on TV."

"In that case, I apologize."

As they moved toward the street, Logan started to put his hand on her back again. He stopped himself before he'd actually touched her. This job was going to be harder than he'd thought, especially when it came to keeping steady company with this attractive young woman.

He didn't know if the temptation to develop a fondness for her would feel less threatening if he were a practicing clergyman, but for the first time in years, he wished he'd gotten more on-the-job experience after his ordination.

He could also use a big dose of divine deliverance, he decided. And the sooner, the better.

Becky watched Logan surreptitiously while keeping up a patter of conversation pertaining to Serenity's history. Anything to mask her nervousness.

"A hill west of here was the site of a battle in the War Between the States. Where you come from they probably call it the Civil War." She paused for a settling breath. "Where *do* you come from, anyway? Fred mentioned Chicago. Is that where you grew up?"

"No. Fred and I met at Seminary. He was one of my professors."

"I know that. Where are your roots? You told me your mother passed away. Don't you have anybody else?"

"No."

She sighed. "I don't, either. Aunt Effie's my whole family. Of course, given her present condition, she's plenty, poor thing."

"You should look into that medication I mentioned."

"I will. Next time she sees Dr. Barryman I'll ask him about it. I imagine it works for some and not for others, depending on the cause of their illness. Being so new, it's probably really expensive."

"Is that a problem for you?"

"We're not destitute, if that's what you're asking. Effie has her Social Security and Medicare and I do as much as I can. I'll get her whatever she needs."

"The church has a fund for that kind of shortfall, doesn't it?"

"That money is for folks who really need it."

"Then let me contribute."

Becky stared at him, incredulous. "Why would you offer to do that?"

"Altruism?"

"Oh?" Her gaze narrowed, her mind in a spin. Why, with all the faith-based answers he could have given, had he chosen such a secular one?

That thought led her further into doubt. Brother Fred often expressed himself in relation to God's work or Jesus' teachings, while Logan had yet to do so. Either that was odd or she'd been hanging around a traditional pastor and living in the Bible Belt for too long. Maybe both.

Becky shook her head slowly, thoughtfully, and chanced a sidelong glance at Logan. Something was wrong. She felt as if her spirit was warning her to keep Logan Malloy at arm's length, just like Effie had wanted her to do.

Maybe that was the crux of the problem. Maybe Effie's distrust of anyone new, especially men, was catching, like the common cold. The silly notion made her smile.

Waving his hand in front of her face to disrupt her glassy-eyed stare, Logan said, "You look pretty pleased all of a sudden. I was starting to wonder if my offer of help had offended you."

"I'm sorry. No. I'm not offended. Just a little surprised, that's all. Effie and I will be fine. We always manage. Thanks, anyway."

"What did your aunt do for a living? Teach? Run a preschool program? Maybe baby sit?"

"Goodness, no. She worked in the old shirt factory over in Salem till it closed down a few years back. Aunt Effie is the *last* person anyone would want to watch their children. She's much too high-strung. Always has been. By the time I was old enough for kindergarten, I already felt like the only grown-up in my family."

"Really? If she was that flighty, I'm surprised the courts gave you to her. Must have taken a real battle to convince a judge she was capable."

"I suppose so. She's never talked about it. I assume we wound up together because she was the only relative I had left." Becky chuckled softly. "You should have heard the stories she used to tell me."

"Like what?"

"My favorite was the one about my grandmother being a princess who had fled to America to escape a forced marriage. That made my mama a princess by birth—at least half of one—and therefore I was supposedly one-quarter royalty. It's silly, I know, but it fit a child's dreams and it made me feel better about myself."

"You don't seem to have any problems with your self-image these days."

"I can't thank Effie for that. Until I realized that God loved and accepted me, faults and all, I wasn't nearly this happy. I don't mean I was miserable. Far from it. I just needed my faith in order to blossom." She smiled at him. "But what am I preaching to you for? You already know all that."

"Sure do."

Even though he had readily agreed with her, she was put off by his averted glance, his quickening steps, the stiff set of his shoulders. Looking after him, Becky wondered how a man who was supposed to be empathetic to a congregation could do his job successfully when he obviously held back so much of himself.

Weary and worried, she wished she were back at her desk dealing with lovable, bumfuzzled Brother Fred instead of traipsing all over town in the company of a man whose true nature was so difficult to fathom. For some reason, she felt as if Logan was keeping things from her. No matter how illogical that idea was, she couldn't seem to shake it.

She shivered. This was going to be a *very* long day. Thankfully, her work week was almost over. Sunday couldn't come any too soon to suit her.

Chapter Five

They stopped for lunch at Bea's Café on the north side of the square. Opening the door and taking in all the wonderful aromas was a treat in itself. The place was small, welcoming and decorated with mostly western-style memorabilia. It was also crowded—as usual.

Responding to hellos, nods of greeting and smiles from nearly everyone, Becky led the way to the only empty table and chose the side that would allow Logan to observe the room when he sat across from her. He removed his cap, even though no other male in the place had bothered to do the same.

Becky noticed his perplexity. "Around here, we have hats-on places and hats-off places. This is a hats-on place. It just means it's very informal."

"I see that. How will I know which is which?"

"The best way is by observation. Like now."

Logan was fingering the stiff brim of his new cap. "I feel like I ought to put it back on so everybody won't stare, but that goes against the way I was brought up."

"Look at this as ultracasual dining," she said with a smile. "Imagine you're at a tailgate party or a picnic and then do as you please. Be comfortable."

"Comfortable? I feel like I'm on a different planet." One corner of his mouth quirked. "And I'm definitely the alien around here. Nobody's paid this much attention to me since I was assigned to foot patrols overseas."

"Excuse me?"

"In the army," Logan explained. "That's why I was away when my mother was failing. Didn't Fred tell you?"

"No. He never said a word about that. Were you a chaplain?"

Logan shook his head, his eyes on the menu instead of his companion. "No."

Although it struck Becky as odd that an ordained clergyman wouldn't follow his chosen profession, even in the military, she didn't comment. What Logan might have done in the past was none of her business, no more than Effie's background was any concern of his. Curiosity wasn't enough to make her ask for details when he obviously didn't want to share them. There was no hurry. She could always quiz Fred about Logan later if she wanted.

"The catfish dinner is very good here," Becky said. "And the hushpuppies are to die for."

"Are those like French fries?"

She giggled. "Oh, brother, you do have a lot to learn, don't you?"

"*Now* what did I say?"

"Nothing. Do yourself a favor and keep your mouth shut till you get used to living around here."

"Must be awfully hard to eat that way."

Chuckling at his silly comment she leaned across the small table to speak more privately. "Half the people in here go to our church and the rest know me from other places. If you want to do Fred a real favor, you'll stop talking like a Yankee who accidentally wandered too far south."

Logan's brow knit. "I did that?"

"*Oh, yes.* For your information, hushpuppies are little fried balls of cornmeal batter. We always eat them with catfish. That, and pickled green tomatoes." Becky leaned back, folded her hands in her lap and smiled. "Just relax and let me order for both of us."

"Suits me. I lived on army chow for three years. I can eat anything."

"I really admire the people in our armed forces. Would you like to tell me more?"

His brow furrowed again. His eyes narrowed. All he said was "No."

That answer was getting far too familiar to suit Becky. If Logan Malloy *wasn't* hiding something, he was certainly giving a good impression of someone who *was*. Honesty and openness were qualities anyone would expect from a man in his profession, so why was he holding back so much of himself? It didn't make any sense.

Logan wiped his mouth and fingers with his napkin and leaned back from the table. "Those little dough balls sure were good. Why in the world are they named after dogs?"

"In the old days folks used to fry up little dabs of batter to toss to their puppies to keep them from begging and whining for food. That's supposedly where the name came from. I kind of doubt they were seasoned like these. They were probably more like corn dodgers."

She could tell from his confused look that she'd lost him again. "Those are kind of like cornbread cookies. You do know what cornbread is, don't you?"

"Of course."

"That's a relief. I was beginning to wonder if we were ever going to find common ground."

As she watched, Logan's amiable expression changed and became unreadable. It was as if he were closing himself off from her, from everything around them. Why? Her conversation had been meant as friendly banter, not ridicule. Was it possible that the man was not only unfamiliar with southern customs and cuisine, but he also lacked the ability to appreciate her easygoing sense of humor? If so, she felt sorry for him. No one should have to go through life so somber.

She thought of Fred, with his bumbling ways

and loving heart. That man had gone through more earthly trials than anyone else she knew, yet he always managed to find reasons to give praise and lift everyone's spirits, including his own.

Becky thumbed the bill off the edge of the table and reached for her purse. "I'm going to go order take-out for Brother Fred. You stay here and finish eating. I'll be right back."

Before Logan could stand, let alone object, she'd hurried off. He watched her zigzag between the tables and head for the counter. Right age, right build, right hair and eyes. She had to be the one he was looking for. Only she was sure no baby anymore.

Becky stopped to speak to the waitress, a middle-aged woman who'd been introduced as the original Bea of Bea's Café, giving Logan a few moments in which to gather his thoughts and relive the past few minutes. When Becky had mentioned finding common ground, he'd nearly choked on his iced tea. She and he had plenty in common already, and if his theories were correct, it was mostly bad—especially for Rebecca Tate and her aunt.

Still, it was his job to dig deep enough to ferret out the truth, for his client's sake, and that was exactly what he intended to do, whether he liked this assignment or not.

Muttering to himself, Logan pushed away from the table and put on his cap. Not *like* this assignment? Hah! He hated it. He'd already started to admire Rebecca far too much for his own good. And he was ninety-nine percent sure Effie Tate was the kidnapper he'd been sent to track down. The question was, how could he remain true to his client without hurting Becky, not to mention sort out this muddle the way poor old Fred wanted?

Logan crossed the room in pursuit of Becky, politely returning the nods of acknowledgement he was getting as he passed. Chances were, everyone knew who he was—or rather, who he was supposed to be. He imagined, when all this was over, the good citizens of Serenity would be ready to run him out of town on a rail.

He snorted derisively. If that was all they did, he'd count himself lucky. He just hoped they were short on tar and feathers when the time came.

Effie confronted Becky as soon as she walked in the door that evening. "I heard where you were today, missy."

"I'm sure you did. I was hoping Brother Fred would call and tell you it was his idea, not mine. I couldn't very well turn him down when he asked me to show Logan around town."

"I'll have to have a talk with that Fred all right," Effie grumbled. "He ought to know better'n to send a pretty young thing like you out with the likes of that new preacher. I don't trust him as far as I could throw him."

"None of us are looking forward to change," Becky said gently. "But we all know Fred deserves his retirement. And Brother Logan isn't permanent. While he's here, you really should treat him with the respect due his calling."

"Bah. Respect, my eye. There's somethin' shifty about that man. Mark my words, he's hidin' something."

How could she admit to thinking the same thing without making Effie's delusional condition worse? "I guess he had a bad time while he was in the army. He doesn't like to talk about it. I hear lots of folks have trouble adjusting to civilian life again after they get out of the service."

"Well, well." The elderly woman plopped down on the settee, grinned at Becky, and gave a noisy, theatrical wheeze. "Tell Fred my asthma's kickin' up again and I'd like for him to stop by."

"You know that's not fair. Fred has other folks to minister to. Ones who are really sick. He only has so much time to give each day. If you monopolize him, somebody else may have to go without."

She began to smile as an idea took shape. "Tell you what. How about I send Brother Logan over, instead? Then you and he can get to know each other."

"No!" It was a shout.

"Why not?"

Seeing the dread in her aunt's expression, the sudden stiffness of her body, Becky realized she'd momentarily dropped her guard and forgotten to choose her words carefully enough.

Seeking to make amends, she joined Effie on the

sofa and put her arm around the elderly woman's thin shoulders. "Never mind. I'll tell Fred, just like you wanted. And I won't ask Brother Logan to come by. I promise."

"You're a good girl," Effie whispered.

"I try." The sentimental compliment nearly brought tears to Becky's eyes.

"We won't let 'em get us."

"That's right," Becky agreed sadly. "You and I will stick together no matter what."

As she gently rocked her aunt to soothe her, she reinforced that vow in her heart. Effie had cared for her when she was a helpless baby. Now that the tables were turned, it was Becky's duty to become the acting parent. The source of strength and wisdom. The decision maker.

It wasn't a position she'd sought. Nor was it one she felt comfortable with. It was simply a necessity. Something she must do.

She was positive the Lord wouldn't give her a task she couldn't cope with, but at times like this, she wished He didn't think quite so highly of her capabilities.

Logan had stopped at the local market to pick up a few things for Fred and was headed home. He flipped open his cell phone as he drove and punched a pre-recorded number. An answering machine picked up the call.

"This is Logan Malloy," he said, giving the date

and time for reference. "Sandra, type this report and fax it to Mr. Dan Keringhoven. The number's in the file. You'll know how to word it. Tell him I'm on the job. I've made some contacts and things are progressing as expected. However, I don't have anything definitive for him yet."

He paused, hoping lightning wasn't going to strike him if he stretched the truth a bit more. "I advise we take our time with this investigation if we want to get everything sorted out to his satisfaction. Be sure he understands that. Tell him I'll phone him as soon as I have positive proof, one way or the other. Thanks."

Logan ended the call as he pulled into Fred's driveway. He found his friend pacing the room he used as his home office and paused in the doorway with the sacks of groceries. "I got most of the stuff you wanted. The chicken was about to go out of date so I bought steaks. My treat. Hope that's okay."

"Sounds great. So, did you find out anything useful today?"

"Not much. Let's go put this stuff away before it spoils." He led the way to the kitchen.

Fred followed. "At least tell me what you think."

"Okay," Logan said with a sigh. "I think I'll be stuck until I have a chance to talk to the aunt. How long has she been mentally unbalanced?"

"I wouldn't go that far," Fred argued. "Effie's had a rough life. I have trouble believing she's as ill as you seem to think she is."

"Tell me more about her." He opened the refrigerator and put the meat away. "Were you living here when she moved to town?"

"Yes. Part of the time. I was attending college over in Walnut Ridge but I came home every chance I got. Serenity Chapel didn't even exist back then." He sighed and shook his head. "Effie Tate showed up here during my summer vacation. She was the prettiest girl I'd ever seen."

That statement got Logan's full attention. "Whoa. What about Gracie?"

"I wasn't married to her then," Fred said. "We hadn't even met. If Effie would have had me, she and I could have raised that baby of hers together. But she wasn't ready for a husband. When I went back to school, I fell in love with Gracie. End of story."

"Not hardly. Do you think Effie had feelings for you?"

"I suppose she might have. She never admitted anything. After I was married, we never spoke of it again."

"But you're friends, aren't you?"

"As much as is appropriate. I've never done anything that would dishonor my calling." He stared at Logan. "And I never will, so don't even ask."

"Hey, don't get defensive. I'm not suggesting you step out of line. But you are a widower. Doesn't it seem natural that you might want companionship in your old age?"

"If I get lonesome I'll get a dog."

Logan laughed. "You don't fool me. There's still a warm spot in your heart for Effie Tate. Admit it."

"I've never denied it. That's why I refuse to help you send her to prison. Don't make me sorry I confided in you and let you come here."

"You're already assuming she's guilty, aren't you?"

Fred's nostrils flared in anger. "I never said that. You're twisting everything. Effie's one of the most loving people I've ever had the privilege to know. I won't be a party to anything that might hurt her."

"Then why did you tell me the truth?" Logan made a face. "Never mind. I know the answer. And I respect you for your honesty. But you're forgetting the purpose of my investigation. A baby was kidnapped. It doesn't matter how long ago the abduction occurred, it's still a crime."

"I know."

Logan was sorry to see the old man's shoulders slump when he made that admission. "Look, Fred," he said, giving his mentor an encouraging pat on the back, "I don't want to see you hurt, either. Don't worry about a thing. I'll handle the girl and her aunt by myself."

"Oh, really?" Fred apparently set his concern aside enough to manage a lopsided smile. "That should be interesting. How do you plan to proceed?"

"I'll get into Becky's good graces and ask her to help me deal with her aunt. It shouldn't take too long." He was surprised to hear the older man chuckle. "What's so funny?"

"Nothing. Just thinking," Fred said. "I'm glad I haven't retired yet. I'm looking forward to seeing you try to manipulate those two stubborn, intelligent women. It should be real entertaining."

Chapter Six

Becky looked forward to Sunday mornings, especially since she'd joined Miss Louella's Extraordinary Ladies class. It was the most popular and the most aptly named group at Serenity Chapel. Becky wasn't certain when the word *Extraordinary* had been added to the description. She simply knew that was where she belonged. And she didn't mind one bit that she was younger than most of the other women who attended regularly.

Walking into that classroom always gave Becky the feeling of a happy family reunion. This morning was no exception. There were usually plenty of aches and pains mentioned, as well as prayer requests for others, yet the welcome aura of peace and love easily overshadowed the negative.

Miss Louella Higgens's smile was as broad as the rest of her when she greeted Becky with a hug and a welcoming, "Glad to see you," followed by a wink and a query. "So, what's new? I notice you've got your best dress on."

Becky ignored the background chuckles. She shrugged. "Not much. I happen to like this dress."

The class's reaction was unanimous disbelief, expressed in several subdued but evident ways, including whispers and snickers.

Miss Louella rapped on the podium. "Now, now. It's none of our business if Becky wants to go cavorting all over town with a handsome stranger and get all those tongues to wagging. We'll love her even if she backslides, won't we? Of course we will." She suppressed a titter of her own. "Maybe we'd best just pray for her real hard and leave the rest to the Good Lord."

Becky blew a loud sigh. "Oh, for crying out loud…." She sank into her usual seat at the end of the second row of folding chairs. "It's no secret. I took Brother Malloy on a short tour around town. We stopped at the chamber and then had lunch at Bea's. Anything else y'all want to know?"

The questions came at her in a rush. She chose to answer the easiest few. "Yes, he's nice. And polite. He has wonderful manners. But Brother Fred is right about his not fitting in here very well. I don't think Logan is the preacher for us. I'm sure he'll make a fine substitute until we can find Fred's replacement, though."

She waved her hands to request quiet. "Simmer

down. I don't know much more about the man than you all do. He's not real talkative."

"All right. Hush." Louella called for order. "Looks like we'd best add finding a new preacher to our list of prayer requests. Anybody else? How's your aunt doing, Becky?"

"She has her ups and downs. Change seems to really bother her. She's having a hard time adjusting to Brother Logan being here, even temporarily. I suppose that's natural. No matter who we choose, we'll always miss Fred."

There was a chorus of agreement.

"I wanted to bring in that young fella from over by Jonesboro and let him show us what he can do," widowed Carol Sue Grabowski announced from the back of the room. "Don't see what's takin' the pulpit committee so long to make a move. You'd think Brother Fred didn't want to let go."

"I suppose he doesn't," Becky said. She pivoted to face everyone. "He doesn't realize it, of course. He's really going to be at loose ends when he doesn't have a job to go to every day."

"Or anybody to come home to," Miss Louella said. "I figured one of us single ladies would've snagged him by now. There's plenty to choose from right here in this room."

"Louella!" Carol Sue blurted, her cheeks reddening. Others merely laughed softly or mumbled.

"Well, I did," the teacher said. "If you can't

speak the truth in the Lord's house, where can you speak it?"

"That's very true," Becky agreed. "I'd like to see him find a nice lady to share his old age, too."

"What about Effie?" Mercy Cosgrove piped up. "Seems to me they need each other. Fred used to be sweet on her. Maybe he still is?"

That revelation took Rebecca by complete surprise. "He did? They were? I mean, Fred and Effie were a couple? That's amazing." No wonder Effie had always run to Fred for advice when she'd had problems she couldn't solve alone. All this time, Becky had assumed Effie was simply relying on their pastor the way everyone else did. Hearing that they might share a deeper friendship was quite a shock.

Continuing to grin like a cat with bird feathers clinging to its whiskers, Mercy nodded. "Yup. I remember it well. You was just a tiny thing back then. Hardly more'n a couple of months old. Fred cut a dashing figure in those days. Every bit as handsome as that Logan Malloy. All the girls wanted to marry him. All except Effie. She got on her high horse about it and poor Fred went off and found him a wife somewhere else."

"Gracie Fleming was a lovely woman. Perfect for Brother Fred," Becky insisted.

"Sure she was. But she's been gone for two years now. Why do you suppose Fred hasn't looked around more? Enough of us have asked him over to Sunday dinner and filled him up with our fried chicken and homemade pies. I think he's still stuck on Effie, more's the pity."

Rebecca took a deep breath and released it as a slow sigh. If that was the case, he'd probably waited too long. Effie's mental state was less than conducive to a happily-ever-after scenario. Still, the Lord did move in mysterious ways sometimes.

"Brother Logan mentioned a new medicine that might help my aunt," Becky said. "I'm going to ask Dr. Sam about it."

"Good." Louella was making notes, as were most of the others. "Now that that's settled, who else has a prayer request or a praise to share? Time's a wastin'."

Logan was hanging back near the sanctuary door, helping Brother Fred greet parishioners who hadn't attended Sunday school. He'd seen Becky breeze into her classroom an hour earlier but he hadn't spotted Effie Tate yet. Hopefully, she'd pass by and give Fred the chance to introduce him on neutral ground. Effie was far less likely to spit in his eye or turn and run if she felt safely surrounded by friends.

Scanning the parking lot, Logan saw the church minibus arrive and begin to disgorge its passengers. His quarry was among them. He elbowed Fred and stepped back. "Here she comes. Ready?"

The older man nodded and reached for Effie's hand, grasping it firmly before he said, "Effie, dear, I'd like to introduce Brother Logan Malloy. You remember him, don't you? He helped you and Rebecca get down off the roof."

Squinting past Fred's shoulder, Effie glared. "I remember him all right. He liked to scare me to death."

"He's an old friend of mine," Fred continued. "A good friend." He stood to one side and passed her hand to Logan as if they were exchanging a precious, fragile commodity.

Logan felt her tremble when he accepted her hand but she stood her ground. He smiled. "Pleased to meet you, ma'am. I wish you and I had gotten off to a better start."

Staring up at him, Effie said clearly, "It's not the beginning that concerns me, young man. It's how everything ends."

He assumed she was referring to spiritual matters. "I'm sure Heaven is a wonderful place."

"Heaven?" The elderly eyes narrowed. "Ha! I'm not near ready to take that trip yet. Got too many things to take care of down here."

"Don't we all. I'm staying with Brother Fred while I'm in town. If you ever need my help or want to talk, feel free to call. Day or night. That's what I'm here for."

Eyebrows arching, she pulled her hand away. "Is it? We'll see."

Watching her walk off, Logan was puzzled. If that woman was senile, she was giving an awfully good impression of cleverness and dry wit. He supposed it was possible she'd been confused and he'd misconstrued her comments as being cunning, but he doubted it. He'd stake his reputation that there was a lot more to Effie Tate than most people suspected. He just hoped he could find out the whole truth and bring this investigation to a suitable conclusion before his employer got impatient and interfered, the way he'd threatened to.

Mr. Keringhoven did deserve to hear that he'd made a little progress, which he had, but he wasn't ready to reveal any details. Not yet. His solemn promise to Fred Fleming took precedence over everything else, even his job. No one was going to storm into town and destroy the Tate family because of supposition. Justice had waited this long. It could wait a little longer. Eventually the real truth would come out.

Rebecca's usual place was in the center of the front row where she could more easily distribute and collect the information cards that prospective members filled out. Consequently, she faced the pulpit. Beside it, to the left, sat Dub Robinson, the gray-haired choir director. Logan sat on the other side. He was wearing a dark suit this morning, and the same kind of plain shirt and tie Brother Fleming favored. That was where their similarity ended. Logan seemed larger than life and twice as handsome.

Her cheeks warmed. Becky looked away, grateful that her back was to the ladies from her Sunday school class. The last thing she needed was to have them see her blush because of Logan.

His eyes met hers. He smiled slightly.

Becky nodded a friendly response, then busied herself with the membership folder she always brought to the service. Anything but continue to look at him, although she didn't have a clue how she was going to listen to Fred's sermon without glancing past him and seeing Logan. The more she tried to avoid doing so, the more her attention drifted in that direction.

She was so intent on *not* looking, she didn't notice she had company until she heard, "Scoot over, girl."

Becky was startled. "Aunt Effie? What brings you down front? I thought you liked to be by the door in the back?"

"Still do. Just don't want you sittin' up here all alone."

Rebecca grinned at the rapidly filling pew as she tucked her skirt closer to make room. "I'm hardly alone, Aunt Effie. But you're more than welcome to join me. I like it in the front. There aren't as many distractions."

"Humph. 'Cept the fellas up there," the older woman said with lifted eyebrows. "Leastwise we can keep track of 'em from here."

"That's true." Becky pulled a face. "And they can watch us. When I was a teenager I used to think Brother Fred was preaching straight to me. It really made me nervous." She laughed quietly. "Especially if I was chewing gum or doing something else I thought he wouldn't like."

Effie snorted. "Why do you think I always sit near the back? That Fred can really get to me when he goes to preachin' serious."

Leaning closer to speak in confidence, Becky said, "I'm looking forward to hearing how Brother Logan does when he finally takes a turn at it. I don't think he's too thrilled with the idea of giving a sermon."

"Don't you think that's a bit strange?"

"Yes and no," Becky answered. "He's from the city. I suspect he knows he's going to have trouble getting this congregation to relate to him."

"Maybe." Effie sat straighter and carefully smoothed her dark navy skirt over her knees. "Or maybe he's afraid everybody'll see right through him."

Before Becky could comment, the elderly woman glared at him and added, "I sure do."

"Aunt Effie!"

"Well, I do. You would, too, if you wasn't so young and foolish. Flo was like that, too. Walked right into the devil's pretty trap with her eyes wide open."

"Who, exactly, is…?"

Before Becky could form the rest of her query, the organist cranked up the volume and the choir began to file in, singing. Resigned, Becky sat back. She'd missed another perfect chance to question Effie. Oh, well, there was bound to be another. This was the first time in recent memory her aunt had spoken of

Flo without sounding confused. That was not only a good sign, it gave Becky hope that she'd soon get an opportunity to ask for more specifics.

Though she stood with the congregation to sing the first hymn, her mind was still puzzling. There had to be a reason why memories of Florence had suddenly begun crowding her aunt's thoughts, why the elderly woman often mistook her for whoever Flo was.

Perhaps if she could convince Effie to talk about the past and identify the personal demons that had started haunting her so vividly, her mental state would improve.

This wasn't the first time that notion had occurred to Becky. Was God answering her prayers by suggesting the underlying reason for poor Effie's turmoil? That seemed almost too simple, too pat. Yet there were cases on record where guilt had eroded sanity enough to cause symptoms of illness.

Rebecca raised her gaze to Brother Fred and found him looking at her with an expression of tender concern. She smiled at him.

Instead of returning the amiable gesture, he shifted his awareness to Effie and began blinking rapidly. When he took out his handkerchief and blew his nose, Becky had to resist the urge to jump out of her seat and rush forward to give him a comforting hug.

Something was really bothering Fred. And he

wasn't the only one. Beside her, Aunt Effie had begun to sniffle, too.

Becky looked back and forth, alternating between the two people she loved most in the whole world. Whatever was wrong, she was going to find out and then fix it, even if that meant she had to use the information she'd garnered in class and play matchmaker for the most unlikely couple she'd ever known.

Chapter Seven

Becky prayed Brother Fred through his sermon, asking the Lord to sustain him and give him the strength to carry on as usual. His struggle became hers. Though the congregation was dismissed a few minutes before noon, the service still felt like the longest one she'd ever sat through.

Gathering up her Bible and the membership file, she stood and waited for Effie. The older woman acted glued to the padded pew. "I need to drop this folder in the office," Becky said. "Want to keep me company?"

"Sure." Effie stood slowly, stiffly. "I want to hang around anyway and talk to Fred before I go. I'm in no hurry to tangle with that new preacher, though. Not again."

"You talked to Brother Logan? When?"

"This morning."

"You didn't give him trouble, did you?"

"No more than he deserved," Effie said flatly. "I

was thinkin' of askin' Fred to come to Sunday dinner today. That okay with you?"

"It's fine. More than fine," Becky said. "He seemed a little out-of-sorts this morning. Probably needs a good dose of your home cooking." *And having Fred there for moral support will give me the perfect chance to ask questions without you getting as upset as usual.*

"Good." Effie seemed to miraculously gain energy. "You get that Logan fella away from our Fred so's I can ask him."

"Don't you think it's impolite to exclude Brother Malloy? I mean, he is staying at Fred's. And they are old friends."

"I don't want that man in my house."

"Why not?"

"I've got my reasons."

"I know. You've told me often enough how you feel about most men. Don't you think we should make an exception in Brother Logan's case? For Fred's sake, I mean."

Effie scrunched up her face. "Humph. Seems to me this whole idea's gotten out of hand. Let's forget it."

"No, no. It'll do us good to have company. And I know the visit will be good for Fred. Let me handle it. We do have enough to feed four, don't we?"

"I put a whole roast in the Crock-Pot. I 'spect it'll do if we mash some extra taters and make gravy. But…"

"All right." Becky worked at acting eager. "Then it's settled. Do you want to ride the bus home or shall I pick you up after I talk to Brother Fred?"

"What're you askin' *me* for? What I want doesn't seem to matter much anymore."

"Of course it does." She patted Effie's hand. "You know as well as I do that excluding Brother Malloy is unkind. You can be a little stubborn sometimes, we all can, but you're not mean-spirited."

Effie's expression showed disgust, followed by reluctant capitulation. "Okay. Do it your way. I'll go home and get busy. Don't hurry on my account. You can set the table when you get there."

"Fine."

She waited for her aunt to start for the side door where the church bus always waited. Instead, the older woman stood motionless, staring into space. "The bus is that way," Becky finally said, pointing.

Effie's head snapped around. "I know."

Watching her amble off, Becky wondered if she had known which way to go or if she was simply covering another mental lapse. Either was possible. If Effie was really that ill, was it fair to Fred to encourage him to renew their courtship?

That question brought a smile. *Why not?* It wasn't up to her to decide the outcome. And if two people were ever suited for each other, it was Brother Fred and Aunt Effie. Talk about two peas in a pod!

Sweet peas, she added, grinning. *Definitely sweet peas.*

* * *

Becky stood aside in the foyer, waiting patiently until Brother Fred and Brother Logan had bid each departing member of the congregation a pleasant goodbye.

As they closed the door, she heard Logan ask the older man, "You okay?" and saw an answering nod.

It was Fred she approached. "Nice sermon."

"Thanks." He blotted his brow. "I think the air-conditioning needs adjusting again. Remind me to ask the custodian to see to it tomorrow."

"Okay."

Logan had stepped so close Becky was having trouble concentrating on her boss. "Uh, Aunt Effie wanted me to invite you to dinner." She gave a nervous little cough. "Both of you."

"Well…" Fred's eyes narrowed.

Smiling, Logan patted him on the back. "We'd love to come. Mind if I run home and ditch this tie first?"

Becky tried not to show how surprised she was that the easy acceptance had come from Logan rather than her beloved employer. "No problem. We'll eat between one-thirty and two. Will that give you enough time?"

All she got from Brother Fred was a nod. It was Logan who said, "Sounds perfect. Can we bring anything?"

"No. Aunt Effie has a roast already cooked. I'm

sure we have plenty of food. Thanks for asking." She backpedaled. "Well, I'd better head home to help."

"Don't go to any trouble," Logan said. "We want you to treat us just like you would family. Don't we, Fred?"

The older man gave Becky a slow, tender smile, his eyes once again beginning to glisten. "We are family. If Gracie and I had been blessed with children, I couldn't love them any more than I do Rebecca."

This time, she was close enough to give him a comforting hug without displaying it in front of the whole congregation. No explanation was necessary. She simply stepped up to Brother Fred and put her arms around him.

"I love you, too," she said, getting misty-eyed herself. "I wish you *were* my real dad."

All he said was, "So do I."

Logan drove Fred home. He waited until they were inside the white, two-story house on Squirrel Hill Road before he said, "You're *not* Becky's father, you know."

The older man's head snapped around. "You don't have to remind me."

"I think maybe I do." Logan dropped his jacket on a chair, then pulled off his tie and unbuttoned the neck and cuffs of his dress shirt. "Try to put yourself in that guy's place. How would you feel?"

Instead of answering, Fred said, "Never mind

how I'd feel. Seems to me you've been assuming too much. How can you be so sure of your client's motives? Suppose it's revenge he wants? And suppose Effie isn't guilty? What if you throw her to the wolves and later discover you're wrong. What then?"

"I'm not throwing anybody to the wolves. My client is only interested in justice."

"I don't want a character reference. I want to know what you intend to do if you realize too late that the man is vindictive."

Fred's query was too perceptive to sit well with Logan. It wasn't his job to judge a client's heart. All he was hired to do was locate missing persons, report his findings, and leave the rest to law enforcement. It had already occurred to him that this job was a special case, particularly when he'd learned that his quarry might be living in the same town his old friend called home.

At first, that news had seemed providential; a walk in the park. Now, however, he was beginning to wonder if this pursuit was going to be more like blundering into quicksand, instead. There wasn't anyone left who meant more to him than Fred Fleming. And apparently, there weren't many people as dear to Fred as Becky and her aunt.

Logan knew he couldn't just walk away, no matter how much he wanted to. If he tried to abdicate his duty, his client would simply send someone else and keep searching Serenity and its environs until he was satisfied.

Ethics—and conscience—precluded Logan's lying. He was, however, open to using delaying tactics when necessary. That was why he'd called in such an ambiguous report.

While Fred was in the bedroom changing into casual clothes, Logan phoned his office to check for messages. He was concluding his business when Fred returned and took up their conversation where it had left off.

"You don't have a shred of real proof," the older man said.

"I know. And I won't act on unfounded suspicions. But I am looking forward to having dinner with the prime suspect."

Muttering, Fred hitched up his slacks. "Then go get changed or whatever you're going to do and let's make tracks. The sooner we get this over with and you see you're barking up the wrong tree, the better I'll feel."

"Barking?" Logan laughed.

"Yeah. I used to have a dumb old hound that acted just like you. He'd get it into his thick head that a squirrel was in a certain tree because he'd seen him run up it. No matter how hard I tried, I couldn't convince that dog the squirrel had jumped to another treetop and was long gone."

"Meaning?"

"Meaning, I'm no detective, but a few ideas have come to mind. One, your caller might have been passing through and just stopped in Serenity to use a pay phone. And two, if Becky wanted to call someone, why wouldn't she use her cell phone? One mysterious telephone call seems like an awfully thin clue to base a whole investigation on."

"It is," Logan said. "But even a hound dog has to start by sniffing around before he can decide which way to go. That's all I'm doing."

Fred bristled. "You just mind where that sniffing leads. My cooperation ends the minute you do anything to upset Effie."

"Even if she's guilty?" Logan asked quietly.

The look of disdain Fred shot his way was all the answer he needed.

"I thought we weren't going to fuss?" Becky arched an eyebrow. "Looks to me like you've gone overboard."

"Nonsense. Brother Fred loves my fried pies." Effie expertly flipped the half-moon-shaped dough pocket bubbling in the skillet. "I made apple. It's his favorite."

"You and Fred have been friends for a long time." She hesitated a heartbeat. "Funny you two never got together. Romantically, I mean."

"The man was married."

"Not when you first met him."

Effie pointed with the spatula. "What do you know about that? Who's been blabbing?"

"Nobody special." Becky continued to lay the silverware beside the plates spaced at compass points around the circular table. "We were talking about it this morning in class. Somebody remembered that you and Fred had been pretty close, once. They said he even asked you to marry him. I wondered why you'd never mentioned it. You didn't turn him down because of me, did you?"

The older woman blanched in spite of the heat from the frying pan. "'Course not. I've told you how I feel plenty of times. Fred's the sweetest man I know but he's still a man. None of 'em can be trusted. 'Specially not…"

"Especially not who?"

"Never mind. I'm a silly old fool, that's all. You got the table set?"

Rebecca squinted at her across the farm-style kitchen. "The table's fine. But you're not. It's high time you told me exactly why you're so dead set against men—particularly good-looking ones."

"Handsome is as handsome does. I got nothin' against 'em, long as they behave themselves."

"Brother Fred has always been polite and kind, to us as well as to everybody else. How can you lump him in with all the others?"

"Self-preservation," Effie said. "There's only one way for a woman to be sure she's safe and that's to take care of herself." She smiled at Becky, then sniffled and turned to tend the frying pan before she added, "Herself, and her innocent babies."

There had been instances, during Becky's childhood, when she'd pretended Effie was her birth mother. She'd never asked directly until now. "Are you my mother?"

"I've done my best to be."

"I know you have." Becky approached and patted her aunt's thin shoulder, taking care to keep them both out of range of splattering cooking oil. "No one could have done a better job of raising me. What I meant was, did you invent the story about my parents so I wouldn't be ashamed of not having a daddy?"

Effie's jaw dropped. "Sakes alive, no. What ever gave you that idea?"

"Partly the wild stories you used to tell when I was a kid. I was never sure whether they were true or whether you were making them up to entertain me." She chuckled. "I am pretty sure I'm not the grand-daughter of a princess."

"Sometimes the truth is a lot harder to swallow than a good, made-up story."

"I'm not a kid anymore. I'm all grown up. I want to know the whole truth, Aunt Effie. Tell me? Please?"

The elderly woman sighed and shook her head. "Not right now. Let me chew on the idea for awhile. Could be the best thing I can do is keep my mouth shut, like I have been."

"That can't be right. The truth is supposed to set us free, remember?"

"*This* truth won't," Effie said flatly.

"How do you know? How can you be so sure?"

Tears glistened in the old woman's eyes. "Because, chances are, this truth got your mama killed."

Chapter Eight

After her aunt's astounding disclosure, it was all Becky could do to act seminormal, let alone carry on pleasant, dinner-table conversation. She not only wasn't sure she was making sense, she couldn't recall half of what had been said, other than, "Please pass the potatoes," or "Would you like gravy?" If she wasn't careful, folks would start imagining she was as dotty as her poor aunt. Right now, that was exactly how she felt.

Effie had clammed up completely after making the comment about Becky's late mother. Fred had arrived with Logan moments later, giving Becky no more private time with her aunt in which to probe for details.

Consequently, Becky was beside herself. The duration of the morning's sermon was nothing compared to the way the afternoon was dragging by. Time was creeping like a snail in January. A frozen snail. That image did nothing for her appetite.

Brother Fred didn't seem hungry, either. Though he'd always loved Effie's home cooking, he wasn't eating enough this time to keep Thelma McEntire's toy poodle happy. Which reminded her of an idea she'd been kicking around.

She voiced it. "I was thinking of getting a dog to keep Aunt Effie company. I was going to wait till Christmas to give it to her but maybe sooner is better."

The astonished expression on her aunt's face was so comical she had to laugh. "It can't be good for you to be home alone all day. Everybody needs companionship. Don't you think so, Brother Fred?"

Fred swallowed wrong and coughed into his napkin. "I, uh, I was just telling Logan the same thing. Dogs make wonderful companions. I used to keep hounds. Remember?"

"Of course, I do," Becky said brightly. "One was a great big black-and-tan dog called Homer. I used to sit on your porch and tell that dog all my troubles while Aunt Effie helped Gracie bake for church suppers. Homer had soft, floppy ears that felt like warm velvet."

"Dogs are nothin' but fleas and hair with an attitude," Effie piped up. "Never did see the use in 'em."

Finally, a subject that everyone could discuss even if their opinions did differ, Becky thought with relief. She glanced at Logan. "Did you have a dog when you were a little boy?"

"No." He shook his head. "But I have worked with a few."

"Really? What's your favorite breed?"

"We used German shepherds. They were great for foot patrols. Never missed a thing," he said flatly.

Oh, dear. He'd told her he'd been in the military and had indicated he didn't want to talk about those experiences. What should she say now? What could she say?

Fred came to the rescue. "Logan was an MP."

"Oh? Military police? How interesting."

No one else commented. Looking from Fred to Logan to Effie, Becky was struck by the difference in each one's expression. Fred seemed to be contemplating poignant thoughts and Effie was scowling like she wished she could boot Logan out the nearest door. When Becky looked at Logan he was staring back at her as if trying to delve into her subconscious and uncover secrets she didn't even know she had. Of all their reactions, his was by far the most unsettling. And the most compelling.

Her heart went out to him. "It must have been very hard to reconcile your beliefs with such a dangerous assignment," she said softly.

A fleeting air of empathy and understanding connected them, giving Becky the shivers. Clearly, she'd touched on a point of conflict Logan didn't often acknowledge. She gave him a smile of encouragement. Instead of the amiable response she'd anticipated, however, he began to scowl.

"There is no way to reconcile my faith with taking a human life," he said. "The only way to deal with it is to close down your rational mind and rely on your reflexes for survival."

"It must feel really good to put all that behind you. I'm glad Brother Fred was able to offer you this chance to get back to preaching. How long have you been out of the army?"

Because she'd expected him to cite a recent date, it was a surprise to hear, "I was discharged five years ago."

"Really?"

Her gaze flashed an unspoken question to Fred. The shake of the older man's head was barely perceptible but his warning was clear. If she wanted to find out where Logan had been and what he'd been doing for the past five years, she needed to choose a better time to ask.

"So, let's get back to the subject of Aunt Effie's Christmas puppy," she suggested. "What kind of a dog should I be looking for?"

"Invisible," the older woman grumbled. "The kind that never makes a mess or chews my shoes or leaves hair all over the house."

Becky chuckled. "Has anybody ever told you you're hard to please?"

"Mostly everybody," Effie said dryly. "But I've saved your bacon, missy. More than once."

Across the table, Fred twitched like he'd been poked with a pin. "Effie!"

"Well, I have," she insisted. "And I'll keep on doin' it as long as there's a spark of life in this old body."

The room stilled. It was as if they'd all stopped breathing. Effie was glaring at Logan. Fred was staring, openmouthed at Effie. And Logan had eased back in his chair as if waiting for further outbursts.

Becky could hear her own heart pounding. What had just happened? Could it be connected to Effie's comments about her mother's death? Waiting with the others, she imagined she saw uncommon apprehension in Brother Fred's eyes. If he was frightened, there had to be good reason. That conclusion alarmed her more than anything else.

Effie had broken the silence by jumping to her feet and announcing dessert. Logan watched her walk stiffly across the kitchen and return with a plate of pastry.

"Fried apple pies," she said, offering the plate to Fred. "Your favorite."

"They certainly are." He patted his ample stomach. "Wish I had room."

"You can take 'em with you if you want."

"Absolutely," Becky agreed. "I don't need all those extra calories." She included Logan, even though Effie wasn't even acknowledging his presence. "How about you, Brother Malloy? They're really good."

He was about to reach for one of the small half circles of puffy dough when his cell phone rang. He got to his feet. "I'll take this outside. Don't let me break up the party."

There was no chatter behind him to cover his pending conversation so he continued to his car, faced the street and leaned a hip against the fender. "This is Logan Malloy."

"I'm sorry, sir," the caller said. "I did as you asked and faxed that report to Mr. Keringhoven, but he's not a happy camper. He insists on speaking to you personally."

"That's okay, Sandra. Tell him I'll call him in a day or so."

"I'm afraid that won't do. He's really steamed." The secretary lowered her voice. "He found out where I live and showed up here."

"At *your* place?"

"Yes. He says he's going to stay till I tell him how to reach you. I figured it was better to place the call myself than to give him your unlisted number."

"You did the right thing, Sandra. Put him on."

Logan didn't give the angry man a chance to say anything beyond, "Malloy?" before breaking in.

"Your behavior is way out of line, Keringhoven. My people take orders from me, not from our clients. I'll give you a full report when I'm ready and not before. Is that clear?"

"Very." The man on the other end of the line sounded gruff, hoarse.

"Good. Then we understand each other. I'll call

you at your home number later today and tell you what little I've learned so far. Be there."

"In other words, get out of your secretary's hair?"

"Exactly. Sandra is my employee, not my confidante. She isn't hiding anything from you." His conscience twitched when he added, "Neither am I," though the claim was essentially true. He hadn't been able to prove Effie's story was false, nor had he been able to substantiate her claim of kinship to Rebecca. Without insisting on DNA evidence or getting the older woman to confess, he was stymied. Temporarily.

"Look," Logan said, "I think I'm getting close. The less I'm distracted by unnecessary interruptions like this, the better. Put Sandra back on."

He heard vague conversation in the background before his secretary returned.

"He's leaving," Sandra said, obviously relieved.

"Good. If he so much as looks at you funny again, I want to know. I'll stay on the line till you're sure he's long gone."

"He's driving away. I'm locking the door now," she said. "Do you think he'll come back?"

"He'd better not. When I talk to him tonight I'll warn him we'll drop his case if he doesn't behave himself."

"I thought you were worried about your old friend."

"I was. I am. I'm going to see this through whether it's an official job or not."

"Okay, boss. But I'm putting in a request for hazardous duty pay."

Logan laughed. "Do it. I'll tell Pete it's okay and have him write you a bonus check. Take care, kid."

Waiting till Sandra hung up, Logan folded the phone and slipped it back into his pocket. Part of him wished he'd never gotten involved in this investigation, while another part knew it had been inevitable. A man didn't turn his back on a true friend, no matter what the personal cost. Once he'd established the connection to Serenity, and to Fred Fleming, he'd been obliged by loyalty to accept the case.

That didn't make his job any easier. If Logan had been dealing with strangers he'd have simply forged ahead according to the usual formula. In this case, however, he intended to take his time and bend as many rules as necessary. It looked like convincing Keringhoven to be patient was going to be the trickiest part of his plan.

Logan heaved a sigh. It was time to head back into the house and see if he could learn anything else relevant.

He straightened, looked up, and stifled an exclamation of self-reproach. Becky was standing barely thirty feet away, quietly watching. This was the second time she'd caught him unawares. The second time she could have overheard too much for her own good. There wouldn't be a third.

She hadn't meant to get close enough to eavesdrop when she'd wandered outside. She'd only wanted to give Fred and Effie a little privacy. When she'd spotted Logan leaning against his car with the phone still pressed to his ear, she'd paused on the front porch and waited politely for him to finish talking.

What little she had heard had sounded a bit odd but not particularly interesting. It was his wary, almost devious expression when he turned and spotted her that made her uneasy.

In seconds, he'd recovered his nonchalant demeanor. The rapid change in him gave her goose bumps and tickled the hair at her nape. She felt like saying, "Will the *real* Logan Malloy please step forward?"

Instead, she waved and held up a plastic bag. "I saved you a couple of pies. Are you ready to eat them?"

His smile was as amiable as ever, yet Becky gave an imperceptible shiver as he approached.

"I'll try one," he said, gesturing at the porch swing. "Why don't we sit out here? The weather's too nice to spend the whole day indoors."

"As long as we keep our feet firmly on the ground that's fine with me. No more ladders, okay?" Her misgivings were rapidly dissolving under the influence of Logan's captivating smile.

"That reminds me. How are Effie's baby birds doing?"

"Fine. Looks like they've all fledged. As soon as I'm positive they're gone for good I'm going to have the chimney cleaned and a better cap installed."

"I could do that for you." Taking a bite of the pie, Logan cupped his other hand beneath it to catch the warm juice. "Hey, this is really good."

"You sound surprised."

"I am, a little. I'd never heard of frying pie. It's kind of like a turnover."

"Only heavier," Becky added.

"That's the truth. I won't be hungry for a week. Aren't you having one?"

"Maybe later." She hesitated, thinking about his offer to bird-proof the chimney. "I hate to ask you to climb up on the roof again, even for a good cause, but since you're going to stay…"

"Stay? What gave you that idea?"

She glanced toward his car and immediately rued the slip.

Logan stiffened, stopped eating. "How much did you hear?"

"Nothing. Well, not much. I wasn't snooping. I may have heard you mention hanging around as long as necessary. I assumed you were talking about staying in Serenity until we found a replacement for Brother Fred."

"What else?"

"Nothing." She scowled. "Don't look at me like that."

"Like what?"

"Like you think I'm guilty of something."

"Are you?"

The hackles on her neck pricked again. "I don't

understand what's gotten into you. One minute you're nice and the next you're accusing me of who-knows-what. Does Brother Fred know you have a split personality? Is that why he didn't recommend you for a permanent position?"

"I'm sure Fred is acting in the best interests of his congregation. You said yourself that I don't belong in a place like this."

"I wasn't being derogatory. I was just repeating something you'd said. I wouldn't purposely hurt your feelings."

"You didn't. I happen to agree with you."

"Then *what* is your problem?"

His eyes darkened. His gaze was so steady, so penetrating, she felt as if it reached all the way to her soul and read her innermost thoughts.

"*You* are," Logan said. "The Word was right. I've discovered for myself how impossible it is to serve two masters."

"You mean the verses that say you'll love the one and hate the other?"

Logan huffed. "Yeah. That's about the size of it."

Chapter Nine

Becky didn't know when she'd been so wrung out. Maybe never. When she'd gone back into the house to get Logan a glass of milk to wash down the fried pie, she'd come upon Brother Fred embracing Aunt Effie while the older woman cried on his shoulder. Literally. They had both regarded her with so much sadness she felt like a first-century martyr about to be fed to the lions.

As soon as their dinner guests had left, Becky began to probe. "Are you feeling better now?"

"Good enough."

"Well, I'm not. I want to know what got you so upset?"

"I wasn't upset. Whatever gave you that idea?"

Becky huffed. "Oh, I don't know. Maybe the fact you were crying all over Brother Fred."

"I was just commiserating."

"About what?" She wasn't ready to give up.

"About bein' between a rock and a hard place,

mostly." Effie managed a tight smile. "I can sure enough identify with him about that."

"Because of me?"

"'Course not. What put that silly notion in your head?"

"You did," Becky said. "Don't you think it's about time you told me about my mother? And not the runaway princess story. The truth about how and why she died."

"I don't know it all."

"Then tell me what you do know. Please?" Becky took her aunt's thin hand and led her out onto the porch she'd so recently shared with Logan. Evening was fast approaching. "Would you like your sweater?"

"No. I'm warm enough."

"Then sit down with me and let's swing while we talk. It'll relax you."

"You aren't aimin' to drop this, are you?"

"No. But I won't rush you. Take your time." Still holding Effie's hand, Becky patted it gently. "It'll be okay. I have a right to know."

Tears glistened in the other woman's eyes. "That doesn't make it wise for me to tell you."

"But it makes it fitting. You won't be telling tales out of school. My parents are both dead, right?"

A tear crested and slid down Effie's cheek before she spoke. "Your mama and I were close. Real close. She was beautiful, just like you, but she wasn't grounded good. She was flighty. Got herself into a terrible mess."

"Is that what you meant by saying she fell for the devil's ways?"

"Sort of. The trouble started when she married your daddy. He seemed like a nice enough fella. I didn't dream he'd turn mean like he did."

Becky's fingers tightened on her aunt's.

Effie returned the squeeze. "You sure you want me to keep on?"

"Yes. Please."

"Well, things just got worse and worse between 'em. Pretty soon Flo was making excuses for supposed accidents and showing up with bruises."

"Whoa," Becky said, "you told me my mother's name was Rebecca, like mine."

"I lied. I had to. It was for your own good." Effie lowered her voice, stared without seeing, and spoke as if narrating a dream. "Flo had that sunshine hair like yours and the bluest eyes you ever saw. It broke my heart to see her gettin' hurt over and over again."

Becky's stomach was churning, her pulse racing. "My *father* did that to her?"

"Yes." Malice filled Effie's gaze.

"Are you positive?"

"Oh, yes. It wasn't too bad at first but after you came along, Flo and me decided to run away. We had it all planned." Effie sniffled and blinked back tears. "I was supposed to take you and meet her at a motel we'd picked out. Only she never showed up. By that time, she was dead."

Becky was so astounded she could hardly speak, let alone think straight. "And you *kept* me?"

"I had to. I couldn't send you back to him. Not after the way he'd treated your mama."

Becky's breath caught, her temples began to throb, her thoughts spun. "Wait a minute. Are you saying my father isn't dead?"

"I don't know what became of him. I don't want to know. That man was as evil as they come."

"But surely he looked for me. He must have." She got to her feet and began pacing the length of the wooden porch. "How did you manage to hide all these years? It can't be easy to just drop out of sight."

"It wasn't. I pulled a lot of shenanigans to keep you safe and sound."

The portent of Effie's confession was beginning to sink in. The person she loved and admired most in the whole world was a fugitive. Unbelievable!

Effie had begun to weep in earnest. Tearful herself, Becky returned to the porch swing, put her arms around the old woman's thin shoulders and pulled her close.

Rocking back and forth, she ached with the anguish of the truth that had been kept from her for so long. All she said was, "Oh, Aunt Effie. What have you done? What have you done?"

The focus of the elderly eyes blurred as present reality faded. "I brought your baby, Flo, just like we'd planned," she said, wiping away the remnants of her tears and looking at Rebecca. "I been waitin' a long time. A real long time. I was beginnin' to think you wasn't comin.' Now you're here, we can get on with our business."

Becky's hold tightened with affection and she began to croon like a mother comforting a distressed child. "Of course we can. You don't have to worry anymore. I'll look after you. I promise. Everything will be fine."

Becky's thoughts were tumbling, refusing to rest. *Florence was my mother's name. But Florence what?* Probably not Tate, especially since she and her aunt currently shared the same last name. No telling where Effie had come up with that alias. Why she'd chosen to fabricate their past, however, was evident.

The most important question remaining was what would happen to poor Effie if the truth came out. Was there a statute of limitations? Becky doubted it. Even if the police were no longer involved, she'd still committed a crime. Reasons or no reasons, valid or not, what Effie had done was terribly wrong.

Going to her room, Becky opened the top drawer of her dresser, dug under her socks and retrieved the old family snapshot. In all the confusion, she'd forgotten about it. Now, the picture made perfect sense—except for the little boy. If she was the baby in Florence's arms, then who was the other child? And what had happened to him?

Asking Effie was out of the question for now. She hadn't been making much sense since her declaration of guilt and Becky didn't want to push her any farther.

She considered taking the picture to Brother Fred. All that was stopping her was Logan's continued involvement in Fred's daily life. Her hands began to tremble.

Logan.

He had arrived shortly after her aborted call to one of the Keringhoven numbers on her list. Was that an innocent coincidence?

It had to be, she reasoned. Logan and Fred were old friends. It was highly unlikely the two events were connected. Still, if she went to Fred with what she'd learned, might he tell Logan? Something told her she shouldn't take that chance.

Becky sank onto the edge of her bed, the photo clutched in her hands. If she were smart, she'd never talk to anybody about this. Ever. The responsibility Effie had been shouldering alone for over twenty-five years weighed so heavily on her she wondered how the poor woman had survived, let alone persevered and brought up a child by herself.

Rising, Becky returned the photo to the bottom of the drawer. Time was on their side. Since they hadn't been found yet, chances were they never would be. Unless...

Picturing Logan, she closed her eyes and sighed. There must be a clue she was missing; a sensible reason why Brother Fred had asked Logan to come to Serenity when so many other qualified men were already vying for the job.

The only result of her troubling thoughts was a twisting in her stomach and a sick feeling that stayed with her the rest of the day.

Going to work Monday morning was one of the hardest things Becky had ever made herself do. Facing Brother Fred wasn't easy, either. The look on his face as he wished her, "Good morning," was anything but *good*.

"Morning," she replied. "Where's Brother Malloy?"

"Um, outside, I guess."

"Probably making another mysterious call," Becky grumbled. "That man does love his little cell phone."

"He mentioned that you'd overheard him. Is there anything you'd like to share with me?"

"Like what?" The hair on her neck tingled. "Don't you trust him, either?"

Fred blinked rapidly and cleared his throat. "What do you mean, *either?* Are you having a problem with him?"

"No, but Aunt Effie sure is. That shouldn't be a surprise to you, seeing as she was crying on your shoulder yesterday. How much did she tell you?"

Clearly nervous, he ran his index finger under the front of his shirt collar as if it were choking him. "About what?"

Becky crossed the room, grasped his arm and pulled him with her into his private office. She shut the door and whirled to face him before she said, "About *me*."

"I don't know what you mean."

If he hadn't seemed so ill-at-ease she might have been tempted to believe his denial. "I think you do." Her voice gentled. "Look, Brother Fred, I'm more worried than angry. I don't want anything bad to happen to Aunt Effie. I love her dearly. I just don't know what to do."

"Nothing," Fred said flatly. "Do nothing." He cast a brief glance over his shoulder at the closed door and lowered his voice. "The best thing you and I can do is nothing at all."

"The committee for next year's Fulton County Homecoming will meet in our church basement tonight." Brother Fred was all business. Becky was taking notes while Logan perched nonchalantly on the edge of his desk and nodded.

"I won't be able to attend, so I've asked Brother Logan to go in my place. You'll be there, of course, Rebecca."

"Of course." The muscles in her neck and shoulders knotted, making her wish she'd followed her inclination to call in sick that morning. Keep up the tension like this and before long she really would be ill.

"Good." Fred rose from behind his desk. "Well, I

have hospital visits to make. One's all the way over in Mountain Home so don't expect me back in the office today."

"What about supper?" Logan asked. "Shall I fix enough for two?"

"No. I'll pick up something if I get hungry." He gave Becky a kindly smile and touched her hand. "Don't you worry about a thing. The Lord can handle any problem, no matter what it is, if we let Him."

The love and concern emanating from Fred warmed her heart and gave her some peace. "Thanks for reminding me."

"That's my job," he said with a wink. "You two behave yourselves while I'm gone, you hear."

"Brother Fred!" Becky was frowning. "You're starting to sound like the women in my Sunday school class."

Logan chuckled. "Trouble in paradise?"

"Nothing I can't handle, thank you." Following Fred to the outer door she asked, "Mind if I go home a little early? Brother Logan's going to be here. There's no sense in both of us sitting around waiting for the phone to ring, is there?"

"Fine with me," the older man said. He leaned closer and cupped his hand to add, "Don't worry about Effie. I'm taking her with me. The hospital chaplain has contacted a specialist who's agreed to meet us there and speak with her. Unofficially, of course."

Becky was overcome with gratitude. "Oh, Brother

Fred." She hugged his neck and kissed his cheek. "I love you."

Behind them, Logan was just stepping into the hallway. He cleared his throat. "Hey, what did I miss?"

"Nothing. Not a thing," she said, waving as Fred walked the final few feet to his car. "I was just reminding Brother Fred what a special pastor he is."

"I know that, and you know that, and Fred knows that," Logan drawled. "My only concern would be what somebody else might think if they saw you acting that way."

"Fred Fleming is like a father to me," she insisted. "And around here, folks are always showing affection. But you are right in a way. It isn't wise for you and me to stay here by ourselves. People might talk."

"More than usual, you mean?"

"Yes." She bustled back to her desk, pulled open the bottom drawer and retrieved her shoulder bag. "Fred gave me permission to go home early and I'm going to take him up on the offer." She pointed. "The answering machine is already on and there are plenty of blank message slips right here. They're the pink ones. The blue paper is for hospital notifications. If anybody calls to tell us about one of those, jot a note for Fred and leave it in the middle of my desk. I'll enter it into the computer and print a fresh list in the morning. Remember to lock up when you leave."

Logan saluted. "Yes, ma'am." He gave her a lopsided grin. "Anything else? Scrub the floors, wash the windows, take out the trash, sweep the parking lot?"

She paused with her hand on the doorknob. "There is one other thing I've been meaning to mention. We're all allowed to make personal calls on the office phone. If you use it, jot down the number, date and time and I'll figure out what you owe when the bill comes."

"Is that what you do?" His smile faded.

"Sometimes. Sometimes I use my cell phone."

"Never a pay phone?"

The question took Becky's breath away. She prayed he couldn't tell she was being evasive when she stood tall and answered, "Don't be silly." The only time she'd used a public phone in past memory had been when she'd foolishly called a perfect stranger to ask about the old photo. Why in the world would Logan bring up using pay phones? The coincidence was more than unsettling. It was scary.

Chapter Ten

Effie still wasn't home by the time Becky had to return to unlock the church for the homecoming committee meeting. She wasn't usually this high-strung but in view of all that had happened in the past few days she supposed it was natural for her hands to tremble slightly when she inserted her key in the lock on the side door.

It wouldn't turn properly. Frowning, she tried again and found she was able to *lock* the door just fine. Logan had apparently neglected to follow her orders and secure the building when he'd left.

Mumbling to herself, she pushed open the heavy door and let it swing closed behind her on its own. The clang and clatter of the latch mechanism echoed down the deserted hallway and drowned out her footsteps.

She flipped on the basement lights and started down the carpeted stairs. It was a journey she'd made countless times. Although she was used to being the first one there and the last one to leave, and to working alone in the cavernous building, this was the first time she'd noticed how quiet the place was. How the tiniest sound echoed. How truly vulnerable she'd be if anyone had a wish to harm her.

"This is the Lord's house," she told herself. "Nobody would…"

Something clicked in the distance. Becky froze, listening. The sound had been so faint she wondered if her imagination was running away with her common sense. This building was like home. As welcoming as her own house. Surely there was no reason to be so jumpy. She never had been before.

Then again, she'd never been aware of her past until yesterday. Remembering chilled her to the core. She was supposed to be the victim, yet she identified so closely with her aunt she felt equally guilty. When had telling the difference between right and wrong gotten so complicated?

Disgusted with the direction her thoughts had taken, she strode quickly to the kitchen in the corner of the basement and began to make coffee for the folks who were expected to attend the meeting.

Noise of running water and the stacking of the metal filter in the coffee urn covered the natural creaks and groans of the floor overhead, giving Becky a chance to relax.

She began to hum an uplifting tune as she carried the coffeemaker to the pass-through counter, plugged it in and stepped back. "There. All ready."

A door latch clattered upstairs. "Come on down," Becky called. "You're early."

No one answered. No one's steps thumped on the stairs.

She strained to listen. Nothing. But that wasn't a sure sign no one was up there. If Logan's carelessness had resulted in the church being vandalized or burglarized and the culprits were still present, he was certainly going to hear about it.

"I think it's time to call the sheriff."

Reaching into her purse she grabbed her cell phone, ready to dial 911. Common sense stopped her. Half the town listened to police and fire department scanners. How was she going to explain a call for help if there was nothing wrong? The least she could do, before riling everybody up, was tiptoe upstairs and take a peek. As long as she had her phone in hand and the emergency number already dialed in, an SOS could be sent with the push of a button.

Feeling more hesitant with every step, Becky climbed the stairs to the ground floor. The few lights she had turned on when she'd arrived still burned. She looked toward the office. It was dark, as expected, yet soft glimmers of colored light flickered through the doorway and danced against the opposing wall.

She held one finger poised over "call" on her phone, while she reasoned things through. Since Logan had forgotten to lock the outer door, there was a good chance he'd also failed to shut down her computer. The light she was seeing could very well be coming from her screensaver rather than an intruder.

"Hello! Anybody here?" she called before starting down the hall.

Each step closer to the office brought a faster pulse. Shorter, more labored breaths. Unexplainable fear. No matter how often she insisted she was being silly, she couldn't seem to overcome the feeling of foreboding. Of danger.

How many times had she lectured heroines who took foolish chances in movies or on television? Bravado only made sense when a person had a backup plan.

And she had one, she reminded herself. Her grip on the phone tightened. Her thumb rested lightly on the button that would complete her 911 call as she crept closer to the office. The door was ajar. She started to ease it open, stopping dead when she realized what she was seeing.

Her computer was on, all right, but it wasn't the light from the screensaver she'd seen. The computer was apparently logged on to the internet, or had been, because it was displaying information from one of the search sites she'd used to garner the information on Keringhoven!

Trembling, she peered into the dimly lit office. Shadows seemed to shift, deepen, threaten. Whoever had been there could still be lurking close by. The smartest thing she could do was take the advice she'd given those idiotic heroines in the movies and *run*.

Becky whirled, the small phone clutched to her chest. The toe of her shoe caught on the bottom corner of the half-open door. She stumbled. Her subconscious was screaming that she'd been grabbed by some unseen monster and her conscious mind was too disoriented to argue.

She gasped. Lurched. Started to fall.

Strong arms grabbed her. Becky took a quick breath and let out a screech that echoed from one end of the empty church to the other. Her heart was pounding so hard and fast she could hear it in her ears and sense it in her temples.

The arms held her fast. Unable to regain her balance she hung suspended and kicked wildly.

"Hey! Whoa. It's just me," Logan said. "Cut it out. That hurts."

Becky hit him with the only weapon she had, her telephone. "Let go of me!"

"Gladly." He stepped back, his arms spread wide. "I didn't mean to scare you. I thought you knew I was here."

She staggered, her head swimming. "How would I know that?"

"My car's parked right there," he said, pointing out the window by the side entry. "Next to yours."

"It wasn't there when I got here."

"No." Logan's voice was slow and gentle as if he were speaking to an irrational child. "I arrived after you did. I figured you'd gone to open the front door so I went looking for you there."

"I was in the basement." Becky's gaze swung to the empty office. "Wait a minute. If you just got here, who's been playing with my computer?"

"What?" He scowled.

"My computer. You left the door unlocked and. . ."

"Hold it." He laid a restraining hand on her arm and eased her behind him as if he were a shield. "I didn't leave anything unlocked. I checked all the doors twice before I went home."

"Well, the side door wasn't locked properly."

"Stay right there. Don't move," Logan said.

Barging past her, he switched on all the overhead lights in the office complex and shoved each door open to its fullest, banging them against the walls.

Becky could hardly believe the change in him. Not only was he giving orders like the military policeman he'd once been, his whole demeanor had hardened. Talk about larger-than-life characters from a movie!

She could see that her computer program had now gone to its usual screensaver, which meant that whoever had been running it must have been there within the past ten minutes.

Logan emerged from Fred's office. "This place is clear. I'm going to go check the rest of the church. Lock yourself in till I get back."

"Gladly."

Still shaky, Becky traded places with him and twisted the dead bolt before rounding her desk. If she could end the search program before he returned, he wouldn't have cause to wonder about the unusual name.

That was, of course, assuming he hadn't been the one to look it up in the first place. She hated to admit it but common sense insisted he was the most likely suspect.

The wail of sirens preceded the arrival of flashing red and blue lights atop the sheriff's car. Though she was still alone, the tension in Becky's shoulders started to ease slightly. Logan must have called the police. He was probably waiting outside to brief them, which would explain why he hadn't returned.

In the distance, several men were shouting. Bracing against the door so she could slam it shut in an emergency, she opened it a crack to listen.

Someone hollered, "Freeze!" followed by thumps and groans. Her heart raced. Had they captured the prowler? Was it safe to open the door? She wished she knew because waiting like this was killing her!

About to succumb to her impatience, she was relieved to hear, "Got him."

Thankful beyond words, she poked her head out of the office. The deputy who stood at the end of the hall guarding the outer door had been one of her classmates in high school. It was an added bonus to see a friendly face.

Grinning, she called, "Hey, Nathan. Fancy meeting you here."

"Stay back, Miss Rebecca. We've got a prowler cornered. Sheriff's bringin' him out now."

"Oh, good."

Her relief was short-lived. The local police had handcuffed Logan Malloy! As the two uniformed men shoved him outside, he shouted, "Becky!"

"Oops." Giggling, she hurried down the hall. "Nathan, wait. That's not a prowler. That's a preacher."

"Hey, Sheriff. Hold on. I think we got the wrong perp," the deputy called.

Becky joined them in time to hear Logan shout, "That's what I've been trying to tell you."

"Then what're you doing with a gun?" the stocky sheriff asked.

"I have a concealed carry permit."

"That wasn't what I asked you, son. I wanna know what a preacher needs with a gun. You care to tell me?"

"No. But if you don't let me go I'll tell my lawyer plenty about false arrest."

"A lawyer?" He reached around behind Logan to free his wrists. "Now what do you need with a lawyer? We're all friendly folks here." Ignoring Logan's muttered reply he turned his attention to Rebecca. "You okay, Miss Becky? When we got your call it sounded like you were scared silly, screamin' and all."

"Me? I never…" She looked back toward the office where all the excitement had begun. Her cell phone was lying on the floor near the door. "Oh, dear. I must have accidentally pushed the button when I ran into Brother Malloy. I'm so sorry."

"You sure about that?" the sheriff drawled, squinting at Logan.

"I'm positive," Becky said. "We were just getting the fellowship hall ready for a meeting and thought we heard noises upstairs. Right, Brother Malloy?"

"That's right." Logan was rubbing his wrists. "And if you two are done with me, I'll go back and finish checking the sanctuary."

"Noises," the sheriff said with a snort. "Right."

Though she'd known the older man since she was a child, she didn't like the inference. She might have been able to convince herself she was imagining his attitude if Nathan hadn't started blushing.

"Yes, *noises,*" Becky said with conviction. "There was a prowler in here. He even messed with my computer."

"Well then, let's go see," the sheriff said.

"I—uh—I turned it off." Her admission didn't seem to surprise the lawmen but it clearly shocked Logan.

He glared at her. "You did *what?*"

"I turned it off. I didn't think it was necessary to leave it on."

"How about fingerprints?" Logan asked. "Didn't you think of that?"

"No. I'm not used to being around devious people." Spine stiffening, she made sure the sheriff was looking right at her when she told him, "I don't lie."

The sheriff nodded his acceptance. "Never said you did, girl. Just doin' my job." His glance settled on Logan, his expression clearly doubtful.

Becky could tell his assessment of truthfulness did *not* extend to Logan Malloy and she had to admit she shared some of the same doubts. Brother Fred might trust Logan implicitly but there was still something about the man that set her nerves on edge.

As soon as the police departed, Logan insisted Becky recheck the office and sanctuary with him to make sure nothing was missing or out of place.

Watching him methodically, cautiously, lead the way through their examination, she started to doubt her earlier conclusions that Logan was the one who had been probing her computer. But if it wasn't him, then who was it?

When she'd used the internet for her original search she hadn't been worried about anyone else checking to see what sites she'd recently visited. Her personal computer expertise wasn't advanced enough to invade anyone's privacy like that—not that she ever would. However, someone else was obviously smart enough to invade hers.

They'd come full circle. Logan paused in front of the outer office door and placed his hands gently on her shoulders so she had to face him. "Okay. There's no prowler in here now." He sighed heavily. "Promise me you will *never* do that again."

Her first thought was of the computer and her real reasons for shutting it down. "I didn't think about not touching anything. I'm sorry."

"Touching anything?" Logan glanced toward her desk. "Oh, that. Forget it. I was talking about walking into a deserted building when there's a chance it's being burglarized. Don't ever take a chance like that again. Understand?"

"Yes." She nodded and tried to look away, embarrassed by the tears of relief misting her vision.

"Promise?" Logan tipped her chin up with one finger. His tender, concerned reaction confused her. If she didn't know better she'd think he was almost as emotionally disconcerted as she was. "I'm sorry," Becky said. "I'll be more careful next time."

Logan's hand brushed her cheek in a light, brief caress before he pulled away and stepped back. His expression hardened. "There'd better not be a next time."

The homecoming committee meeting was short and productive. Rather than argue, everybody simply deferred to Miss Louella Higgens, who assigned Carol Sue Grabowski to head the booth space group and gave Mercy Cosgrove charge of the food committee, in spite of the elderly woman's polite protest. Leaving the details to Louella made perfect sense to

Becky. If a job needed doing, Louella would either handle it herself or draft an unwitting volunteer.

Miss Mercy had brought homemade cookies to go with the coffee, calling for added fellowship after the meeting proper. Logan was chatting with Mercy, leaving Becky a victim of the others' questions.

Louella drew her aside. "What was going on here tonight? I heard sirens."

"It was a false alarm. We thought there was a prowler."

"And?"

"And, we never turned up anybody."

"Who's we? You and Brother Logan?"

"Yes. Why?"

The older woman grinned. "Oh, nothing. It just seemed to some of us that he was spending a lot of extra time with your family. Is old Fred trying to match you two up?"

Becky's eyes widened. "I certainly hope not!"

"Where is Fred tonight, anyway? I expected his input. Homecoming will be here again before we know it."

"He had some hospital visits to make. I doubt he's back in town yet."

"That poor man," Louella crooned. "He's got more miles on him than my old clunker. He deserves his retirement. I'm just not sure how we'll get along without him."

Becky smiled and nodded. "I'm not, either."

"Well, don't you worry," Louella said, emphasizing her comment with a pat on Becky's shoulder, "I'm on the pulpit committee. I'm sure we'll find a good man before Christmas. And he'll be handsome and single. No sense wasting a perfectly good chance to bring new blood into Serenity."

"Louella!"

"Oh, posh. You know as well as I do that there are way too many unmarried women in this church, you among them. Why should we pass up an opportunity like this?"

Becky was chuckling and shaking her head. "I hope you're joking. We need a strong spiritual leader, no matter what his marital status happens to be."

"Okay. I'll go along with that. Who says our future pastor can't be available, too? Certainly not me." She hid a snicker behind her hand. "Look at Brother Logan, for instance. Now there's a good catch for some young woman."

Becky's smile waned. She wouldn't say anything that might taint Logan's already tenuous status in Serenity Chapel, but that didn't keep her from forming her own opinions. Brother Malloy was Fred's close friend, had rescued her off the roof, had protected her from burglars and was doing his best to fill the void Fred's departure would soon create. All of that was in his favor.

On a personal level, however, he was holding too much back for her to view him as a good marriage prospect, assuming she was looking for a husband, which she certainly wasn't. The man was too mysterious. Too reclusive when it came to details about himself or his past. He was too...

She glanced across the room, meaning only to reinforce her conclusions that Logan was many things, all of them troubling. He was openly staring at her.

Though she quickly turned away and began straightening up the kitchen, Becky felt his eyes continuing to follow her every move.

By the time she managed to usher everyone out the door so that she could lock up, she was a nervous wreck. Plus, she was mad at herself for taking the situation so to heart.

Must be leftover anxiety from the prowler scare, she decided as she headed for the parking lot with the others.

Recalling that episode intensified her edginess. There was still the unanswered question of who had been fooling with her computer. If it truly hadn't been Logan, then who had it been? And why?

Chapter Eleven

Becky wished she hadn't disposed of her original list of the Keringhoven contacts she'd found on the internet. Not having a computer at home meant she'd have to use the one at work again if she wanted to replace those phone numbers and renew her search now that she had more information.

Before she did anything, however, she intended to learn how to guard against prying eyes, which meant a visit to someone more knowledgeable than she was. The first person who came to mind was Belinda Randall.

Office hours for the chamber of commerce were the only complication. If Becky aimed to sneak off to visit her friend during the day she'd have to do it at lunchtime.

Rather than share her plans with Brother Fred and give him another chance to suggest she take Logan along, Becky left a note on her desk, grabbed her purse and was out the door at eleven-thirty sharp.

Logan heard her car start and drive away. He raised an eyebrow at Fred. "I think our chicken has flown the coop."

The older man chuckled. "You're beginning to sound like the rest of us country folks."

"Never." Logan snorted. "Next thing you know, you'll be asking me to preach."

"Why not? You're ordained."

"I'm also seriously out of practice."

"So?"

"So, it's not my calling. I've told you that before."

"You also told me you were happy being a private investigator."

"I am."

The old man cocked his head and raised a gray eyebrow in contradiction. "Are you? I wonder. Can you honestly tell me you haven't started to feel like you've come home since you've been here?"

Logan rose and paced across the office before answering. "If I do feel like that, it's because of you, not because of the job. It's been good to see you again."

"And you're telling yourself that's a lucky accident?" Fred asked wisely.

"What else could it be?" Logan raised his hands, palms out. "Oh, no. You're not going to suggest this was all meant to be, are you?"

"Why not? You said it yourself. If you hadn't stumbled on this case in the first place, your client might have sent people who would have torn this town apart."

"That doesn't mean it was all providential."

"No," Fred said. "But it sure does point to that conclusion. If you weren't so stubborn you might be able to see the writing on the wall." He smiled. "Don't forget what happened to old Belshazzar when he didn't pay attention. He lost everything."

"I have nothing to lose," Logan countered.

Fred smiled. "I wouldn't be so sure."

"I need to find out how to hide the sites I've visited if I use the office computer to look things up on the internet," Becky told Belinda.

"Why? What are you checking that's so secret?"

Becky was sorely tempted to confide in her friend. Perhaps she would—later. "Don't look at me like that. I'm not doing anything wrong. I think somebody's been fooling with my computer when I'm not there and I need to safeguard the data files."

"So, set up a password."

"That might help at night. During the day we usually leave everything up and running. Anybody could use my desk if I stepped away."

"Anybody?" The dark-haired woman was scowling. "Who's there besides you and Brother Fred." Her eyes widened. "Ah-ha. Has Brother Malloy been giving you trouble?"

"I don't think it was him. He said it wasn't."

"You believe him?"

"I want to." Becky made a silly face. "I've been

trying to treat him the same way I do Fred. Can't say that's working very well, though."

"Surprise, surprise," Belinda drawled.

"Stop leering. I know what everybody thinks. It's not true. Brother Logan and I are hardly even friends. That's part of the problem."

"You don't like him?"

"I didn't say that."

"Then what's bothering you?"

Becky shook her head and pressed her lips into a thin line while she considered the question. "He asks too many questions."

"What's wrong with that? Lots of people are curious by nature."

"I suppose so."

Thoughtful, Becky strolled to the window of the chamber office and gazed at passersby. Older folks were lounging in the sun on benches that framed the courthouse lawn. The usual complement of farmers, ranchers and merchants was going in and out of the courthouse on business. Children too young for school were playing hide-and-seek around the gazebo on the southwest corner.

Everything seemed normal but *her*—and the two men she'd just noticed standing next to a shiny black car parked across the street. They were trying to act nonchalant but their clothing gave them away. It was too citified, too *GQ*. And the black car was far too clean to have traveled the dirt roads in and around Serenity.

Becky motioned to Belinda. "Come here a sec. Do you know those guys?"

"Nope. Never seen 'em before. Have you?"

"I'm not sure. I may have. Guess I'm just jumpy after last night."

"I heard there was quite a commotion at the church."

"Everybody in town probably knows about it by now." She shivered and wrapped her arms around herself.

"Was there really a prowler?"

"I don't know. We never found anybody. I'd gone to open the fellowship hall for a meeting when I thought I heard noises upstairs. If Logan hadn't been there, too, I'd have bailed out and waited for the police."

"What did you do?"

"Locked myself in the office while Logan searched the place from top to bottom."

"That was stupid, if you don't mind my saying so. He was risking your life as well as his own."

"Yes and no," Becky explained. "He used to be an MP." She lowered her voice to add, "And he was armed."

"Armed? You mean he had a *gun?*" Belinda sounded astonished. "On him? In church?"

Becky huffed. "Yeah. The sheriff was surprised, too. Brother Logan had a permit to carry a concealed weapon so nothing came of it."

"The guy must have come from a pretty tough area. I'm glad I'm not a part of *that* congregation."

"I know what you mean. My heart tells me I should love every believer, no matter what their background, but my head keeps arguing for self-preservation. I think that's part of my problem with Brother Logan. He makes me nervous."

Belinda began to smile. "Oh? You mean tingly all over and butterflies in your stomach? Chills? Shakes? Dry mouth?"

"Yes, but don't go making more out of it than there really is, okay?"

Laughing, the slightly older woman put her arm around Becky's shoulders, gave her a squeeze and led her away from the window. "Honey, that's not up to me. Sounds like you've got it bad, whether you're ready to admit it or not. I think you're in love."

"No way. I hardly know the man." Becky twisted free and distanced herself from her friend. "He scares me."

"Okay. If you say so."

"I do."

"Fine." Belinda led the way to her computer terminal and sat in front of the monitor. "While I show you how to access your history and change preferences on the main program, you can decide exactly what you're afraid of."

"I'm afraid I'll erase data, among other things."

"I wasn't referring to the computer, Becky, I was

talking about you. I suspect you're a lot more scared of your own feelings than you are of Logan Malloy."

Becky opened her mouth to protest, then snapped it closed without saying a word.

The private line on Brother Fred's desk rang just after one. Logan was alone in the office. The minute he answered with the words, "Serenity Chapel," Becky started babbling.

"They're after me!"

"Who is?"

"Logan? Is that you? Oh, thank God," she said prayerfully. "Two men were loitering outside the chamber office. They followed me when I left. They're still behind me!"

Logan gripped the receiver. "Are you sure?"

"Positive."

"Okay. Calm down. Where are you now?"

"On 62-412, going west. I'd planned to stop at the post office."

"Don't," Logan said firmly. "Stick to well-traveled streets and come straight back here. Don't speed or take chances. And whatever happens, don't let them force you off the road."

"Maybe I'm imagining things."

"And maybe you're not. Are they still behind you?"

"Yes. I'll turn back toward the square and see what happens." In seconds she added, "They turned, too!"

"Okay. Stay cool. I'm going to break this connection and call you back on my cell phone so I'll be mobile, too. Hang up and wait for my call."

Logan hoped and prayed she wasn't too distressed to follow his orders. He hated to stop talking to her but if she needed his help, he'd have to be able to take directions on the move.

Running for his car, he punched her name on the speed dial. He was slamming the door of the red convertible when she answered.

"Logan?"

"It's me. I'm leaving the church now. Which direction?"

"Make a right. Go to the signal and turn right again. "I should get to the square about the same time you do." She hesitated for a few heartbeats. "The other car is big and black. A Caddy or something like that. I noticed it first because it was too clean. It didn't fit in."

"Gotcha. I'm on my way. Stay on the line."

He arrived at the traffic signal in seconds. It was red. Logan banged his fist on the steering wheel, then spoke into his phone. "You still there? I'm stuck at the light."

"I'm here," Becky answered. "So far, so good. I've passed the old Laundromat on Church Street and I'm almost to the grocery store."

"Are your friends still with you?"

"Oh, yeah. They haven't tried to catch me, though."

"Good." Logan made the turn. "Okay. I'm moving again. Which side of the square shall I take?"

"Go straight, past the courthouse, then left at the pet store. We should pass each other in that block."

Logan heard her fumble, grumble and recover. "Sorry. I dropped the phone. I see your car. What should I do?"

"Go back to the church and lock yourself in."

"Wait a minute. What about you? What are you going to do?"

"Talk to your new friends. Or try to."

"Be careful."

He was touched by the concern in her voice. "I won't take chances as long as I know you're safe."

Nodding acknowledgement as she passed, he pulled wide, cut the wheel tight to the left, and slid the convertible into a U-turn in the middle of the street. The sound of his squealing tires drew plenty of attention. That couldn't be helped. By the time the black car passed a few seconds later, Logan was headed in the right direction to slip in behind it.

He hadn't recognized the faces of the driver or passenger. He had, however, recognized their type. They were cheap hired hands, maybe bounty hunters, though he doubted it. If he'd had to guess, he would have started by assuming they were flunkies sent to hurry his cautious investigation. Chances were good Keringhoven had carried out the threat to bring in additional investigators, and if that were the case, he was going to have to intervene in order to protect Becky.

How had he gotten on the other side of this? Logan

suddenly wondered. The answer was basic. He'd chosen the side of innocence; the side he'd begun to care for. Nobody was going to hurt Rebecca Tate if he could help it, starting with the guys in the black car.

Logan hung back, letting them get several car lengths ahead. He was close enough to see Becky turn in at the church driveway.

He picked up his phone. "So far, so good. Keep going. I won't follow you all the way up unless they do."

There was a short pause. "I think it's okay, Logan. They just drove by."

"I know. I'm right behind them. Go on in and lock the door, like I told you."

"What about you?"

"I'll be back soon."

"Wait! What if they're just tourists or something?"

"Then they're going to get the kind of welcome you southerners are *not* used to handing out. Leave the rough stuff to us Yankees."

"That's not funny," she said. "I don't want you or anybody else causing trouble on my account."

"Then think of it as retribution. They followed you and scared you. The least I can do is return the favor."

"Logan!"

The line went dead.

Becky's first inclination was to turn around and go after him. That was such a dumb idea she immediately talked herself out of it, which left following his orders, like it or not.

Muttering to herself, she entered the chapel building and flipped the dead bolt inside the main door.

"Okay. Now what?" she asked the empty air.

No answer was forthcoming. Her cell phone was still clutched in her hand. Knowing that Logan would probably try to contact her that way again, she took it with her to the office where she dialed her aunt on a landline.

Each ring of the unanswered phone made her heart beat faster. She was about to hang up when Effie barked, "You better not be sellin' anything. I'm in the middle of bakin' cookies."

"Aunt Effie, it's me. Are you all right?"

"'Course I am. Why wouldn't I be?"

"I was just checking on you."

"Don't give me that, Rebecca. I know you too well. Something's wrong. What is it?"

"Nothing. Really." She was rapidly realizing she shouldn't have contacted Effie until she'd calmed down more. There was no easy way to explain what had occurred without unduly upsetting the older woman. Given Effie's tenuous mental state, stories about being chased by strangers were definitely out of the question.

"Who's been telling you tales about me this time?" Effie asked.

"Nobody. I just had a minute and thought I'd give

you a call." She changed the subject. "What kind of cookies are you baking?"

"Oatmeal with raisins. Fred's favorite. I figured to take him some when I got done. Thelma can drive me."

"Don't do that," Becky said abruptly. "Brother Fred's not here. I don't have a clue when he'll be back, either. Why don't you and I deliver the cookies to him later?"

"Well…"

Becky could tell there was still too much emotion behind her responses. For Effie's sake, she fought the urge to confess everything the way she used to when she was a little girl, though she wondered if it was wise to continue to keep her aunt in the dark about what had just happened. Would she be taking a chance with the old woman's safety if she didn't warn her?

Warn her about what? Surely there wasn't anything serious going on. Becky shivered, remembering Effie's recent ramblings about unseen danger. Was paranoia catching? If it was, she'd apparently been infected all the way to the roots of her hair because it was prickling at her nape.

She made a snap decision. "Look, Aunt Effie. You stay put and finish your baking. I'll run home for a few minutes and explain everything. Okay?" There was no response. "Okay, Aunt Effie?"

The receiver clattered as if it had been dropped. When it was picked up again, Effie said, "I'm back."

"Why didn't you answer me just now? Where were you? You scared me to death."

"I went to lock the doors," the older woman said in a subdued tone. "Hurry home. I'll be waiting."

Chapter Twelve

Logan was frustrated. He'd been hot on the trail of the black car and about to intercept it until an enormous green tractor hauling a set of implements had pulled out ahead of him. The lumbering rig had taken up most of both sides of the roadway. By the time Logan had found a place to pass, his quarry was long gone.

Already on edge, he headed the few miles back to Serenity, roared into the church parking lot and skidded to a stop. Eyes wide, he swallowed past the lump in his throat. Becky's car wasn't there!

He immediately tried to telephone her. Inside the building, a phone rang.

Straight-arming the door, he raced down the hall. His heart fell. Her cell phone was ringing all right. She'd left it lying on her desk. Wherever she'd gone, he wouldn't be able to contact her that way. Worse, she'd left in such a hurry she hadn't remembered to lock the door. That was so totally out of character for her it gave him chills.

Logan slammed the side of his fist into the door-jamb, trying to mute his fury and decide on his next move. The black car had gotten away so he had no idea if Becky had been right about being followed. Since she was now missing, he had to assume she was in further jeopardy. As frightened as she'd sounded, it was hard to believe she'd disregarded his good advice and left the church without being forced to.

"Unless she was worried about somebody else," Logan muttered. He grabbed her cell phone. The last number it had dialed was his. He threw it down, snatched up the desk phone and pushed the redial button.

A shaky voice said, "Hello?"

"Effie? Is that you?" he demanded.

"Who is this?"

"Logan Malloy. Brother Malloy," he said quickly. "I'm looking for Becky. Is she there?"

To his astonishment, there was a click on the line. Logan stared at the receiver. The old woman had hung up on him! What that meant was anybody's guess, although he'd long suspected Effie Tate wasn't nearly as addlebrained as she pretended to be.

Leaving Becky's cell phone on her desk in case she returned for it, he hurried back to his car. He was beginning to understand the rustic analogy about running around like a chicken with its head cut off.

He was certainly feeling plenty brainless and undirected at the moment.

Every instinct screamed at him to slow down. To think. To plan. To gather more information before rushing off to Effie's house like an idiot. But his emotions overruled his good sense. Becky might be in trouble. She might need him. He had to go to her.

That was all he could think about. The only course of action his heart and mind would accept.

Effie opened the front door to her niece as soon as Becky arrived, then locked it behind her. Though Becky was breathless and agitated, the older woman seemed completely in control.

"I told you," Effie said. "For years I told you. *Now* do you believe me?"

"About what?" Becky was still trying to quiet her pounding heart.

"Strangers. They're here. I seen 'em. One called, too, but I hung up on him."

"Are you sure?"

The gray head nodded sagely. "Sure as the world."

"Maybe you'd better sit down." She managed a smile. "Actually, maybe *I'd* better sit down. I feel kind of shaky."

Effie led the way to the kitchen. The aroma of freshly baked cookies made the room seem so welcoming, so safe, it was hard for Becky to stay focused on her earlier concerns. Still, there was nothing imaginary about the men who had followed her all over town. Something odd was definitely going on. And since none of this had started until after her calls to the people named Keringhoven, she had to assume that was in some way tied to their present predicament.

She eyed her aunt. The elderly eyes were bright, clear, piercing in their intensity. If there was ever a good time for probing questions, this was it.

Taking a seat at the table she cleared her throat. "Um, Aunt Effie? Please sit down. I need to ask you something. It's about my past. Our past. What does it have to do with anyone named Keringhoven?"

A long pause. "Nothing."

If Effie's shoulders hadn't slumped like a marionette whose strings had been cut, Becky might have believed her. She reached across the table and grasped her aunt's thin hands. "Please? I found an old photo and I wondered…"

"Where? Where'd you find it?"

"In the trunk in the garage. I was looking for the quilt top you started when I was little. I was going to try to finish it before Christmas and surprise you."

Tears glistened. "Show me that picture."

Becky went to her room and returned. She laid the faded snapshot on the table in front of her aunt. "Here. I look so much like the woman I thought we must be related. Is that my mother? The one you told me about?"

Effie nodded. Her hands were trembling as she gently touched the image. "Yes. That's Flo."

"Was her maiden name Tate?"

"No." Slowly, hesitantly, she looked up. Tears welled. "Effie Tate was a girlhood friend of mine. She died when we were both very young."

Becky sank to her knees beside the old woman and once again reached for her frail hands. "Then who are you? And who am I?"

Instead of answering, Effie pulled away, folded her arms, put her head down on the table and began to sob uncontrollably.

The banging at Becky's front door was so violent it shook the house. If she hadn't recognized Logan's shouts of "Open up!" she'd have met him at the door swinging their heaviest iron frying pan as a defensive weapon.

She hated to leave Effie crying like that but she didn't want the neighbors to panic and call the police over Logan's assault on the door. One false alarm featuring her and their substitute preacher was plenty.

"Hold your horses," she yelled back. "I'm coming."

When she opened the door she could see he was livid. Not only was his face flushed, his gaze was piercing. She stepped back. "You want to come in, or are you going to stand out there and holler at me all day?"

"I haven't even begun to yell," Logan said, shouldering through the doorway. He wheeled. "Where were you? Why didn't you stay at the office like I told you to? Were you trying to give me a heart attack?"

"No, of course not. I just…" There was moisture gathering in his eyes! His expression touched her soul. The man might be hard as nails on the outside but there was no denying his kindhearted, compassionate inner nature.

Becky reached to caress his cheek, to impress upon him how truly sorry she was. The fervor in his gaze seemed to darken, intensify. Her hand sank to his chest as he reached out and drew her closer.

"Do you have any idea what you did to me?" he whispered against her hair. "I went crazy when I couldn't find you."

She laid her cheek on his chest. "I'm so sorry. I didn't mean to make you worry. I got to thinking about Aunt Effie, being here all alone, and I knew I had to see for myself that she was okay."

Logan kissed the top of her head, his lips lingering. "I know what you mean."

What was he saying? That he cared for her as much as she cared about Effie? It had sounded that way. Then again, he'd suffered a fright and could be overreacting.

Such a logical train of thought struck Becky as ironic. There was certainly nothing levelheaded about the way she was beginning to feel about Logan Malloy. Even if Belinda was right and she was falling in love with him, it still didn't make any sense. Of all the men she knew, he was the least likely to bring her happiness. They had nothing in common, except their faith and a fondness for Brother Fred, and that didn't seem like a very firm foundation on which to build a life together.

She sighed. Snuggled closer. Listened to the beating of Logan's heart and smiled. Never mind the future. Being in his arms was not only amazingly comforting, it was just the kind of support she needed right now. Tomorrow would have to take care of itself. She was busy enjoying today. So much so, in fact, that she leaned back slightly and lifted her face to him.

Logan loosened his embrace and eased her away. "No, Becky," he said hoarsely. "Don't."

She knew he was thinking of kissing her because the same notion had taken up residence in her mind. "We have a chaperone. Aunt Effie's in the kitchen."

"You don't know me."

That brought a deep, noisy sigh. "Well, Brother Malloy, I hate to tell you this, but I'm not very well-acquainted with myself, either."

"What do you mean?" He started to ease away.

"It's a long story. I just found out that Aunt Effie isn't a Tate. Neither am I. It's no wonder her mind gave out. I can't imagine hiding a secret like that for so many years."

"How do you know she's not just confused again?"

Becky took his warm, comforting hand and started to lead him toward the kitchen. "Because I have a picture to prove it. Come on. I'll show you."

Logan didn't need urging to accompany her. He was so relieved to have found her alive and well he wouldn't have left her side if the house had caught fire.

When her hand tightened on his he thought she was being affectionate until he noticed that the kitchen was empty. No wonder he'd been subconsciously thinking of fire! Smoke was beginning to seep out of the oven and billow into the room. A smoke alarm started to beep.

Becky grabbed a potholder and rescued the charred sheet of cookies, then turned on the vent hood over the stove. She was about to start for the back door till she noticed that Logan had already thrown it open.

One quick scan of the smoky room told her that both Effie and the photograph were missing. She clutched at Logan's arm. "Effie's gone!"

"Evidently. Could she have forgotten she was baking?"

"It's never happened before."

He was about to suggest they search the house when Becky bolted past him. He waited in the hallway while she ran through each bedroom. By the time she rejoined him, her eyes were wide and her already fair skin was ashen.

"She's not here?" Logan asked.

Becky shook her head. "But why would she leave? I know she was afraid to go out."

"Maybe she was more afraid of staying here after I arrived," he said. "She never has liked me. I almost scared her into pitching off the roof the first time we met."

"I'm sorry to say you're right." Becky was wringing her hands. Her gaze was darting from the inside of the house to the windows and doors. "She can't have gone far. Even if she hadn't lost her driver's license the last time she took the test, she was too beside herself to drive."

"We should check with the neighbors first," Logan said.

"Right." Becky raced to the door and paused only long enough to point. "You take Miss Mercy's. I'll check Thelma's."

Logan was jogging across the lawn when he skidded to a stop. "Becky!"

She glanced over her shoulder. "What?"

"Come back. I know what happened to your aunt."

"What?" She froze.

Logan was shaking his head while standing in the driveway beside Becky's car. It was the only vehicle present. "Why did Effie flunk her driving test?" he shouted.

"Bad peripheral vision," Becky answered. "Why?"

"Because, she stole my car."

Brother Fred Fleming had been visiting the local nursing home and was on his way out. He wasn't surprised to see a familiar red convertible approaching. He nearly swallowed his dentures, however, when he recognized the diminutive woman behind the wheel.

Effie skidded to a stop practically at his feet. She jammed the car into Park and jumped out, hollering, "Praise the Lord! I found you."

If Fred hadn't been braced she might have bowled him over when she threw herself into his arms. "Take it easy, Miss Effie. What's wrong? Is Becky hurt?"

"No," Effie said with breathlessness and rancor, "but that Logan Malloy is about to get the best of me." She paused long enough to take a few shaky breaths, then plunged ahead. "Rebecca found out who we really are. She must of told him, 'cause he showed up at the house right after."

"Who you really are? I don't understand." Fred's voice was little above a whisper.

Effie continued to babble. "She showed me a picture of her and Flo and the others. I knew I should of burned it. But it was the only picture I had of her mama and I thought maybe someday she'd want it. I never dreamed it'd stir up all this trouble."

Keeping his arm around her shoulders, he guided her away from Logan's car and toward his own. "What do you say you and I go for a ride and talk? Sort this all out by ourselves?"

"Suits me," Effie said. "I've got plenty to say."

"I wish you'd confided in me years ago," Fred said gently.

"I wish I had, too. Maybe now you'll see why I couldn't marry you, no matter how I felt. It wouldn't have been fair, you bein' a preacher and all."

Nodding, Fred said, "I knew there had to be

more to it than you'd let on. Why couldn't you have trusted me?"

"Because you were too honorable." There was a catch in her voice. "If you'd married me and then found out what I'd done, you'd have had to turn me in. Your conscience would have made you. I know it and so do you."

"I'm still the same person," Fred said.

"But the girl's not a helpless baby anymore." Effie sniffled, swiped at her tears in frustration. "She can stand on her own. She knows what kind of a man her father is and she can tell him she doesn't want anything to do with the likes of him."

"Is he that bad?"

She snorted in disgust. "Bad? Guess so. He killed her poor mama. And maybe her brother, too."

Chapter Thirteen

Becky and Logan had located his car, abandoned at the rest home, and had decided to leave it there for the present. By evening, the only place they hadn't checked was Fred's new home on Lake Norfork because they lacked an exact address.

Becky was driving. She pulled over and stopped on the shoulder of the highway. "We have some decisions to make."

"For instance?"

"Do we keep driving around like we have been or do we go home and wait for Aunt Effie to turn up?"

"She's your aunt. What would you like to do?"

"Right now?" Becky gave a quiet, "Humph," then said, "I don't know. Scream? Tear my hair? Cry? Pick one."

"Are those my only choices?" Logan asked with a lopsided smile.

"Probably. They seem to be mine."

He laid his hand over hers, meaning to offer comfort. There was unspoken compassion in the act, in his heart. When she looked at him, however, he saw a more complicated mix of emotions, especially in the glistening blue of her eyes. Her lips were parted slightly. The lower one quivered.

Logan knew he'd be ten times the fool if he gave in and put his arms around her. He also knew he was losing the battle to hold himself in check. He started to lean toward her. Their warm breath mingled. Logan imagined he could already taste the sweetness of her kiss.

Becky laid her fingertips against his lips. "Wait. There's something I have to tell you."

Her words splashed like icy water over his ardor. He straightened, pulled away. "All right."

"It's about Aunt Effie and me," she said slowly, deliberately. "Remember what I said about not being a real Tate?"

"Vaguely." Logan's gut twisted.

"Well, I don't understand it all yet, but apparently Aunt Effie changed our names when she adopted me. She said she was afraid of my father, only…" Becky paled. "Wait a minute. If my mother was killed and my father disappeared and doesn't care, like she told me, then why would she be so afraid?"

"Maybe your father does care."

"Could he?"

"Anything's possible." Logan wanted desperately to confess his part in the subterfuge. He took her hand. "Listen. There's something I need to say, too."

The faraway look in her eyes told him she wasn't paying attention. No wonder. The safe little world she'd grown up in had been fractured by her aunt's partial confession. Once Becky got all the facts and realized how badly she'd been deceived by the person she loved most, she was going to be devastated. This was clearly not the time for him to clear his own conscience and add to her misery.

Logan got out of the car and circled around it, opening the driver's door. "Scoot over. I'll drive you home."

Her lack of objection told him he'd made the right choice when he'd held his peace. Poor Becky was bewildered, as well she should be. It wasn't every day a supposed orphan figured out she might have a surviving parent.

And if that news had stunned her, wait till she learned the rest.

Brother Fred's tan car was parked in the Tate driveway when Logan pulled up in front of the house.

Becky leaped out and ran toward the front door. She burst in before Logan could catch up to her. "Aunt Effie?" Her vision misted in relief when she spotted her aunt. "I thought I'd lost you."

Effie was seated on the sofa. Brother Fred left his place beside her and motioned for Becky to take it. "Here. You two have a lot to talk about," Fred said. "We'll wait outside so you can have some privacy."

He caught Logan's arm and urged him to back off. "Come on, son. I'll tell you all about it."

Loathe to leave Becky, Logan resisted. "Are you sure?"

"Positive," his mentor assured him. "They need a few minutes alone. It'll be all right."

Logan refused to go farther than the front porch. "This'll do. I think there are other operatives in the area. Guys I don't know. We shouldn't leave the women unguarded."

"Our prowler?" Fred asked.

"Probably. Whoever he was, he was interested in what was stored in Becky's computer files. I'm positive somebody had been snooping around her office."

"That wasn't *your* doing?" Fred asked soberly.

"No. If it had been, I wouldn't have been careless enough to have left the information displayed. I'm sure she's the missing Keringhoven baby. I just haven't decided what to do about it."

"Maybe what I have to say will help you make up your mind." Fred sighed. "Effie's explained everything."

"Go on."

"Not until I have your word you won't act without taking it all into careful consideration."

Logan scowled. "I'm already doing that."

"You're right. You are."

Waiting for Fred to speak seemed to take eons. Logan forced himself to take deep, settling breaths

and bide his time when what he wanted to do was shout at the older man to get on with it.

Finally, the story began. "Effie was the nanny, just like Keringhoven told you. She was in charge of both children, baby Rebecca and her older brother, Cody. Florence had been an unhappy wife and mother for a long time but she'd stuck it out. Effie was her confidante. That's how she learned about the physical abuse."

"He beat his wife?" Logan had considered himself a good judge of character and was astounded he'd misjudged the man so badly. Then again, a lot of years had passed since Becky's disappearance. People could change.

"That's what Effie told me," Fred said sadly. "Flo was too afraid of her husband to leave him lawfully, so the two women planned an escape. They were going to run away together and take the children."

"That would have been legal. Messy, but legal."

"I know." The old man's shoulders slumped. He sat down on the porch and leaned forward, elbows on his knees, fingers laced. "Only Flo never made it."

"Right. There was an accident and she was killed. That's all in the file."

Nodding, Fred stared at his clasped hands. "Suppose the crash wasn't an accident? Effie thinks Flo was murdered."

"No way." Logan began to pace the porch. "There was an investigation. The woman drove her car into a bridge abutment. If it wasn't a mistake, it was suicide."

"That was my first thought. But Effie's positive Flo was looking forward to her freedom. Effie had already gone into hiding with the baby. Flo was supposed to bring the older child, Cody, and join them. When she didn't show up, Effie panicked and ran. She was thinking of going back until she heard Flo was dead."

"So she kept running."

"Exactly."

Sighing, Fred looked at Logan, silently pleading for understanding and sympathy. "She figured she'd be caught unless she changed her name, so she got the birth certificate of a childhood friend and assumed her identity. That only left what to do about the baby. She bribed somebody to falsify a birth certificate. How she got away with that is a mystery, but she did."

"If Keringhoven was so bad, how could she stand to leave the little boy behind?"

"That tore her up. It still does. But she knew she didn't dare try to rescue him, too. If she had, she could very easily have lost Becky."

"Unbelievable."

"That's what I said when she told me." He rose. "So, what are you going to do? Go to the police?"

"I should," Logan said flatly. "Laws were broken. People were hurt."

"Is there any hurry after all this time?" Brother

Fred asked. "Can't you take awhile? Probe a little deeper? Make sure you have the right information?"

That had already occurred to Logan and he'd come to the conclusion he was up against an immense challenge, both to his secular principles and to his faith. Separating the two was getting harder and harder. If he didn't eventually reveal Effie's crime, he'd be abdicating his vow to uphold the law. If he turned her in too soon, however, he might be thwarting the Lord's plans for this sticky situation. Far be it from him to assume he knew the mind of God, especially this time.

"I'll give it some thought," Logan finally said. "I won't make my move without consulting you first. Will that be good enough?"

Fred rose and shook his hand, clapping him on the shoulder at the same time. "I couldn't ask for more. Come on. I'll drive you back so you can pick up your car. It won't take us five minutes."

Becky was thunderstruck. It was as if all her fantasies about happy family life had been melted in the fires of reality. No wonder Aunt Effie was so distrustful of men. After all she'd been through, who wouldn't be?

It was hard for Becky to believe her father could have purposely caused her mother's death. The whole story seemed unreal, impossible, though it did explain a lot of things she'd wondered about ever since she'd gotten old enough to ask questions. Questions like, where did her parents live? How had they died? Did she have any other living relatives?

The fanciful stories Effie had told about their family had been far-fetched and changeable, leading Becky to doubt them all. Now, her reasons for telling tales made sense in a sad sort of way.

If Effie was being truthful this time, she and Becky weren't even remotely related. That was the harshest truth of all.

Though she didn't want to admit any change in her affection, Becky noticed an emotional distancing that made her heart ache with loss.

She took Effie's hand and squeezed it as she said, "I need to get away. Take a walk by myself. Think things through. Will you be okay?"

Effie nodded. "I'd like to see Brother Fred again. Would you ask him to come back inside, please?"

"Of course."

Rising, Becky walked slowly to the door, opened it, and stepped onto the porch. Fred and Logan had just returned and greeted her with expectant looks. She managed a smile. "Effie wants to see you again, Brother Fred, if you don't mind."

"Not at all." After a brief glance at the younger man, he went back into the house.

Left alone with Logan, Becky stood tall, chin up. "You heard?"

"Fred filled me in. I'm sorry."

"Boy, me, too," she said. "When I said I didn't know myself, I didn't realize how right I was!"

"What are you going to do now? Look for your father?"

Her brow furrowed. "Why would I want to do that?"

"I don't know. Maybe for Effie's sake."

"It's for her sake that I won't. I made the mistake of looking into the past once. I don't intend to make it again."

"What about your brother?"

Becky cocked her head and studied his expression. "Effie assumes he's dead. Why would you think otherwise?"

"Logic," Logan said with a shrug. "She obviously heard plenty about your mother's accident. Why not keep tabs on the family to find out how the boy was doing?"

"I think she was afraid to," Becky explained. "She's still beating herself up about not rescuing him. If she'd learned anything bad about him, in a newspaper or whatever, it might have driven her over the edge."

"You mean before now?"

"Yes. I'm no doctor, but I'm beginning to think the cause of her mental lapses may be more because of guilt than because of aging brain cells."

"How long has it been since she's seen a doctor?"

Becky purposely refrained from mentioning Fred's recent attempt at intervention via his chaplain friend. "Not long. Since all this has come out, I'm going to make sure she sees her regular doctor soon, though."

"And then what? Confess?" Logan asked. "Think for a second. Are you sure you want Effie to come clean to everybody the way she did to you and Fred?"

"Well…"

He cupped Becky's elbow and guided her off the porch, lowering his voice when he finally paused at the edge of the street. "I wouldn't encourage it. Not yet. Make a doctor's appointment if you want, but keep the sordid details of your aunt's story to yourself, at least until we're sure what really happened. I'll make a few calls, look into it for you."

"Thanks. I suppose you're right." Becky looked up at him with appreciation. "The fewer the people who know, the better off we'll all be, especially poor Effie." She smiled slightly and reached for his hand. "I'm glad you're here. Fred's too close to Aunt Effie to see things clearly. He may need your counsel."

Who's going to counsel me? Logan wondered. *Who's going to tell me how to get out of this mess without hurting the only woman who's ever been this important to me?*

This was a foxhole moment. The kind of epiphany he'd had as a young soldier afraid of making the wrong move. Or as a seminary graduate questioning his career choices. Each instance had been bathed in prayer, yet he hadn't been nearly as certain then as he was right now.

He'd come to Serenity thinking he was working for a man, when in reality he'd been working for the

Lord. Perhaps he'd never stopped, even when he'd left the pulpit to follow a different path.

That conclusion settled in his heart and cocooned him in peace.

Fred was right. It did feel like coming home.

Chapter Fourteen

Continuing to go to work every day as if nothing had changed seemed surreal to Becky. If the truth were told, her emotions were in such an upheaval she could hardly think straight, let alone work efficiently.

The urge to confide in her friend Belinda or one of the women from her Sunday school class was strong. Stronger still was the gut-level warning she kept getting every time she considered saying anything to anyone other than Fred or Logan.

Fred had been spending most of his free time with Effie. They'd sat at the Tate kitchen table, talking and drinking coffee, for hours every evening. When Becky had awakened at 2:00 a.m. the night before, they were still at it. She knew she should be happy for them, but she couldn't help wondering what was going to happen to their renewed closeness, if and when Effie had to pay for her crime. That thought sent shivers skittering along her spine like a dry leaf tumbling in a gale.

Logan was passing her desk. He hesitated. "You okay?"

"Fine. I was just thinking."

"I thought I saw steam coming out of your ears."

"Couldn't be that." She made a silly face. "Steam is for when you're mad. The way I've been grinding my gears, I think smoke is more likely."

"At least it wasn't as bad as burning cookies."

Becky chuckled. "I hope not. If it looks like it's getting worse, don't call the fire department, okay?"

"Okay." Logan laughed with her and settled a hip on the edge of her desk. "How's Effie doing?"

"As good as can be expected, I guess. Have you found out anything about my family?"

"A little. It turns out your brother Cody is alive and well. He was secure in the backseat when your mother had her accident. Didn't get a scratch."

"That's wonderful." She studied his closed expression and decided he was hiding something. An eyebrow arched. "Okay, out with it. What else?"

"Nothing else, for now."

"Oh, no, you don't." Becky stood to face him. Since he was still half seated, they were close to eye-level. She put her hands on his shoulders to keep him there while she made her demands. "I want to know it all. Right now. No glossing over, no holding back. Got that?"

Logan didn't look pleased. "Where's Fred when a guy needs him?"

"Probably with my counterfeit aunt," Becky said.

"If you know that much about my brother, you should know whether Effie was telling the truth about everything else."

"She was," Logan said with a sigh. "At least the truth as she believed it." He placed his hands at Becky's waist. "There's more. I'm just not sure you're ready to hear it."

"I'm ready, believe me. *More* than ready. Now give, mister, or I'll conk you with the door again, like I did when we first met in Brother Fred's office."

He laughed quietly, appreciatively. "You're quite a lady, Miss Rebecca."

"Well, at least your southern accent is improving. Come on. Talk. I may be easygoing about most things but I've never been accused of having too much patience."

Nodding, he gazed into her eyes, hoping she'd accept what he had to say without misunderstanding. "I do know more about your father. His name is Dan Keringhoven. He's been searching for you for years without any luck. He had no idea your mother was unhappy, so when she took off with your brother and wrecked her car, it was a shock."

"That's not what Effie said."

"I know. Bear with me for a minute. After you and Effie disappeared, he started checking with your mother's friends and discovered she'd been having an affair."

"No way."

"You don't even know her. How can you defend her?"

"Aunt Effie says she was wonderful."

"I'm sure she was. That's no guarantee she didn't have flaws. None of us is free of sin."

"Sorry," Becky said. "Go on. What else?"

"Years went by without a clue. Then, a month or so ago, your father received an anonymous telephone call. His caller ID let him trace it to a booth in front of the grocery store, right here in Serenity."

"That was me."

"We figured that out."

"We? You mean you and Fred?"

Logan took a deep breath and tightened his grip on her slim waist. "No," he said, "me and Dan Keringhoven. I came here because he sent me. I work for him."

It took a few seconds for Logan's words to register. When they did, she tried to twist away. He held fast.

"Let me go!"

"Not till you calm down."

"Calm down? You're crazy if you think I'm going to stay here with you." She gritted her teeth and pushed against his chest. Anger surged. It blotted out everything else.

"I'm still on your side," he vowed.

"Oh, sure. Tell me another lie. You might as well. Everybody else does." She was disgusted with the emotional quaver in her voice. "I thought I knew you."

"You do know me."

The urge to yell at him was strong. "No, I don't. I thought Effie was the only one who was pretending. You're worse. At least she did it for me. You did it for the man who killed my mother."

A slight slacking of Logan's grip was all she needed to wrench free. Whirling, she ran.

"Don't condemn him till you've heard all the facts," he called after her.

"I've heard plenty," Becky shouted back.

Logan stopped in the hallway and watched her straight-arm the outer door, letting it slam behind her.

His hands fisted. So much for the subtle approach. Chances were she'd never trust him again. He didn't blame her. If he'd been in Becky's shoes, he doubted he'd have handled everything half as well, although why she didn't want to seek out her father and be certain of the facts was perplexing.

Logan had always wished he'd known his own dad better. A little boy's dreams and faded memories were a poor substitute for a real father. Good men like Fred had helped some, of course, but there was still a hollow place in his heart that even his faith hadn't fully filled. He supposed that was why he was having so much trouble understanding Becky's reluctance to come face-to-face with her father, even if the man was as despicable as Effie had claimed.

Picking up his cell phone, Logan contacted his

office. "Sandra? It's me. Any more problems with Keringhoven?"

"None. He's been good as gold since you talked to him. Very polite."

"Glad to hear it. Anything else?"

"Not to speak of. I knew you didn't want him to have your private number but he was really insistent, so I gave him the number of the church. I hope that was okay."

Logan huffed. "It may explain a few things."

"Uh-oh. I goofed, huh?"

"It's nothing that can't be handled on this end," Logan said. "Just don't let clients scare you into being too helpful again, okay?"

"Okay. Sorry. Do you have any messages for Mr. K.?"

"None I can't deliver in person."

"You sound upset."

That brought a wry twist to Logan's smile. "Not half as upset as I'm going to be if I find out he hasn't kept his promise to leave this case to me."

Becky was driving too fast. She knew it. She didn't care. Right now, pointing her car down the highway and going as far as she could before she ran out of gas sounded like a great idea. If she hadn't had Aunt Effie to consider, she might have actually done it.

That train of thought made her grit her teeth. *Aunt Effie.* The one person she'd been positive she

could rely on had turned out to be the biggest liar of
all. Now that the truth had come out, Becky had to
wonder what else was hidden in her past. How many
other nasty surprises were waiting to be uncovered?
Tales of runaway princesses weren't at all outlandish
compared to the real facts, were they?

And what about Logan? He'd admitted coming
to Serenity to search for her so there was no telling
what else he was hiding. She was already blinking
back tears of regret and betrayal when her thoughts
progressed to Brother Fred.

Her heart leaped, lodged in her throat like bitter
gall. *Fred had had to know!* He was the one who had
vouched for Logan and included him in their office
staff from the start. Fred was in on the subterfuge,
too! There wasn't one person left she could count on.
Not *one.*

Fighting tears and blurred vision, she slowed and
eased her car to the right, thankful that particular
stretch of highway had recently been widened. Swip-
ing angrily at her damp cheeks she rued the day she'd
opened her heart to *any* of them. Nobody could be
trusted. *Nobody.*

God can, her heart told her.

"But what about those *people?*" Becky murmured.
"I loved them. All of them, even Logan, and look
what they did."

What have they done besides love you in return?

Becky was sobbing. "They lied to me."

She used the back of her hand to wipe her eyes.

The tears flowed so freely it was a losing battle. Aware that she had no business driving when she was posing a hazard to others as well as herself, she started to pull to the side of the road.

A car had been passing on her left. It, too, slowed.

Becky barely glanced at it through her veil of sadness until it began to match her pace. Then, she blinked and stared. The car was black. Clean. And the same men who had chased her before were looking straight at her!

Overwrought, she sped up. So did they. Her foot pressed harder on the gas pedal. Who were they? Friends of Logan, maybe? It was possible. If he'd lied about other things, why not assume he'd lied about those men, too? When he'd claimed to be chasing them off he could have been meeting and exchanging information instead. What a horrible possibility!

And what about all those mysterious phone calls he'd made? No wonder he'd been so secretive. He'd been plotting against her all along. And she'd believed him. That was what hurt the most. She'd given him her total trust and he'd played her for a fool. How could she have been so stupidly blind?

Fresh tears blurred her already hampered sight. She wanted to hate them all, Logan and Fred and even Effie, but she couldn't seem to do it. All she felt was used up, abandoned and alone.

There was no way to express the absolute emptiness in her heart. All she had left was tears—and plenty of them.

Angry at herself as much as anyone, she rubbed her eyes roughly and sniffled. The community park was to her right. If she stayed on this road she'd soon be out of town and thus more vulnerable to whoever was tracking her. *Nobody* was going to get the best of her. Not while she still had breath in her body and a brain she could use to think.

One thing was certain. She wasn't going to keep running blindly to who-knows-where. No matter how many people disappointed her, they weren't going to drive her out of town or make her decide to disappear the way Effie had. Serenity was her home. She belonged there. If anybody was leaving, it was going to be Logan Malloy—and he could take the fancy suits in the black car with him.

She checked the side mirror. The other car was still following, though not as closely as it had been. That gave her the room she figured she needed.

Coming up on a barely visible crossroad, Becky suddenly hit the brakes and whipped her steering wheel hard to the right.

Her car went into a skid. The rear slid around and fishtailed, then straightened out. She thought she'd made it. Then disaster struck. Meaning to accelerate coming out of the sharp turn, she accidentally hit the brakes.

That was the last straw. Gravity and centrifugal force took control. Her body strained against the seat belt. The countryside seemed to be spinning and tumbling until she couldn't tell what she was seeing. All

she could do was grit her teeth, hang on and ride it out.

Her tires bounced over the mounded shoulder of the highway. Briefly airborne, she hit the ground and started to skim down the grassy embankment.

That was enough to bring on an instinctive, "Father, help! Don't let me roll over," which sounded a little informal, but seemed to suffice.

The last thing she saw through the windshield was the rough bark of an oak.

Everything went white for a split second.

Then all was black.

Logan heard sirens. Normally, he wouldn't have paid much attention but since he still had Becky on his mind, the wail of the passing fire engine spurred him to action.

Running for his car, he slid behind the wheel and was on his way in seconds. No matter how many times he insisted he was being foolish, he couldn't convince himself to disregard the urge to investigate. Chances were slim that Becky was the cause of the alarm, yet he had to see for himself, had to know she was all right. And if there was a chance to minister to whoever was injured, he belonged there for that reason, too.

Such a spiritual conclusion took him by surprise. Apparently Fred had been right. There was a part of Logan Malloy that missed the ministry; missed being able to help troubled souls find their way.

"Starting with myself," he admitted cynically.

The traffic light was green and he sailed through. A fire truck up ahead was rounding a bend. Logan accelerated enough to keep the flashing red lights in sight. With no smoke in the air he had to assume the volunteer crew was on its way to an accident. He didn't want to hamper their rescue efforts or cause further problems. However, now that he'd made up his mind to help he wasn't about to let them get away, either.

Traffic was slowing. Some drivers were turning off on side streets rather than wait for the upcoming snarl to be cleared. If his memory served, there would be a widening of the highway soon, right about where the Serenity Park began. If the accident scene was near that place, he could leave his car on the park grounds. If not, he'd find a driveway or some other safe place to stop.

An ambulance appeared in his rearview mirror. Logan pulled to the side of the road to let it pass. Just ahead of him the ambulance started to slow. Looked like this was the place. He decided to leave his car right where it sat and go the rest of the way on foot.

In less than a hundred yards, a man in a tan sheriff's department uniform signaled to him and shouted, "Over here!"

Logan recognized the deputy he'd met the night he'd been mistaken for a burglar, so he knew he wasn't going to have to explain his presence or provide identification in order to offer assistance. There were some advantages to living in a small town, weren't there?

"Nathan, isn't it?" Logan asked, extending his hand.

The other man ignored his greeting, grabbed his arm, and pulled him along, instead. "Boy, am I glad to see you, Brother Malloy. The medics can't do a thing with her. Maybe she'll listen to you."

"She?" Logan's heart was in his throat. Was Becky the victim after all?

Sliding down the steep incline behind the deputy, Logan fought to keep his balance while he scanned the scene below. A car was bunched up against an enormous oak at the base of the hill. It was the only tree for hundreds of feet. If the driver had aimed for it she couldn't have hit it any squarer or done more damage.

The color of the car was the same as Becky's. That was where the similarity ended. This vehicle was so bent up, folded over and buried in the long grass it was impossible to tell its make and model. The expression on the young deputy's face, however, explained plenty.

So did the loud, familiar, "No!" coming from the gaping door on the driver's side.

Logan skidded to a stop just short of a collision with the mangled car. He leaped around the rear bumper and shouted, "Becky!" as he dropped to one knee beside her.

She reached for him and wrapped her arms around

his neck as if he were Heaven-sent, then quickly let go and recoiled. "Leave me alone. I never want to see you again."

"No way, lady. I'm not going anywhere until you get medical treatment."

"Why should you care? I'm just another job to you. One more case to solve. Well, you've solved it, so scram."

"You can yell at me all day and it's not going to make any difference. If you want to get rid of me, you're going to have to let the medics put you in the ambulance."

"Fine," Becky said, grimacing. "Call off your goons and I'll cooperate."

Logan's spine stiffened. His jaw muscles clenched. He scowled. "What goons?"

"The ones in the black car. Remember? You pretended to chase them away the last time."

"*They* did this to you?"

"They sure didn't help."

Logan's fists clenched as he stood and scanned the crowd that was gathering. "I don't see them. That doesn't mean they aren't here." Lowering his voice he looked directly into her puffy, red-rimmed eyes and willed her to believe him. "I came to Serenity alone," he said. "I'm still working alone. Those men aren't with me."

"Hah! You've done nothing but lie to me from the minute we met. Why in the world should I believe you?"

Before he had time to consider the consequences or temper his answer, Logan blurted, "Because I *love* you."

Chapter Fifteen

Becky blinked. Had he really said what she thought she'd heard or was her imagination working overtime? Maybe she'd hit her head harder than she'd supposed and was hallucinating.

She licked her bruised upper lip and took a moment to study Logan's expression. He seemed sincere. Did she dare believe him? Was there room in her wounded heart for that much forgiveness?

The concern she saw in Logan's eyes was touching. Still, it was much too soon to tell whether or not he was being unduly influenced by the aftermath of her accident. He also might be saying whatever he thought she wanted to hear in order to regain her confidence. She wasn't ready to let her guard down. Not yet.

"Sorry. I don't buy that," she said as one of the paramedics fastened a cervical collar around her neck to stabilize it. "Of course, you can't go by my opinion. I just drove my car into a tree." A cynical chuckle made her wince. "Ouch. That hurts."

"Then hold still and don't get hysterical," Logan said.

"Hah! I might as well laugh at myself. Everybody else is going to. I was stupid. I never should have been on the road when I was so upset."

"It's just as much my fault for letting you go," he said. "I thought it would be best to give you room to think things through on your own. I was wrong."

"No, you weren't. I did need time by myself. I just chose the wrong way to go about it."

"That's for sure."

"You don't have to rub it in."

"Sorry."

"Me, too." She let out a shallow sigh. "I don't recommend this method of dealing with problems. It's too hard on the machinery."

"It's plenty hard on your friends, too," Logan said. "Good thing the airbag deployed or…" He cleared his throat and looked away. "Want me to ride shotgun on the way to the hospital?"

"That's not necessary." Her voice sounded harsh in spite of her burning desire to keep him near. "I'll be fine."

"Like you were fine a few minutes ago?" he snapped back.

"I thought you weren't going to rub it in."

"Just looking for some way to help."

"Tell you what you can do. Make sure Aunt Effie

has a ride to the hospital. I don't want her to think she has to steal another car to get there."

It tore Logan up to see Becky wince and bite her lip when they transferred her from the stretcher to the gurney. As soon as he could take Effie safely to the hospital and make sure Becky was going to be all right, he intended to find out if she'd simply had an accident or had been forced off the road. If it was the latter, heads were going to roll.

It wasn't a very forgiving attitude, though it did prove he was human. Even the most spiritual men had weaknesses. Rebecca Tate was one of his. A big one. Besides, it was a husband's duty to protect his wife.

That brought Logan up short. *Whoa.* First he'd admitted he loved her and now he was thinking about marriage? How dumb could he get? After all that had transpired he'd be lucky if Becky didn't tell him to get lost for good. Asking her to be his wife was out of the question. She'd never be happy in the city—or married to a detective whose life could be in danger every time he stepped out the door.

He did love her. Immeasurably. And because of that he wanted the best for her. Unfortunately, that didn't include him. What Becky needed was a gentle soul, a man like Brother Fred had been in his younger days, someone who lived his sermons every day.

It had tied his gut in a knot when he'd first caught sight of the collision. He felt even worse now. Becky was beginning to tremble due to shock. One of the attendants covered her with a gray blanket while the other secured the ambulance door, shutting him out.

Logan was instantly bereft. If parting from her temporarily was tearing him apart like this, what was it going to do to him when he had to bid her a final goodbye?

He couldn't imagine that kind of agony.

There was no answer at Effie's when Logan tried to telephone with news of the accident. He was trying to decide where to look next when he spotted Effie and Brother Fred driving by.

Logan caught up to them in the hospital parking lot and followed them inside while they checked with a nurse and were told they'd have to wait for news of Becky's condition.

Effie seemed less befuddled than Fred, at least for the moment, although she did allow Logan to put his arm around her shoulders when he greeted them both.

"How is she? Do you know?" Fred's voice cracked. "They won't tell us a thing."

"A little sore but probably fine," Logan said. "She was awake and talking to me when I got to the accident scene. We'll know more once a doctor has looked her over."

Effie's "Praise the Lord" sounded totally appropriate. Logan smiled at her. "My sentiments exactly, ma'am."

The old woman's eyebrows arched. "You didn't have nothin' to do with this, did you?"

"In a way. I said something that upset her," Logan admitted, "but I didn't cause the accident. Becky isn't sure what happened. I'm hoping she'll remember more later."

"What was it you said to her?"

Logan considered being evasive, then decided against prolonging the inevitable. Once the elderly woman found out who and what he was, he knew she'd feel the same aversion Becky had. This was a no-win situation. Nothing he said or did was going to change the facts or make him good enough for Becky. A biblical leper would have had a better chance of being accepted by her friends and family than he did.

Looking to Fred for moral support, Logan said, "I told her I was a private detective. I came to Serenity looking for her. And for you, Miss Effie." He lowered his voice. "I'm sorry."

"*You're* sorry?" She yanked free of Fred's grasp and began to back away, looking from one man to the other as if struggling to decide which of them was worse.

She settled on Fred. "I trusted you. I told you everything. How could you let me ramble on and on like that when you *knew?*"

"I never believed you were guilty of a crime," he told her, his hands outstretched pleadingly. "I still don't. I don't care what the law says, I know you acted purely out of love." He took a step closer.

"Stay away from me," she screeched. "Both of you."

Logan intervened. "Fred never told me anything you shared with him in private. He didn't have to. Becky's looks and age provided enough evidence."

"How did you find us?"

"Through an anonymous phone call Becky placed herself," Logan said. "Once she did that, it was only a matter of time till somebody figured it out and came after you."

Effie faltered, swayed.

Fred was instantly at her side, guiding her into a chair and taking the one next to her. "I didn't betray you," he said. "When Logan explained what was going on, I decided it would be best if he took charge of the situation instead of leaving it to people we didn't know. I wanted to be sure it was handled fairly."

"Nothing's fair," she wailed. "A man can abuse his wife, kill her and go free. I saved her baby and *I'm* going to be sent to jail." She looked to Fred. "I'm supposed to be forgiven. How can God let this happen?"

He patted her frail hands. "Being forgiven doesn't mean we don't have to bear the consequences of our mistakes."

"I know, but…"

When Fred put his arm around her shoulders and drew her closer, she let him. "I'll stand by you no matter what," he vowed. "We'll make it. Together. You'll see. Now that I'm retiring, you won't have any more excuses to send me packing. Face it. You're stuck with me, old girl."

Effie sniffled and took an ineffectual poke at him. "Old girl, my eye. I'm younger than you are."

"And twice as feisty," he said.

Logan was so engrossed by the tender, playful scene, the doctor's arrival took him by surprise.

"Becky's going to be fine," the white-coated man said, addressing everyone. "I don't foresee any problems. I'd like to keep her here for another hour or so though, just for observation. She should be able to go home soon."

Effie pushed forward. "I want to see her."

The doctor stepped up to block her path. "I'm sorry. She says she doesn't want to talk to anybody right now."

Placing a steadying hand on the older woman's shoulder, Logan assured her, "She's just upset. She'll get over it. She asked me to be sure you got here safely so I know she cares. I'll go tell her you're waiting."

It looked as if Effie was going to argue until Fred intervened. "Let him do it. If Becky's going to pitch a fit at any of us, I'd rather it be Logan, wouldn't you?"

"Well, since you put it that way," Effie answered.

Logan rolled his eyes. "Thanks, Brother Fred. I'll do a favor for you, sometime."

"You know what favor I want," Fred said, hugging Effie to his side.

With that plea echoing in his heart, Logan entered

the cramped examination cubicle. Becky was lying on a table with her head and shoulders slightly elevated and a blanket tucked around her. Her hair was mussed, her face was smudged and her upper lip was slightly puffy. He'd never seen her look more disheveled—or more beautiful.

Approaching, Logan noted her grumpy expression. During the time they'd been apart she apparently hadn't changed her mind about him. That was undoubtedly for the best but it wasn't easy to take.

"Go away," she said, scowling.

Instead of bowing to her wishes, Logan took her hand. Her fingers were icy. He cupped them with his to try to warm them. "How are you feeling? The doctor says you're in pretty good shape."

The touch of his warm hands, the tender look in his eyes and his mellow voice melted her reserve enough to keep her from pulling away.

"I have a cracked rib, a bruised shoulder and a fat lip, which I could have told him without X-rays. Other than that, I'm in great shape. A lot better than my poor car."

"It's just metal."

"Easy for you to say. I finished paying off the loan last month. That pile of junk is all mine."

"It can be replaced. You can't."

"Humph." She was still cynical and self-derisive. "I'm definitely one of a kind, that's for sure, even if I'm not sure who I really am."

"It's who you are inside that counts." Logan

glanced in the direction of the waiting room. "Effie and Fred are waiting to see you."

"I don't think I'm ready to talk to them. Not till I get some straight answers." She was gazing deeply, pleadingly, into Logan's eyes.

"I'll tell you whatever I can," he said.

"How about starting with my real name?"

"Okay. All your birth certificate says is baby girl Keringhoven. Because you were born in December, your parents were still arguing over whether to choose Carole, Noel or Holly when you left the hospital. Dan says he just called you sweetheart."

"Terrific. How old was I when Effie ran off with me?"

"Less than a month."

"That young?" Her fingers tightened on Logan's.

"Yes. Your mother had apparently made her escape plans long before she delivered you. That was one of the things that caught your father off guard. At first, he thought her emotional problems were caused by postpartum depression. It was only later that he found out what was really going on."

"You're sure she was cheating on him?"

"As sure as anyone can be after the fact."

"Did my father really abuse her, like Aunt Effie thinks he did?"

"I doubt it," Logan said with a thoughtful shake of his head. "I've met the man. He can be stubborn and unreasonable but I don't think he's violent."

"What about my brother?"

Logan smiled. "Ah, now we're getting to the best part. Cody's been making his living guiding white-water raft trips. A real outdoor type guy. You'll like him."

"Is there a family resemblance?"

"Well, he's taller and has a lot bigger muscles," Logan said with a wry chuckle. "Your eyes and hair are about the same color as his, though. You may want to do DNA testing just to be sure. As far as I'm concerned, you're definitely his missing sister."

"What will happen to Aunt Effie? Are you going to turn her in?"

"No. When I make my report to your father I'll try to influence him in her favor. And Fred's definitely in her corner. As a matter of fact, I think he asked her to marry him a few minutes ago."

"What?" Forgetting her soreness she sat bolt up-right. "Are you sure?"

"Well, it sounded like a proposal to me."

"What did she say?"

Logan shrugged. "I don't know."

"Isn't that just like a man!" Becky threw off the blanket and swung her legs over the side of the narrow bunk.

"Whoa. The doctor didn't say you could get up yet."

"I don't care. Either you go get Aunt Effie and Brother Fred or I will."

"I thought you didn't want to see either of them."

Becky made a silly, cynical face. "I didn't. I should

be furious—with all of you. But I'm so glad to be alive after the crash I can't seem to stay mad. Guess that makes me the biggest fool of all."

"Or the most loving," Logan told her with a smile of admiration. "You're quite a lady, Miss Rebecca."

"Either can the southern charm and fetch me Effie or get out of my way," Becky insisted, attempting to stand.

Logan intervened by gently placing his hands on her shoulders. "Simmer down. I'll go." He hesitated long enough to add, "And speaking of going, I'll be heading back up north soon."

"When?"

"Probably in the next day or so. Don't worry. I won't leave till I've found out who's been following you and taken care of them."

"They really weren't working with you?"

"No. I didn't lie to you, Becky."

Releasing his hold, he backed away and headed for the door. That wasn't the only time he'd told her the absolute truth lately. His only hope was that in the confusion after the crash she either wouldn't remember what he'd confessed or would assume she'd imagined it.

He, however, wasn't imagining a thing. He'd never forget his assignment in Serenity—or the young woman he'd fallen head over heels in love with in spite of himself.

Chapter Sixteen

A tearful Effie rushed into the room and right into Becky's arms. Logan and Brother Fred stood back and let the women embrace without interference.

Finally, Becky spoke to Effie. "All right. What have you been up to while I was stuck in here? What's this I hear about marriage plans?"

"Fred was just jabbering. He knows it would never work. What kind of a wife would I make if I was stuck in jail?"

"Maybe you won't have to go to jail." She looked pleadingly at Logan. "Brother Malloy says he'll have a word with my—my father, on your behalf."

"Won't do no good," the older woman said flatly. "My goose is cooked for sure."

"Not if Logan can make him see the truth."

Approaching footsteps drew everyone's attention to the doorway, where a middle-aged man had appeared. He glowered at Logan. "I'm looking forward to hearing that."

Effie squealed and tried to hide behind Fred, setting Becky on edge. When Logan once again placed himself between her and perceived danger, the way he had when they'd been looking for the prowler at church, she didn't object.

"I think some introductions are in order," Logan said formally. "Mr. Keringhoven, I'd like you to meet your daughter, Rebecca. You already know me and I think you recognize Miss Effie. The other gentleman is Brother Fred Fleming."

Peeking past Logan, Becky sized up the man who was supposedly her father. In spite of his wrinkled forehead, thick, gray eyebrows and thinning hair, he didn't look menacing. Certainly not dangerous. In fact, judging by the tears glistening in his eyes, he was anything but irate.

When she stood and nudged Logan aside, he steadied her with an arm around her shoulders.

"I never thought I'd see my girl again," the man whispered. "Why didn't you tell me how beautiful she was? She looks just like her mother."

"I thought so, too," Logan said. "That was one of the things that helped convince me."

Effie was quivering but far from silent. "Don't you listen to that man. He's the devil himself!"

"Why?" Dan asked, finally turning his attention to his accuser. "How could you do this to me? I treated you like a member of the family. Why did you steal my baby?"

"Flo's baby, you mean," Effie answered. "You

didn't deserve to have her. Not after the way you acted."

Logan watched their exchange with interest. Clearly, the man was confounded by her accusations rather than being defensive.

Speaking quietly so Effie would have to hush to hear him, Logan said, "Suppose Florence had a different motive for wanting to leave. I know it was a long time ago but try to remember. Think, Miss Effie. Was there something else going on in your friend's life back then? Something she might have been embarrassed to tell you?"

"No. Of course not. She…"

Waiting, Logan saw doubt cross her face, saw her blink rapidly as she began to consider his question.

"Why would she lie to me?" Effie asked in a near whisper.

"To keep her children?"

"She didn't have to run away to do that."

"Didn't she? If she'd divorced my client and gone to another man, especially one she'd been having an affair with, she might have lost custody on moral grounds. By getting you to help, she not only covered her tracks, she set you up to watch the kids while she continued to have her fun. If she hadn't had that fatal accident, her plan would have succeeded."

The older woman's eyes widened. "It can't be."

"I never laid a hand on my wife," Keringhoven vowed. "Never. Not even when she laughed in my face and taunted me with her affairs. I loved her too much."

Behind him, the outer door banged. In seconds, a younger, taller version of Becky's Nordic-looking father poked his head in the room and said, "Sorry it took me so long to park the car, Dad. I had trouble finding an empty spot."

Effie gasped, made a grab for Brother Fred's arm, and wilted like a plucked daisy on a hot summer day.

Fred had refused to leave Effie's side, even after she was admitted to the hospital for observation. Finally, her doctor had stopped trying to convince him to go home and had had a reclining chair brought in so he could doze nearby in comfort.

It had taken Logan hours to convince Becky that she'd be foolish to stay, too. He knew it was more her pain than his persuasiveness that had pushed her to let him drive her home. That was okay. Anything was fine with him as long as it was best for Becky.

She'd laid her head back and closed her eyes as soon as he'd helped her into the car. Logan had decided not to insist she use the seat belt. The one in her car had probably saved her from more serious injury but it had also caused her cracked rib and a very sore left shoulder. All in all, it seemed like a pretty fair trade, considering how badly she could have been hurt.

That terrible thought tied his gut in another knot and made his palms clammy. Every instinct told him to take her in his arms and tell her he loved her, over and over again. The only thing stopping him was the realization of how unfair it would be, especially to her.

Tenderly, he asked, "Are you riding okay?"

"Fine." There was a slight lift to the corners of her mouth. Her eyes opened lazily. "How slow are you driving, anyway?"

"I didn't want to jostle you."

"I think a little faster would be all right. It would be nice to get home sometime today."

"I see you haven't lost your sense of humor."

"Guess not. So, tell me more about my family. How soon can I see them again?" Her blue eyes widened. "You didn't send them away, did you?"

"No." Logan gave her a smile of encouragement. "After Effie fainted, your dad thought it best to make himself scarce. He hasn't gone far. Neither has Cody."

"A brother," Becky murmured, "I have a real brother. I've always wanted one."

"And a father?" Logan asked.

"I don't know about that part. It's a lot to get used to all at once."

"True enough. I'm not sure how I'd react if my father popped back into my life. Probably not as well as you have."

"My situation is different. In a way, my father and I were both victims."

"If I can make him realize that, too, it should make things easier for everyone."

Becky's brow furrowed. "What's next for you?"

"File my final report and go back to Chicago, I guess. My work here is done."

"Whoa. What about the men in the black car?"

"I'm working on that."

"I certainly hope so." Laying her head back once again she started to take a deep breath. Pain cut it short. "Do you have any leads?"

"Not that I'm ready to share."

She gave him a disgusted look. "Here we go again, huh? Guess I'll never learn."

"What's that supposed to mean?"

"Nothing," she said wearily. "I'm just overtired. Forget it."

Weariness of her soul caused her to hold her tongue. She was tired, all right. Tired of being sheltered. Tired of being protected. Just because someone else had made a decision, supposedly in her best interests, didn't mean it was right.

She sighed. Someday, hopefully, the people she loved were going to wake up and realize she needed the truth a lot more than she needed to be coddled.

Except for hearing the truth about Logan's plans, she added. She'd *never* be ready to hear he was leaving for good. Never.

The old house seemed empty without Effie. Normal creaks and groans stood out the way the noise of the prowler had at church. If Becky hadn't been suffering the aftereffects of the accident and dulled senses due to the mild painkiller the doctor had prescribed, she would have been too fidgety to doze. As it was, however, she soon fell asleep propped on pillows piled at one end of the living room sofa.

Night came. She awoke to a stab of pain when she tried to turn over. Pressing her hands tightly against her side she waited for the ache to go away. It merely eased.

Moving with care, she sat up. Obviously the pain medication had worn off and it was time to take more, so where had she left her purse? Come to think of it, what was she doing in the living room?

Vague memories of Logan dropping her off drifted through her muzzy mind. She'd meant to go to bed after sending him away. Apparently, she'd been so worn out she hadn't gotten any farther than the comfort of the couch.

She was about to get to her feet and go searching for the purse containing her prescription when she thought she heard a muffled sound at the rear of the house.

"Aunt Effie?" she called.

Wait a minute. Effie wasn't there. No one else was. So what was she hearing?

A stab of pain shot through her as she stood. Clutching her ribs, she paused to catch her breath. This was one time she wished she had bought Effie a dog—only not a lap dog. What they needed was a big, protective German shepherd with an attitude, preferably in her favor.

Switching on the lamp and reaching for the telephone on the end table, she put the receiver to her ear. Dialing 911 wasn't going to help this time. The line was dead!

Frantic, she realized her cell phone was her only remaining connection to the world outside—and it was in the purse she'd misplaced.

So now what? Flee? How far would she get when the slightest move hurt so much it took her breath away?

Hide? That was out of the question, too. Any closet or cupboard that had had a bit of room was stuffed with Effie's hobby supplies, Christmas decorations and the spare clothing they'd been saving to give to a homeless shelter.

Becky gritted her teeth. *Stand and fight? How?* Lifting their biggest iron frying pan had taken two hands before she'd cracked a rib. Now, it would be impossible.

China crashed to the floor in the kitchen. Someone groaned.

Run! her most basic instinct shouted.

No. Somebody might need help.

"Yeah, somebody like me," she muttered.

Disgusted with herself for being so self-centered, Becky scooped up one of the throw pillows and hugged it to her side. It cushioned her movement enough to allow her to tiptoe silently to the kitchen and peek in.

The beam of a flashlight was sweeping the room. The place was in shambles. She ducked back too late when the light swung her way. She'd been seen!

"Wait!" a hushed voice ordered.

Becky didn't listen. Bent on escape, she zigzagged past the living room furniture and burst out the front door, no longer mindful of her injuries.

She was almost to the base of the porch steps when a shadow loomed beside her. One strong arm grabbed and held her while a hand muffled her scream.

Though the hand was clad in a leather glove she tried to bite it. The nip was enough to loosen the man's grip. Becky tossed her head and used his momentary lapse to let out a piercing screech followed by "Help!"

Suddenly, she was loose! Falling to her knees on the dewy lawn she crawled away, fully expecting to be caught and assaulted again. Instead, she was able to reach the base of the flower bed and tuck herself beneath the heavy branches of a cascading forsythia, long past its yellow bloom.

The moon slipped from behind a drifting cloud, partially lighting the scene. Two large figures in dark clothes were struggling at the foot of the porch steps. At first, she wondered if the men who had followed her might be the ones fighting. Logic refuted that possibility.

She edged farther into the shadows and waited,

hoping and praying the victor would be someone who was on her side. Someone like Logan Malloy. She'd give anything to see him drive up about now, even if she was still distressed over his announcement that he was leaving Serenity for good.

One of the men drew back and landed a punch that rocked his opponent. The other man fell. Lay still. Becky held her breath. There was something familiar about the way the victor moved. The set of his shoulders reminded her of Logan. So did the way he ran his fingers through his tousled hair to comb it back.

She was already certain she wasn't imagining things when he said, "Rebecca? Where are you? Are you all right?"

"Yes." It was a verbal sigh. "I'm here."

He dropped to his knees in front of her.

She came to him without hesitation and slipped her arms around his waist. Laying her cheek on his chest she listened to his racing heart and felt him gently caressing her hair.

"I was afraid I'd lost you," Logan said breathlessly.

"Was that you in the kitchen?"

"Yes. I took care of one of them in there. You ran off before I could warn you. I knew the other one had to be close by. I just couldn't be in two places at once."

"Seems to me you did a pretty fair job of it."

"Not good enough." He held her away long enough to give her a relieved look. "Did you call the police?"

"No. The line was dead and I couldn't find my cell

phone. I don't know what happened to my purse after the accident. I thought I had it at the hospital."

"You did. You left it in my car when I drove you home." Logan got to his feet and took her hands to help her up. "I was parked down the block, watching your place, when I noticed the purse and remembered your pain medication was in it. I was bringing it to you when I caught those guys breaking in. I don't know how they got past me."

She saw him press his lips into a thin line. His jaw muscles clenched. She caressed his cheek, mindless of the beard stubble. "It's okay. I got what I wanted."

"What was that?"

"You," she said softly. Her lips parted. Her hand slipped around the back of Logan's neck and she urged him closer. She knew she wasn't being over-confident. Not this time. She might not have had much experience with men but she could tell enough to know that Logan wanted to kiss her as much as she wanted to kiss him. She was right.

His mouth barely brushed hers, then lingered. When he finally leaned away he was clearly moved. "I don't want to hurt you," he whispered.

Becky knew he was referring to her injured lips but her heart gave his words deeper meaning. If something didn't happen to change his mind about leaving town he *was* going to hurt her. Terribly. She just didn't know how to keep that from happening— or if she should even try.

Rather than dwell on such a depressing scenario

she concentrated on imagining a humorous side to her dilemma. She wasn't desperate enough to throw herself bodily in front of his car to stop him from going away, so that idea was no good. And she had too much pride to cling to him and beg him to stay.

There were only two things she was ready and willing to do; pray with every ounce of faith she could muster, and kiss him again, preferably more than once.

Praying wasn't going to be difficult.

Giving Logan a few tender kisses, then calling a halt and distancing herself from him was going to be much, much harder.

Chapter Seventeen

They'd used Logan's cell phone to summon the police. Naturally, all the commotion had brought the neighbors out in droves, giving Becky and Logan no more private time.

It was the next morning before she saw him again. Her first thought was that he must have dropped by her house to bid her a final goodbye. She preempted the strike with a cheerful, "Hello."

"Hi. How are you feeling this morning?"

"Like somebody threw me off the porch." She laughed when she saw he was taking her too seriously. "I'm fine. Fred called."

"Did you tell him what happened last night?"

"Yes. Effie wanted to come straight home when she heard about it. I convinced her to stay in the hospital till her doctor runs those tests he had planned."

"Good. I stopped by to tell you our mystery is solved. Your visitors last night were private investigators."

She instinctively wrapped her arms around her waist and held tight. "Who hired them?"

"Your father."

"What?"

"It's not as bad as it sounds. Dan got impatient. I didn't move fast enough to suit him so he brought in another firm. They weren't supposed to do anything but keep an eye on you."

Becky huffed. "I'd hate to see what they'd do if they were told to get rough." Noticing that Logan was staring at the way she was favoring her sore side, she added, "I'm okay. Honest. You don't need to go knock them in the head again."

"They're fortunate that's all I did."

While he was in such a protective mood she decided to forge ahead. "I'm glad you dropped by. I need to talk to you. Fred wants you to preach this coming Sunday."

"Why? What's wrong with him?"

"Nothing. He doesn't plan to come back to work until Effie's out of the hospital so he wants you to take over his duties, including worship services."

"What put that idiotic notion into his head? Fred knows better than to ask me to preach. I don't belong in a pulpit. I realized that a long time ago."

Becky was smiling wryly in spite of her tender upper lip. "Did you? Well, I guess we'll see, won't we?"

"No way. Call somebody else."

"I suppose I could. If I was of a mind to," she

drawled. "But I've been injured, you know. I doubt I'll be well enough to go to the office for quite some time. Sorry."

He grimaced. "I'm getting the idea Fred's not the one who's really behind this sudden request to hear me make a fool of myself in front of the whole congregation."

"You'll do fine."

"That's a matter of opinion."

Becky nodded sagely. "Exactly."

Late that afternoon, Logan once again appeared at Becky's door. He wasn't smiling. Nevertheless, she greeted him pleasantly. "Hi, again. Trouble at work? You could have phoned if you had questions."

"That's not why I'm here."

His demeanor was sobering. Her smile waned. "Okay. Are you going to tell me what's wrong or do I have to guess?"

"Dan wants a meeting."

"When?"

"Now. I'll drive you."

"Just like that? No *please* or anything?"

Logan nodded. "I tried to convince him it would be better to wait."

"Well?"

"He blew up at me and started yelling. I backed off so he'd calm down. He says he's made up his mind and wants to get everything settled before he goes back to Chicago."

"What is it with you people?" Becky complained. "Seems like you can't wait to get out of Serenity. Is it *that* bad here? Have we made you feel unwelcome or something?"

"Not at all," Logan said. He checked his watch. "Grab your purse and let's go. We don't want to be late."

"Of course not." Her voice was tinged with sarcasm. "So, where is this important meeting, anyway?"

She almost gasped when Logan said, "In Effie's hospital room. Everybody's going to be there."

Becky thought she was doing well to even speak, let alone ask pertinent questions during the short drive to the hospital. Trouble was, Logan refused to give her straight answers. His reticence was more than worrying. It was frightening.

She tried again as they left the car. "You must have some idea what he's planning."

"Not much."

"Then at least tell me what you think. Is he going to have Aunt Effie arrested?"

"I honestly don't know."

"What about Brother Fred? Will he be in trouble, too? I mean, if the authorities thought he'd been protecting her all these years, wouldn't he be considered guilty of aiding and abetting?"

"Probably. If that happens, we can swear under oath that he was as much in the dark as you were."

"Will they believe us?"

"I hope so." Logan held the door for her, then followed her onto the elevator and pushed the button for the second floor. "Unfortunately, it's been my experience that our justice system can be fallible. Are you ready for a long, hard fight?"

"If it comes to that," Becky answered. "I won't let anything bad happen to Aunt Effie if there's any way to prevent it. She doesn't deserve to go to prison."

"I'm glad to hear you're still calling her your aunt. I was worried about your relationship."

Becky managed a slight smile. "So was I. After the initial shock wore off, I realized how much she must have loved me, and my mother, to have done what she did for us. I'm just sorry everything turned out so badly."

The door to Effie's room stood open. Becky halted outside to gather her courage and felt the light touch of Logan's hand at the small of her back. This time, she didn't object. Considering how much she was dreading entering that room, she was more than glad she wasn't alone.

"I feel kind of like a teenager who's late getting home from a date," she told Logan. "Only this is worse. I have to face an irate father I don't even know. How can I hope to reason with him when we're strangers?"

"I'll be right here with you."

Becky made a cynical face. "Terrific. You're the

one he just yelled at. He's probably even madder at you than he is at me."

"Possibly." Logan gave her a nudge.

"Don't push. I'm going."

"Yes, ma'am."

The hint of teasing in his voice helped her step forward. Curtains were drawn between Effie's bed and the door. Beneath the curtain, Becky counted three sets of men's shoes. Only one set belonged to Brother Fred.

She called out, "Aunt Effie? I'm here."

The curtain slid partway back on squeaking overhead rollers. Dan Keringhoven held it aside. He was glaring at Logan. "What took you so long?"

"You're early," Logan countered.

Cody stepped between them. "That's my fault. I don't have much patience. I figured we might as well wait here instead of pacing rooms at the motel."

Becky greeted him with a smile and offered her hand. "Must be a family trait. I'm the same way."

Her brother shook hands warmly. "Well, at least we're seldom late."

"True." She transferred her attention to Effie and Fred. They were grasping each other's hands as if they were afraid to let go. Clearly, Effie had been crying.

"You two okay?" Becky asked.

Fred nodded, obviously desperately worried.

Struck by the unfairness of the location Dan had chosen for their meeting, Becky whirled and faced him. "Okay. I've had about enough of this. I'm not going to stand here and let you torture these poor people any more. If you have something to say to me, I'll be out in the hall."

"Wait," Dan said. "Don't go. You'll miss the best part."

"Of what?" Becky wasn't about to capitulate without good reason.

"I've consulted my lawyer in regard to this whole situation," he said.

Effie began to sob softly in the background and Becky went to her side before saying, "The only way to be fair is for you to forget everything that's happened."

"I'll never forget," Dan said with emotion. "I wouldn't want to. I loved my wife. I love my son." He hesitated. "And I want to get to know my daughter. Maybe, someday, we can build the kind of relationship we should have had in the first place."

"Not if you send Aunt Effie to prison!"

"I see that. That's why I talked to my attorney. I had already decided not to reveal any secrets or press charges but I was worried about legalities. If there is a problem, my lawyer will be ready to provide a good defense. Florence was the one who's really guilty. She set up the scheme and gave the orders. That should put Effie in the clear even if the police stir things up later."

"Really?" Becky was awed. "I don't know what to say. I thought…"

"You don't have to explain. I understand. You'd spent so many years hating me, you assumed I'd want revenge." He made a self-deprecating noise. "I *was* mad. Furious, as a matter of fact. Then I got to thinking about what might have happened when you were a baby. If Effie hadn't taken you away with her before Flo's crash, you could have been in that mangled car, too."

Dan paused to blow his nose. "All that was brought back to me when I heard you'd been in an accident. The similarity to your mother's death was appalling. I could have lost you all over again. I never want that to happen."

Becky was dumbfounded.

"I know we have a lot of obstacles to overcome," her father said, "but I'd like to try."

Her gaze swept around the room. Everyone was staring at her, waiting. No one moved. No one spoke.

Finally, Becky released the grin she'd been holding back and centered it on her father. "So would I," she said. "What do you say you and I go get a cup of coffee? Looks like we have a lot to talk about."

"I'd love to."

It pleased her to note how relieved Dan seemed. Whatever his reasons for offering to help Effie, the result would be for the good. That was what mattered.

"We'll have to take your car. Mine's in the shop," Becky said lightly. "Probably permanently."

"Aren't there any car dealers around here?"

"We have little used car lots all over the place. I'll

be able to find something I can afford. I just haven't had time to look yet."

"I take it nobody's told you what I do for a living," Dan said.

"Sell used cars?"

"No, new ones. What's your favorite color?"

Becky pulled a silly face. "Don't tease. I might take you seriously."

"I expect you to," Dan said. "My hired idiots caused your accident so I figure I owe you a car. I have some sales brochures with me. All you have to do is take a look, pick one out, and I'll have it shipped down to you."

Her glance darted to Logan for affirmation. The look on his face was a cross between shock and amusement.

Becky's already frazzled nerves were making the whole situation seem unduly amusing. She giggled. "I thought kids were supposed to have a lot of trouble talking their parents into getting them a car. I don't know what to say. This is way too easy."

From across the room came a chorus of encouragement. Logan's "Stop arguing and take the car!" carried best.

She turned to her father with a wide grin. "I'd be pleased to look at your brochures and choose. I'm especially fond of blue."

"Done."

Dan offered his arm and Becky took it as they left the hospital room. It seemed strange to have a father beside her, let alone such a benevolent one. She was so overwhelmed she couldn't stop grinning at him like a silly child.

Which isn't so bad, she decided easily. It looked like Dan Keringhoven had a softer side to his gruff persona after all. Given enough time, maybe they would find common ground and become like the family she'd missed.

It was certainly worth the effort to find out—and *not* just because he was giving her a new car!

Chapter Eighteen

Brother Fred had kept his promise and stayed away from the office for the remainder of the week. The only time Becky had seen him was when she'd spelled him at Effie's bedside. Effie was playing up her supposed frailty for all it was worth. Becky suspected she was relying on her hospitalization to keep from accidentally running into Dan while he was in town, even though he'd promised he wouldn't prosecute.

Part of the credit for that happy decision went to Logan. Some obviously lay with Cody, too. Thoughts of her newfound brother made her smile. He was not only polite and handsome, he radiated an aura of kindness and easygoing acceptance that was harder to see in their father. That was why, when she decided to invite both of them to church, she chose to call Cody first.

He answered his cell phone immediately. "Hello?"

"Cody? It's me, Becky."

"Hi, kiddo. What's up?"

"Actually, I was wondering if you and Dad would like to come to church with me tomorrow?"

"I would. Dad's gone."

"Gone? Where?"

"Home. He took off like a shot this morning. I know he tried to call your house before he left. I heard him."

"Oh, dear. I dropped by the hospital to see how Effie was doing. I wasn't home."

"So, how is she? Has she settled down any?"

"Yes. It's wonderful. The doctors have decided which medications will help her and she's actually making sense almost all the time now."

"That's great."

"You really mean that, don't you?" Becky was touched by her brother's sincere concern.

"Of course I do. She raised my baby sister."

"I wish we could go back," Becky said.

Cody took a moment to reply. "I don't. It was different for me, being a boy and being older when Mom died. I'm not sure how Dad would have coped with raising a daughter, especially one who grew up to look so much like Mom. He'd have done his best, I know, but he's human. Being with Effie may have been the best place for you."

"I hadn't thought of it that way." She paused. "I wish I'd had a chance to say goodbye to him before he left."

"Chicago's not that far away. When you get your new car why don't you drive up to visit him?"

"I might," she said with a smile. "I don't know how I'd fare in heavy traffic, though." She chuckled softly. "I have enough trouble avoiding trees that jump out in front of me."

Cody had promised to meet Becky in the church parking lot. She spotted him walking toward her and mirrored his smile. "Welcome. I'm glad you could come."

"Thanks for inviting me," Cody said. "This church is a lot smaller than the one I go to at home."

"Really? Serenity Chapel has just about the biggest congregation in Fulton County, although size isn't what makes it so special."

He fell into step beside her. "I agree. That Brother Fred of yours is quite a guy. Real likeable."

"Fred's the sweetest, kindest man in the world but he's getting old, bless his heart. He's definitely earned his retirement. Getting him to take it is what's going to be hard. He hates to let go. That's one of the reasons I asked Logan to step in and preach this morning."

"Logan Malloy? The detective?"

"The same. He's actually an ordained minister."

"You're kidding! I never would have dreamed he had it in him."

Becky laughed. "You're not the only one. Logan isn't real sure, either."

* * *

The church filled up quickly. Becky wasn't at all taken aback when Carol Sue Grabowski and Trudy Lynn Brown squeezed into the pew directly behind them and tapped her on the shoulder with a cheery, "Good morning!"

Becky pivoted and smiled. "Well, what a nice surprise. I'd like you ladies to meet my brother, Cody. Cody, this is Carol Sue and Trudy. They're members of my Sunday school class." Her grin widened. "My *singles* class."

He stood briefly and acknowledged the attractive women. For his sake, Becky was thankful the service was about to begin. As usual, the members of Miss Louella's Extraordinary Ladies Class were the first to answer a challenge. If her eligible brother didn't leave Serenity soon, as planned, he'd be the object of plenty more flattering female interest.

Becky stifled a grin. Maybe she should take lessons from those other women and try batting her eyelashes at Logan Malloy to get him to hang around. *That would be the day!*

And speaking of Logan, she hadn't seen him since they'd passed in the hall before Sunday school. That was worrisome. If he'd ducked out on her—or on Brother Fred—she was going to be very disappointed. In more ways than one.

Everyone stood for the opening hymn. Still no Logan. Becky was starting to get antsy. Where was he? Come to think of it, why hadn't he stayed out front to greet parishioners? He knew that was what Fred always did.

But Logan isn't Fred, she reminded herself soberly. No matter who took over the pastorate of Serenity Chapel, some things were bound to change. Life was like that.

Eyes widening, she realized the wisdom of what she'd just told herself. She'd been fighting against that very thing, resisting any changes to her safe little world without giving the subject conscious consideration. She'd been going about this all wrong. Getting Logan to stay in Serenity and change his lifestyle to suit her wasn't the answer. If she *really* loved him, she wouldn't care where they went or what he did for a living, as long as they were together.

And she *did* love him. That much was undeniable. Given his admission that he felt the same way about her, his plans to leave Serenity made no sense. The least he could do was stick around long enough to give their relationship a chance. That was only fair.

She was about to make a dash for the side door, hunt him down and tell him exactly that, when he appeared. Becky had never seen him look more handsome, more appealing, or more ill-at-ease. As soon as his gaze met hers, she gave him her most encouraging smile and wiggled the fingers beneath her hymnal in a surreptitious wave.

Logan reddened and looked away, giving her a glimmer of hope. Maybe he hadn't changed his mind about what he'd said at the accident scene. Her heart soared in the few moments it took for logic to intervene.

More likely, his flushed complexion was a reaction to the sight of the packed sanctuary. Even the most seasoned pastor was bound to struggle with nervousness from time to time. In Logan's case, his battle seemed to be within himself as well as with the job, so it was no wonder he looked so uncomfortable.

Loving him, she quietly bowed her head and began to pray for his success. And for his peace. Personal concerns would wait.

Logan laid his note cards on the lectern when he rose to speak. This sermon was going to be his first in a long time—and also his last. He'd agonized over what he should focus on, changing his mind again and again. Something inside him kept insisting his future was wrapped up in what he was about to say and he didn't like that feeling one bit.

Squinting against the bright lights trained on the pulpit, he stared at the congregation and quietly cleared his throat. To his chagrin, the microphone he wore was sensitive enough to pick up even that. Too bad he hadn't forced himself to eat breakfast. The way his clerical career had gone so far, this congregation was liable to hear his stomach growling loud and clear before he was through.

It's not about me, he suddenly thought. *It never was.* That was what was so different this time! It didn't matter how he spoke or whether his delivery was as perfect and eloquent as Fred's. The message was what was important. He must have known that once, long ago. Why had he forgotten?

The note cards fluttered to the floor. Logan ignored them. His voice as strong as his conviction, he began to speak from the heart.

"I didn't come to Serenity to preach to you," he said boldly. "I came to help Brother Fred in another way. At the time, I thought my motives were pure. I meant them to be. But I was wrong. About a lot of things."

Pausing, he peered through the brightness to settle his gaze on Becky. She was giving him her rapt attention.

"I met Fred Fleming years ago, in seminary," Logan continued. "He was more than my teacher. He was my mentor. I know many of you see him as a father figure. I did, too. And a very special friend. So, when I got an opportunity to step in and help him, I jumped at it."

In the congregation, heads were nodding in agreement and appreciation.

"I thought I was doing it as a favor for Fred but I was fooling myself. You see, I'm an imposter."

A murmur of unrest started to rumble through the room. Logan held up his hands. "It's not as bad as it sounds. I was ordained a long time ago. Then life intervened and I fell away from the ministry. Or maybe I should say I turned my back on it and walked away. The bottom line is, I was making my living as a private investigator when one of my cases brought me to Fred's doorstep. I guess that was when my outlook began to shift. I'm a slow learner. It's taken me this long to realize it."

Stepping out from behind the lectern, Logan spread his hands wide, palms out. "I'm supposed to stand up here and tell you you're lost sinners in need of Christ. Well, so am I. I've been lost for a long time. God's been telling me I needed to come home and I've been doing my best to ignore Him. That's over."

His head bowed. "I'm done running, Father. If You want me back You can have me. I don't have a clue what You'd want with a guy like me but that's okay. I know You'll show me."

Stepping down off the podium and turning to face the altar, he knelt and began to pray silently.

Becky was awed. Logan's brief, poignant sermon had gone beyond her fondest hopes. He'd preached it with his own life. And judging by the stirring she heard behind her, his example of faith was already producing results.

She stood, paused, then quietly went forward to kneel beside him. Others were filing down the aisles, too; some with great joy, some with tears, some alone and some accompanied by family members.

The choir director began to sing a praise anthem. The congregation joined in.

At the altar, Becky reached out to Logan and grasped his hand. No words were necessary. Sharing that moment was enough. If she'd had her way, it would have lasted for an eternity.

"But you have to stay now," Becky argued as they locked up after the service. "Everybody wants you to."

Logan wouldn't be swayed. "It's not that simple. I have other responsibilities."

"You said you were giving your life back to God. Didn't you mean it?"

"Of course I did. But it doesn't follow that I'm supposed to immediately pack up and go become a missionary in some distant land."

She followed him up the main aisle of the sanctuary and waited while he checked the locks on the front doors. "Serenity is *not* a distant land."

"No, and I'm not a missionary. At least I don't think I am. Time will tell."

"That's it? That's all? You're just going to walk away after what you did this morning? We've never had a revival like the one you just started. Folks who hardly ever go to church were coming up to me afterward and volunteering to help with whatever we need. It's amazing."

Logan was slowly shaking his head and smiling at her. "I didn't do a thing, Becky. God did. You can have a continued revival with Brother Fred or whoever takes his place. You don't need me."

"Wrong," she said, steeling herself for the worst.

"Maybe Serenity Chapel doesn't need you but *I* do." She saw his eyes begin to narrow, his jaw set.

In spite of that, she decided to forge ahead. This was not the time to give up or back down. "I may have been a little woozy after I tangled with that tree and scrunched my poor old car," she told him, "but I heard *exactly* what you said."

"Uh-oh."

"Don't try to deny it. You said you loved me." Hands fisted on her hips, she stood firm and faced him. "Well? Do you or don't you?"

One corner of Logan's mouth quirked in a suppressed smile. "We're standing inside a church. If I say, 'I do,' does that make us married?"

"If I thought it would, I'd say it, too."

"Is that what you want?" he asked softly.

She had to talk fast before she lost her nerve or leaped into Logan's arms like a lovesick teenager. "Yes."

"Well, well. And would you be willing to leave here and follow me if I decided to go be a missionary in Africa—or Chicago?"

Trembling and stepping closer, she gazed at him. "Yes. I would."

"Okay. I accept. I'll marry you."

"What?" Eyes wide, she planted her palms on his chest and gave him a push. "That's not how it's supposed to go. You're supposed to propose to *me*."

Logan grinned. *"Now* she tells me."

"Logan…" She'd started to smile at him in spite of herself.

"Oh, all right." He took her hand and dropped to one knee. "Miss Rebecca, will y'all marry up with me?"

Of all the romantic moments she'd ever imagined, none had begun to measure up to the pure delight of this one. If Logan expected her to take exception to his theatrical actions or his exaggerated southern drawl he had another think coming.

With a grin so broad her cheeks hurt, she said, "I'd be proud to."

"Even if you have to live in the big city?"

"Even there. I'll follow you anywhere."

He stood and took her in his arms. "I believe you would. So, tell me, how soon do you want to become Mrs. Logan Malloy?"

Becky rested her cheek on his chest and sighed. "I don't know. Yesterday?"

Her silly answer made him laugh and she took a moment to revel in the surge of pleasure his good humor gave her before continuing. "Actually, I was thinking of a Christmas wedding. Maybe around the time of my birthday?" She tilted her face to gaze at him. "I hope you know when that is, because I'm not real sure."

"Early December," Logan said. "And I think it's a wonderful idea. We can invite your whole family to celebrate the holidays with us."

"Effie and Fred, too," Becky added. "I just hope they're up to traveling that far in the winter."

"Far? Who said anything about going far?"

"But, I thought…"

Logan kissed her silent. "You think too much, honey. I wouldn't dream of taking you away from Serenity, except maybe on our honeymoon. We'll live here, even if I have to commute all the way to Chicago!"

"You mean that?"

"Absolutely. And if it's okay with you, I'd like to ask Fred to marry us."

Astounded, Becky nodded. If life got any better she was going to burst from trying to contain such sheer joy. Blinking back tears of happiness she whispered, "I love you, Logan."

Just before he bent to kiss her he grinned and said, "Bless your little heart. I love you, too, darlin'."

Epilogue

Becky had thought Effie and Fred might want to combine their nuptials and join her and Logan for a double wedding but the older couple had declined. They'd said they couldn't bear to spend time apart, and who could argue with that? In his first official act as the church's new pastor, Logan had performed their ceremony in front of the entire Serenity Chapel family, much to everyone's delight.

Fred had gladly come out of retirement for Becky's Christmas wedding a few months later. At that time, the chapel sanctuary had already been decorated with banks of rich red poinsettias and evergreen boughs. Those colors had set off her white gown like snow against the cedars on the Ozark hills, and the sun streaming through the stained glass windows had added a rosy glow.

Best of all, her father had agreed to give her away. Walking down the aisle on Dan Keringhoven's arm, she'd felt like all her dreams had come true. And now that the reception was over and she and Logan were finally at home, surrounded by close family and a few friends, she was sure of it.

"Aunt Effie's been cooking for days," Becky told her guests. "I'm surprised she was able to tear herself away from the stove long enough to come to the wedding this morning. I tried to help her but she said I had enough to worry about and banished me from my own kitchen."

Logan chuckled. "Probably just as well."

She made a face and took a mock swipe at him. "My cooking's not that bad. I baked the pies last night."

"After you took them out of the freezer?" her new husband asked knowingly.

That brought gales of laughter from everyone, especially Dan and Cody.

"I'm so glad you could come," Becky told them. "I've never had Christmas with anyone but Aunt Effie." She blinked rapidly to hide her overflowing emotions. "It was always wonderful, of course, but I never thought I'd have a whole family to celebrate with like this."

Logan stepped closer and put his arm around her shoulders. "There's more good news," he said. "That's why I've asked Effie and Fred to come out of the kitchen and join us for a minute."

Looking past Dan, Becky smiled at the older couple standing in the doorway. Their closeness mirrored the way Logan was hugging her and made her appreciate anew how truly blessed they all were to have each other.

Logan deferred to Becky's father. "Dan, would you like to tell them?"

The older man cleared his throat and sniffled. "I'd rather you did it."

If Logan hadn't tightened his grip on her shoulders at just the right moment, Becky might have trembled. Obviously, something important was about to be revealed.

"Okay," Logan said. "It's like this. Dan's had a team of attorneys working on the abduction case for months and they've managed to iron everything out. Effie's in the clear. For good."

Squeals of joy and applause filled the room while Fred drew his wife closer and kissed her cheek.

"The mixed-up birth certificates have been correctly filed and all criminal charges have been withdrawn," Logan continued. "Becky is—I mean, was—a Keringhoven before she became a Malloy this morning. Dan left Rebecca listed as her first name to simplify things." He grinned down at her. "We figured she was already confused enough about her identity."

Becky winked at her father. "As long as I get to belong to this crazy family, you can call me anything you want." She giggled. "Within reason."

"I think it's time to share the rest of your surprise," Logan told his new father-in-law. "I know you were going to wait till after we'd eaten and were exchanging our regular gifts but this seems like a perfect opportunity."

"I agree," Dan said. "Everybody stay right where you are. I'll be back in a jiffy."

Becky frowned. "The man already gave me a brand-new car. How in the world can he top that?"

"You'll see."

She was surprised to see Dan bearing a gift the size of a small shoebox when he returned. He handed it to her without comment so she asked, "What is it?"

"Open it," her father said hoarsely.

The faded holiday wrapping paper was so brittle it crumbled when she pulled on it. Letting the scraps fall to the floor at her feet, Becky carefully lifted the lid off the box. Her vision blurred. Inside, resting in a bed of yellowed tissue paper, was a simple baby doll dressed in pastel pink.

"I bought that for your first Christmas," Dan said, his voice breaking. "I've kept it all these years, hoping…"

"It's the best present I've ever gotten," Becky said, beaming through unshed tears. "I'll treasure it always. Thanks, Daddy."

Logan pulled her closer, lifted the doll from its nest of paper and held it up, cradled in one hand. "She has your beautiful hair and eyes. I hope our kids look just like this." He paused for a low chuckle. "Of course, they'll all have to be boys."

Becky played along by pretending to be astonished, as if they hadn't discussed eventually starting a family. "All? How many do you want?"

"Oh, no more than five or six," he joked. "If we decide to form our own little league team we can always wait till Cody gets married and provides us with a few cousins."

"Sounds good to me," Becky said, snuggling closer to her new husband and grinning at her embarrassed brother. "So, any plans along those lines, Cody? Any prospects?"

The ensuing silence was almost palpable. Becky had invited a few of the unmarried members of her ladies' Sunday school class to join them that evening. Those women were especially interested in hearing her brother's answer. When he said, "Yes," their sighs were audible.

Becky shrugged. "Oh, well. I tried." She looked to Logan, her gaze filled with tenderness and adoration. "I wish everyone as much happiness as we've found."

"And a blessed Christmas," he added, "the first of many to come."

* * * * *

Dear Reader,

It's easy to say we're walking by faith when everything in life is going our way, yet it's those other times, the harder times, when we need to focus most on trusting God.

No matter how bleak things look, we aren't alone in our troubles if we've given our lives to Christ. I don't have the answer to why bad things happen. Nobody does. But I do know that God has been with me through many trials and that every time I trust Him completely, I grow stronger in my faith. It's always easier to look back and see the handiwork of God than it is to step into an unknown future unafraid. But that's when we most need to do just that.

The characters and stories I create are meant to convey a sense of the joy—and of the problems—we believers share. If you belong to Him, trust Him. If you're questioning whether or not you're truly His child, all you have to do is surrender your pride, ask Jesus to forgive and accept you right now, and He will. It's that easy.

I love to hear from readers. You can write to me at P.O. Box 13, Glencoe, AR 72539, contact me via my website, www.ValerieHansen.com, or send an email to Val@ValerieHansen.com.

Blessings,

Valerie Hansen

OUT OF THE DEPTHS

Count it all joy when you fall into various trials,
knowing that the testing of your faith
produces patience.
—*James* 1:2, 3

I never get tired of saying that Joe is the
most important person in my life. He always will be.

Prologue

"She's the last one."

"I told you she would be. She's real stubborn. We're gonna have more trouble with her than we did with the others."

"Nonsense. She's a woman. Alone."

"Not exactly. She's got a lot of friends." He winced at the string of curses that erupted from his surly companion. "Well, she does. And folks around here stick together. You oughta know that."

"I don't want to hear any more lame excuses. If you can't handle this job, I'll hire somebody who can."

"You threatening me?"

"I never threaten. I promise."

"Give me a few more weeks. I'll up the pressure. She'll cave. I know she will."

"She'd better. I'm sick of waiting."

"I don't know why you're in such a big hurry all

of a sudden. It's gonna turn out just the way I said. It's a sweet setup. She doesn't suspect a thing."

"Yet."

"Hey, don't talk like that. She'll be ready to pack her bags and head for the hills before much longer. She's already jumpy as a cat."

"She should be," the man said with a self-satisfied snort. "She has plenty to be scared of."

"You said there'd be no rough stuff."

"That was before. Things are different now. I'm running out of patience. And time. I'll step in and clear up the problem myself, once and for all, if I have to."

"You wouldn't!"

"Try me."

"Whoa. Don't get all het up." He waved his hands in front of him, palms out, in a placating gesture. "You won't have to do a thing. Two or three more weeks and Trudy Lynn Brown will be finished. She'll be so down in the dumps she'll be beggin' for a chance to sell out."

"Selling's not enough. I want to see her business closed. Period. End of story."

"Yeah, that's what I meant."

"Good. You'd better make sure that's exactly what happens or she won't be the only one in deep trouble."

"I know, I know. But don't forget about those kids

she's got workin' for her. If they get in my way it might slow down our plans a tad."

"Humph." He raised his boot and brought it down on a passing beetle. Its shell collapsed with a sickening, deadly crunch. "Anybody who causes too many problems for me gets the same treatment as that bug. Including you. Best you remember that when you're dealin' with the lady."

"Just promise me you won't hurt her."

"I'm through making promises, especially to you. Get her out of my way—or else."

Chapter One

"Good morning! What a beautiful day," Trudy Lynn said, stepping out onto the porch of her cabin to greet her elderly hired hand. "Don't you love the Ozarks this time of year?"

"Yes'm." Will took off his sweat-stained baseball cap and held it in front of him. "Morning, Miz Brown. Can't say it's too good, though. Maybe you'd best sit down."

She shaded her eyes and braced for the worst. "What now?" The look on Will's leathery face made her heart sink. "Not more of the same?"

"'Fraid so."

"Oh, no."

It wasn't fair. Not after all the sacrifices she'd made to keep this business going. She'd hung on and finally prospered when other campgrounds and canoe rentals around her had closed. This year, she'd even managed to buy a bit of new equipment.

"What did they do this time?" Trudy asked nervously.

"Took out three more of them new red canoes. Looks to me like we'd best put 'em in storage and use the old ones for now. You can't keep buyin' new ones if somebody's gonna go knockin' holes in 'em."

"I know."

Pensive, she stood at the porch railing and gazed fondly at the neat campsites arrayed beside the Spring River. Oaks and hickory had greened up, while dogwoods were almost done with their blooms. Every day, new varieties of wildflowers appeared, some with blossoms so tiny they could hardly be seen. The only thing spoiling the picture was the knowledge that someone despised her enough to try to ruin her.

"Okay," Trudy told Will. "Take Jimmy and have him help you load what's left of my best canoes on the spare trailer. I'll tow it down to Serenity and rent a storage spot to park it. I just hate to back down like this."

"What else can we do?"

"Nothing. We can't stay up every night to stand guard and still hope to function well during the day, especially not when peak season gets here. Besides, it's too dangerous for amateurs like us. And hiring a real security man would cost way too much."

"How 'bout that ornery little dog of yours? We could tie him down by the boats. He's sure to make a racket if anybody strange comes around."

Trudy Lynn laughed softly and shook her head. "You know Widget barks at everything, including rabbits and deer. He'd sound false alarms and keep us running all night long."

"Prob'ly." The stooped old man nodded sagely. "Okay, Miz Brown, I'll fetch Jimmy and we'll load up them new canoes for you. He's not gonna like doing it, though."

"What my cousin likes or doesn't like isn't your problem, Will. It's time he learned that his brains aren't the only reason I hired him. It shouldn't take all day to keep our accounts current. When he's not busy in the office I expect him to lend a hand outside, not sit around playing computer games."

"That, I gotta see."

"You will. I promise," Trudy Lynn said, smiling. "He's my kin. I can always threaten to tell Grandma Earlene if he doesn't behave. Otherwise, I'll fire him, just like I did that Randall boy."

The old man put his cap back on and hesitated, squinting against the bright sunlight. "You be careful who you rile up. So far, all we've lost is a few boats. I don't want to lose you, too." Smiling wryly he added, "I'd never find another job as easy as this one. Not at my age."

She chose to take him seriously in spite of his jesting tone. "You be careful, too, you old coot. I'd never find another helper as savvy and hardworking as you are." Will's throaty chuckle warmed her heart. "Now get going."

"Yes, ma'am. You gonna be tending the camp store?"

"No. The new girl's a fast learner. She can cope with the store. Farley's had enough training to handle canoe launches by himself till you're free. As soon as you and Jimmy get that trailer hitched and loaded, bring the truck up here, and I'll head for Serenity."

"Yes'm."

Watching Will shuffle away, Trudy Lynn marveled at his devotion. He was a jewel, all right, but he was no kid. How much longer could he keep working? Every spring she had to train a new batch of local teens because her prior employees had either grown up and moved away or sought better-paying, year-round jobs. Trying to operate both the campground and canoe rental without Will's steady support seemed like an impossible task.

She huffed in disgust. If the vandalism kept on as it had been—or escalated—she might not have to worry about doing without Will. There wouldn't be any business left to run.

Once in Serenity, Trudy Lynn decided to stop at Becky Malloy's to unwind before driving back to camp. She knocked on the screen door of the old stone house and was welcomed with a pleasant, "Come on in! I'm in the kitchen."

"It's just me." She pushed open the screen. "Mmm. Smells good in here. Has your aunt Effie been borrowing your fancy oven to bake again?"

Becky stuck her head around the corner from the kitchen. "Hi there! Nope, I'm the one making the mess. I hope my cookies turn out as good as Effie's always do. I've got company coming tonight."

"In that case, I won't keep you," Trudy Lynn said. "I just stopped by for a little commiseration."

"I'm getting real good at that. Never dreamed how often I'd be called on to help people now that I'm a pastor's wife. I'm busier than when I was church secretary."

"How's Logan doing? As a preacher, I mean."

"As well as can be expected. There'll always be problems. All churches have them, even Serenity Chapel." She tittered. "Congregations would get along a lot better if they were made up of perfect saints. Unfortunately, there aren't any of those available."

"Amen. Which reminds me of why I stopped by," Trudy Lynn said. "We were vandalized again last night."

"No way!" Her friend's mouth fell open. "What happened?"

"Somebody knocked holes in more of my canoes. I just dropped off the rest of the new ones at the storage yard over on Highway 395."

"That's unbelievable. What did the sheriff say this time?"

"I haven't told him yet. Why hurry? He never finds any clues. I figured I'd stop by his office while I'm in town and fill him in."

"Do you want me to ask Logan to look into it for you?" Becky asked.

"And distract him from his church work? Absolutely not. He's not a detective anymore. Besides, he never did have connections around here—and I doubt anybody back in Chicago has it in for me."

"You're probably right about that." A timer dinged and Becky went to the oven to remove a sheet of finished cookies and replace it with another that was ready to bake. "Well, if you change your mind, all you have to do is ask," she said, resetting the timer.

"I know. Thanks." Trudy Lynn eyed the tray. "I could be talked into tasting a few of those if you have extra. I was so upset I forgot to eat breakfast."

"How about having a cup of tea with me, too? I need a break. I've been at this all morning."

"Sure." Trudy Lynn got two mugs from the cupboard and added tea bags while her friend put a kettle of water on to boil. "So, who are you expecting? Must be important to make you go to all this trouble. You *hate* cooking."

"I can do anything if I set my mind to it. Dad told me oatmeal raisin cookies are Cody's favorite so I made lots."

"Cody? Your brother's coming?" She felt the flush of her reddening cheeks. "I thought he was long gone."

"He was." Sighing, Becky joined her at the table. "He got hurt."

"Oh, no! When?" Trudy Lynn immediately reached for her friend's hand. "Why didn't you tell me?"

"I didn't even hear about it until yesterday. I guess Cody didn't want anybody to feel sorry for him. Dad didn't find out till Cody called and asked if he could spend a few weeks recuperating at his place."

"How badly was he hurt?"

"Bad enough. His leg was broken. But that's not the worst part. When he told his girlfriend he might always have a little trouble getting around, she ditched him."

"The one he told everybody he was going to marry? That's awful!"

"No kidding. Dad says he's really down in the dumps. That's why I invited him here. My father's at work all day and Cody has nothing to do at Dad's condo but brood about everything he's lost. I figure, if he's here with Logan and me, we can at least keep his mind occupied."

"What about physical therapy? Won't that help?"

"It probably would if he hadn't refused to keep doing it." Becky made a face. "He is one stubborn Viking."

"I'd never thought of him that way before. He does kind of look like paintings of Eric the Red. So do you." She blushed. "The reddish-blond hair part, I mean, not the Viking-raider-swinging-a-sword part."

"Glad we got that straightened out." Becky was chuckling. "Why don't you stop by for supper tonight? Dad will be here and I've already invited Carol Sue to keep him company. We could use a fourth. You liked Cody when you met him, didn't you?"

"Sure, but—"

"Then come. Will won't mind babysitting your camp for a few hours. I don't expect the party to last long. Dad wants to head back up north and Cody'll probably be worn-out, especially after the long drive."

"What if he's not up to being in a crowd?"

"Then I'll just wag my finger in his face and tell him to get over himself, like any spoiled baby sister would." Her smile grew. "I'll probably get away with it, too, since we don't have a lot of history together. At least I hope I will."

Trudy Lynn thought back to Becky's odd past, being kept away from her brother and father because of her mother's lies. She took a bite of warm cookie and chewed thoughtfully before answering, "I hope so, too."

By the time she'd finally made up her mind on what to wear that evening, Trudy Lynn was disgusted with herself for being so uneasy. She was only having supper at a friend's house, not going to a real party. It didn't make any difference what she wore as long as she was presentable.

She made a face as she pulled the camp pickup into Becky's driveway and parked. Apparently, her subconscious disagreed. She couldn't recall feeling this concerned about her appearance for ages. Not that she wasn't always dressed properly, especially on Sunday mornings. She just wasn't usually as aware of the details, like whether her long, brown hair lay perfectly in place or her nails were neatly filed.

The muted silk dress she'd chosen for that evening was a favorite, partly because it brought out the misty-green of her hazel eyes. An attempt at high-lighting her lashes with mascara, however, had had disastrous results. The brush had slipped and her right eye was still smarting.

Peering at her reflection in the truck's rearview mirror, she ran one finger gently beneath her sore eye. At least it had quit watering so the remaining mascara was no longer making black smudges. She didn't want Becky's big brother to take one look at her and conclude she'd been the loser in a fistfight!

Thoughts of Cody Keringhoven made her pulse jump. He was handsome, in a rugged sort of way. And when he'd smiled at her and his blue eyes had sparkled so mischievously, she'd tingled all over, in spite of her vow to never get involved with another man.

Funny, Trudy mused, stepping down out of her pickup and starting toward the house. She hadn't thought of Ned, her ex-fiancé, for ages. Perhaps she was finally getting over the disappointment of their breakup. It was high time.

Climbing the porch steps, she was about to knock when Logan pushed open the door and greeted her.

"Trudy Lynn! Glad you could make it. Becky told me she'd invited you."

"Am I early? I didn't see any other cars."

"No. Not at all." He ushered her inside. "Dan drove around back so Cody wouldn't have to wrestle with the front stairs while he's on crutches. Can I get you something to drink? We have iced tea, soda and lemonade."

"Nothing now, thanks. Where is everybody?"

"Becky's in the kitchen, chiseling supper out of the roaster, and Dan's showing Carol Sue the newest model of those fancy cars he sells. The last time I saw Cody he was parked on the couch in the living room. Why don't you go keep him company till everybody else gets back?"

"Maybe I should help your wife?"

"There is no help for her when it comes to cooking," Logan joked. "Besides, that's my job. I've gotten really good at salvaging burned food."

Trudy Lynn took a mock swing at him. "Cynic."

"Realist, you mean. Come on. I'll introduce you to Cody, just in case he doesn't remember meeting you before."

"Oh, that's flattering," she retorted, grinning. "I met him at church, and again right here in this house last Christmas, besides your wedding. If he doesn't remember me after all that, I'll be really disappointed."

They entered the modest living room together. Cody was seated on the brocade sofa with one leg propped stiffly on the coffee table atop a throw pillow. Dejection had affected him so deeply he barely resembled the vital man he'd been. It broke her heart to see such a dramatic, negative change.

Logan made brief small talk, then excused himself.

"Nice to see you again," Trudy Lynn said, trying to sound upbeat.

Cody barely glanced at her. "You'll pardon me if I don't get up?"

"Sure. No problem. Mind if I sit here?"

He shrugged. "It's a free country."

Choosing to ignore his moodiness she perched at the opposite end of the sofa, taking care to avoid bumping the coffee table or his elevated leg. "I'm certainly glad it is. And I'm thankful for the folks who keep it that way, too. Were you in the army like Brother Logan?"

"No."

"Oh." Trudy Lynn tried a different subject. "Becky tells me you guide raft trips."

He glanced at his injured leg, then scowled at her. "I used to."

"You will again."

"Not according to the doctors."

Oh dear. No wonder he was bitter. Becky hadn't told her enough about his injury to keep her from saying the wrong thing and now she had her foot planted firmly in her mouth.

"Have you gotten a second opinion?" she asked, hoping to salvage something encouraging from their conversation.

"What for?"

Trudy Lynn couldn't help the tiny smile that threatened to spread as she said, "To see if the second doctor is as sure about your leg as the first one was? I think that's what second opinions are supposed to do."

"Very funny."

"I figured it was worth a try." Leaning closer, she lightly touched the back of his hand. "Look, Cody, I know you've had it rough lately. We all face problems we can't understand, especially when we're stuck in the middle of them. It's how we let those situations influence us and shape our future that matters."

He pulled his hand away. "You have no idea what I'm facing. Don't preach to me, lady. I get enough of that from my family."

"I see."

Trudy Lynn's initial urge was to apologize and commiserate with him. She quickly decided that would be the worst thing she could do. If he wasn't ready to look for the bright side of his troubles, then so be it. She didn't intend to sit there and argue with him.

Chin up, she got to her feet and smoothed her flowing skirt. "Okay. Have it your way. You can wallow in self-pity all you want. I'm going out to the kitchen to help your sister. It's her I feel sorry for. I can go home. She's going to be stuck here with you for who knows *how* long."

The last thing she saw as she whirled and flounced from the room was Cody's expression of utter astonishment.

As soon as he was alone, Cody sank back against the sofa cushions. That woman didn't understand. Nobody could. He was still struggling to accept what had happened—and he'd been there—so how could anyone else have a clue as to what he was going through?

That fateful day had seemed perfect for running the rapids. "This is it," he remembered shouting. "Paddles inside!"

The bow of the raft had cut through the high side of the channel and plunged straight into an eddy. Behind him, the Slighman brothers had been whooping it up like the seasoned veterans they were. It was the two younger men in the front of the raft who'd had Cody worried. The guy on the right looked strong enough to bench press a semi truck, but he was acting way too nervous.

"Okay. Brace yourselves," Cody ordered. "Here comes the *Widow-maker.*"

Busy keeping the raft away from submerged rocks, he only half saw his panicky client let go of the safety ropes, drop to the floor and curl into a fetal position.

"No! Get up! You're throwing our balance off!"

The pliable raft's pitch and yaw tossed the loose passenger around like a knot of dirty laundry in an overloaded washing machine. Cody strained to plot a safe course through the approaching cataracts. The trick was to be in the right place at the right time and let the river do the navigating. His biggest concern was how much deviation his passenger's erratic behavior had already caused.

"Sit on the floor and stay there," he roared. "Before you get us all killed."

Cody's muscles strained to master the treacherous river. His lungs labored, his body ached. Determination welded his cold, stiffening fingers to the oars. Squinting, he spotted a narrow, clear path ahead. *Thank You, God.*

Suddenly, the man he'd ordered to stay on the floor gave a strangled cry and thrust his head over the side. Cody had only two options: make a course correction and hope the water was high enough to skim submerged rocks, or press through narrows where the fool might be decapitated. He chose the rocks.

Blinding spray stung like tiny hailstones. Momentum lifted the raft high on the left side, depressing the right till it was pushed underwater, sick man and all. Helpless to do more, Cody watched his passenger wash over the side. Then, to his enormous relief, he noticed the man's hand was fisted around the safety rope.

"Feet first!" Cody shouted. "Lead with your legs."

Instead, the frightened man grabbed an oar shaft.

Cody passed his free oar to one of the experienced rafters behind him and dropped to his knees. "Let go before you wreck us!"

Instead, ice-cold fingers closed around his wrist. Already off balance, Cody was easily jerked out of the raft.

The frigid torrent closed around him, hammered against his chest, stole his breath. Muscles instantly cramped despite the protection of his wet suit. Something was wrong. Very wrong. Plunging into a glacial watercourse like the upper Tuolumne was always a severe shock, but he'd never experienced anything this excruciating.

Nearly out of his head from the knifing pain, he'd gritted his teeth and forced his eyes open. One of the Slighman brothers had taken over the oars and was steering toward shore. He'd thought then that everything would turn out all right.

How wrong he'd been. With every muscle nearly as knotted as it had been during the accident, Cody struggled to free his mind from the past. Perspiration dotted his forehead. He had the same intense reaction every time he was foolish enough to recall the events of that horrible day.

He had to get hold of himself before someone came back into the room and detected his temporary loss of self-control. Closing his eyes, he took a deep, settling breath and purposely visualized how he'd finally surrendered to his pain and had let the river carry him where it would.

Even now, he realized with chagrin, that terrible trip was far from over.

Chapter Two

By the time Trudy Lynn reached the kitchen she was contrite enough to relate her whole conversation with Cody to her hosts. "And then I snapped at the poor guy and told him off. I always babble too much when I don't know what to say. I feel terrible."

"Don't," Becky said. "Sometimes the best way to show love is to disagree, especially when the other person is wrong. So, how did he take it?"

"I'm not sure. His mouth was still hanging open when I left him."

"Good."

"Good?"

Becky nodded sagely. "Sure. He's a lot more likely to listen to sensible advice coming from someone like you."

"He did say his family was getting on his nerves. I assumed he meant his father, but I suppose that could include you and Logan, too."

"Probably. Right now, everything bothers Cody more than it normally would. He's already gone through plenty."

"What, exactly, is wrong with his leg? He said he won't be able to go back to work. Is it that bad?"

"Could be. His knee was smashed. There's a lot of scarring and stiffness. According to Dad, he'd have to regain a wide range of motion in order to be qualified to guide the kind of trip he loves. Might eventually have to undergo more surgery, too."

"Oh, dear." Thoughtful, Trudy Lynn glanced in the direction of the living room. "Now I feel even worse about the way I talked to him."

Logan chimed in with a smile of encouragement. "Don't worry. From what I've seen so far, Cody can take criticism as well as he can dish it out."

"He certainly can dish it out." Trudy Lynn gave Becky a pat of commiseration. "Like I said, it's you I feel sorriest for. You'll be stuck here with him."

"Maybe. Logan had an idea. Until you told us how you stood up to my stubborn brother just now, I didn't think it would work."

Trudy Lynn took a step backward. "Whoa. I don't like the sound of that. What kind of an idea?"

"A brilliant one."

"That's what I'm afraid of." Looking from Becky to Logan and back, she was struck by how in tune they seemed. Thoughts, expressions and actions meshed as perfectly as if they'd been married for decades instead of mere months.

"Tell you what," Logan said with a smile, "I'll go keep Cody occupied while you ladies discuss how we can all work together to help him through this."

Watching him walk away, Trudy Lynn felt decidedly uneasy. Logan Malloy was not only her pastor, he was married to one of her dearest friends. It was going to be hard to deny either of them anything, even if she hated their idea. And they knew it.

Folding her arms across her chest, she raised an eyebrow at her hostess. "Okay. I can already hear the train whistles, so if you're going to try to railroad me into doing something, let's get it over with."

"It's just a thought," Becky insisted. "We don't expect you to commit yourself right away. All we ask is that you consider doing it."

"Consider doing what?"

"Hiring Cody."

Trudy Lynn's glance darted in the direction of the living room. She lowered her voice. "To do what? He can't even walk, can he?"

"Not without crutches. But we all know it's bad for him to sit around and dwell on his problems. If he doesn't get out and try to do something for himself soon, he may never regain his agility."

"Okay. Bring him down to the river to visit and I'll have Will entertain him with stories about the old days. That'll be plenty distracting."

"Thanks. I'm sure it will help. But I was thinking about a job."

"I *can't* hire him." Trudy Lynn was adamant. "I can barely afford the staff I have—and they're fully capable of doing any job I assign."

"I understand. It's all right."

"No, it isn't. Why don't you beg or plead or yell at me or something?"

"I told you there was no pressure," her friend said. "There isn't. Logan and I will be glad to take care of Cody for as long as he needs us."

"Even if he never walks on his own again?" It was almost a whisper.

"Yes," Becky said. "Even then. I may not have known him when we were children because of my kidnapping but he's still my brother. I'm not going to give up on him."

"Wow." Trudy Lynn gazed at her friend through misty eyes and gave her a brief hug before she spoke from the heart. "I wish I had a sister like you."

As soon as Becky had finished arranging a platter of roast beef and had filled serving bowls with the rest of the meal, she picked up the two largest dishes and gestured to Trudy with a nod of her head. "Grab those mashed potatoes and bring them along, will you? I'll come back for the gravy in a sec."

"No problem. This bowl isn't that heavy. I can carry the gravy boat, too."

"Okay. Just be careful, it's…"

Trudy Lynn didn't hear the rest of Becky's comment because her voice had been muted when she'd passed through the archway to the dining room. Oh, well. At least they were through talking about Cody's problems. That was a relief.

Following her hostess, Trudy was surprised and happy to note that the injured man was up and about. Logan hovered close behind him, obviously ready to assist if Cody had difficulty managing his crutches in the crowded room. Dan and Carol Sue, another of the Malloys' friends from church, had already taken their seats on the opposite side of the beautifully set table and seemed engrossed in a private conversation.

Cody approached laboriously. Pausing to let him pass, Trudy Lynn smiled for his benefit. She knew she had to continue to treat him as if he were just like everyone else. The hardest part was subduing the tender feelings that welled up every time she looked into his eyes and read the depth of his suffering.

Still carrying the food she'd brought from the kitchen, she stepped back to give him extra room to pass. On the opposite side of the table, Becky gasped.

Scowling, Trudy Lynn gave her friend a questioning glance and mouthed, "What?" Was she still too close? She thought she'd allowed Cody adequate space to get by, even with his crutches, so why was Becky acting nervous?

Drawing back, Trudy felt her heel hit the base

of the wall. The only way to get completely out of Cody's path now would be to duck back into the kitchen. Regrettably, she'd sidled away from the doorway while trying to accommodate him. There was no easy exit.

She pressed her back against the wall as he started to pass and raised both arms, meaning only to carefully lift the potatoes and gravy out of harm's way.

Becky shouted, "Be careful!"

Startled, Cody faltered.

Trudy Lynn followed her friend's line of sight. If the pitcher and saucer of the gravy server had been one unit, the way she'd assumed they were, she'd have had everything under control. Unfortunately, they were two separate pieces. And the gravy-filled section was starting to slide!

She had only an instant to make a correction. Cody was too close! She had to protect him, even if that meant absorbing the worst of the mishap herself.

Dropping her arm, she pushed the leading edge of the saucer forward and gave it a quick flip. That wasn't enough to right the shallow pitcher but it did alter its trajectory and keep its contents from showering the injured man.

Everyone was shouting. Trudy couldn't use both hands to halt the spill because she was still holding the bowl of mashed potatoes. Her only recourse was to press the small pitcher against her chest and wait for rescue. Thankfully, the discussion in the kitchen had delayed the meal long enough to cool and thicken the gravy.

Cody quickly tucked one crutch under his arm and reached for the potatoes. "Here. Give me that."

"Gladly."

"Are you all right?"

She answered without looking at him. Now that she had a free hand she was focused on wiping globs of gravy off her bodice and catching them without dripping on the carpet. The task was daunting as well as disgustingly messy. "I've been better," she said wryly. "How about you?"

"Never touched me. I hope that dress isn't a favorite."

"Actually, it was." His undertone of mirth caused her to pause and look up. Amazingly, the corners of his mouth were starting to twitch into a smile. "I thought it matched my eyes."

"Only if they're part brown," Cody replied. He inclined his head to study her more closely. "They are kind of brown, with specks of green and maybe a little blue. The right one looks irritated. Did you burn it just now?"

Trudy Lynn made a face. Considering the state she was already in there was no use keeping up any pretense of poise or refinement. "No. The gravy wasn't that hot. If you must know, I jabbed myself in the eye with a mascara brush when I was getting ready to come over here."

"Are you always this accident-prone?"

"Not usually. I did want to be entertaining tonight, though. How am I doing?"

"Pretty good, actually."

The humor in Cody's voice reflected his smile and warmed her heart. "Glad to hear it." Her gaze briefly passed over the others and returned to him. "I'm sorry I made such a mess. If everyone will please excuse me, I think I'll go see if I can salvage my dignity—and my dress."

Her hostess had dashed to the kitchen for a handful of paper towels and was thrusting them at her. "Here. Blot."

Trudy Lynn shook her head. "It's too late for that. Just stand back so I can make a run for it before I start dripping on your floor."

"I'm not worried about the carpet," Becky said. "I'm worried about you. Want me to come help you get cleaned up?"

"No. Stay with your guests. And please don't wait dinner for me. The way my clothes feel right now I'll probably give up and go home anyway."

"And miss my sister's infamous cooking?" Cody asked, still smiling. "They tell me she's been working on this meal all day."

"I know. I can't apologize enough for being such a klutz." Starting to turn away she paused and stared directly at Cody. Careful to deliver her remarks with a straight face she added, "Even if my dress was okay

I probably wouldn't stay to eat. I don't much care for roast beef and mashed potatoes without lots of gravy."

She could hear him chuckling softly as she hurried from the room. Good. At least *one* positive thing had come out of the worst social disaster of her life.

Reaching the guest bathroom on the ground floor, Trudy Lynn heard a ruckus behind her. Poor Becky. It sounded as if there was more trouble brewing.

She was turning the knob to open the closed bathroom door when Cody's strong, deep voice rose above the clamor.

"No!" he shouted. "Don't open that door!"

What a strange thing to shout, Trudy Lynn mused. She knew Cody couldn't be yelling at her. All the guests and their hosts were accounted for in the other room, so she certainly wouldn't be intruding on anyone. The sooner she got her dress rinsed out and could assess the damage, the happier she'd be.

An odd clumping sound echoed in the hallway. Ignoring it, she stepped into the bathroom and shut the door. Her eyes widened. Her breath caught. She *wasn't* alone.

An animal as big and furry as a black bear was napping on the floor. Before she could decide what to do, the creature opened its warm brown eyes, saw her, yawned and began to pant.

"You're a *dog*?" Trudy whispered. Her voice rose

as she realized she was right. "You're a dog. What a relief!"

The animal apparently took her words as an invitation. It leaped to its feet with a lot more agility than she'd imagined anything that size could possess and in one lumbering, tail-wagging stride was crowding against her, clearly begging for attention.

Deciding to assert authority before the situation got out of control, she said, "Good boy. Settle down," and tried to push the overly affectionate canine away.

Using her hands was a mistake. The dog took one whiff of the traces of gravy on her fingers and proceeded to lick them with a pink tongue as wide as her palm.

Trudy giggled. "Hey, that tickles."

To her delight, the dog cocked its head and looked up at her as if it were in on the joke. Its nostrils twitched, sniffing the air. "Oh, no. Not the dress," she said firmly. "If you want any more gravy you'll have to wait till I bring you some in a dish."

The impromptu training session was going quite well until Cody banged on the door.

"What?" Trudy Lynn called.

"Are you okay?"

"Of course."

"Stand back. I'm coming in."

The sound of his voice had already excited the dog so much it was spinning in circles. When he burst through the door, it raised on its hind legs and put its broad front feet on Trudy Lynn's shoulders, bringing their faces nose-to-nose.

She twisted away. "Phew! Dog breath. Down boy."

"Sailor. Stop that." Cody gave the dog's collar a tug. It landed on all four feet with a soft thump.

Once again, Trudy Lynn held out her hands to her new canine buddy and let him lick her fingers. "He wasn't hurting anything. We were getting along fine till you showed up and distracted him."

"Nonsense. Sailor only listens to me. I took him to obedience school, but he's been a lot harder to manage since I got hurt."

"I'm not surprised. You've probably been acting overly cautious and he's sensing an opening to become the alpha dog. He'll gladly be the boss if you let him."

"You're crazy. He knows I'm still in charge." Cody tried to grab the dog's collar again and was almost pulled off balance for his trouble. "Go on. Get out of here," he told her gruffly. "I can handle this."

"Oh really?" Forgetting her stained dress and disheveled appearance, Trudy Lynn faced him, hands fisted on her hips. "And who's going to handle you when you wind up in a heap on the floor or break your leg all over again? It won't be your dog's fault if that happens. It'll be yours."

Sailor had left his arguing companions and was cavorting around the cramped room like a hamster in an exercise wheel. A very large hamster. In a very small wheel.

"Sailor. Get over here," Cody demanded.

The dog looked at him as if to say, *You've got to be kidding. I'm having too much fun.*

Trudy Lynn stepped forward and calmly said, "Sailor?" She pointed to the floor at her feet. "Come here." As soon as he obeyed she added, "Good boy. Sit."

"Beginner's luck," Cody muttered.

"Maybe." She nodded toward the door. "You go first. I've decided to wash in the upstairs bathroom, instead."

"Good decision."

As soon as they were both safely in the hall and the dog was isolated in the bathroom again, Trudy apologized. "I didn't mean to usurp your authority. I just wanted to show you how being firm will work with a big lummox like that. He's a Newfoundland, isn't he? I love him. I saw one like that win Best-in-Show at Westminster a few years ago."

"Yes. I'd heard they were an easy breed to train. Too bad Sailor's not as intelligent as he's supposed to be."

"Oh, I don't know. He's smart enough to have you buffaloed."

"I told you. It's different since I've been on these stupid crutches."

"I imagine a lot of things are," Trudy Lynn said.

"And since I know you don't want to hear my opinion about making adjustments to change, I'll save my breath."

"Thank you."

"You're welcome."

"Are you about ready to eat?"

She glanced at her dress and grimaced. "I refuse to come to the table looking like this. Folks in Serenity may be relaxed and casual, but this outfit is way over the top. Give your sister my regrets, will you?"

"Nope."

"What?"

"You heard me. I'm trying your training method. No."

"That's for dogs, not people."

"Whatever works. Becky can loan you some clean clothes if you want. She's already warned us we'll sit there and wait for you till we starve, if necessary."

"It would serve her right if I came to the table just like this," Trudy Lynn said with disgust.

"That's okay by me," Cody drawled, raising an eyebrow and looking her up and down before breaking out in a quirky smile. "I think you should consider changing, though. Sailor's losing his winter coat. I don't mind gravy stains, but that black dog hair all over your skirt is probably a bit much, even for laid-back folks like Becky and Logan."

In the end, Trudy Lynn gave in and accepted an oversize shirt and slacks from her friend's closet.

Hurrying to the table, she was relieved to see that the others had already begun to fill their plates.

Becky quickly explained. "Dad has to get going soon, so we finally started without you. I'm sorry."

"Not a problem," Trudy Lynn replied, smiling across the table at the older man. "Why don't you stay over and leave in the morning when you're not so tired? I know it's a long drive." She shot a quick wink at the woman seated beside him. "Besides, I'm sure Carol Sue would like to get to know you better. She's a widow, you know."

"Can't. Cody's going to need the extra bed," Dan said pleasantly. "I suppose I could get a room at a motel."

"Absolutely not." Becky was adamant. "If you want to stay over we'll make a place for you here. Somehow."

"Or, I could put him up," Trudy Lynn offered. She took a spoonful of mashed potatoes, then set the bowl down. "I almost always have a few empty cabins, Dan. If you stayed overnight at my campground, maybe you could help us by listening for the vandal who's been wrecking my canoes."

The platter of meat came her way and she grasped it firmly. Fork raised to choose a slice, she suddenly froze in midmotion. Her gaze met Becky's, then darted to Cody and lingered.

He noticed immediately and scowled. "What?"

"Just thinking," Trudy Lynn said.

"About what? Have I missed something?"

"No. I was just wondering. I do have some available cabins, like I said, and I could use help. Would you be interested in spending some time at my campground?"

Cody cast a disgusted look at the crutches he'd propped against the wall. "Doing what?"

Her growing enthusiasm made Trudy Lynn grin in spite of his dour expression. This was the answer to everyone's prayers, including her own. "Watching. I can use an extra pair of eyes. That's all you'd have to do. In exchange, I'd give you free room and board."

"I can get the same deal right here," he argued.

"Okay. What about Sailor? I have a river and woods for him to explore that are far from dangerous traffic. And you'll get a rustic cabin he can't possibly hurt, even if he sheds a truckload of hair. It's perfect. How can you turn down an offer like that? Your poor dog can't spend weeks shut up in a bathroom."

"I know." Cody was pensive. "What's the terrain like?"

"Flat, mostly. My basic operation is down by the Spring River on an old floodplain. You'll have to climb to get to the camp store, but if you need groceries or anything, I'll be glad to bring them to you."

"It might work." He looked to his sister. "I know you had your heart set on having me stay here. At least you did until you found out I was bringing my dog. Would you be too upset if Sailor and I spent a little time roughing it?"

"Well, I suppose it would be okay, if that's what you want. A city lot with no fence isn't a good place for a dog. I'd hate to have to chain him up to keep him safe."

Trudy could tell her friend was having a terrible time suppressing a satisfied grin. No wonder. Becky and Logan were getting everything they'd asked for, with one notable exception.

"There is a small catch," Trudy Lynn said seriously. "I can't pay you anything. I'm sorry."

"When I worked, it wasn't because I had to, it was because I loved my job," Cody replied. "I have some investments that provide income. If you have internet access I can tap into once a week, I'll have everything I need."

"I do! My cousin Jim uses it all the time. He keeps the camp books for me." She smiled and arched an eyebrow. "I hate math. Give me a sunny afternoon, a picnic lunch, a cool river for swimming or canoeing and I'm as happy as can be."

It wasn't until Cody clenched his jaw and looked away that she realized how her innocent banter must have hurt him. Granted, her stretch of the Spring River wasn't a thrilling rapids but the comparison was there just the same. She'd have to remember to watch what she said, at least for a while. There was healing for Cody Keringhoven in the peaceful beauty of her campground. She could sense it. That was the most important thing.

And if he actually managed to help identify the vandal who'd been plaguing her lately? Trudy Lynn bowed her head and let her hair swing against her cheeks to hide her insightful smile. If that did happen, she might consider his success a very surprising answer to prayer, but she wasn't going to hold her breath waiting for it.

Chapter Three

Getting Sailor into the back of her truck hadn't been nearly as difficult as Trudy Lynn had imagined it would be. Loading his master into the front seat, however, had turned out to be a real trial. Cody's behavior had been far too stoic to suit her. There was no way to tell if she'd accidentally caused him pain in spite of her monumental efforts to be careful, and that upset her greatly.

"You don't have to pretend you're invincible when you're around me," she told him after they were underway. "I'm not your sister or your father. If your leg hurts, I expect you to say so. I want to know what you're thinking."

"No, you don't. You may think you do, but you don't."

"Try me."

"Not in a million years, lady."

"I'm only trying to help. Why do you insist on being so difficult?"

"I'm not hard to get along with. All I want is to be left alone. I thought you'd figured that out. Isn't that why you offered me a free cabin? To get my sister off the hook and give me some privacy."

"That was part of the reason."

He huffed. "You don't think I bought that crazy story about vandalism, do you?"

"It's not a crazy story. It's true. I've had six new canoes ruined already." She absently kneaded the back of her neck as they drove farther from the heart of Serenity. "I get a headache every time I start to think about it."

"Headaches? Hah!"

The irony and contempt coloring his otherwise simple exclamation made Trudy Lynn stare. Cody was shaking his head and peering out the window as if he could see something terrible hidden in the darkness. Something invisible to her.

She was about to ask him if the bumpy road was bothering his leg when he shivered, then said quietly, "If you think a few wrecked canoes can give you a headache, you ought to try killing somebody, like I did, and see how much it hurts."

Trudy Lynn didn't know how to respond to his startling confession so she said nothing. Chances were, Cody was referring to an accidental death. She wasn't going to press him about it. Not yet. There would be plenty of time to assess the root cause of his depression after they became friends. And they would be friends, she decided. Even if she had to beat him over the head with tough love and kill him with kindness!

That thought made her want to smile. She would have surrendered to the urge if she hadn't been worried about giving Cody the wrong impression. The last thing the poor guy needed was to think she was laughing at his plight.

The most entertaining element of their situation was her own reactions to everything about him. It had been a long time since anyone had flustered her enough to bring out her klutzy side, nor had she been this personally interested in any man for ages. She wasn't a prude. She was simply fed up with exaggerated male egos, thanks mainly to her recent disappointment in the one person she'd thought she could trust to be faithful. Ned's disloyalty had taken her completely by surprise. Thus, she no longer trusted her instincts the way she used to.

Cody had been staring at her ever since he'd dropped his bombshell. "Well? Aren't you going to say anything?"

"About what?" Trudy Lynn huffed. "If you think I'm going to stick my nose into something that's none of my business, you have another think coming." One eyebrow arched and she gave him a cursory glance.

"However, if you want to tell me what happened, I'll be happy to listen."

"Never mind."

"Okay." She shrugged and concentrated on the curving road ahead.

"You really aren't curious? I mean, suppose I'm dangerous?"

That brought a soft chuckle. "If I thought you were, I wouldn't be here with you."

Cody agreed. "If I had my choice, *I* wouldn't be here with me, either."

"That might be a little hard to accomplish."

"No lie." He was slowly shaking his head. "You know, as many times as I've gone over that day in my mind, I still haven't figured out what I could have done to avert the accident."

"Maybe it was meant to be." Trudy Lynn saw his fists clench, so she elaborated. "What I mean is, maybe there wasn't anything that could have been done, at least not on your part. Most disasters are the result of a combination of errors. You can't hold yourself totally responsible."

Cody snorted in disgust. "Maybe not, but the dead man's relatives sure blame me plenty."

"I'm sorry to hear that. Have they been giving you a lot of grief?"

"Not as much as they've said they're going to give me. I've been warned I'll be sued. And so will the tour company I used to work for."

"What did happen, exactly?"

He gave her a swift, telling glance. "I thought you weren't interested."

"Hey, I never said that. I just told you I wasn't going to pry. You're the one who kept talking about it."

"True. I suppose it wouldn't hurt to get your take on it. You are in sort of the same business."

Trudy Lynn listened patiently, stifling any urge to interrupt his story by asking for details. By the time he was through, she'd heard enough to clarify the main points and make sensible comments.

"Surely, your clients signed a waiver of responsibility. Even I require that, and my trips aren't nearly as hazardous as whitewater rafting."

"Of course they did. The victim signed one just like everybody else. Only he lied about his age. He was big enough to be every bit as old as he claimed."

"But he wasn't eighteen?"

"Bingo. Just seventeen."

"Do you have a lawyer?"

"If I need one. I'm still hoping his family will cool off and not file suit." He unconsciously rubbed the knotted muscles in his thigh as he spoke. "I did all I could. If my knee hadn't snapped when he flipped me onto those rocks, I might have been able to save him."

"You did your best, in spite of being hurt, right?"

"Of course."

"Well, then…" Trudy Lynn shrugged. "What more do you want from yourself?"

The look of disdain Cody shot at her was a clear rebuke. Trudy Lynn took her hands off the wheel long enough to hold them up in a gesture of surrender. "Okay, okay. No more unsolicited advice. But I'm right, and you know it."

"Do you *always* have to have the last word?"

She laughed softly. "I try to."

Fireflies were blinking a pale, luminescent green welcome when Trudy Lynn pulled through the double gates of her Spring River Campground. Thanks to the lateness of the hour and scarcity of overnight campers this early in the season, the place was unusually quiet.

The dirt drive meandered in a lazy, back-and-forth pattern toward the flats beside the river. "I'll put you in a cabin near the canoe storage to give you a better view of the area where we've had most of our trouble," she told Cody.

"You were serious?"

"Very. I really do need someone to watch for vandals." She smiled over at him. "And, yes, I actually do have that problem, in spite of your doubts."

"Okay by me. Sailor and I will be delighted to stand guard. Figuratively speaking, in my case."

"Don't sell yourself short," Trudy Lynn said.

Pulling up in front of a darkened cabin she killed

the engine, set the parking brake and climbed out. Sailor had been patient till they'd stopped. Now, he was straining at the safety tether that held him in place in the truck bed.

"Just a minute, boy. Settle down," she said, pausing to give him a pat and ruffle his ears. "Daddy first. Then you."

She circled in time to meet Cody face-to-face as he braced himself on his crutches and slid off the seat. "I could have helped you do that," she said.

"I may be crippled but I'm not helpless," he replied stiffly.

"Good. Then I suppose you can get your own bags?" Her eyebrows arched.

"Gladly." Cody groped behind the front seat and pulled out both his canvas duffel-type bags, letting them drop to the ground at his feet.

Trudy Lynn reached for one of them. He stopped her with an outstretched hand. "I said, I can handle it."

"I know what you said. But this is my camp and you're my guest. I'm not pampering you. I'd offer to help carry anybody's bags, whether they were able to or not."

"That's nice. Tell you what. Why don't you let Sailor loose before he goes nuts? He gets really agitated if he thinks I'm going to wander off and leave him."

"I can see that." Trudy Lynn ordered the Newfoundland to sit before she unfastened the tether and lowered the tailgate. His exuberance in scrambling out almost bowled her over.

The dog had made two galloping circuits of the pickup and had come to a stop at Cody's feet before Trudy Lynn rejoined him. "Looks like he's happy now."

"It doesn't take much to please Sailor. Food, water and my company. They definitely are a family breed, just not suited to my sister's fancy new carpet and furniture."

"Well, we fixed that."

She was about to reach for his bags again when Cody waved her off. "Wait. Watch this." He pointed to the strap of the largest one. "Sailor. Bring it."

The enormous dog took the handle in his mouth gently, as if it were as fragile as a kitten, and, with his bushy tail waving, proudly bore it along while his master headed for the cabin.

"What about the other one?" Trudy Lynn asked.

"He'll go get that, too."

She hurried ahead to open the door and flip on the lights. Any worries she'd had that Sailor might get excited and knock his master down were dispelled when she noted how cautiously the lumbering dog proceeded. When the first bag was safely delivered, Cody sent him back for the second.

"Wow. I'm impressed," Trudy Lynn said. "How did you teach him that?"

"I can't take credit. He was a natural. From the time he was a pup he carried things around. Loved my socks. I used to leave them on the floor just so he'd have something to pick up and bring to me."

"A furry valet?"

"Something like that. He added more to the mess than he cleaned up, but his heart was in the right place so I encouraged him." Cody's smile widened as Sailor returned with the second bag, mission accomplished, and placed it at his feet. "It would have been a lot nicer if he hadn't drooled, though."

"So what? You were going to wash the socks anyway."

"Right." He surveyed the one-room cabin approvingly. "Looks cozy. Any special instructions?"

"Not that I can think of. If I'd known anyone was going to be staying here I'd have made up the bed ahead of time." She was already moving across the room. "It'll only take me a second."

"Don't bother."

Trudy Lynn sent him a grin over her shoulder as she whipped the plaid bedspread aside, unfurled a clean sheet and bent to her task. "Why? Does your dog make beds, too?"

"Not yet, but I'm working on it."

"Should be an interesting trick. Especially if you can teach him to stop slobbering while he works."

Cody made a face. "Yeah. There is that problem."

"This cabin has its own private bathroom," Trudy

Lynn explained while smoothing out the last wrinkle in the bedding. "Towels are in the cabinet over there. So are more clean sheets if you decide Sailor needs to practice his tucking skills."

"Thanks. I think I'll wait on that till we get home."

"In that case, I'll say good-night and leave you in peace."

She was almost to the door when Cody said, "Thank you."

There was so much true relief in his tone she turned and smiled. "You're quite welcome. Both of you. I'll get Sailor's food and dishes out of the back of the truck before I go. Sleep as late as you want in the morning. When you're up and about, I'll introduce you to my staff. There aren't many of us. Will and I stay overnight. The rest come to work when I need them."

Cody's eyebrow arched. "Will? Your boyfriend? Husband?"

"Will's old enough to be my grandpa," she said with a subdued chuckle. "There've been lots of times when I've wished we were kin. I guess *old friend* describes him best. He takes a real proprietary interest in this place. I don't know what I'd do without him."

"I hope he doesn't mind my staying here."

"Don't worry. First thing in the morning, I'll explain everything to him."

"While you're at it, would you mind explaining it to me, too? I'm still not sure how I wound up here."

"Providence," Trudy Lynn said with a wide, satisfied grin. "I needed more security and God sent you."

That brought a wry chuckle from her guest. "If I'm the best God can do, I think you'd better start questioning His wisdom. I have."

"What an awful thing to say."

"Maybe. But I meant every word."

She sobered, eyes wide, and nodded. "I know you did. That's what makes it a lot worse than it would be if you were joking."

Cody was so exhausted he didn't bother to unpack. He sent Sailor outside, briefly, then lay across the bed, fully clothed except for his shoes. The Newf made himself comfortable on the floor and quickly fell asleep.

Sailor snored, as usual, while Cody stared at the rustic pine ceiling and wondered why his dog had so much more peace than he did.

Because he doesn't think of the future, Cody decided. No worries meant no stress. Too bad he couldn't share the dog's easy ability to drop off to sleep anywhere, anytime.

Relating the details of the fatal accident to Trudy Lynn had brought the tragedy vividly to mind for the second time that night. Not that the young man's death was ever far from his thoughts. That moment would never leave him, never let him rest the way he once had.

Why kept nagging at him, refusing to be rationalized away. Too bad it wasn't a question that could be solved like a riddle that had an actual solution. There was no answer to his conundrum—at least not one that included the benevolent, loving God he'd sought and believed in as a lonely, motherless child.

In that respect, his sister, Becky, had more faith than he'd ever possessed. He wasn't about to pretend he still had a strong belief in the Lord, even if that meant he didn't fit her idea of the perfect brother. As far as Cody was concerned, God had deserted him. Twice. No, make that three times. First when his mother had been killed, second when he'd prayed for the safety of his clients on the raft while fighting for his own life, and third, when Stephanie had walked away from the love she'd once sworn would last forever.

He looked down at his injured knee. It was throbbing in time with his heartbeats. Must be time for another pain pill, which meant he'd also need a glass of water. Well, so what? Why baby himself? He was going to ache all night anyway, just as he always did. At least the cabin was small enough to hop to the sink without crutches.

He swung his feet over the side of the bed and spoke to Sailor so the dog wouldn't be startled, leap up and topple him. "That's it, old boy. Scoot over. I'll be right back." The thick, black tail thumped on the bare floor.

Cody pulled himself upright by grabbing the headboard and stood quietly for a second to make sure he had his balance. The brace on his knee would keep it from giving out on him but there was always the chance of a sharp pain causing him to falter. He switched on the bedside lamp and started across the room. Seconds later, he heard a throaty growl behind him.

Grabbing the edge of the sink for support he stared at Sailor. The usually amiable, laid-back dog was fully alert. Had the vandals returned? Now that he'd switched on the cabin light, they'd know someone was close by. Would that be enough to scare them away? Cody hoped so.

Leaning against the kitchenette counter, he listened. Other than Sailor's rumbling, silence reigned. Whip-poor-wills had stopped calling to their mates, frogs had ceased their rhythmic chirping, and even the noisy cicadas were still.

He tensed. The first thing he needed to do was grab his crutches so he'd be more mobile. Second, he had to keep Sailor from going on the defensive and getting into trouble.

"Sailor, come," Cody whispered, giving a hand signal as well. Hackles up, the dog had risen and was facing the closed door, clearly standing guard.

"Sailor," he hissed, "get over here."

The protective canine reluctantly obeyed, edging closer until Cody was able to grab his collar.

The door creaked on rusty hinges. The first thing that poked through was the long barrel of a shotgun! Cody tightened his grip on Sailor, braced himself and waited.

A weathered old codger stepped into the room and took shaky aim. The man was clad only in boxer shorts and a sleeveless undershirt. At the ends of his spindly legs, his unlaced hiking boots looked as though they were at least as old as he was. Maybe older.

Before Cody could decide whether to yell at him, surrender, or burst out laughing, the old man commanded, "Freeze, mister. And call off your dog."

"I've been trying to," Cody said. "Don't shoot. We're unarmed." He raised his free hand. "You must be Will."

"What if I am?"

"Trudy Lynn, Ms. Brown, told me about you. She was planning to introduce us in the morning."

"Says who?"

"It's the truth. I'm Becky Malloy's brother, Cody Keringhoven."

"I s'pose you can prove it."

"I have my ID right here." Cody produced his wallet and held it out.

Will motioned with a jerk of his head. "Bring it over here. Real slow."

"That's about the only way I *can* move." He

pointed to the crutches propped at the foot of the bed. "I'll do better if you'll hand me those first."

"You don't look crippled."

"Well, I sure feel it," Cody replied. "I just got up to take a pain pill. Mind if I do?"

"Guess not." He lowered the muzzle toward the floor so it wasn't pointing directly at Cody or the dog. "Miz Brown didn't say nothin' about puttin' nobody in this cabin." He scowled. "We hardly ever rent it, 'specially not this time of year."

"So she told me. I'm supposed to be watching out for vandals while I'm here. I guess you know all about that."

"Sure do. That's what I figured you was when I saw the light." Bushy gray eyebrows knit. "I tried sittin' by that there window all night. Couldn't keep my eyes open. That what you're plannin' to do?"

"Not tonight," Cody said, drawing water and downing his medication. "Dad and I just drove all the way from Chicago. I'm beat. Maybe tomorrow."

Thumbing the shotgun open to extract the shells, the old man nodded. "Suits me. Sorry if I scared ya. I'm goin' back to bed. You be all right?"

"Fine. Thanks. See you in the morning?"

"You betcha," Will said. "In case you're wonderin', I'm gonna go talk to Miz Brown before I turn in, see if your story checks."

"I wouldn't have it any other way," Cody said with a grin. "She's lucky to have you."

"Sure is." He eyed the now complacent-looking, panting dog. "Big fella, ain't he? What's his name?"

"Sailor."

Will chuckled. "Well, well. Me, too. Spent many a happy year as a merchant seaman before I finally decided to settle down. I take it he loves the water."

"I think he'd rather swim than eat," Cody said. "Newfoundlands are related to Labrador retrievers, just bigger and a lot more hairy."

"That's the truth. Sure glad he's yours to feed and not mine. What all does he eat?"

Cody immediately thought of Trudy Lynn's messy introduction to Sailor's fondness for beef gravy. Rather than mention it, he laughed then quipped, "Anything that doesn't eat him first."

"You'd best watch him around Miz Brown's little mutt, then. That Widget's got a nasty attitude."

"Uh-oh. She never mentioned having a dog."

"He's more like family to her. 'Specially since that fiancé of hers, Ned What's-his-name, took off." Will grimaced and blushed. "Forget I said anything about that, will you? Don't want her to think I'm carryin' tales."

"We won't mention it again," Cody vowed. "I had wondered why she was so fixated on this business. Guess she put all her energies into it after Ned left, huh?"

"Nope," Will said. "Always was nuts about canoes and camping. This place was perfect for her, right from the start. I think that's one of the things Ned didn't take to. Miss Trudy liked the outdoors a lot more'n he did." He lowered his voice to add, "You ask me, she loved the Ozarks every bit as much as she loved him, maybe more, and he knew it. Didn't surprise me when their wedding didn't pan out."

Cody nodded sagely. "Thanks for telling me. It'll keep me from putting my foot in my mouth." He managed another chuckle in spite of the growing discomfort radiating from his sore knee. "Good thing, too. These days, it's about all I can do to make my feet work together to hold me up. I can't afford to be chewing on one of them."

"And I'm standin' here keepin' you up and makin' it worse. Sorry, mister…what'd you say the name was?"

"Just call me Cody. Keringhoven's too hard to remember."

"Cody, it is. I'll look in on you in the mornin', 'fore I start my chores, case you need anything."

"Thanks. I'd appreciate that."

"Glad to do it. Any friend of Miz Brown's is a friend of mine."

Nodding, Cody bid him a polite good-night and waited till the door had closed before gritting his teeth. The pain tonight was worse than it had ever been, except perhaps for the hours immediately following the physical therapy sessions he had submitted to while hospitalized.

Seeming to sense his master's need for solace, Sailor licked his hand.

"Yeah, it hurts something awful," Cody admitted. "You know that, don't you?"

Sailor wagged his tail so vigorously his entire rear half swayed.

"Just be sure to keep it to yourself, okay? I don't want my sister and her church ladies fussing over me."

That much was true. Still, he'd agreed to come to Serenity for a recuperation period, knowing Becky would undoubtedly try to meddle and insist she was doing it for his own good.

"I must have been taking way too much pain medication when Dad recommended this trip," Cody muttered. "I can't believe I agreed."

In the back of his mind, however, another idea was jumping up and down and screeching like a squad of teenage cheerleaders at a pep rally. Could Trudy Lynn have been on the right track when she'd mentioned the possibility of divine intervention?

Cody immediately rejected that notion. If God had wanted to intercede on his behalf, He was too late. About two months too late.

He snorted derisively. Make that a whole *lifetime* too late. Considering all that had happened, there was no way he could ever go back to the unquestioning faith he'd leaned on as a lonely, confused child.

Of all the losses he'd experienced, that loss of faith left him feeling the emptiest.

Chapter Four

Trudy Lynn made sure she was the first person to knock on Cody's door the following morning. Her arrival was heralded by a chorus of deep woofing and a call of, "Hang on. I'm coming."

Fidgeting, she waited. When Cody opened the door she greeted him with a wide smile and a cheery, "Good morning." His clothes were wrinkled. His day's growth of beard was nearly invisible due to his light coloring but his tousled hair showed he hadn't expected such an early visit.

Nevertheless, he smiled. "I thought you said I could sleep in?"

"I know I did. I'm sorry. I just wanted to apologize for Will. His mistake was my fault. I should have stopped by his cabin last night and told him you were staying here."

"At least he didn't shoot me. Or my dog."

"Thank God—literally." She pointed to Sailor who

was sitting behind Cody and panting so heartily he looked as if he was smiling. "Want me to walk him for you?"

"Not a good idea. He hates leashes. He'd probably wind up walking you. Besides, he's already been out once this morning. You're not the only one who's an early riser. My furry friend got me up at dawn."

"Did you rest okay? Is the bed soft enough?"

Cody nodded. "Actually, it's almost too soft. The less I accidentally move while I'm sleeping, the better."

"How about now? How are you feeling?"

"Fine."

Trudy Lynn could tell he was far from fine but she figured, if he wanted to deny his pain, that was okay with her. Dwelling on it was probably worse for him, anyway.

"Glad to hear it. Have you eaten?"

"No. To tell you the truth, I haven't even brushed my teeth yet." He rubbed his palm over his cheek. "Feels like I need a shave, too."

"And a change of clothes. Did you sleep in those? They look like it."

"Sure did. After your friend Will scared us silly, I didn't have enough energy left to get ready for bed." He glanced at his dog with affection. "Sailor was a great watchdog. Stood right in front of me and kept the dangerous old codger at bay."

"Poor Will," Trudy Lynn said. "He was really disappointed when he discovered you weren't the bad guys, come to ransack a cabin."

"I hope he put on more clothes before he went to your place to tell you about it. When he showed up here he was dressed in boxers and hiking boots. If he hadn't been pointing a gun at me I'd have laughed out loud. He has the skinniest, ugliest legs I've ever seen, except maybe on a scrawny chicken."

"That's because you haven't seen mine." Trudy Lynn was instantly sorry she'd been so glib. Cody was now looking her up and down as if he'd just discovered she was a woman, and she didn't like the awareness his assessing blue eyes revealed.

"You look nice in those jeans," he finally said.

Flustered, she averted her gaze and unnecessarily smoothed the denim. "Thanks. Now, about breakfast. How soon do you think you can be ready?"

"Ready? Ready for what?"

"The best biscuits and gravy in Fulton County."

"Are you asking me to go out to breakfast?"

"No." Her brow wrinkled. "I'm cooking. Actually, it's all made. I took the biscuits out of the oven before I came down here." She brightened. "Oh, I get it. You're thinking of your sister's cooking. Don't worry. Mine has won prizes at the county fair."

"That's a relief. But really, you don't have to coddle me. I'm perfectly capable of taking care of myself."

"I know that." She rolled her eyes. "Look, Cody.

You might as well get used to folks being nice to you for no particular reason. Around here, people are friendly, period. It's not because you have a problem or because we feel sorry for you. Okay?"

"Okay." He shrugged. "I am a little hungry. How far is it to your place? Up the hill, right?"

"Right. But don't try to walk it." Trudy Lynn pointed to a squat, green, four-wheel-drive vehicle parked in the drive. "I'll do a few chores, then bring the ATV back and pick you up. How much time will you need to get ready?"

"Ready to ride that? About six months should do it."

"Cynic. I'll do the driving. All you'll have to do is shut up and hang on."

His wry expression when he said, "That's what I was afraid of," was so funny she couldn't help laughing.

Cody managed to shower and shave in short order. He didn't think it would hurt to humor Trudy Lynn just this once. Besides, he wanted a chance to ask her more about the vandalism before he got Will's opinion. He knew there wasn't a whole lot he could do to apprehend whoever had been damaging the canoes but there was no reason he couldn't at least try to get a description of them for the police. To his surprise, he was looking forward to having something constructive to occupy his mind for a change.

He was positive that he'd be able to mount the ATV successfully. How he'd stay on it once they were moving promised to be a bit trickier.

Trudy Lynn arrived in a cloud of dust and slid to a stop right in front of him. "Hop on."

"What about my crutches?"

"We'll clip them across the rack with a bungee cord. Come on. Gravy's getting cold."

Cody got on easily by keeping his injured leg straight and swinging it around and over, brace and all. Once he was in position behind Trudy Lynn, however, he was faced with the decision of whether or not he should slip his arms around her waist. His balance was off due to the knee brace and he didn't want to wind up flat on his back in the dirt, yet he hardly knew the young woman.

"You'd better hang on to me," she said, solving his dilemma. "This road's kind of bumpy."

"You don't mind?"

"Not at all," Trudy Lynn said. "I trust you."

"Thanks."

Cody did as she'd instructed, keeping his touch as light and gentlemanly as he could. Only in an emergency would he tighten his hold, he promised himself. Grabbing her like that would be a last resort.

It was a narrow waist, he noted. Yet Trudy Lynn wasn't delicate or prissy the way Stephanie had been. She was a healthy, active woman who treated men as equals, neither elevating them to sainthood nor denigrating them for being male. Though her casual acceptance was going to take some getting used to, he found he liked it, liked keeping company with a woman who had no hidden agenda. Trudy Lynn wasn't the type who picked out an engagement ring and started making wedding plans by the second date.

Whoa! Where had that thought come from? He didn't intend to start dating anyone for a while, especially not his sister's best friend. He'd been cured of any tendencies toward romance when Steph had dumped him. Besides, according to Will, Trudy Lynn was sort of in the same boat. Maybe that was why being with her seemed so pleasant. It was a welcome change to relax and not have to worry about whether or not he should consider a lasting relationship—or try to keep one from developing.

She broke into his thoughts with a question. "How're you doing? Am I going too fast?"

"I'm fine." Out of the corner of his eye he saw a dark blur. "Uh-oh. I must not have shut the cabin door tight. We have company. Sailor came along."

"That's okay," Trudy Lynn said, raising her voice to be heard over the roar of the ATV's motor. "He's a sweetheart. I'm sure he won't be any trouble. He might pick up a few bugs if he wanders into the woods but you can always wet him down with flea and tick repellant if you have to."

"Does the stuff come in fifty-five gallon drums?"

Her light laughter drifted back to him on the wind, lifting his spirits further.

"It must. They dip sheep, don't they?"

"Guess so. Since I won't be able to wrestle him into accepting the treatment, I'll have to leave it to you."

"In that case, we'll get him a flea collar instead. We can always fasten two together, end to end, if we can't find one big enough to go all the way around his neck."

"Clever. Are you always this smart?"

"Sure am."

She stopped the ATV beside a single-story off-shoot tied to a larger log building. "That's our store, camp office and laundry. I got tired of having to run over here to take care of late arrivals, so I built myself a connected apartment. Might as well live here. I'm on call night and day, anyway."

"It's very impressive," Cody said. "The whole campground is. No wonder you're proud of this place." The small yard bordering the private portion of the building was bursting with color. "I see you like to garden."

"Not if I have to fuss much. Those are all wild-flowers that I've either transplanted from other parts of the property or started from seed. It seems like every day I notice something new starting to bloom." She shut off the engine. "Do you want to get off first or shall I?"

"Better hand me my crutches before I try anything fancy," Cody answered.

"Right." She giggled when Sailor galloped up and slurped the back of her hand. "I guess he remembers me."

Before Cody could answer, a yipping ball of brown-and-white fur raced around the corner. Teeth bared, it charged straight for the clueless Newfoundland.

Trudy Lynn screeched, "Widget! No!" and lunged, half on and half off the ATV, to intercept her little terrier. She'd have been successful, too, if Sailor hadn't practically bowled her over making his lumbering getaway.

Cody was hopping on his good leg so he could extend one of his crutches as a barrier between the dogs. When he saw Trudy Lynn losing her balance he redirected his efforts. Unfortunately, he bumped her with the tip of the crutch and removed any chance she might have had of righting herself.

She twisted in midair and landed on the back pockets of her jeans with an undignified, "Oof!"

Widget leaped into her lap, barking and growling while she clasped him tightly to her chest and told him, "Hush!"

Crutches set wide like outriggers, Cody half turned to check on Sailor. "You okay, boy?"

The big dog had laid its ears back, ducked behind him and was just sitting there, head down, quivering like a bowl of Jell-O in a California earthquake and staring up at his master with soulful brown eyes.

Cody glanced back at Trudy Lynn. She looked at him and grinned. Widget kept yipping. Sailor kept trembling. In moments, both humans had recognized the humor of their situation and burst into riotous laughter.

Trudy Lynn laughed so hard tears rolled down her cheeks. She'd almost regained her composure till Cody held out his hand and asked, "Want some help?"

That set her off again. When she quieted down enough to catch her breath, she answered, "No, thanks. I can manage. The first time you helped me was plenty."

"I didn't mean to bump you. I was trying to keep the dogs from fighting."

"I know. Poor Sailor. I don't think we need to worry about him attacking Widget, do you?"

"Probably not. I hope you can keep that ankle-biter from harassing my innocent dog. I came up here so he could enjoy a little freedom, not be traumatized by a psychotic terrier."

"Widget's a great watchdog," Trudy Lynn said, getting to her feet with the wiggly little dog tucked under one arm. She dusted off her jeans with her free hand. "Will told me I should tie him by the canoes at night and let him sound the alarm if we had prowlers."

"Did you?"

"No. Widget barks at everything, even fireflies. He'd keep me up all night, investigating nothing."

Cody followed her toward the apartment. There were already customers going in and out of the store. "Looks like business is good."

"It's picking up. This time of year is always kind of slow." She ushered him inside.

The place was small but cozy, with a definitely feminine decor, including lace curtains and floral-printed chair cushions. Through an open interior doorway he could glimpse activity going on in the store, proper.

"This is my kitchen. Guess you can tell."

"The stove and refrigerator were a dead giveaway," Cody teased. "Something smells great."

"Fresh biscuits. I told you I was a good cook." She pointed to another door. "My living quarters are through there. I wanted the kitchen out here so my staff could use it as a break room, too, if they wanted."

"You don't have problems keeping others out?"

"Not at all. The access is behind the counter so everybody can tell it's private space. I've never had campers wander in."

"Amazing. Aren't you worried about staying here alone at night? I mean, what kind of security does an arrangement like this give you?"

"All I've ever needed."

"Till now." Cody rounded the table and seated himself where he could keep an eye on the open door. "While we eat, I want you to tell me everything strange that's happened so far. Don't leave anything out, even if you think it's trivial."

"That might take a long time."

"Humph. Suits me. I seem to have a lot more leisure time than I need. If you've got the time to brief me, I have plenty of time to listen."

Trudy Lynn was carrying their dirty plates to the sink when she finished airing her concerns. "The only person I can think of who might have a grudge against me is a teenager I had to let go about a month ago. Name's Ronnie Randall. He was pretty upset. His father phoned me the next day and accused me of blaming the wrong person."

"What did the kid do?" Cody took a sip of his coffee.

"Petty theft. He helped himself to a case of sodas. I couldn't let it slide. It wouldn't have been fair to Ronnie, or to the others who work here."

"I totally agree. What makes you think he may be the one behind the damage to your property?"

"Mostly a gut feeling. Jim has seen him hanging around here more than once. Ronnie said he was just waiting for his girlfriend but I'm skeptical."

"Tell me more about Jim."

"There's not much to tell. He's a second cousin on

my mama's side. A real math whiz. I hate book work. I'm lucky to have him."

"He uses a computer program, you say?"

"Yes. I used to write everything in a ledger. Boy, do I love letting Jim fiddle with the figures, instead. And is he fast! You should see him work."

"I probably will," Cody said, pushing away from the table and rising. "I'll want to borrow your internet connection to do a little work of my own while I'm here. Remember?"

"Of course. I'll tell Jim to let you know when he's not going to be using the computer."

"That'll be fine. I'd also like a list of names and addresses for all your employees, even the seasonal ones, for the past two years. I don't want to overlook any angle." He noticed her quizzical expression. "What?"

"You're taking this a lot more seriously than I thought you would. What if there's no big, scary conspiracy? What if it's just a couple of kids who think it's fun to break things?"

"Then we'll catch them in the act, and they'll find out differently," he said.

"I don't want you to go to a lot of trouble. I mean, our deal was for you to watch from the cabin in exchange for rent. That's all I expect."

Thoughtful for long moments, Cody finally said, "Look. When I opened my eyes this morning it hit me. This is the first time since my accident that I've looked forward to getting out of bed and doing something. Anything. Being useful is a feeling I've missed and I don't want to lose it. Can you understand that?"

"Yes. Completely. I feel the same way about running this campground. Even bad days are better than my life was before I opened. And the good days are wonderful. The Lord's blessed me beyond my wildest dreams. That's one reason why I'll never sell or quit, no matter what."

"Quit? I thought you said business was good."

"It is. And believe me, I'm not complaining. I just don't understand why all the other canoe rentals on this part of the river have closed in the past year or so."

Cody scowled. "*All* of them?"

"The closest ones," she said. "There were three others when I opened. I'm a little farther upriver but that shouldn't make any difference. If a client wants a longer ride, we just drive them to a distant point, launch from there and pick them up when they drift back down."

"Makes sense. We used to do the same thing on the Tuolumne. For Class I, II or III rapids we used a different stretch of the river."

"You ran Class IV and V, didn't you?"

"Usually." Cody glanced at his knee and gritted his teeth. "I really miss it."

"I'm sure you do."

He stared at her, waiting. "Well?"

"Well, what?"

"Aren't you going to tell me how lucky I am to be alive? Everybody else does."

"Hey, not me." Trudy Lynn held up both hands, palms out. "You warned me not to preach so I'm not preaching." She gave him a sweet, knowing smile. "But don't expect me, or Becky, or any of our friends to stop talking about God's influence in our lives. This part of the country isn't called the Bible Belt for nothing."

"Yeah. I didn't think of that when I decided to visit my sister." He turned and started away. "Thanks for breakfast. I'm going to go outside and check on Sailor. Hang on to your ankle-biter when I open the door, will you?"

"Sure. No problem. Come here, Widget. That's a good boy." She lifted her little dog in her arms. "Got him."

Though she'd sounded glib and unconcerned, Cody knew she was watching him laboriously making his way across the room and he wished mightily that he had his formerly steady gait. He'd always taken strength and agility for granted. Now that he was having to grit his teeth and work for every step, he realized just how much he'd lost.

It made him angry. Especially toward God. If there really was a God.

Chapter Five

❧

Cody spent the better part of the day sitting on the porch of his cabin with his heel propped on the railing and Sailor dozing beside him. He'd read the information Trudy Lynn had provided. Everything seemed pretty straightforward. Her operation was small but well run and her seasonal staff members were teenagers drawn from the local community. Good kids. He'd made it a point to talk to as many of them as he could when they'd passed his cabin. One more was on duty in the camp store. He'd observed her working while he ate breakfast and couldn't imagine any threat originating with such a polite young lady. That only left getting to know Will and cousin Jim.

Cody smiled. The old man had failed to look in on him that morning as promised. Maybe Trudy Lynn had told him to stay away, or maybe he was embarrassed over their initial confrontation. Either way, talking to Will was going to be imperative. And the sooner the better.

He hailed a passing young man. "Hey there! You're Sam, aren't you? Have you seen Will lately?"

"Yes, sir. He's up by the office. You need him?"

"I'd like to talk to him," Cody said, "but not if he's busy."

"He always says he's busy, even if he's taking a nap." Sam sported a grin that accentuated the sunburn and freckles on his cheeks. "I'll tell him to come on down."

"Thanks. Make sure he knows there's no hurry."

"Yes, sir."

The warm sun and the ambience of the camp had been bathing Cody in Southern contentment all day. Compared to the cold wind off Lake Michigan at his dad's place or the icy waters of the Tuolumne, this was sure a pleasant place to lounge around. He sighed and closed his eyes. His knee wasn't throbbing ceaselessly, the way it had been. That, alone, was enough to make him glad he'd come.

"Afternoon," Will said, startling him back to alertness. "You wanna see me?"

The weathered old man was clutching his dingy baseball cap in his hands and looking as if he expected to be chastised. Cody smiled and gestured to the porch. "Yes, I do. Join me?"

"I guess I can spare a few minutes. What did you want to talk about?"

Cody waited until Will was seated in the other pressed-metal chair. "Trudy Lynn's prowler," Cody said. "Have you ever gotten a good look at him?"

"Nope. Comes sneakin' around at night. I've seen shadows. That's about all."

"Where was he when you spotted him?"

"Down closer to the river." Will peered past Cody. "Don't think you can see that place from here."

"That's what I was afraid of. Okay. Tell me where you'd go if you were planning on sitting up all night."

"I ain't plannin' to."

"I am." He lowered his stiff leg and rubbed his thigh through the khaki fabric of his slacks.

"That's clear dumb if you ask me. Wanna borrow my twelve-gauge?"

Cody shook his head. "No. I don't intend to try to capture anybody. I just want to get a good look at them so I can give the sheriff a description."

The old man cackled. "Okay. It's your funeral."

"I certainly hope not," Cody gibed. "What makes you say that?"

"I'm not laughin' at you," Will said. "I'm laughin' because around here, our county sheriff is elected. Anybody can run. Most times, the fella what wins ain't much of a lawman. We figure we're lucky if he knows which end of a gun shoots and where to put the bullets."

"How about the man who's in office, now?"

"He's kin to just about everybody so I can't say."

Will continued to laugh softly. "We only got two police cars for this whole county. Last I heard, one of 'em was broke down. That tell ya what ya need to know?"

"Pretty much," Cody answered, nodding thoughtfully. "Okay. Here's what we'll do. As soon as it starts to get dark, you come get me and help me find a place where I can hide and watch. Think you can do that?"

"Sure. But why ask me? Why not get Miss Trudy Lynn to help you? Be lots more fun."

Cody ignored the other man's knowing expression and conspiratorial wink. "Because I don't want her to know what I'm doing. You're not to tell her. Understand?"

"She'll throw a hissy fit when she finds out."

"Unless I spot a prowler, there's no need for her to know anything about it. Ever."

"There ain't much about the Spring River Miz Brown don't know. But I figure I owe you a favor after bustin' in on you last night, so I'll keep mum."

"Thanks. See you at dusk."

"Yeah. See ya." Will started away, then paused and turned back to Cody. "That fella Ned I told you about? The one Miz Brown was figuring on marryin' someday? He used to keep a lot of secrets. She didn't like it."

"This is for her own good," Cody replied.

"Don't matter. She still ain't gonna like it. Not one little bit."

* * *

Cody had let the old man help him to the river's edge and settle him comfortably behind a fallen tree. Moonlight reflecting off his metal crutches had made them too noticeable in the dark so he'd sent them back to the cabin with his cohort. There would be no need to walk until Will returned for him in the morning, anyway.

Smoke from a distant campfire layered across the lowlands, bringing back childhood memories of his father showing him how to cook hot dogs and roast marshmallows over an open fire. He smiled. Dad's love of the outdoors had certainly rubbed off on him, hadn't it?

Suddenly, a twig snapped. Cody slowly turned his head in the direction of the noise. Instead of the vandal he'd expected, he saw Trudy Lynn. Judging by her direct course she knew exactly where he was hidden.

Her "Hi, there," sounded far too cheerful for the circumstances.

"Get down before you blow my cover," Cody ordered. "What are you doing here?"

"Bringing you hot chocolate. I made a whole thermosful. I brought an extra cup, too. Mind if I join you?"

"Yes, I mind. How did you find out where I was?"

"Don't blame Will. I caught him putting your crutches back in the cabin. Even if he hadn't told me what was going on, I'd have found you sooner or later. Will said I was better off sitting with you than poking through the bushes alone in the dark. Don't you agree?"

"The only thing I agree about is how dangerous it is for you to be out here. Go home. Now."

"You don't have to yell."

"I'm not yelling. I'm stating a firm opinion. There's a difference."

"Not in my book there isn't." She plopped down on the ground beside him and ducked her head below the level of the fallen oak. "This is my campground. I pretty much go where I want and do as I please."

"Fine. Then catch your own vandal. I'm leaving."

"Oh, yeah? How? If I remember right, your crutches are back in your cabin."

"I'll crawl."

"Not on that sore knee, you won't," Trudy Lynn said.

Cody thought he saw a flash of sorrow in her eyes. When she immediately mellowed, he was certain of it.

"Look. I'll go back soon if that's what you want. Just have some hot chocolate with me first. Please?"

"If I do, you'll go home?"

"Yes."

"And stay there?"

"Cross my heart."

Sighing in resignation, Cody said, "Okay. Pour.

But no funny business. One cup and you're on your way."

"Absolutely." She pulled a large thermos out of her pack and twisted off the lid. "I'll leave the rest of this with you so you can warm up through the night. It gets pretty cold out here sometimes, depending on the season, of course. I see Will talked you into wearing a jacket. That's good. I was afraid you'd be cold."

Cody scowled. "Don't you ever stop talking?"

"Not often."

"Then I know why you never spotted your prowler. He could hear you long before he got close enough to see you."

"Very funny." Trudy Lynn made a silly face.

"And very true." Cody waited till she'd poured herself a drink, then raised his cup to his lips. The liquid was scalding. "Ouch!"

"You don't have to chug it down and burn yourself just to get rid of me faster."

"I wasn't."

"Right."

"You calling me a liar?"

"Of course not. I just think you have a skewed view of life, of what's really important, that's all."

"For instance?" He took a more cautious sip.

Trudy Lynn blew on her hot chocolate and waited a few moments to answer. "Well, you might want to start by appreciating the good things. Didn't it occur to you that you were spared for a reason when you were pitched into that river?"

"I was lucky, that's all."

"Okay. Let's say you were lucky. Does that mean the man who drowned was unlucky?"

"I suppose so." He saw her start to smile. "What's so amusing now?"

"You are. Don't you see? If it's all a matter of luck, you just exonerated yourself. And if it isn't, if God is in charge of life and death, the way I happen to believe, you still can't take the blame."

Cody huffed. "Fine. Does that mean I should blame God for my limp?"

"If you want to. He can take criticism." She paused for another sip. "Later on, when enough time has passed that you can look at the whole situation objectively, maybe you'll see that what happened was for the best."

"I doubt it."

Trudy Lynn's smile was sweet and sympathetic when she said, "That's okay, too."

They sat in companionable silence till each had finished a second serving of cocoa. Stretching, Trudy Lynn zipped her empty cup back inside her pack.

"Well, guess I'd better keep my promise. You sure you'll be all right if I leave you here?"

"I have a bad knee, I'm not unconscious. Of course I'll be all right. Why wouldn't I be?"

She had to admit he had a valid point. "You win.

I'm going. But don't blame me if you're freezing by morning and wishing you were back in your nice, cozy cabin."

"I promise to hold you blameless."

Clearly, he was teasing—and enjoying every word. Well, so what? If their back-and-forth banter amused him, she'd pretend he was winning their contest of wits. She knew she could give as good as she got. Truth to tell, she was enjoying Cody's wry sense of humor and the way his eyes twinkled when he was expecting a weird reaction to something he'd said or done.

If Cody wanted weird, she thought, he'd certainly come to the right person. More than one man had told her she was crazy, including her former fiancé. Thinking back on it, she was surprised to find the memory of Ned's censure no longer made her sad. Her spirit soared. What a wonderful, unexpected gift!

"You look awfully happy. What're you up to?" Cody asked.

"Just counting my blessings, like I told you to," she said. "I—"

A crash behind them made Trudy Lynn jump. Her eyes widened. "What was that?"

"I don't know. Hush." Cody pushed her head down. "Stay out of sight."

"Where did the sound come from?" she asked in a stage whisper.

"Down by the dock, I think."

Holding her breath and listening, she winced when a second blow echoed. The crunching, brittle sound was all too familiar. "That's one of my canoes!"

Cody hoisted himself up to peer over the top of the log. "Are you sure? I can't see anything."

"Positive. Fiberglass hulls always sound like that when they smash against a rock. Somebody's breaking up a canoe."

"Okay. Take a quick look. Can you make out who's there? Maybe give the cops an idea of what to look for?"

On her knees, Trudy Lynn eased higher so she could peer over the horizontal trunk. Rough bark flaked off on her palms. It was no use. Even with the help of moonlight it was too dark to see details that far away. "No."

She felt Cody's hand on her arm as he said, "Then get back down here before they spot you."

"If I can't see them, they can't see me," she argued. "We have to get closer."

"Absolutely not. We're staying right here."

"In a pig's eye." Without giving Cody a chance to talk her out of it, she vaulted over the fallen tree and started creeping, bent low, toward the sound of chaos.

"Wait!"

Trudy Lynn knew he was being sensible, but someone was tearing her life apart with every blow. She couldn't merely stand by and let them. No, sir.

Not when she had a chance to intervene before too much more damage was done.

Near the rack of inverted canoes stood a bin filled with extra paddles. Trudy Lynn grabbed one in passing, hefted it like a batter stepping up to the plate, straightened and charged.

Cody heard her yell. His pulse had already been racing. When Trudy Lynn screeched as if she was either demented or under attack or both, he thought his heart would pound out of his chest. He'd never felt so helpless in his entire life.

Using his arm and chest muscles, he levered himself into a standing position. Deadwood littered the ground. Choosing a stout limb to use as a walking stick, he leaned on it and began to hobble toward the echoes of demolition and mayhem.

The energy Cody had to put into his efforts was tremendous. Sweat beaded on his forehead and trickled into his eyes, making them sting. Although the brace kept his knee from buckling, he still had to keep as much weight off it as possible, meaning his balance was poor.

He staggered. Tripped. Recovered. Pressed on. There she was! He could see her, silhouetted by moonlight. It looked as though she was alone. "Trudy!"

"Over here," she called back.

By the time Cody hobbled up to her she was sitting on the bare ground trying to catch her breath. "You okay?" he asked.

"Yeah. That was scary."

"Tell me about it."

She glanced up. "Hey! You walked."

"Correction. I hobbled." He gritted his teeth. "What the… What did you think you were doing?"

"Chasing off the bad guys." She rolled onto her knees and got up cautiously, wearily. "I could ask you the same thing. How come you followed me? Isn't that hard on you?"

"Not nearly as hard as sitting back there and listening to you scream," Cody said. He saw her start to sway and put out a steadying hand.

"I'm okay. Really," Trudy Lynn insisted. "The guy took off running the minute he saw me."

"What was he using on the canoes?"

"I don't know. I haven't had time to look." Taking a few steps closer to the dock she hesitated, then bent and picked up a metal object. "Probably this. I don't think it's one of Will's."

Cody stared, first at her, then at the crowbar in her hand. He blanched. "What if he'd turned it on you?"

"I never thought of that." Leaning slightly toward Cody, she dropped the crowbar. "Pretty dumb, huh?"

"Yeah." There was a catch in his voice that betrayed his emotional involvement. He didn't try to hide it. All he wanted to do at that moment was take this foolish, brave, outspoken woman in his arms and hold her tight, as much for his own consoling as for hers. Only his sense of propriety held him back.

When she put her hand to her forehead and began to act woozy, however, he set aside his reservations, gave in to the urge and reached for her.

Trudy Lynn stepped into his waiting embrace as if she expected it. Needed it. She slipped her arms around his waist, laid her cheek on his chest and shivered. "I won't be stupid like that again, I promise."

His hold tightened briefly. "Good. I don't think my heart can take much more excitement."

"Mine, either."

He heard a stifled sob and began to soothe her the way he would a frightened child. "It's okay. Nothing bad happened. I've got you. You're safe."

She leaned back slightly to look at him through teary eyes and said simply, "I know."

Chapter Six

The taller man clenched his fists and glared at his companion. "I don't believe it!"

"She surprised me, that's all."

"And you turned tail like a cur."

"What was I supposed to do? She came out of nowhere, yellin' and swingin' that paddle. She could have killed me."

"You had the crowbar, you idiot. Why didn't you stand your ground?"

"I told you. I wasn't expectin' anybody to get down there till I was long gone. She must have been waitin' for me. How do you suppose she knew I was comin'?"

"I've been wondering the same thing. Who did you tell?"

"Nobody. I never said a word about what we were up to."

"Not *we*. You," the first man said flatly. "I'm in the

clear and I plan to keep it that way. Don't make me change my mind or get somebody else to take your place."

"I told you I'd handle Trudy Lynn, and I will."

"Like you did this time?" He spat into the dirt at their feet. "I should have known better than to include you in my plans. You're the one weak link."

"No, I'm not. I just had a little trouble, that's all. Next time, I'll finish the job, even if a whole posse comes chargin' after me."

His eyes narrowed menacingly. "Suppose you're arrested? What then?"

"They can't prove I was doing anything wrong."

"What if she chases you again? What will you do?"

"Do?"

"Yes, do. If she comes after you, I expect you to defend yourself. Understand? I want you to hit her. Hard. Got that?"

"But…what if I hurt her bad or…kill her?"

The taller man snorted cynically before he answered, "Then I'll go to her funeral and shed a few tears before I buy the place at auction and close it down." He smiled. "The more I think about it, the better that plan sounds."

"No way!"

"I was afraid you'd chicken out," he said with a thoughtful nod. "Okay. I'll give you one more week."

"Then what?"

Turning away he said, "You don't want to know."

The beam from a flashlight was bouncing down the hill, signaling the arrival of help from the main camp. Trudy Lynn stepped away from Cody, feeling like a teenager caught kissing her boyfriend good-night on her parents' front porch.

"I hope that's Will," Cody said. "I'm not looking forward to heading back to my cabin without my crutches."

"You did okay just now."

"Only because I was afraid for you," he said. "I imagine I'll pay for it later."

"I'm so sorry. I only brought you the hot chocolate to be neighborly."

"I know." He pointed to the place where she'd dropped the vandal's weapon. "Better not touch that again. We'll let the sheriff handle it. There may be fingerprints."

"Uh-oh. I never thought of that when I picked it up."

"That's because you're an upstanding citizen, not a crook." He cleared his throat noisily. "Speaking of your sterling reputation, I'm sorry about what just happened."

"What?"

"You know."

She certainly did. And a wonderful hug it was, too.

Good thing it was dark enough that Cody couldn't see her face very well because there was an unusual warmth to her cheeks.

"Oh, that," she said, trying to sound nonchalant. "Don't worry. Around here, everybody hugs everybody. It's practically a given, especially among friends. No one thinks a thing about it."

"Really?"

"Really. You were just making sure I was okay, not making a pass at me, right?"

"Right."

"Well then, no problem."

Although Trudy Lynn was being totally honest with him, a hidden part of her heart wanted the circumstances to be otherwise. She'd thought she'd permanently cast aside all romantic notions long ago, yet Cody's nearness kept urging her to reconsider. Given his physical and emotional scarring, not to mention his hardheadedness, that was not a good idea. Not good at all. Then again, as long as she kept her wandering thoughts to herself and merely befriended him, what harm could it do? Even cynics like Cody needed faithful friends and compassionate comrades.

Speaking of which…a furry black blur the size of a pony galloped up and started to circle their legs with panting, drooling enthusiasm.

Will joined them a few seconds later. "Sorry 'bout the dog, Miz Brown. He must'a heard the ruckus and busted out of the cabin. I know I shut him in."

Cody sighed. "I don't doubt it. Sailor's strong enough to break the links in chains made to tether normal dogs. There isn't much that stops him when he makes up his mind to go somewhere."

Trudy Lynn patted the dog's broad head. "That's okay, Will. Mr. Keringhoven needs his crutches. Would you mind fetching them?"

"Glad to. You folks all right? I heard an awful commotion a few minutes ago."

"We're fine. Did you call the sheriff?"

"Yes, ma'am. Was that okay?"

"Perfect." She smiled at him. "We think we finally have a clue."

"Well, well. About time."

"That's for sure." Trudy Lynn noticed that Sailor had wandered away. She frowned at his master. "Where's your dog? He wouldn't have tried to track the vandal, would he?"

"I doubt it. He's no bloodhound." Cody cupped his hands around his mouth and broadcast a firm, "Sailor! Come."

Silence followed his call.

"Where could he be?"

"Best guess?" Cody sounded disgusted. "Swimming. It takes his coat forever to dry, too. That's why I keep him inside at night. The last thing I want sleeping in the cabin with me is a soggy dog."

"Can't argue with that. For your sake, I hope he's just sniffing a tree or something."

"Me, too. Sailor! Sailor, get over here." The words were barely out when Cody followed them with, "Here he comes."

Trudy Lynn looked around in time to see the Newf bound over an upside-down canoe and head straight for them. She didn't realize what he was going to do next until he stopped between her and Cody and started to shake himself. Repeatedly.

She gave a little screech and turned away in time to keep the flying drops off her face. The rest of her, however, was well showered. So was Cody.

"I told you," he said. "I should have known any dog with webbed feet would behave like a duck."

"No wonder he loves swimming."

"The mud he tracks in is the worst." Cody's eyes widened. "Oh, no."

"What's wrong?"

"The crowbar," he said, pointing. "Sailor's been stepping all over it. If there were any good finger-prints, after you handled it, they're smeared, now."

The sheriff arrived shortly, visited the scene of the crime with Will and took brief statements from Trudy Lynn and Cody before leaving. They remained seated on the porch of Cody's cabin, talking and unwinding, until long after the rest of the camp had quieted down.

"Later in the summer we'll need bug repellant to

sit outside like this," she warned. "Mosquitoes can be deadly around here."

"They're deadly everywhere these days," he said. "Might as well be cautious."

"Right."

Cody was studying her profile in the reflected light from the cabin window. "What's wrong? You're awfully quiet."

"Maybe I ran out of things to say."

"That's never stopped you before."

She took a playful swing at him. "I'm not that bad."

"Could have fooled me." His smile faded. Now that they'd discussed recent events and he'd gone over her list of employees, there was a suggestion he wanted to make. He just wasn't sure how to broach the subject without putting her on the defensive.

"Listen, I know you like to handle things yourself, and I commend you for it," he said, "but after what happened tonight, don't you think it's time to call in some professional help?"

"Like what?"

"Well, how about we start by asking Logan to do some background checks for us?"

"We? Us?" Her eyebrows arched.

"I just thought, since he's my brother-in-law, it would be best if I did the asking. You're welcome to approach him yourself if you'd prefer."

Trudy Lynn shook her head. "Becky already suggested it. The main reason I haven't is because I don't want to interfere with his pastoral duties. I can't believe how busy that poor man is, day and night."

"He won't be too busy to make a few inquiries for us, will he? After all, you do go to his church."

"I suppose it won't be so bad if we make sure he understands we don't expect him to drop everything and go back to being a private investigator."

"Then it's settled. We'll give him a call tomorrow and put him on the trail." Cody saw her make a comical face that was half frown, half smile. "What?"

She pointed to a sliver of sky visible through the oaks. "I think we'd better call Logan today. That sure looks like the glow before sunrise." She yawned. "No wonder I'm so tired."

"We've both been running on adrenaline. Now that its effect is wearing off, we're bound to feel exhausted."

"How's your knee?" Trudy Lynn asked.

"Not as bad as I'd thought it would be by now," he confessed, eyeing his propped-up foot. "Ask me again in the morning."

"I just did. It *is* morning, remember?" Stifling another yawn, she stood and stretched. "Get some rest. As soon as I finish my chores I'll call Becky and see if she knows what Brother Logan has scheduled for today. If he's not too busy, I'll ask for his opinion. Okay?"

"Sounds good to me."

Cody purposely waited until she'd left before he tried to move. The calf muscles in his injured leg were tied in knots, but at least his knee wasn't throbbing. He used his hands to support and cautiously lower it. So far, so good. At least he hadn't had to stifle a shout of pain.

He pulled himself upright by tugging on the porch railing, then tucked a crutch under each arm before starting for the door.

Tail wagging, Sailor was already waiting there, ready to go in.

When Cody turned the knob, it came off in his hand! Disgusted, he looked at his dog. "So, that's how you got out. What'd you do, eat the inside handle?"

The Newfoundland wagged his tail and panted, his sad, brown eyes giving him a totally innocent expression.

Cody pushed open the door. Expecting the worst, he was relieved to note that the only thing Sailor had done to escape was chew at the knob and make a series of scratches below the lock.

Correction, Cody thought. *Not below the lock. Below where the lock would have been if the interior knob was still attached.*

He picked up the pieces and reassembled them as best he could, mostly to make sure Sailor hadn't ingested anything dangerous. When he was satisfied his dog had merely chewed the lock set apart and spit out the mechanism, he hobbled wearily to the bed, lay across it and closed his eyes.

In the morning, he'd use his cell phone to call the local hardware store and have them send out a replacement. That thought brought a quiet chuckle. Make that later *this* morning. Much later. Right now, he didn't care if the sun was rising or not. He had to get some sleep.

Although Trudy Lynn had made the initial request for Logan's professional advice, Cody had followed it up with a friendly call of his own, and the pastor had used that ready-made opportunity to pass along the results of his brief investigation.

Cody suggested Trudy Lynn drop by his cabin to discuss Logan's findings. She found him sitting on the porch in his favorite position, foot elevated, and paused at the base of the wooden steps. "Okay. I'm here. What was so bad that Logan couldn't tell *me* about it?"

"Like you said, he's a busy guy. We happened to be talking and he asked me to pass along some data, that's all. There's no conspiracy to leave you out of the loop, honest."

"I'll reserve judgment on that. Go ahead. What did Logan say?"

"Sure you don't want to sit down?"

"No thanks. I can't stay."

"Have it your way." Cody unfolded a slip of paper

and began reading. "William Garfield Wilson, age sixty-seven, paroled after serving three years of an eight-year sentence in…"

"Whoa! You're telling me Will, *my* Will, has a prison record? Are you sure?"

Cody nodded. "The information came straight from the state police website. Logan was surprised, too."

She sank onto the porch step, shoulders slumping, and laced her fingers together around her bent knees. "What was Will arrested for?"

"Maiming a man in a brawl. It happened when he was in the Merchant Marines."

"That was ages ago."

"I know. There's more."

"I can hardly wait."

"Hey, I'm just the messenger. Don't grumble at me. I didn't make this stuff up."

"I know. Sorry. Go on."

"The other info you may already have heard through the local grapevine. Ronnie Randall? The kid you fired? His whole family has a reputation for being pretty unforgiving when they think they've been wronged. The boy's father and uncles have been arrested for getting belligerent numerous times. One of the kids working on the canoes told me they've been spreading the rumor you let poor Ronnie go because you're prejudiced against folks who have more influence than you do."

"Humph. That would be just about everybody in Fulton County, if it were true," Trudy Lynn said. "What I'm prejudiced against is thieves. I don't suppose anybody mentioned the little problem of missing sodas and candy from the camp store, did they?"

She was surprised to see Cody nod and refer to his notes again. "Matter of fact, they did. Ronnie swears he's innocent. Naturally, his family believes him."

"Naturally." She sighed. "Is that all?"

"Not quite."

The tone of Cody's voice caused her to glance up at him. "Uh-oh. What else?"

"Did you know that your cousin Jim is on probation? He was convicted of drug possession."

"Of course I knew. That was all a mistake. He was just holding a backpack for a friend. He had no idea there was anything illegal in it."

"That's the oldest excuse in the book, but okay. If you say so."

"I have to give him the benefit of the doubt. Jim can be kind of reckless when he's hanging around with the wrong crowd but he's not a criminal. If anything, he's a genius. I've never known anybody so gifted with a computer."

"Which reminds me," Cody said. "When did he say he could spare me an hour or so of time on the internet?"

"I didn't get around to asking. Tomorrow's his day off. Anytime then should be fine. Let me know when you want to come over to the office and I'll send Will to get you on the ATV. Is that okay?"

"Sure. No problem. It'll give me a chance to ask him about his prison time."

"Don't you dare!"

"Why not? Aren't you interested in hearing his side of the story?"

"Not if it means making him think I don't trust him. People's feelings are more important to me than dredging up details of a past that can't possibly have any connection to my vandal."

"How do you know it can't?"

"I just do," Trudy Lynn insisted. "In all the years Will has worked for me, this is the first time I've had any problems. If he were involved, the trouble would have started long ago, and you know it."

"Probably. Unless whoever's been smashing your canoes was incarcerated till recently."

"A cell mate, you mean?"

"Maybe."

"I'd sooner believe fish could fly."

Cody chuckled. "As slippery as fish are, I imagine they'd have a real hard time roosting in trees. Birds wouldn't like the competition for food, either."

In spite of her worry over Will, Trudy Lynn couldn't help joining in. "Neither would the squirrels. Big catfish actually eat acorns if the nuts happen to drop into the water. I've seen them do it." She giggled. "You know, you have a very strange sense of humor."

"So I've been told. Doesn't it bother you that you always laugh at my crazy jokes?"

"Not at all," she said with a broadening grin. "After my trick with the gravy boat the other night, I figure my reputation has nowhere to go but *up*."

Chapter Seven

After thinking it over, Trudy Lynn decided that even if his closeness was a bit unsettling, Cody would be safer riding the ATV with her than with Will. The older man was cautious, sometimes to a fault, but his peripheral vision and reaction time left much to be desired.

She picked Cody up at 10:00 a.m. and drove straight to the camp office. Instead of making him climb the front steps and enter through the store, she ushered him through her kitchen and out into the central hallway.

"Like I said before, the computer is in that room over there. I've locked Widget in the bathroom so he won't bother you." At the arch of Cody's eyebrow she added, "It's a trick I learned from a guy with a *really* big dog."

"Glad to be of service."

"Speaking of service, Anne's on duty in the

store. She's a sweetheart. I'll tell her you're working in here. If you get hungry or thirsty, just holler and she'll bring you whatever you want."

"I should be fine. All I want to do is access my accounts and see if I need to make any modifications. It won't take long."

"Investments like that have always scared me," Trudy Lynn admitted. "I prefer to put my money into things I can see and touch, like this place."

"I'm glad it's worked out for you."

"Me, too. It's been a long, hard road but I'm finally starting to see a small profit."

"Good. Well…"

She gestured toward the open office. "Right. I'm keeping you. Go on in. Make yourself at home. If you want privacy, just shut the door. I won't mind. If I need anything, I'll knock. Just promise you'll be careful. I almost never touch that computer. Jim gets really upset if he thinks I'm fiddling with his programs."

"Understood," Cody said.

Trudy Lynn noticed that not only was she babbling again, her hands were making exaggerated, fluttery motions to accent her words. That fit with the way the butterflies in her stomach were behaving. She'd been unnecessarily on edge all morning and it was beginning to rile her. What a ridiculous response to doing a simple favor. Surely, there was no need to be worried about Cody accidentally losing or corrupting important files, so why be nervous?

She solved her fidgeting problem by stuffing her hands into the pockets of her jeans. "Okay. Have at it. I'll go do some chores. See you later."

"Okay. Thanks."

Trudy Lynn paused to watch him turn and make his way to the office. He did seem to be getting around a little better. Was he? Or was that just wishful thinking on her part?

Make that wishful *praying.* Cody Keringhoven had been in her prayers ever since Becky had told her he'd been hurt, and there was certainly nothing wrong with affirming a positive result. She didn't need the equivalent of thunder and lightning to convince her the Lord was working in Cody's life. She knew He was.

Though she still wasn't sure what part she might play in Cody's recovery, she was open to heavenly inspiration, just as long as it didn't require the kind of trust she'd once placed in Ned. Becoming involved with one overly controlling, pigheaded man had been an honest mistake. Falling for a second one who was carrying even more excess emotional baggage would be totally idiotic.

Besides, until she and Cody had recovered from the disappointments in their respective love lives, neither of them could count on thinking clearly. Enter-

taining the notion of becoming romantically involved
again, let alone acting on it, scared her silly.

Trudy Lynn felt a sudden, overpowering urge
to flee. She was outside, taking gulping breaths of
fresh air, before she realized that no matter how much
distance she put between herself and Cody Keringhoven, her tenderhearted sympathies would remain
with him.

Okay. She could live with that. There was nothing
wrong with well-placed compassion and concern. So
what if she happened to like the man? That didn't au-
tomatically mean she was falling for him, did it? Of
course not.

Letting her thoughts gel, Trudy Lynn began to
smile and relax. She cared about a lot of people, her
friends, her pastor, her employees, even the folks
who rented canoes and campsites from her. Why not
extend that same innocent sentiment to Cody? He
might be grumpy at times but who wouldn't be, given
his past? When he was in good spirits, he was a lot
of fun to be around. There was nothing wrong with
enjoying his company.

Satisfied with that logical conclusion, she skipped
down the steps, feeling more lighthearted and more
alive than she had for ages.

Cody was still seated in front of the computer
monitor when Trudy Lynn returned and rapped on
the doorjamb before poking her head in. "You busy?"

"No. Just finishing up. Am I in your way?"

"Not at all. As a matter of fact, maybe you can do me a favor. I called my insurance agent about the canoe that was damaged last night. She says she needs the date of purchase and the unit price before she can process my claim."

"How can I help?" Cody pushed back from the desk to give Trudy Lynn access when she approached.

Instead, she paused and held up her hands. "Oh, no. I'm not touching that thing. The last time I tried I messed up days and days of Jim's work."

"Don't you have the information you need on paper?"

She shrugged and quirked a lopsided smile. "Somewhere. Your guess is as good as mine. See those stacks of storage boxes over there? The white ones? Once Jim started putting all the data into the computer, I kind of quit keeping up any other files."

"Kind of?" Cody arched an eyebrow.

"Don't look at me like that. The stuff is in groups. I kept adding to a box till it was full, then started a new one. If I could remember approximately when we ordered those older canoes, I could probably locate the invoice. Eventually. Trouble is, the longer I take, the longer it'll be till I get any reimbursement. I thought, since you're good with computers, you could look it up for me."

"I'm not sure I want to. How big is your cousin?" Cody teased with a wry smile.

"Not big at all. He's a skinny teenager. Smart, but no muscleman like you."

Cody couldn't help feeling good about her description of him, especially when she began to blush. He laughed. "Muscleman? Thanks, I think."

"You know what I mean. You're taller, and... Oh, never mind."

To his delight, her rosy cheeks darkened even more. "Okay. Enough compliments," he said, carefully rolling the chair closer so it faced the desk. "Tell me how to access the accounts payable file and I'll see what I can find."

"I don't know." Trudy Lynn leaned over his shoulder to peer at the screen. "The thingie was already running when I got myself in trouble the last time."

"The *thingie?*" Cody chuckled low as he disconnected from the internet and checked the listings of files. There were two with almost identical names. "Here you are. Which is it?"

"Beats me." She scowled. "One must be from last year. Open the one with the most recent activity and we'll work backward from there."

Cody checked dates. "This shows they've both been accessed in the past few days."

"Jim was probably looking for the insurance information on the other canoes that were ruined," she said. "Just pick either one."

"You could wait till your cousin comes back to work."

"I could," Trudy Lynn said, "but why dawdle when I have an expert sitting right here?" She pulled a face. "You are an expert, aren't you?"

"I won't accidentally erase anything, if that's what you're asking. I use a similar program to keep my investment portfolio. It's a pretty simple system once you get the hang of it."

"Not for me it isn't," she said with a smirk. "All machines hate me, even my vacuum cleaner. The only reason I can keep the ATV running is because Will uses it more than I do and it likes him. I think it's a guy thing."

"If you say so." Cody had been trying to open the chosen file and had failed. "What's your password?"

"Password? For what?"

"This file. It's password protected. Didn't you know that?"

"No." She laid a hand lightly on Cody's shoulder and leaned closer to read what was on the screen. "That's weird."

He forced himself to pay no heed to the warm touch of her hand. It was harder to ignore the light, floral fragrance of her long brown hair as it neared his cheek.

"Not if Cousin Jim was worried you'd mess with the program again and cause him extra work," Cody said, fighting to concentrate on anything but his companion. "What's his last name? When's his birthday? Who's his current girlfriend?"

None of those answers proved to be the password so he began to try more eclectic terms. It wasn't until he used *weed* that he got a positive response. "Hmm. Not good. I'd rather he'd chosen something non-drug related."

"You don't know that's what that stands for."

"I have a pretty good idea," Cody argued, "unless you're going to tell me Jim is into horticulture."

"Unfortunately, no." Trudy Lynn squinted at the data. "Page down. Again. That can't be right. I didn't net nearly that much last month."

He looked up and noted her scowl. "Are you sure?"

"Positive."

"Okay. Let's print this page and check it against the other file."

"What good will that do?"

"Maybe none. Shall I go ahead and try it?"

"Sure." She shook her head, clearly confused. "Things were a lot simpler when I used to save my receipts in a shoe box and pay the bills myself."

"This system is more efficient," Cody told her.

"I suppose so. I just miss having a clear picture of how the business is doing. Looking at the printouts Jim gives me is not the same."

Cody clicked on the second file. To his surprise, it opened without difficulty. He leaned back in the chair and whistled softly.

"What?"

"Look at this. Is that more like what you think you earned last month?"

"Yes, but…"

"Wait a second," he said. "I want this on paper, too. Then we'll do some comparing."

"How will that help?"

Cody started the printer, then turned to study Trudy Lynn's expression. She was his sister's close friend. He couldn't imagine she'd be in on any scheme to defraud the government by keeping two sets of books in order to avoid paying income taxes. Although dishonest businesses did it all the time, or tried to, this woman didn't fit the pattern. She was too open. Too honest. Too clearly perplexed. Besides, if she'd been involved in cooking the books she wouldn't have invited an outsider like him to examine them.

Picking up the second printed sheet, Cody carefully compared it to the first, then laid them both facedown on the desk. He could see at a glance that part of the net difference was in the amount of hourly wage charged to her summer help.

"How much do you pay Anne and the other kids?" Cody asked.

Trudy Lynn quoted a figure far above what he'd seen on one of the sheets.

"How about Will?"

"I pay him about twice what the kids get. And I gave him a raise this year. Why?"

"One of these sets of books shows a good-sized increase. The other doesn't show nearly that much."

"So, one has to be from last year."

"Nope. Sorry." Cody could tell she was stunned. Good. That spoke well for her character. "I can't be positive without doing some serious math, but I suspect your cousin has been siphoning off cash for himself and charging it to other sources. The teens who work for you are only getting part of what you think you're paying them."

Cody displayed his findings and pointed out the discrepancies. "See? According to this posting, Will hasn't had a decent raise in at least two years, either."

"That's impossible!" Trudy Lynn snatched the papers from him, her glance darting back and forth between the two lists. Her eyes grew misty. "I can't believe it. There must be another explanation."

"I sincerely hope so," Cody said. "For your sake and for Jim's. Because if there isn't, you have more than one crime to worry about. You're a victim of embezzlement."

Trudy Lynn had ferried Cody back to his cabin and was sitting alone in her office, mulling over the morning's startling discovery, when her private phone rang. So few people knew that number she assumed it had to be a personal call. "Hello?"

"Ms. Brown? This is Billy Joe Potts, down at Serenity Realty, on the square. I brokered sales for several of your competitors last year. Remember?"

She tensed. "Vaguely."

"Well, Ms. Brown, I have great news for you. I've had an offer on your place that you won't be able to turn down. Isn't that amazing?"

The fine hairs at the nape of Trudy's neck were bristling. Her grip tightened on the receiver. "Amazing."

"Then you'll consider selling? That's wonderful! I knew you'd appreciate the chance to make a big profit. I'll bring the offer right over and get your signature. Say, in an hour?"

"No," Trudy Lynn said, masking her wariness as best she could. "I'm not free this afternoon. And tomorrow is Sunday. Why don't I stop by your office sometime Monday?"

"I don't mind working on the weekend."

"Well, I do. I'll be in church Sunday morning and evening. If you can't wait till Monday, perhaps we'd better just forget the whole thing."

"No, no! Don't…don't do that. Monday's fine."

His nervous, stammering protest was enough to prove to Trudy Lynn that something fishy was going on. She hung up and headed for Cody's cabin without hesitation.

As usual, she found him and his dog lounging

on the porch. "Don't you ever go inside?" she asked pleasantly.

"Not if I can help it. At least not in nice weather like this."

"Well, since this is Arkansas, you might as well enjoy it while you can. Folks say our weather changes every twenty minutes." She joined him by sitting on the top step, as before. "Personally, I think that's an exaggeration. It usually takes at least thirty."

"I'll keep that in mind." He started to lower his propped-up leg.

"Sit still and be comfortable," Trudy Lynn said. "I can't stay. I just need a second opinion. Since you're the only one aware of the mess my finances are in right now, I thought you could give me the best advice."

"I'll try. What's up? Did you talk to your cousin?"

"Not yet. I did just get a call from a real estate agent, though. He says he's had an offer on this place."

"You told me you'd never sell."

"I still feel that way. But if I'm going to owe back taxes or be fined for filing erroneous tax returns or something like that, I don't know if I can afford to stay."

"I wouldn't make any rash decisions," Cody said. "I'd hate to see you give up when none of this mess was your fault. That's not like you. Where's that faith you keep talking about?"

"Sometimes it's hard to see God's plan. I have a tendency to try to second-guess Him."

"Must mean you're human."

"I guess so." She laced her fingers together around one knee and leaned back. "So, what do you think? Should I even bother talking to the real estate agent? He wants to see me Monday."

"Do you want to sell?"

"No. Of course not."

"Then turn down the offer, no matter how good it is. If you're meant to sell, there'll be another one."

"Trust God to work it out, you mean?" Trudy Lynn tilted her head back to grin up at him.

"I didn't say that."

"Yes, you did. But don't worry. I won't tell anybody. It'll be our secret, just you, me and Sailor." The Newf thumped his tail at the mention of his name.

"That's big of you."

The comical, cynical face Cody was making spurred her to chuckle quietly. "My pleasure. And speaking of things that are nice, how about letting me drive you to church tomorrow? I'm sure your sister would love to see you."

Cody huffed. "Yeah. Especially in her husband's church." He shrugged. "Oh well, why not? I want to talk to Logan, anyway."

"Not about the discrepancies in the books. Not yet," Trudy warned. "I don't want you to say anything to anybody till I've had a chance to hear Jim's side of it."

"I think you're wrong to wait. The sooner you get to the bottom of things, the less opportunity your cousin will have to erase the files and destroy the evidence."

"I've been thinking about that," she said. "Why would Jim want proof of his theft? It's nonsense to think he's that stupid."

"Not stupid," Cody replied, "overconfident and egotistical. He's sure he's smarter than anybody else and he wants a record of his accomplishments."

"Maybe he's keeping track because he means to return what he's taken."

Cody stared at her for a moment, then burst into laughter. "That's the most naive thing I've ever heard."

"Oh, yeah? Well, he deserves the benefit of the doubt, and I intend to give it to him."

"Because he's *kin,* as you all say around here?"

"Not entirely. I like to think I'd be that fair with anybody."

"What about the Randall kid? Were you positive he was a thief when you fired him?"

"Of course. Jim even saw…" Trudy realized what she was saying and broke off before Cody had a chance to interrupt. "Uh-oh. Jim again. You don't suppose…?"

"I don't know. But I do think I'd look into it if I

were you. Just because a kid's family has problems, that doesn't mean he or she has to end up the same."

She scowled, studying Cody. His expression was innocent enough. However, if he'd been gossiping with Will there was no telling what tales he'd already heard about *her* parents.

Straightening and getting to her feet, she faced him. "Speaking of families, I want you to know my father was a fine man. He did the best he could for me and my mother. She was just fragile, that's all. It wasn't Daddy's fault."

"I'm sure it wasn't," Cody said.

If he'd shown any sign of puzzlement she would have stopped explaining. Since he appeared to know what she was referring to, she continued. "After Mama died, Daddy was never the same. I was barely in my teens but I did all I could to help him. I took over cooking, cleaning, paying the bills, everything. It was like he didn't care anymore. I know he couldn't stop blaming himself, wondering what more he could have done. In the end, I think it killed him, too."

"So, you've had to be strong for everybody else."

"Yes. I'm proud to say I'm nothing like my parents. I never give up."

Nodding, he spoke quietly and with compassion. "I understand. No wonder you kept insisting my client's drowning wasn't my fault. You knew what harboring guilt like that can do to a person."

"Yes. Firsthand."

Trudy Lynn was watching him closely, waiting for an argument, when she saw the clear blue of his eyes grow misty. She wasn't sure whether he was letting go of his misplaced blame or merely appreciating her opinion when he said, "Thank you," but she took it as a very good sign.

Chapter Eight

Sunday morning dawned bright and clear. Cody had been planning to catch Logan after church and ask him more about good old Cousin Jim. Now that he'd heard Trudy Lynn's sad tale of her childhood, he had a few questions for his sister, too.

Personal inquiries about his hostess were probably out of line, he realized, yet her revelation had touched him deeply. No wonder she was so determined to be self-reliant. At a time when she should have been enjoying childhood she'd been forced to step into a grown-up's shoes. Her skill and perseverance spoke well of her, yes, but there were still invisible scars.

Cody smiled as he dressed. Early success in an adult role had made Trudy Lynn the most hardheaded woman he'd ever met. Although he now understood some of the reasons for her stubbornness, she still drove him crazy. For instance when she'd charged the prowler with only a canoe paddle for defense!

He raked his fingers through his hair, venting his frustration. Much more excitement like that and he'd be turning gray before his time, as Sailor was starting to do around the muzzle.

One glance at the placid canine brought back Cody's smile. "You're going to be on your own this morning, boy. I'm going out. Think you can be good while I'm gone?"

The dog's head drooped. He laid his ears back and settled a pitiful gaze on his master.

"That's right. I'm leaving. And you're staying here. I want you to behave. I'll leave you plenty of food and water. Just don't break down any more doors, okay? Will wasn't real happy about fixing this one the last time."

His dog's expression made Cody shake his head and chuckle. "Now I know where the saying, hang-dog-look, came from. That's the most miserable face you've ever made." He paused to ruffle the silky fur on the dog's ears. "Cheer up, fella. I'll bring you a treat. I promise."

He was still petting the dog when he heard a knock. Gathering up his crutches he called, "Come in. I'm ready."

Trudy Lynn eased the door open. The smile on her face grew to a grin when she saw him. "Morning."

"Good morning. I was just telling Sailor we'd bring him a treat. Will that be okay? I don't want to put you out, but I wouldn't want him to think I'd fib, either."

She giggled. "That's fine. We'll find something. Some of the stores are open on Sunday. And a few restaurants serve brunch after church, then close about two o'clock."

"They close early?" Cody joined her on the porch and secured the door. "Why?"

"Because it's Sunday, silly. The Sabbath."

"Ah, yes. Sunday in the Bible Belt. You weren't kidding about this part of the country being different, were you?"

"Nope." She led the way to her pickup and opened the door for him.

Cody scowled. "You don't have to baby me."

"Sorry. My mistake."

He watched her flounce around to the driver's side, her skirt swinging gracefully against her calves. If the green dress she'd ruined had actually been her favorite, this blue one deserved to be number two. It looked wonderful on her. Then again, everything she wore did.

Trudy Lynn slipped behind the wheel and peered over at him. "Well? Get a move on."

"Yes, ma'am." He positioned the crutches against the seat, parallel to his leg, and slammed the door. "Sorry I snapped at you."

"No problem. Sorry I was too nice. I'll do my best to be much meaner in the future."

"Thanks."

"You're welcome." She glanced at him as she drove out of the campground. "That's a nice jacket. You clean up pretty decent for a Californian."

"I was born in Illinois, remember?"

"I wouldn't tell that to too many folks till they get to know you better. I'm okay with it but some people think, *once a Yankee, always a Yankee.*"

"I'll keep that in mind."

"I doubt it." She laughed. "You tend to do things your way most of the time, no matter what."

Cody stared at her. "*I* tend to? What about you?"

"I can't help it if my way's the best way."

"Not always," he said firmly.

"Oh, yeah? Name one time when it wasn't."

His voice rumbled with emotion as he answered, "The time you charged an armed man and risked your life for a stupid canoe."

Remembering, she shivered in spite of herself.

The parking lot surrounding Serenity Chapel was already crowded when they arrived. Trudy Lynn considered stopping near the front doors so Cody wouldn't have to walk so far, then decided against it. She wasn't being mean, as she'd jokingly threatened, she was merely making him exercise. His mention of their misadventure while guarding the canoes had reminded her of how well he'd managed to get around when he'd been forced to. She didn't think for a minute that he was faking his disability and pain. But she did suspect he might be subconsciously punishing himself for the outcome of the original accident. If that were the case, it helped explain his refusal to continue physical therapy.

She found an empty space and parked. To Cody's credit, he didn't comment on how far they were from the entrance. By the time she'd gathered up her Bible and her purse, he was out of the truck, waiting.

"You've been here before, right?" she asked, leading the way.

"You know I have. This is where we first met."

"That's right. You were visiting Becky."

"Yes. You and Carol Sue sat in the pew behind my poor sister and me, giggling and whispering during the service."

"We did not!"

"Maybe not the whole time. But you two were sure enjoying yourselves."

"Why not? Church is a happy place," Trudy Lynn said.

"For you, maybe. Sometimes, I sit there feeling so much like an outsider I want to make a break for the door long before the sermon is over."

"Try to avoid making that kind of an exit this morning, will you? Becky and Logan would be embarrassed."

"Speaking of which, isn't that Logan standing inside, shaking hands?"

"Sure is. Go grab a pew for us. I'll join you in a few minutes. I need to pop into my Sunday school class first and explain why I wasn't there this morning so they won't worry."

Before Cody had time to ask if she'd missed the class on his account, Trudy Lynn had dashed off down the hall.

He approached Logan. "Good morning. Where's Becky?"

"Home," Logan said. "I think she's got a touch of the flu. We didn't give you our germs the other night, did we?"

"Nope. I'm healthy as a horse." He paused for a wry chuckle. "Of course, if I were a horse, they'd have shot me by now."

"How is your leg?"

"Sore." Cody shrugged. "But I didn't come here to discuss my troubles. I need to have a private chat with you about my landlady."

"Trudy Lynn? Why? More vandalism?"

"I wish it were that simple," Cody said. "What else do you know about her cousin, Jim?"

"Nothing more than what I've already told you. That's public record so I wasn't violating a trust. Is Jim causing problems?"

"You have no idea." Cody lowered his voice and spoke aside. "I'm not going into any detail till you and I are alone, but it looks like he's been stealing from her."

"Really? Humph, that is a surprise. If I'd been asked to choose the person most likely to try to swindle her, I'd have picked her ex-boyfriend."

"Whoa. That's one suspect I hadn't considered." Cody was frowning. "I thought he was out of the picture."

"He's supposed to be. The thing is, my wife tells me Ned was never one to give up without a fight, even when they were kids. He had too much pride."

"Will says the guy dumped Trudy, not the other way around. Isn't that what happened?"

"In a manner of speaking. Once he'd graduated college, Ned let her know he wasn't coming back to town. When she refused to join him, he apparently insinuated she didn't measure up to his new standards of sophistication any more than Serenity did."

"Ouch. That had to hurt."

"If it did, you sure couldn't tell. She didn't even seem to care, which is why I wondered if Ned got his pride hurt and decided to cause trouble for her."

Logan paused to welcome some late arrivals, then said, "It's almost eleven. Come on. We can talk a little more on the way to my office."

By then, Cody was so involved in their conversation he'd have accompanied his brother-in-law if he'd had to crawl.

Logan stopped just inside his office door and checked his watch. "I can give you all of three minutes. What makes you think Jim is stealing?"

"Two sets of books, for starters. He's been doing all the accounts payable and giving Trudy's staff lower wages than she thought."

"He's pocketing the difference?"

"Looks like it. I didn't have time to go over all the records. Who knows what else he may have done? She insists she wants to talk to him before we go to the sheriff. If Jim finds out we're on to him, I'm afraid he'll panic and erase those files."

"A good tech can almost always get them back for you if you need them," Logan said. "That's a mistake lots of criminals make. They think data that doesn't show up in their computer's active memory is gone. Trust me. It isn't. It may be hard to access but it's still there."

"That's good to hear."

"So, tell me," Logan said with a knowing smile. "When did you start referring to yourself and our Ms. Trudy Brown as *we?*"

Exiting Miss Louella's Class for Extraordinary Ladies, Trudy Lynn was grinning. They'd teased her about coming to church with Cody that morning, as she'd expected. She didn't mind. The women in that class had the biggest, most loving hearts of any group she'd ever belonged to and it was their serious prayers she desired most.

Though she was loathe to admit it, especially to him, Cody had frightened her with his constant talk of danger. She'd never felt personally threatened before. Now, it was all she could do to make herself accompany Widget outside after dark. Having a spirit of fear was supposed to be wrong, so why was she unable to shake it?

Hurrying into the sanctuary, she paused at the rear. There weren't many tall, blond men in the congregation so she expected to spot Cody easily. Puzzled when she didn't see him, she started slowly down the center aisle, responding to greetings from fellow worshippers as she went.

She came upon Becky's aunt Effie and her new husband, Brother Fred, seated in the first row. "Hi. Have you seen Cody? We rode together."

"And you lost him?" Effie teased. "A big guy like that? My, my." She sobered. "How's he doing, anyway? We haven't heard much lately."

"Pretty well," Trudy Lynn said. "We expected to visit with Becky this morning. Have you seen her?"

"She's sick, I reckon. Nothin' else ever kept her out of church."

"That's too bad. Cody'll be disappointed. Assuming I ever locate him, that is."

"When you do, you'd best keep a close eye on him," the elderly woman warned. "Turning a handsome, single fella like that loose in here with all these unmarried ladies is like wavin' a pan of fudge under the nose of a gal who's been on a starvation diet.

Anything might happen." She squeezed Fred's hand. "I always hold tight to this good catch of mine."

It warmed Trudy Lynn's heart to see the fond look the older couple exchanged. "I'll keep that in mind." Her already generous smile widened as she spotted her guest. "There's Cody. In the back. Safe and sound. If you talk to Becky, tell her I asked about her. I'll phone her later."

"Y'all could sit down here by us," Effie suggested. "There's plenty of room."

"I know. But it looks like Cody's having a little trouble balancing on the sloping aisle. We'll visit after the service, okay?"

Trudy Lynn didn't wait for an answer. She quickly joined Cody and motioned to an empty space in the back. "I was just talking to Effie and Brother Fred."

"Do you want to go sit with them?"

"That's not necessary. I said we'd talk later." Entering the pew, she left room for Cody and his crutches. When he was comfortably seated she added, "I guess Becky's sick this morning."

"That's what Logan said."

"You had a chance to talk with him? You didn't mention those problems we found, did you?"

"I certainly did."

Trudy Lynn was irritated. "I told you I wanted to speak to Jim before we said anything to anybody. I should have known you wouldn't listen to me."

"I listened. Calm down and think for a second.

Logan was already aware of some of Jim's problems and he also has a professional background. There was no reason to keep our suspicions from him. We need his advice."

Trudy Lynn pulled a face. She had no plausible grounds to disagree. "Okay. I suppose you're right. *This* time. So, tell me. What did Logan have to say?"

"Not to worry about the files being erased, among other things."

"What other things?" Scowling, she tried to be patient. Expecting a man to make sense was problematical. Getting this one to reveal anything was like waiting for Widget to spit out a grasshopper— whatever parts did finally show up, it probably wasn't going to be the whole insect.

Cody leaned closer. He lowered his voice to ask, "What are the chances your ex-boyfriend could be our vandal?" She drew back and scowled.

"Ned? That's ridiculous."

"Is it? Why?"

"Because."

"That's not a very good reason."

"It's good enough for me. Ned insisted nothing would ever make him set foot in this hick town again and I believed him. I'm sure that opinion extends to my campground. He never did like the place."

"He's a fool," Cody said flatly.

Trudy Lynn's cheeks warmed. No wonder it was so hard to stay upset with this impossible man. Every time he made her mad he seemed to follow up with something so endearing, so unexpected, it instantly negated her annoyance.

She smiled. "What a nice thing to say. I'm glad you appreciate the beauty of this area. I love it here."

The service was starting, giving Cody barely enough time to cup his hand around his mouth and add, "I wasn't referring to the real estate."

To Trudy Lynn's credit she managed to listen to most of Logan's sermon, although if anyone had asked her, she knew she couldn't have recalled its content. She figured she was doing well to accompany Cody out the door afterward without grinning so broadly her cheek muscles cramped.

They chatted briefly with Effie and Fred before bidding them goodbye and starting for the parking lot. Trudy Lynn stopped in surprise when she saw her supposedly nefarious cousin leaning against the side of her pickup truck. His nonchalant pose made her wary. Jim never relaxed. His manner was usually comparable to that of a nervous hummingbird. Seeing him standing so quietly, obviously waiting for her, was a bit unnerving.

She would have reached for Cody's arm if his crutches hadn't been in the way. Instead, she put her hand lightly on his shoulder. "See that guy by the truck? That's Jim. I wonder what he wants." She shuddered. "You don't think Brother Logan called him, do you?"

"Not for a minute. Logan takes his job too seriously. He'd never betray a confidence." Cody started forward. "Come on. It's high time I met your cousin."

Trudy Lynn had to hurry to keep up. She reached the truck at the same time Cody did and forced a smile. "Hi, Jim. I'd like you to meet Cody Keringhoven. He's Becky's brother."

"I heard you'd taken in a stray." The wiry teen snorted, obviously passing judgment.

Before Trudy Lynn could object to Jim's lack of respect, Cody said, "I'm not freeloading, if that's what you're thinking. I'm working for my keep."

Jim eyed him up and down. "Oh, yeah? Doin' what?"

"Looking out for prowlers, to start with," Cody said evenly. "I'm also pretty good at bookkeeping."

"Hey! That's my job," Jim blurted, abandoning his lackadaisical facade.

Trudy Lynn could tell how worried the younger man was. Good. Let him sweat. If they'd made a mistake and Jim was innocent of the suspected theft, she'd apologize. Unfortunately, it didn't look as if she was going to have to. Jim was giving a perfect impression of a naughty kid who'd been caught with his hand in the cookie jar. *Her* cookie jar. And she wasn't ready to forgive what he'd already done to her staff.

The worst part was, she couldn't afford to make it up to them retroactively.

"Those books are mine," Trudy Lynn said. "I can look at them anytime I want to. Right?"

"Sure." Jim's bony shoulders twitched. "No problem. I'll print you out whatever you want."

"From which file?" she asked without smiling.

Her cousin's glance darted to Cody. When he began to glare at the man, any lingering doubt Trudy Lynn had was swept away. Jim was as guilty as if he'd robbed her at gunpoint. That would have been hard enough to accept coming from a stranger. This boy was *family.*

Saddened, she said, "We haven't gone to the sheriff, Jimmy. Not yet. But we will if you don't have a *very* good explanation for what you did."

"You owed me the money," he said, as if that made his thievery acceptable.

"I gave you as much as I could afford. You knew what the job paid when you took it."

"Yeah. I knew." He snorted derisively. "I knew a lot of other stuff, too. You don't have a clue."

"I want to understand." She gently laid her hand on his thin forearm and felt it tremble. "Don't be afraid."

Jim jerked free. "I ain't afraid of nothin'."

"Then calm down and come back to the office with us. I want you to show Mr. Keringhoven everything—all the duplicate files you set up. Then we'll talk. I'm sure we can work something out so you won't have to go to jail."

"Yeah, sure." He was backing away. "Later."

Trudy Lynn stood beside Cody and watched the teen cut across the lawn to the street. She sighed. "Do you think he'll show up?"

Cody shook his head. "Not in a million years."

Chapter Nine

That Sunday afternoon had begun sultry and ended wet, thanks to a surprise storm. The rain didn't have to last long to impress Cody. Drops as big as quarters were driven horizontal by a gale that looked as if it was strong enough to snap the tops off the trees. He waited it out in the camp store with Trudy Lynn while Anna tended to the few customers daring enough to brave the deluge.

"Does it always come down like this?" Cody asked.

Trudy Lynn laughed. "No. Sometimes it's worse. Our storms are very unpredictable. This is the kind of weather that can spawn tornadoes, too."

"Terrific. And for this I left California?"

"Why did you leave, anyway?"

"Lots of reasons."

"One of them wouldn't happen to be similar to my story about Ned, would it?"

"Maybe. I haven't met Ned so I can't judge his motives. I imagine Stephanie was prettier, though."

To his chagrin, he saw the twinkle fade from Trudy's eyes. "All her beauty was on the outside," Cody quickly explained. "There was a callous element to her personality that I never saw till I wound up on crutches."

"I'm sorry."

He smiled. "I used to be sorry, too. Now, I'm glad I found out before it was too late. When—if—I ever do decide to get married, I intend for it to last the rest of my life." He raised an eyebrow. "Admit it. Haven't you felt the same kind of relief about Ned?"

"Truthfully? Yes. I can't picture myself tagging along after him and pretending I like being in the city. Even if I could have managed to please him temporarily, I'd eventually have resented him for taking me away from all this." She swept her arm in a wide arc. "I belong here the same way those oaks and sycamores belong in the forest. Or the Spring River belongs in its banks. They just do."

Cody nodded. "I know exactly what you mean. I felt the same about the Tuolumne."

"Felt? Past tense? I thought you were looking forward to going back there as soon as you were able."

"Not anymore." He shrugged. "I've accepted my limitations."

"You can still enjoy being on the water. How

about going canoeing with me as soon as the weather clears?"

"No thanks."

"Why not? It would do you good to get out. Our river may not be as exciting as you're used to but it's not boring, either. There's lots to see—birds, deer, all kinds of wildlife."

"I said, *no.*"

Cody didn't like the way Trudy Lynn was studying his face, trying to read him. It was embarrassing to admit, even to himself, how his stomach churned every time he thought about getting back into a boat. Any boat. On any watercourse. The last thing he was going to do was confess those irrational feelings and open himself to ridicule. He gritted his teeth. Worse than that, Trudy Lynn might decide to help him overcome his hang-ups, with or without his consent.

Moments later, she said, "Fine," as if it didn't matter.

"I couldn't even get into a canoe with this brace on my knee," he said, hoping to soothe her bruised pride. "Maybe later." *And maybe never.*

"Okay. If you decide you want to take out one of my canoes by yourself, just tell Will. He'll fix you up."

Cody took her hand. To his relief, she didn't resist his easy grasp. "I'm not turning down your offer because I don't want to ride with you, Trudy Lynn. I'm turning it down because…" Her clear, trusting gaze unnerved him. "Just because I don't want to go, okay?"

"Okay." She pulled her hand free, got to her feet and peered out the window. "It's still raining. Looks like that terrible wind has eased, though, so we can probably quit worrying about getting hit by falling limbs. It's safe enough to drive you on home. Let's go."

Cody's conscience was doing backflips. If he voiced his apprehension about boating, he'd have to admit to the possibility it might never go away. Plus, he'd have to continue to face Trudy Lynn, an extraordinary woman who was as fearless as any man he'd ever met. That notion didn't set well in his already churning gut.

Mulling over his predicament, it occurred to Cody that he cared too much what his hostess thought of him. Way too much. In the space of a few days, staying in her good graces and ensuring her welfare had become the most important goals in his life. It was nice to know he could accomplish that by relying on his brain, even if his knee never healed properly. And he wouldn't starve. His investments would see to that. So why was he so downhearted?

Because I never appreciated what I had before, he decided. And now there was no way to reclaim it.

Watching Trudy Lynn lead the way to her truck, he paused on the porch and began to smile. It might be too late to be grateful for his past but it wasn't too late to give thanks for the present. For being here. For being dragged into the intrigue surrounding his hostess.

Cody *was* grateful. Sincerely so. Yet his heart held back from actually acknowledging the benevolent influence of a higher power. Although the idea of a universal God did make sense, he still doubted any deity cared for him personally or noticed if he stumbled. That premise was okay for women and children. It was too far-fetched for him.

Trudy Lynn had dropped Cody in front of his cabin, then returned to the main lodge to transmit her grocery order by phone to the computer at the warehouse which supplied her store. She'd just finished when Will thumped up the steps in his rubber boots and flung open the door. He was dripping rainwater and panting.

His demeanor was enough to alert her. "What's wrong? More vandalism? Surely not on a Sunday."

"No, ma'am." The old man mopped his wet face with his hands. "It's worse."

"What could be worse?"

"Plenty. We're missin' a canoe."

"That's not too unusual after a storm like the one we just had. The rain probably floated it off. Don't get yourself in a tizzy. I'm sure it didn't go far."

"This one did," Will said, still breathless. "Jim

took it. Farley saw him push off and head downriver, right as the rain was commencin'."

"Then we'll pick him up at one of the landings as soon as he calls. If he doesn't phone before I leave for services tonight, wait till I get back. I want to be the one who goes and gets him."

"You ain't thinkin' of goin' by yourself, are ya?"

She hadn't given it a lot of thought. "Why not?"

"I don't like it," Will said, scowling. "That boy ain't been actin' right for months. Mark my words, he's up to something. I wouldn't trust him no farther than I could throw him. Maybe not that far."

"If you were so worried, why didn't you tell me?"

"Because he's your kin."

"The only thing Jim and I have in common is our ancestors and I'm about ready to disown him. What, exactly, has he done to make you suspicious?"

"Sneakin' around for one thing. Seems like he's always turning up. For a while there I thought he was spyin' on me, checkin' to see if I was workin' hard enough."

"What else?"

"Those friends of his. Bunch of no-goods if I ever seen 'em. Always hangin' around and moochin' free rides. If I had a nickel for every time he let one of his buddies take a canoe without payin', I'd be a rich man."

"Didn't you say something to him about it?"

"Sure did," Will told her with pride. "I took him aside and gave him what for."

"And?" Trudy Lynn was beginning to think Will would never finish his story to her satisfaction.

"And, he cussed at me. Said you gave him permission. If I'd of run to you about it after that, I'd of sounded as spoiled as he is. It's none of my business if you want to let him treat his friends."

"Only I never said he could." The more she probed, the worse Jim's sins got. What else was waiting to be uncovered?

Will looked apologetic. "I'm terribly sorry, Miz Brown. I shoulda known."

"Don't worry about it. You're not the only one who was fooled. Is that all Jim did?"

"All that I know of. 'Course, that don't mean there ain't more. What're you goin' to do? Wait him out?"

"For now." She nodded, thoughtful. "If we don't hear from him by nightfall, we'll call the sheriff and report the canoe stolen."

"Jim'll be fit to be tied."

"Good. He needs shaking up. I wouldn't be doing him any favors if I let him get away with this."

The truth of that statement entered her subconscious and began to bounce around as Widget's favorite tennis ball had done the time it had accidentally ended up in the clothes dryer. Maybe Jim did need to be forced to face his misdeeds and right them— before she granted him forgiveness. There was a lot to be said for standing up and taking your medicine, even if it was hard to swallow.

Like Cody needs to do, she thought. Jim wasn't the only one who should be made to face facts. In a way, Cody's task was more difficult. His problems had resulted from an accident, while the origin of Jim's was his own missteps.

Which is probably why Cody blames God, Trudy Lynn mused. That wasn't as terrible as she'd first imagined. In his misplaced anger he was at least acknowledging a basic belief in the Lord. That was a start. She knew she couldn't argue him into a renewal of his faith, though the urge to try was strong. Too bad Christianity wasn't catching like the common cold or genetic like his light-colored hair.

Will was still standing by, waiting for orders, when her thoughts returned to the problem at hand. Wherever her cousin was, chances were good he was okay. The storm had arisen fairly suddenly but Jim was a native of Arkansas so he knew how severe the weather could get. Surely, he'd have beached the canoe and waited it out when the heaviest rain had begun. He'd have had to. Seeing where he was going and piloting the boat in the midst of such a deluge would have been impossible.

"Okay, Will," she said. "I'll stay close to the phones in case Jim calls. You go ask Farley if he mentioned anything that may give us a clue to where he was headed."

"Yes, ma'am. You want me to tell Mr. Cody what's goin' on, too?"

The old man's keen perception amused and embarrassed her. "Yes. You can tell Cody. He's going to be helping me in the office for a while so he should be kept informed about camp business."

"You fire ol' Jim?"

"Not yet," Trudy Lynn said, "but I'm going to."

"What'll his grandma Earlene say?"

"I doubt she'll be too surprised. She's had eighteen years of watching after him while his mama worked." Trudy Lynn began to smile. "I don't suppose you'd like to drop by Earlene's place and tell her for me, would you?"

"Who? Me?"

To her delight, the old man's face reddened. "Yes, you. Word around town is, you've been goin' to church with her on the Sunday evenings you don't have to work."

"I mighta gone a few times."

"Uh-huh. Well, as soon as I can get things squared away here, you'll have every Sunday off. Tell Earlene that for me when you see her, too."

"I didn't say I was goin'."

"You're going. Consider it an order. I'd rather have you break it to her about Jim than have to do it myself."

"In that case, I think you'd best pass the word to Mr. Cody." Will began to grin. "If I have to run into town and break the bad news to Earlene, it could take me hours, by the time I get her settled down and all."

Laughing softly, Trudy Lynn assented. "I suppose that's fair. I'll go tell Cody and you go tell Earlene." Pausing, she shook her head. "But don't think I'm not wise to you, old man. You can pretend you're not interested in her all you want. You don't fool me one bit."

Will was chuckling when he answered, "You don't fool me, either, missy."

If Cody was surprised by Trudy Lynn's visit he didn't show it. He joined her on the porch and dried the pressed-metal chairs with a towel before offering her one. That show of hospitality didn't impress her nearly as much as the fact he was getting around nicely with the aid of a cane he'd borrowed from Will.

"Jim's gone," she said, sinking into the closest chair with a sigh. The cool dampness felt good.

Cody lowered himself into the other chair. "I figured he'd run. So, what now?"

"We wait. Since he stole a canoe instead of taking the ATV, his trail will be easy to follow. Even if he decides to beach the boat downriver and take off on foot his options are limited. When he gets tired of hanging out in the woods with the ticks and chiggers he'll come back. I know Jim. He won't rough it for long. He's spoiled rotten."

"We have ticks in northern California," Cody said. "Tell me what a chigger looks like so I can avoid them, too. I've heard they really make you itch."

Trudy Lynn gave him a lopsided smile. "*Oh,* yeah. If you ever find one big enough to see, I'd like to take a peek, too. The first inkling you'll have that you've been bitten is a little red spot, usually somewhere near your ankles. I put home remedies on my chigger bites, not that anything works very well. You kind of have to tough it out till the itching finally stops."

"How long does that take?"

"Well," she drawled, smile spreading, "I'm usually through scratching my summer bites by Christmas."

"No wonder Sailor's been acting uncomfortable. We forgot to buy him a flea collar."

"Or two. I left Widget home so he wouldn't traumatize your gentle giant again. Where is he, anyway?"

"Inside. Sleeping," Cody said. "I've been thinking."

"*That's* a good sign."

"Be serious and let me finish, will you?"

"Sorry." She made a comical face to show she was far from being intimidated.

"Did Widget like Jim?"

"Not particularly," Trudy Lynn said.

"I wish Sailor had met him."

"Why? Is he out of tasty snacks or chew toys?"

Cody gave a wry chuckle. "No. But he is intuitive,

especially about people he doesn't already know. I've seen it before. He's the best judge of character I've ever met."

"And he loved me the minute he saw me!"

"You were covered in gravy at the time. That's hardly a fair test."

"True. He did seem to like me after that, too, didn't he?"

"Yes." Cody blessed her with a grin. "He liked you. I told you he was a great judge of character."

Her cheeks grew rosy. "Thanks. Widget told me he liked you, too." It pleased her when that far-fetched comment made Cody laugh.

"So," he said a moment later, "what's Plan B? Are you going to call the cops on Jim or let him off?"

"I'm not going to let him get away with stealing, if that's what you mean. It isn't just me he cheated, it's my employees. Too bad none of them questioned their wages."

"Maybe they did and Jim gave them some lame excuse."

Trudy Lynn had already considered that probability. When all this was over and things were back to normal, she intended to give as many raises as her budget would allow, even if it meant no new equipment for several seasons.

She nodded in agreement. "That's entirely possible. I don't want to discuss it with the kids until I know for sure how much damage has been done, but I may tell Will. He'll understand."

"Because he's been on both sides of the law?"

"Of course not!" Trudy Lynn stared at Cody as if he'd just delivered a personal insult. "Will's my friend. I trust him, even if you don't."

"I'm sorry if I offended you," Cody said evenly. "You asked for my help solving your mystery and I've been doing my best to give it. If you'd rather deal with fairy tales than hear the truth, I'll stop."

"I didn't mean that."

"Then what did you mean?"

Good question. She sighed. Everything was getting too complicated. Not only had she been disappointed to learn negative aspects regarding people close to her, she was having to come to grips with her own vacillating point of view on a minute-by-minute basis. Was she or wasn't she interested in developing a personal relationship with Cody Keringhoven? And if she was, how did he feel about it? Given the severity of her other tribulations, that should have been the least of her worries, yet she couldn't help constantly wondering.

Clearly, Cody was waiting for an answer. "I don't know what I meant," Trudy Lynn said. "This whole business has me so bumfuzzled—confused—I don't even make sense to myself. And believe me, I've been talking myself silly."

"I don't doubt that."

It was a relief to see his good humor returning, even though she was once again the focus of his taunt. "I do not talk too much."

"Oh?" He glanced at his watch. "I've been timing you. The longest you can go without having to say something is about twenty seconds."

"That's ridiculous."

"Is it? Try keeping still."

The man was exasperating. Did he really expect her to believe she couldn't stop talking, any time she wanted, for as long as she wanted? Of course she could. She pressed her lips together and waited. And waited. Finally, her patience was at an end.

"All right. How was that? Can I talk now?"

Cody was laughing. "Nineteen seconds. You just proved my point."

Waving her hands like a demented butterfly caught in a whirlwind, she got to her feet and faced him. "Oh, who cares? I'm going to go back to the office and see if Jim has called from one of the landings downriver. If he hasn't, I'm going to drive the usual route and check each one. Do you want to come along or are you afraid to be cooped up in a truck with somebody who chatters like I do?"

"I think I can stand it," Cody said. "Give me a few minutes to be sure Sailor's going to be all right while I'm gone."

"Fine. I'll be right back."

Hurrying away, Trudy Lynn was struck by the fact

she was suddenly so elated she wanted to jump for joy. Her life was falling apart, her business might go down the tubes, she still hadn't figured out who was trying to ruin her new canoes, and her cousin had absconded after embezzling who-knows-how-much from her accounts, yet she was ecstatic to the point of being giddy.

There could be only one reason for that, she admitted ruefully. Like it or not, her spirits were up because she and Cody were about to spend more time together.

Chapter Ten

Cody could have predicted they wouldn't find any trace of Jim no matter how many landings and byways they searched. Night was fast approaching when Trudy Lynn voiced the same conclusion. "I guess we should give up and go home."

"Guess so." Cody tried to sound supportive. "You've done all you can. It's probably time to involve the law."

"I know." She sighed heavily. "I kept hoping. We'll stop at the sheriff's office when we go through Serenity. I'd rather talk to him in person than by phone."

"On Sunday night?"

She blinked rapidly and peered at the digital clock on her dash. "Oh, no. We've missed church. I was so involved in looking for Jim I let the time slip by."

"That's okay. Why don't we stop at Becky and Logan's and tell them what's been going on? I'd like to see how she's feeling, anyway. Do you think they'd be home by now?"

"Undoubtedly, even if they stopped for ice cream. Evening services don't last all that long."

Cody's stomach growled. "Ice cream? Sounds good. I didn't eat lunch."

"You mean, *dinner*. Around here, dinner is served right after church, around noon. Supper is the late meal."

"No lunch?"

"Nope."

"How—Southern." He'd been going to say something less genteel but changed his mind. After the way his hostess had bristled when he'd reminded her of Will's prison record, he'd decided to choose his words more carefully in future conversations. Judging by her amiable reaction to his latest efforts to subdue his candor, he'd succeeded.

Turning slightly to stretch his stiff knee, Cody draped his left arm across the back of the seat between them and studied Trudy Lynn's profile as she drove. It was amazing how her freshness and natural beauty remained so compelling despite the trying day she'd had.

The driver's side window was partially open and the wind was lifting wisps of her long, silky hair. It feathered against his forearm like butterfly wings. He knew he should move away. And he would. He just didn't see any rush.

Trudy Lynn shot him a bemused glance. "What?"

"Ice cream," Cody said, seizing on the first excuse that came to mind. "I'll buy. I'm starving."

"I thought you wanted to go see your sister."

"Let her get her own ice cream," he joked. "I never treat more than one pretty lady at a time." The glib words were out of his mouth before he fully realized what he'd said. There was no hope that Trudy Lynn had missed the inference. Her cheeks were flaming. Anything he said now would only make matters worse.

Hunkering down in the seat and facing forward, arms folded across his chest, Cody used the remaining miles to try to figure out how he'd turned into such a blithering idiot in just a short few days.

Trudy Lynn left Cody talking with Logan and followed Becky into the kitchen. "How are you feeling?" she asked.

"Mostly okay," her friend said. "It comes and goes. I can be fine one minute and woozy the next."

"Then sit down and let me make the coffee," Trudy Lynn said. "I wanted to get you alone, anyway."

"Uh-oh. Sounds serious. More trouble?"

"I hope not." She busied herself with the coffee-maker while she organized her thoughts. "I'm really starting to like your brother."

"That's *bad*?"

"It could be. We hardly know each other."

"How does he feel about it?"

Trudy Lynn's eyes widened. "I don't know. I don't want to know. We're both on the rebound. It's way too soon for either of us to be having any serious ideas."

"Then what's the problem?"

"I haven't been leading him on. At least I don't think I have. But on the way over here he said I was pretty."

"How awful. I'll have Logan tell him to mind his manners."

"Stop teasing. It's hard to remember exactly what Cody said and how he said it."

"Try." Becky leaned her elbows on the table, rested her chin in her hands and grinned knowingly.

"And stop staring at me like that. I happen to *like* the man. I never said I was falling in love or anything."

"Perish the thought. Go on. Protest as much as you want if you think it'll help. I'm a pastor's wife. You'd be amazed at the secrets people tell me."

Trudy Lynn was adamant. "There's no secret. Nothing. I'm probably imagining things. Cody and I were talking about how you and Logan sometimes go get ice cream after evening services. Cody said he was hungry and offered to pay if I'd stop for ice cream for us."

"So far, so good. That all made sense."

"I know. But then, he said you should get your own ice cream because he only treats one pretty lady at a time. I know he was just kidding around. I suppose I shouldn't take it so seriously."

Becky laughed softly. "Well, well. He stuck his foot in it that time, didn't he?"

"What do you mean?"

"Reason it out, honey. I'm not only married, I'm his sister, so that leaves only one pretty, available lady. You."

"We're *not* on a date," Trudy Lynn insisted. "Nothing like it. We've been driving around looking for Jim that's all." She sobered and sighed. "I suppose I might as well tell you. You'll hear the gossip soon enough. Jim's been embezzling from me. When I confronted him, he promised to come to the office and talk. Instead, he took a canoe and disappeared downriver."

Becky whistled. "Wow. What're you going to do now?"

"Cody's getting Logan's advice, for starters. Then, I guess we'll have to call the sheriff."

"I should hope so. Is there anything I can do to help?"

"No. Thanks anyway." Trudy Lynn began frowning. "Except maybe tell me why your coffeemaker isn't starting to drip. I filled it with fresh water."

Laughing, her friend stood and reached across the counter. She held the end of a brown cord in front of her face and wiggled it as she said, "I think it works better if you plug it in. Always has for me."

* * *

If Trudy Lynn had envisioned the turmoil and confusion that would descend upon her formerly peaceful camp as a result of Jim's vanishing act, she might have considered writing off the monetary loss after all.

The local police had been the only ones involved in the search to begin with. After they'd located a bloody life vest and splintered paddle, however, they'd called in a state investigative team which had come equipped with its own mobile command center and full staff. That team's activation caught the attention of the Arkansas newspapers, followed by wider distribution on the newswires. Soon, a number of reporters from nearby towns began to set up camp in Serenity.

Trudy Lynn didn't mind the extra business for her store and cabins. What disturbed her was the cancellations from her regular customers. She was just hanging up the receiver after another disappointing conversation when Cody entered the office.

"Hi. Any news?"

Trudy Lynn shook her head and gestured toward the phone. "Not anything good. That was the Millers. They've had reservations since they were here last summer. Suddenly they've changed their minds. Lots of my usual campers aren't coming this year."

"Because of what happened to Jim?"

"Yes. Everybody's positive he's been murdered or come to some equally horrible end." She scowled and pursed her lips. "If you ask me, he faked his disappearance. Anything to get out of being held responsible for his crimes."

"That's highly possible," Cody said. "But if he intended to hide, he sure went about it the wrong way. With all these people looking for him, one of them is bound to turn up a clue. It's only a matter of time." He approached and reached for Trudy Lynn's hand before he went on. "Unless Jim really has met with foul play. There is that possibility. The sheriff tells me some of your cousin's friends have bad reputations."

Head bowed, she stared at the gentle way Cody was holding her hand and stroking his thumb over her knuckles. It was the kind of unspoken comfort she'd craved and never received after her mother's death. Even later, when she'd begun to seriously consider spending the rest of her life with Ned, he'd never touched her with quiet compassion the way Cody had.

"I wish I'd never hired Jim," she said softly. "Earlene convinced me to give him a chance. She's Jim's maternal grandmother. She's been a better parent to him than his mom ever thought of being."

"What about his father?"

"Long gone."

"Too bad. I know what it's like to grow up in a one-parent home. Dad did his best for me but it still wasn't as good as it could have been with a mother in the house, especially when I was younger."

"I know what you mean." Trudy Lynn felt instantly bereft when Cody released her hand and stepped back.

"Tell you what," he said. "Let's check all the landings again and do our own snooping. It'll be better than sitting here stewing over the lack of progress the professionals are making."

"Great idea. We can take a canoe. The weather's perfect for it. And I need a break. You can hardly hear yourself think in the store or on the porch with all the police activity."

Although she'd started toward the outer door, Cody hadn't budged. She looked back. "Aren't you coming?"

"I'll take a rain check."

"Why? This was your idea."

"I meant we could drive."

"What's the difference?" She saw him glance down at his knee. "Don't worry. You'll be able to get into a canoe. I'll be there if you need help."

"No, thanks."

Puzzled, she tried to read his closed expression. If she didn't know how daring he'd been before, she might suspect he was afraid. That was impossible of course. Cody was used to taking chances. A little canoe ride on a peacefully flowing river wouldn't scare him one bit. Therefore, the only possible conclusion was that he didn't want her company. So much for the silly notion the man was growing fond of her.

Pride came to her rescue. She lifted her chin and squared her shoulders. "Okay. Have it your way. I should relieve Anne for her afternoon break instead of going on a wild-goose chase, anyway. I may not have a business left when all this is over, but we're sure raking in the money right now. Better make the most of it."

"Right. Guess I'll take Sailor for a swim. It beats bathing him in the bathtub."

"And it's easier on the plumbing," Trudy Lynn said. "I've had clogged sinks in two of the cabins since the reporters showed up. I suspect they forget we don't have garbage disposals so they dump food scraps down the drain."

"I'll mention it to them for you."

"That won't be necessary."

"It's no bother. Glad to do it."

Trudy Lynn's hands fisted on her hips. "I said, it won't be necessary. I've already handled it."

"Who put the burr under *your* saddle, lady?"

"Nobody. I appreciate your offer, but…"

"But?"

"I was running this place all by myself before you came to Serenity. Nothing has changed. I can still do it."

"I never said you couldn't. While I was delivering my speech about the cabin sinks, I thought I'd try to get the reporters talking, maybe piece together some clues."

"Good idea. I'll do that as soon as Anne gets back from her break. Now, if you'll excuse me?"

The dumbfounded expression on Cody's face reminded Trudy Lynn of the time she'd stood up to him at Becky's. Back then, he'd been the grumpy one. This time, it was she who had set the strident tone of their exchange. She was already penitent. How could she hope to influence Cody for the good if she didn't treat him with civility? Moreover, the example she was setting of loving Christian behavior was sorely lacking.

She knew she should apologize. The trick was deciding what to say. In this case, blurting out the plain truth would be embarrassing to all concerned. She could just picture Cody's astonishment if she told him, "I was short-tempered because I apparently have a crush on you and you hurt my feelings when you wouldn't go for a canoe ride with me." Talk about a lame excuse for being uppity! Explained that way, her reaction was on a par with the temper tantrum of a spoiled brat. That comparison made her shudder.

Okay, so she wasn't perfect. At least she kept trying to be kinder and more understanding. Later, when she'd cooled off and was thinking clearly, she'd seek out Cody and tell him she was sorry she'd snapped at him. Given the tense atmosphere in the camp, he'd probably be able to accept that excuse for her being on edge. As long as he didn't insist she explain further, she'd be satisfied.

The afternoon passed in a blur. Trudy Lynn had long ago lost count of how many soft drinks, candy bars and bags of ice she'd sold. Doing an inventory and ordering another truckload of supplies midweek was going to be a top priority.

First, however, she was going to do herself a favor and escape. Her urge to grab a canoe and get away from the chaos in camp had been building ever since she'd suggested the trip to Cody. Just because he didn't want to accompany her didn't mean she had to sit there and go quietly nuts while the nosy reporters and concerned searchers looked at her askance, as if she might hold the answers to what had become of Jim.

The only person she confided in was Will. Trudy Lynn slipped down to the dock and took the old man aside. "I'm going downriver. If anybody asks, just tell them I stepped out for a few minutes."

"I don't know if this is such a good idea," Will said as he helped her launch a red canoe. "Jim might be out there, waitin' for somebody to drift by alone so's he can steal their boat or something."

"He'd have to catch me, first. You know I'm a wiz with a paddle."

Will started to mutter under his breath. She couldn't help teasing him. "One word about women being weak and I'll bean you with my purse. A blow like that could be fatal."

"That's 'cause it's full of all that heavy money you've been takin' in. Never knew you to carry a purse on the river, though, so I'll take my chances. Just see *you* don't take any."

"I won't. I plan to drift awhile, calm down and try to get my head on straight. This whole experience with Jim has made me way too irritable."

"You ought to take that Cody fella with you."

"I invited him. He turned me down."

The old man shrugged. "Okay. You're the boss. Where do you want me to send the van?"

"I don't know. I haven't decided how far I'll go yet." She patted her pocket. "I have my cell phone. I'll call after I land and tell you where to pick me up."

"Before nightfall?"

Chuckling, she nodded. "Yes, *Papa*. Before the sun goes down. I promise." A person in a familiar, bright blue jacket caught her eye. "Uh-oh. One of those stubborn reporters I've been avoiding is headed this way. Gotta go. Don't worry. I'll be fine. And don't let anybody follow me." She pointed. "Especially not her."

"Yes, ma'am."

Pushing off, Trudy Lynn paddled furiously. She hadn't believed there was any limit to her capacity for hospitality until recently. Now, she knew otherwise. All she wanted was for everybody to pack up and go home. Well, *almost* everybody. She wouldn't mind if Cody Keringhoven stayed a while longer.

Cody again, she mused. *Always Cody.*

As her paddle slid silently into the water with hardly a ripple she realized that Cody had slipped into her mind, into her heart, as effortlessly as that smooth paddle bisected the clear, cold water. He was already an integral part of her thoughts. And, like the river that flowed into the emptiness left by the retreating paddle and obliterated all sign of its passing, she couldn't look back and see how it had happened.

Cody finished turning the tables on the reporters, in spite of Trudy Lynn's admonition against it, and headed for the little store to report what he'd learned. By the time he'd worked his way through the crowd to talk to Anne, he was positive Trudy Lynn wasn't in the building. Widget was raising the roof in the back room.

He greeted the teen with a smile. "Hi. Boss lady gone?"

"Yup."

"You wouldn't happen to know where I'd find her, would you?"

"No. Sorry."

Cody leaned closer. "Want to give me a hint?"

The girl giggled. "You might ask Will. He knows everything."

"Thanks. I'll do that. Where would he be?"

She whispered behind her cupped hand. "He was supposed to help Farley work on the dock this afternoon."

"Got it. Thanks."

When he ducked out the door he noticed a few reporters gathering like turkey vultures circling fresh roadkill. Little wonder Trudy Lynn had felt the need to make herself scarce. If she'd given him any choice besides going by water, he'd have gladly joined her.

The Spring River was nothing like the Tuolumne, he reasoned, hoping to come to grips with his uneasiness. He'd never been hesitant to grab a boat and try to navigate any watercourse, no matter how dangerous, so what was stopping him now? What, indeed?

It wasn't fear. Not the way he'd felt it before. Only a fool would deny being afraid during a whitewater trip. That was what heightened the excitement, made the adrenaline flow. It was a familiar part of the exhilaration.

These current emotions were different. Unlike anything else he'd experienced. It was as if he loathed the water so much he didn't even want to look at it, let alone trust himself to enter it. Where before he'd seen beauty and power, he now saw ugliness and malice. His injured knee wasn't the only thing keeping him on dry land, was it? Part of his heart and soul had also died when his client had drowned so tragically, so needlessly.

Cody was grim from retrospection when he reached the dock where Will and Farley were nailing down replacement planks. He waited on shore till one of the men looked up.

"Anne sent me to see you, Will."

"Come on out, son."

"That's okay. Looks like you're almost done. I don't mind waiting."

The old man rose stiffly to his feet. "I see my cane worked for ya."

"Very well, thanks. It's been a pleasure to get rid of those crutches."

"Glad to help." Will walked closer, inspecting their work, board by board, as he came. "So, what can I do for ya this time? You ready to paddle your own canoe?" He cackled at the stale joke.

"No. Thanks anyway. I can't seem to find your boss. Anne told me you might know where she's hiding."

"I might."

"Well?"

"Miz Brown told me not to say." Drawing his fingers and thumb slowly down his cheeks to meet at the point of his chin, Will looked Cody up and down. "She didn't want no reporters buggin' her. But since she asked you to go along, I reckon it'd be okay to tell ya."

Icy needles of fear prickled along Cody's nerves. "She didn't take a canoe?"

"She sure did. 'Bout ten minutes ago. Say, you okay, son? You look kinda pale."

"I'm fine," Cody lied. His heart was pounding, his mouth so dry he could hardly swallow, let alone sound casual when he spoke. "Did she go alone?"

"Yep. I tried to talk her out of it but she's one stubborn lady. There's not a lot of traffic on the river this late in the day, especially not till the time changes to daylight saving next month. She promised me she'd go ashore and call for the van before dark."

Concerned, Cody shaded his eyes and squinted at the setting sun. "How long does she have?"

"An hour and a half. Maybe two. Depends on the lay of the land."

Something inside Cody kept insisting he had to act, even though the thought almost made him gag. He pointed to an empty canoe. "How hard is it to man one of those?"

"Not hard at all," Will said. "It might be a little tough to balance or kneel to paddle with that stiff leg of yours but I wouldn't worry. Compared to them rapids you're used to, this river's easy as pie. Want me to set you up?"

"Yes," Cody said. He gritted his teeth. "Give me the works, life vest and all. If I turn the thing over I don't want to have to try to tread water."

"Might do you good," the old man offered. "I hear swimmin' is good fer bad joints."

"In warm water," Cody replied. "Trudy Lynn told

me this comes from an underground spring about thirty miles north. She says it's so cold when it hits the surface they built a trout hatchery at the headwaters."

"True enough. Them trout love it. The colder the water the better."

"I'll take your word for it," Cody said flatly.

Shrugging into the bright orange life vest he slipped a map of the river into his pocket, then cautiously climbed into the waiting canoe while Farley and Will steadied it. Thankfully, there was enough room to stretch his sore leg as far as he needed for comfort.

"Okay. I'm in," he said. "I've been to all the landings with Trudy so I know what they look like. I'll catch up to her unless it gets too dark to see."

Will handed him the cane. "Better take this, too. Some of that country's pretty rugged."

"Yeah, I know." Cody gritted his teeth and steeled himself for what he was about to do. "Push me off," he said hoarsely. "I'm ready."

Chapter Eleven

Peace flowed over Trudy Lynn like the ripples bathing the smooth rocks beneath her canoe. She dangled her fingertips in the water and drifted with the slow current. Few course corrections were necessary in this deeper portion of the river. Water levels were holding higher than normal since the heavy rain they'd had the day Jim had disappeared, and she skimmed along above submerged hazards she'd have had to paddle around in drier times.

A red squirrel on the east bank realized he had company and scampered up the closest oak. Watching him, Trudy Lynn noticed dozens of robins. Spring was here all right. Soon, the flock would pair off and the migrating purple martins would arrive. The meadowlarks would begin their morning serenades and the steady calls of the whip-poor-will would lull her to sleep every night.

She sighed. Too bad *her* life wasn't that simple.

Just when she thought she had it all figured out, along came another problem. A vivid image of Cody Keringhoven popped into her mind. *Speaking of problems.*

One quick assessment of the river told her it would be safe to close her eyes for a moment of prayer. Where should she begin? What should she ask? If she knew *that,* she'd have the dilemma half-solved.

Finally, she whispered, "Father, thank you for all this. For letting me live here." Gratitude filled her heart to overflowing. "This is a beautiful place and I am grateful for everything. I just need help dealing with the people."

Boy, was that the truth. Give her birds and squirrels and Widget and she'd be totally content, she told herself. Was that true? Was she really happy single? She'd certainly thought so until very recently. Until she'd been given the chance to spend time with Cody. Was the Lord using him to try to tell her she was on the wrong track?

Trudy Lynn's eyes popped open. She blinked in the brightness. *Whoa.* Cody might be someone's idea of the perfect husband but he certainly wasn't hers. For one thing, he was way too opinionated. Too bossy. Then again, maybe God merely wanted her to open her mind to the possibility of marriage. Even Adam had needed his Eve. It would be comforting to have someone to share both her good times and her burdens. Yeah. Like now.

Her worried musings turned to her cousin. How could Jim have vanished so completely? Finding a life vest and damaged paddle was worrisome enough. Losing a full-size canoe was nearly impossible. Even if it had floated further than normal due to the flooding, it would run aground eventually. Her camp ID and logo were stenciled on it. It should have turned up by now and so should Jim.

Lost in a fog of contradictory thoughts, Trudy Lynn had quit paying much attention to the passing scene. A cloud of aggravating gnats buzzed around her head. A hungry one landed on her forearm.

"Ouch!" She swatted and missed. The tiny insect's escape route took it up and away, to her left. Waving her hands to disperse the swirling mass of insects she caught a flash of unusual color in her peripheral vision.

Seconds passed before she reacted. Her head snapped around. Eyes wide, she scanned the bank. Nothing seemed amiss. Still, if she let herself continue to drift on by, she'd always wonder if she should have stopped to take a better look.

Grabbing her paddle, Trudy Lynn dropped the blade into the water and used its drag like a rudder to swing the bow of the canoe toward shore. Rather than fight against the current, she'd hit the beach and hike back. It wouldn't take long. All she wanted to do was assure herself that what she'd glimpsed was unimportant. Chances were good it was nothing but a pile of trash a group of campers or picnickers had left behind.

She was ashore before she realized what a poor choice the rocky, wooded terrain was for socializing. Flying insects would be enough to discourage most tourists, and the bugs hiding on the forest floor, more than ready to dine on man or beast, would deter the diehards.

Removing her life vest and leaving it behind so it wouldn't catch on the undergrowth and slow her down, she headed into the forest. The sooner she satisfied her curiosity and got back on the river where she belonged, the happier she'd be.

Cody easily mastered maneuvers with the paddle. Now that he was committed, his misgivings were lessening. If he'd had any choice he still wouldn't have wanted to go canoeing, yet he did seem to be coping pretty well. That was a relief, given his earlier uneasiness.

Trudy Lynn hadn't exaggerated when she'd claimed it was peaceful on the Spring River. After the Tuolumne, this trip would have seemed almost boring if he hadn't been on a mission. Catching up to Trudy was the most important quest Cody had undertaken in ages. If he'd had any inkling that his hardheaded landlady was going to wander off alone, he'd have forced himself to accompany her no matter how disconcerted he'd felt. If anything bad happened…

He paddled faster. Muscles that had once piloted him through raging rapids and over foaming cataracts adopted a familiar rhythm. Cody likened himself to a marathon runner who was so focused on reaching a goal he refused to acknowledge fatigue. Good thing, too. Judging by the rosy glow in the west he was running out of time.

Brambles caught in Trudy Lynn's T-shirt and scratched her bare legs, making her wish she'd worn jeans instead of walking shorts. She could tell how high the river had most recently crested by noting the undulating piles of dead leaves and twigs it had deposited along the upper banks. No wonder poor Jim had lost some of his equipment. He must have been caught in a fearsome torrent.

One foot slipped in the slick mud, dropping her to her knees. She righted herself and grabbed a deadfall for balance. Leaving her canoe had been a mistake. Here she was, in the middle of nowhere, covered with gummy, red mud, rotting leaves and disgusting slime, chasing figments of her imagination that had probably never existed in the first place. If she hurt herself, no telling how long it would be before rescuers found her.

"I should turn back and forget it," she muttered. That was excellent advice. Unfortunately, a contrary part of her character refused to be deterred by logic. It couldn't be much farther to the place where she'd seen the flash of color. As soon as she was satisfied it was nothing, she'd gladly make for the nearest landing and phone Will to come get her.

The vegetation grew thicker, harder to traverse. A stand of young hickory trees was almost impenetrable. Trudy Lynn was about to call it quits when she spied another bright spot of paint. It was red, as she'd thought, but it wasn't trash. Even without seeing a number or name, she knew. It was one of her canoes. And the only one unaccounted for was the one Jim had taken the day he'd disappeared.

It took Trudy Lynn several more minutes to fight her way to her goal. Flood or no flood, it was clear the canoe hadn't wound up that far out of the water by accident. Though it may have floated in this direction while unmanned, it hadn't pulled itself up the bank and covered its own hull with loose brush for camouflage.

Uneasy, she stopped and peered into the surrounding woods. Shadows had deepened while she'd been on foot. Details were dimmer. Not only was the sun obviously setting, nearby trees were so close together they blocked out the usual patterns of dappled, filtered light on the leaf-strewn ground.

An unexplained tingle skittered up her spine. The fine hairs on the back of her neck tickled. She wrapped her arms around her torso and shivered, head to toe, before finding enough willpower to re-claim her self-control.

Being afraid was ridiculous. These woods were her home, her solace, her place to hide when the out-side world began to close in.

Dwelling on that truth, she managed to relax a bit, though she couldn't totally banish the innate urge to chatter whether there was anyone else present or not.

"What I do next is critical," she told herself, calmed by the sound of her own voice. "I have to tag a tree next to the water so I can locate this place again when I bring the police. And I need to back out of this thicket so I don't disturb the ground any more than I already have."

Such sensible planning triggered a smile. At last she had a plausible excuse for reading all those mys-tery stories Will kept teasing her about. Hopefully, she'd learned enough from them to do her—and the police—some good.

She took several steps backward, then halted. "What if poor Jim is in the canoe? He could be hurt. Or worse."

If she crept closer to peek, she'd know for sure. If she didn't let curiosity get the better of her, however, any footprints or other clues to his disappearance would be preserved. Which choice made the most sense?

Trudy Lynn had encountered dead animals in the woods a few times. Their stench was unforgettable.

The air she was currently breathing was clear, fresh, unsullied, proving there were no dead bodies close by. And since no one who was incapacitated could have buried the canoe that well with himself still inside, she was reassured.

Satisfied, she gave in to the growing urge to turn and flee. Since her hands, knees and shoes were already covered with mud she took no pains to proceed slowly and avoid getting dirtier. Her impulsiveness led to a slipping, sliding descent to the river, punctuated by an occasional "Oof," or "Ugh."

She'd almost reached her beached canoe when a guttural, angry-sounding "Stop!" stood her hair on end.

She froze. Whirled. Stared, openmouthed. The man crouched on the low bluff directly above her was terrifying! He had wild, stringy hair and a beard in the same condition. His shadowed figure conveyed so much malice it took away what little breath she had left. In his hand was a rifle or shotgun, she couldn't tell which, and his clothing looked as if he'd put it on years ago and hadn't taken it off since.

"You're trespassing!" he roared. "Who are you? What are you doing here?"

Trudy Lynn hoped the good Lord would forgive her for telling a bold-faced lie because this seemed like a very dangerous moment to admit the truth. "I got lost," she called back. "Don't worry. I'm leaving."

Instead of the chastising she'd expected, the man gave a bearlike bellow and charged!

Trudy Lynn didn't know she was screaming till she heard the piercing wails and realized they had to be coming from her! She planted both hands on the prow of the canoe and shoved it into the river as far as she could wade, then gave one last mighty push and heaved herself aboard.

Instead of continuing forward, the canoe came to an abrupt halt and began rocking. Violently. She knew what she'd see before she looked back. Her pursuer had her! And he was starting to reel her in like a helpless fish.

Her paddle lay on the floor beneath her. She grabbed it and flailed wildly at him. The edge of the blade cracked against the metal rim of the canoe. With a maniacal laugh the man yanked the splintered weapon out of her hands and turned it on her.

Trudy Lynn ducked, stumbled, backpedaled. She had only a split second in which to decide. If she dived over the side she might have a better chance of survival. Staying in the canoe like a sitting duck was out of the question. There was no telling what her attacker might do if—when—he got his filthy hands on her.

I knew I should have polished up my swimming skills. Well, it was too late for regrets. From here on she'd have to either wade, swim as best she could or drown. Given this man's aura of rage and menace, any of those choices would be preferable to letting him get close enough to touch her.

A woman's screams echoed up the river and across the hills, confusing the direction the sound was coming from. Cody strained to listen. He had no idea if Trudy Lynn was the one yelling. He didn't care. Anyone that scared needed help. Fast. Hopefully, he was close enough to give it.

He plied the paddle skillfully and sent the canoe skimming along, faster and faster. In the distance, a male voice was shouting curses. Something crashed. Splintered. Banged. It sounded like a dozen men were brawling just around the next bend in the river. He had to be getting close.

The woman's screeching suddenly ceased. Cody's heart leaped, bringing the bitter taste of gall to his throat. Silence was a bad sign. It meant the situation had changed, probably not for the better.

Slewing around a curve he spotted another canoe. A man was standing in the water next to it, hip deep. Perhaps he was trying to rescue someone. That would explain the shouting.

Cody continued his rapid approach. He saw the man climb into the canoe and kneel to use his hands as oars. Sighting along a line to where the other boat was headed, Cody saw a figure splashing in the water.

He was farther away but his pace was much faster.

Chances were good he'd reach the swimmer first. Elated, he shouted, "Hang on. I'm coming!"

When the person in the water screamed, "Cody!" then went under, his gut tied in a knot. He'd found Trudy Lynn.

If this is what it's like to die I don't like it. Where are the bright lights? The comforting feelings?

Trudy Lynn's toes touched bottom. Instinct spurred her to bend her knees enough for a powerful jump.

She popped to the surface, gasping and spitting. Had she really seen Cody a moment ago? Or was hallucinating an element of death by drowning?

Wet hair plastered to her face and hampered her vision. She managed another "Cody?" and a few wild strokes with her arms before going under again. This time, however, she'd grabbed a gulp of air and knew what to do.

Using the uneven riverbed as a springboard she bobbed up and down like a fish on a Pogo stick. Current kept pushing her along, yet every time she surfaced, both canoes were definitely closer. To her great relief, the one coming at her from the bank wasn't moving nearly as swiftly as the one from upriver— the one she hoped and prayed Cody was in.

It took three more bounces and a mouthful of water before Trudy Lynn was certain. It *was* Cody! She'd never been so glad to see anybody in her whole life. She didn't care if he had refused to come with her in the first place. He was here now, when it counted.

Suddenly, it occurred to her that she wasn't the only one in danger. She and Cody both were. Her attacker had dropped his gun on shore when he'd grabbed her canoe but that didn't mean he wasn't armed with a knife or something equally deadly. Plus, he was built like a grizzly bear and had an even nastier disposition. The chance of Cody being able to pull her on board with him and facilitate an escape before they were attacked was slim. Very slim. He wouldn't even try to get away because he didn't have a clue how much trouble they were in.

"Look out!" she screeched.

Down she went, this time without a full breath. It seemed like hours before she returned to the surface. Between racking coughs she hollered, "Bad!" and gestured wildly at the slower canoe.

Had Cody understood? Dog-paddling she tossed her head to flip her dripping hair away from her eyes and blinked rapidly to clear her vision. It was no use. She couldn't see his face well enough to judge.

The constant, simple prayer, *God, help us,* kept running through her mind. Even if she'd been able to come up with a more spiritual-sounding plea, this was clearly not the time for fancy words. They were in deep trouble. Getting out of it was going to take more than mere physical ability. If any situation in her life had ever needed divine intervention, this was it.

Cody was confused. Will had been certain his boss had set out alone. So who was the other rescuer? What had happened to Trudy Lynn's canoe? And why had she removed her life vest and gone into the water when she knew she was a poor swimmer? None of it made sense, especially not the guy trying to row after her using nothing but his bare hands.

"It's okay. I'll get her," Cody called.

He wouldn't have taken his eyes off Trudy Lynn for an instant if the other man hadn't cursed in reply. He chanced a swift glance. The malice reflected in the dark glare that met his was all the clarification Cody needed. Whatever the guy's motive was for going after Trudy Lynn, it sure wasn't benevolent.

The scenario took on a totally different connotation. Cody stiffened, wary. Getting Trudy Lynn out of the water and into his canoe should be pretty easy. Doing that while facing opposition promised to be trickier.

He'd planned to steer to her right, positioning himself so the other canoe could assist. Now, his plans changed.

He turned the blade of his paddle to add drag at the last second, altered course to put himself between Trudy and the other man and reached for her. One of her hands was all that wasn't submerged. Grabbing it and hanging on, he pulled her over the side so she hung beside him, head down in the boat, feet still in the water.

"Breathe!" he ordered. "Breathe."

The sweetest sound he'd ever heard was her gagging, hacking cough. "That's it, honey. Don't fight it. Get it all out."

She raised her head slightly and tried unsuccessfully to speak.

Cody thumped her between her shoulder blades. "I know. He's bad news. I figured that out." The other canoe was nearing. "I'll take care of it."

Her faint "Be careful" warmed his heart.

"I will. Hang on. I'm going to pull you the rest of the way in just in case things get rough."

To his delight and further relief, Trudy Lynn had regained enough strength to help him. Though she still sounded as if she was trying to imitate Sailor's barking, she sat up as soon as she was fully aboard.

Her eyes were red and wild-looking. Her hair was streaming river water. Her arms and calves were covered with welts and scratches. Cody's heart rejoiced. He had never been so glad to see her.

There were only a few seconds left before the other canoe would pull alongside. Cupping her cheeks, he drew her closer and placed a light kiss on her forehead.

Tears filled Trudy Lynn's eyes and slid, unnoticed, down her already wet face. She was so relieved, so thankful, she just wanted to throw herself into Cody's arms, cling to him and sob. A shred of sensibility held her back. Cody was already at a physical disadvantage. Adding emotion to the mix and distracting him from the danger, even for an instant, would be idiotic.

Cody swiveled his torso and faced his foe. "We're fine. Everything's under control. You can go."

"I ain't goin' nowhere. I'll take care of both of you if I have to," came the gravelly reply.

Nothing about the man's threat struck Trudy Lynn as a show of false bravado. She could tell that Cody agreed, because his fists were clenched and he was clearly bracing for an attack. If the two men had been standing, toe-to-toe, Cody's injured knee would have been a significant negative factor. Seated, however, they were more evenly matched.

"Oh, please, God," she whispered prayerfully.

Cody didn't look a bit worried, certainly not as frazzled as she felt.

"I don't see the problem here," Cody told the man evenly. "Suppose I take the lady on down the river with me? Would that satisfy you?"

"Humph." He let out a string of curses. "Don't suppose it would. She was trespassin' on my land."

"In that case, we apologize. If there was any damage done we'll be happy to make restitution. Just contact the Spring River Camp or send a bill. You know where that's located, don't you."

"Oh, yeah," the swarthy man drawled. "I surely do."

Trudy Lynn laid her hand on Cody's arm to get his attention and felt his skin twitch beneath her touch. "Don't tell him any more."

He cast a sidelong glance in her general direction while continuing to focus most of his attention on their accuser. "Why not? It's no secret. All he has to do is look at the names printed on your canoes."

"I know, but…" She cupped her hand around her mouth and leaned closer to whisper, "I found the one Jim took. Somebody tried to bury it. It's right over there."

Although she didn't actually point, Trudy Lynn did stare at the thicket where she'd uncovered the missing canoe. Too late, she realized she'd inadvertently done the very thing she'd vowed to avoid. She'd distracted Cody.

A dark blur rose up on one side of them. The other man leaped and tackled Cody squarely in the chest.

Trudy Lynn shouted, "Look out!" but her warning came too late. Momentum carried both men over the side with a sickening splash.

Stunned, she watched them sink. Together.

Chapter Twelve

The shock of hitting the water wasn't incapacitating. The vivid recollection of the last time he'd been catapulted into an icy river was. Cody didn't feel pain, only sorrow and deep regret. His brain tried to shelter him by shutting off all thought while his life jacket gave him the buoyancy to rise to the surface without trying.

The pressure of strong hands grasping his throat snapped him back to reality. He slipped both hands between his opponent's arms and shoved upward, breaking the viselike grip.

Instead of immediately resuming his efforts to strangle Cody, the man clutched at his life vest and tore it away, then grabbed him again and pulled him under.

Cody kicked and tore at his opponent, oblivious to anything but the danger to Trudy Lynn. He didn't even want to think about what might happen to her if he was defeated.

Freeing himself once again, he struck out for the surface. For life-giving air. As soon as his head was out of the water he rejoiced. Trudy Lynn was still safe in his canoe. What a relief!

He gulped down a quick breath and shouted, "Stay back!" while he waited for his attacker to pop up nearby.

Something grabbed his ankle instead. Pulled him under. Kept him there till he thought his lungs would burst. It was impossible to throw a forceful punch through water. If this fight came to a contest of brute strength, Cody wasn't positive he'd win. He wasn't filled with brilliant ideas for outsmarting his opponent, either.

The top of his head banged against a hull, making a hollow thud. The attacker's empty boat must be directly above them. He didn't know exactly how canoes behaved when inverted but he could guess. Large inflatable rafts were hard to get out from under, especially in a swift current, and this stretch of the river was gaining speed. If he could turn the canoe over unexpectedly, maybe that would give him an advantage. It was worth a try. At this point, anything was.

Cody lunged. Twisted into position. Set his feet. Using his opponent as a springboard he managed to thrust one arm out of the water far enough to grab the side rim of the empty canoe. If the other man continued to try to drag him down, the combined mass of Cody and the canoe should provide the necessary counterbalance.

It did. Cody would have cheered if he hadn't been submerged. Experience told him a small pocket of air was waiting beneath the overturned hull. Gasping, he bobbed into the empty space and filled his aching lungs while his confused enemy swam away. The question was, which way had the guy gone? Toward Trudy Lynn?

Frustrated with himself for being unsure, Cody took one last gulping breath before ducking out from under the inverted hull. As his head broke the surface he swiveled. His heart stopped. "No!"

The attacker had grabbed onto the side of the canoe Trudy Lynn occupied and was working his way toward her, hand over hand.

"The paddle!" Cody shouted. "Use the paddle!"

"No! I won't leave you." She dodged the grasping fingers that kept clawing at her.

"Not to *row* with," Cody bellowed. "Hit him!"

Trudy Lynn didn't have to be told twice. Loving her neighbor had ended the minute said neighbor had tried to drown Cody.

The oar shaft fit her fists like a baseball bat. She wasn't going to make the mistake of swinging at the man's hands and breaking this paddle the way she had the other one. No, sir. She was going to do what she had to do.

Thoughts of personal accountability made her hesitate for an instant. Was it really right to bash him? What if she *killed* him?

"Leave us alone," she shouted shrilly. "Just leave us alone. We weren't hurting you."

The man's laugh was abrasive. "You are dumber than dirt, aren't you?" He wiggled his fingers. "C'mon. Give me that thing. Hand it over. Or else."

While she and the swarthy man had been arguing, Cody had swum into reach. Trudy Lynn's wide-eyed gaze touched on him. Too late, she realized her carelessness had cost him the element of surprise.

The attacker's eyes narrowed. Looking over his shoulder he grinned with malevolence. "I thought I was rid of you. Guess I'm gonna have to whup you some more."

Trudy Lynn could see pain in Cody's eyes. There was no telling how badly this encounter had affected his injured leg. Well, she wasn't going to just sit there and let him be hurt anymore.

The man let go of the canoe and made a lunge for Cody's throat.

That did it. Trudy Lynn drew back and swung. The horrible noise of the broadside to the man's head echoed in her ears and lingered in her conscience. It had sounded for all the world like a ripe watermelon being dropped onto a hard surface!

Cody lifted his foe's face out of the water.

"Did I kill him?" Trudy Lynn asked breathlessly. "I didn't mean to hit him so hard. Honest, I didn't."

"He's not dead, just groggy," Cody answered. "He'll probably have a headache, though. Help me get him out of the water. Then we'll call the sheriff. This time, we have proof."

Trudy Lynn peered into lengthening shadows along the shore. "Not exactly. We've drifted way past the place where I found Jim's canoe. I'm pretty sure I can locate it again if we start upstream and float down in the daylight, but it's way too late to go back and try it, now."

"Okay." Cody rolled the man's limp body onto its back and hooked one arm under the bearded chin. Held that way, his burden floated safely and with little effort. "Think you can tow us in like this?"

"Sure. After the day I've had I can do anything."

"I'll settle for hitching a ride to shore and finding the quickest way out of this jungle," Cody said. "I don't know about you, but I'm beat."

Trudy Lynn's heart swelled with pride in her rescuer. "You were wonderful. I don't know what I'd have done if you hadn't come along when you did."

"I don't even want to think about it."

"I do," she replied. "I'll never forget today. I have no doubt you saved my life. If there's ever anything I can do to pay you back, just let me know. No matter what it is or how much it costs. All you have to do is say the word and I'll do whatever I can. I promise."

"Good. Then how about you stop talking and start rowing. Our friend is beginning to wiggle. The sooner we get him tied up so he can't cause any more trouble, the happier I'll be."

"I'm pretty happy already." Trudy Lynn grinned. Plying the paddle skillfully, she rowed them toward shore at an angle, using the current to assist.

"You should be happy," Cody said. "Looks like we're finally going to get some answers about your cousin."

"Oh, that. Right." A rush of embarrassment colored her cheeks. They'd reached the shallows where Cody was able to stand. Vaulting over the side of the boat into the waist-deep water, Trudy Lynn helped him haul his semi-conscious burden onto dry land.

"We'd better hurry. He's waking up," Cody said. "Grab the mooring rope off the canoe. We'll tie him to a tree till the sheriff gets here."

Her head snapped around. "Oops. Looks like I'm going to have to get wet again."

"You let it drift? I don't believe this."

"Don't get excited, okay? I didn't take time to beach it because I was in a hurry to help you. It's no big deal. I'll get it back." She was already moving that direction.

"You can't swim well, remember?"

The gruffness of his voice rankled her. "I'm not

likely to forget. I'm just going to wade out a little way."

"No. You stay here. I'll go."

"Don't be silly. I do this kind of thing all the time."

Trudy Lynn quickly retrieved the canoe, dragged it up the bank and untied the braided nylon rope at its bow.

Jaw set, eyes narrowed, Cody stared at her. "You don't have to keep reminding me you're more capable than I am."

"What? What are you talking about?"

"Chasing that loose canoe. I may not be as fast on my feet as you are but I could have caught it."

"I know that."

"You don't act like you do."

Trudy Lynn rolled her eyes to emphasize how silly she thought he was. "You were busy. I certainly didn't want to trade places with you and have our friend wake up while you were gone. I chase loose boats all the time. If I'd waited till we were done arguing about who should go, the stupid canoe could have drifted out of everybody's reach. *Then* where would we be? On foot, that's where."

She thrust the coil of rope at him. "Here. Do you want this or don't you?"

Cody's initial hesitation and the begrudging way he finally accepted the rope told her he wasn't convinced she'd meant no disrespect. Well, too bad. He was going to have to get used to the way she took charge when something needed to be done. She wasn't about to sit back and act like a helpless female in need of coddling. Her mother had been that kind of woman and look what had happened.

Thinking of her father's kindness reminded her of how much she'd sensed the same tender concern from Cody. He cared. That was why he'd snapped at her for going into the river again.

Approaching as soon as he'd finished trussing their captive to a tree, Trudy Lynn placed her hand on his forearm in a show of conciliation. "I'm sorry. You were right. It was stupid of me not to stop and put on a life vest."

His astonished reaction made her giggle. "Hey, don't look so surprised. I do occasionally make mistakes. There just wasn't time to explain. Your canoe was about to break out into the faster current and…"

"I know that," Cody said. "I shouldn't have jumped to conclusions. I'm sorry, too." A half smile began to lift the corner of his mouth. "So, are you done scaring me to death?"

"I hope so."

"Good. Then let's call the sheriff. My cell phone's so full of water it gurgles. Do you have a dry one?"

"No. My pack was in the canoe that turned over."

"Terrific. How far is it to the next landing?"

"Less than a mile." Eyeing their captive she noticed he was beginning to struggle against his bonds. "Will it be safe to leave him for a little while?"

"He won't get away," Cody said flatly.

"I'm more worried about his head. He acts like he's okay but I conked him awfully hard."

"The sooner we get to a phone and call, the sooner he can be checked out by a doctor. Come on. Let's go."

Trudy Lynn paused and stopped him with a gentle touch. "Wait. I want to thank you."

"You already did."

"I mean properly."

Standing on tiptoe, she slipped her hands around his neck, tilted her head back and felt his warm breath on her face. Ever since he'd hauled her out of the river and kissed her on the forehead she'd wanted to do this. There might never be a better time than right now.

"I was coughing so much you got it all wrong." She smiled as she pointed to her lips. "It goes right here."

"What does?"

There was no question he was teasing. The sparkle in his azure eyes confirmed it. "This," she said, an instant before she kissed him gently, briefly. "Thank you for saving my life."

The ambulance got lost on unmarked dirt roads so the sheriff loaded the injured man into his car and personally delivered him to the hospital.

Trudy Lynn had called Will from the landing and

told him to bring the truck with the overhead rack to haul the canoes home. She and Cody had instructions to report to the sheriff's office as soon as possible.

Wedged into the front seat of the pickup between Will and Cody, she shivered. "I may never get warm again."

Cody's arm had been draped across the back of the seat. He lowered it and patted her opposite shoulder. "It's probably shock more than temperature that's making you feel cold. Maybe we'd better take you to the emergency room for a checkup, too."

"Oh, no. That's where the sheriff took that man. I'm not going anywhere near him."

To her left, Will chuckled. "Scared ya good, did he?"

"You could say that."

She gazed up at Cody, supremely grateful for his strength and levelheadedness in the recent crisis. "I'm thankful we both survived. I had my doubts for a while there, especially when that canoe flipped over on top of you. It never dawned on me you'd done it on purpose."

"I was kind of short of options." His hold tightened just enough to let her know his arm was still around her. "I'd have preferred working in a faster current. I'm more used to handling myself in that kind of situation."

"I think you did just fine," she said.

"So did you. That's quite a swing you have."

She grimaced. "Don't remind me. I feel awful about it."

"You shouldn't."

"Yes, I should. I'm supposed to trust the Lord to take care of me."

Cody's rich laughter rose above Will's accompanying chuckle.

Trudy Lynn scowled. "Okay, you two. What's so funny?"

"You are," Cody said. "I can't help thinking of how handy that paddle was when you needed it. I doubt God expects us to sit back and act like helpless victims, especially not when He's provided a means of self-defense."

"Right," the older man said. "The Good Book's full of teachin' like that." He cackled. "'Course, it's also possible He was usin' *you* to take care of our girl."

Trudy Lynn let centrifugal force slue her against Cody as the truck rounded a corner, then stayed close to him by choice. "I have to agree," she said, nodding. "If you hadn't pulled me out of the river when you did, I wouldn't have been alive to swing a paddle."

She saw his eyes close briefly before he sighed and said, "I know."

There was so much poignancy and heartfelt relief in his voice she almost wept.

"I may have seen the man before," Trudy Lynn told the sheriff a little later, "but I can't place him. The important thing is, I found Jim's canoe."

"So you say. Are you sure?"

"Positive."

"You saw the name and number on it, then?"

"Well, no, but…" She looked to Cody for moral support. There was rancor and disbelief in the way he was staring at the lawman.

"If Ms. Brown says she found one of her canoes, she found one. Period," Cody said firmly. "What're you going to do about it?"

The portly sheriff shrugged. "Tonight? Nothing. Buford swears that boat is his and he caught you two trespassing. They're keepin' him in the hospital at least till tomorrow. For observation, they said. That's some knot on the head you gave him. You'll be lucky if Buford don't press charges."

"Press charges for self-defense?" Cody was scowling.

"Your word against his. He is the one who landed in the emergency room."

"For good reason," Cody argued.

"Maybe. No sense gettin' carried away. A little neighborly kindness might settle the whole thing."

Cody got to his feet. "We'll see what the state police have to say about that." He looked to Trudy Lynn. "Come on. Let's go before I say something I'll be sorry for."

"Good luck," the sheriff drawled. "Those state boys packed up their trucks and lit out while you two were beatin' up poor ol' Buford. I reckon they're all the way to Little Rock by now."

"Then we'll phone their office in the morning," Trudy Lynn said. Head high, spine stiff, she led the way out of the building. Once she and Cody were back on the street, however, she began to show fatigue and disillusionment.

"You okay?" he asked.

"Fine." She gave him a wry smile. "No, not fine. Did he just call me a liar?"

"Not exactly. But it did sound like he thinks you're a hysterical female who was imagining things."

"That's almost as bad."

"*I* believe you."

"I know you do. Thanks. That means a lot to me."

Trudy Lynn saw him start to reach for her hand, then stop himself. Little wonder. She'd probably scared him to death when she'd kissed him. What had come over her? She wasn't the kind to pass out affection carelessly so why in the world had she given in to such an irrational urge? The man must think the worst of her.

Well, why shouldn't he? she countered. *I certainly think it.*

Try as she might, Trudy Lynn couldn't come up with an acceptable rationale for the unusual way she had behaved. Thankfulness didn't cover it. Neither did being free from danger. She'd been beholden to others in the past and hadn't felt the need to throw herself into their arms as a result. What was it about Cody Keringhoven that brought out the wild side of her?

Perhaps *wild* wasn't the right term. She hadn't felt out of control. On the contrary, she'd sensed a strength of purpose, a need to reveal her emotions and see what Cody's response might be. Now that she'd seen his reaction, however, she was beginning to wish she'd kept her distance.

She sighed. "Well, what now? I suppose we should let Will take us back to camp."

"Sounds like a good idea to me." Cody used the cane as he walked beside her toward the waiting truck. "We're both dead tired. And we need a phone."

"To call Little Rock?"

"Yes. Are you up to it or shall I do it for you?"

"Whatever." Trudy Lynn shrugged. "I'm too tired and sore to care." She paused, her hand on the door handle of the pickup. "Shame on me. Here I am, complaining over little aches and pains like a sissy when it's you I should be thinking of. How's your leg?"

"Forget it. It's okay." Cody reached to open the door for her.

"No, it's not okay."

"Yes, it is." He swung the door back and gestured as Will started the motor. "In you go."

"But you're limping."

"I always do," Cody said solemnly. "That's never going to change."

"Like the color of your eyes. They'll always be blue."

"I beg your pardon?"

Giving him a satisfied smile she scooted to the center of the bench seat to make room. "Blue eyes are part of how you're made. You're used to them because you've always had them but there's really no difference between that and your limp. It just *is*. Like being tall or short, blond or brunette—you get the idea."

"There's no comparison." Cody climbed in and slammed the door.

"Sure there is. You've been so busy thinking about what's wrong or different, you've lost sight of the stuff that's wonderful."

"Wonderful?" He tapped the tip of the cane on his shoe. "You call this wonderful? Humph. I sure don't."

"Maybe that's because you've forgotten who made you in the first place. Or who kept you out of the accident that killed your mother. Or who guided your sister to look for her birth family and reunited all of you. Or who put you in the right place at the right time to come to my rescue."

"You mean God." It wasn't a question.

"Yes, I do. Think about it. Every time you complain you dishonor your creator. You're as worthwhile in God's eyes as you were before. It's time you recognized your value as a human being and started thanking Him for sparing your life instead of griping about a little limp."

Cody stared at her. "Are you through?"

"Yes." She pulled a face and bowed her head rather than continue to make eye contact with him. "I guess so. I can't think of anything else to say."

Will guffawed when Cody said, "Now that I *am* thankful for."

Chapter Thirteen

Cody hadn't dozed off till nearly dawn. As long as his brain was racing, there was no way he could unwind enough to sleep.

He'd spoken to a dispatcher at the Arkansas State Police headquarters as soon as he and the others had gotten back to camp. The men who had been looking into Jim's disappearance had other duties. It seemed that Jim was no longer considered a high priority according to the local sheriff.

Cody couldn't blame them for pulling out; he just wished their orders had come through a day or two later. He flexed his knee. It hurt. That figured. The big surprise was how little its condition had changed. In spite of all the stress of the fight and subsequent short hike to the landing, he didn't feel any worse than before.

"Trudy Lynn would call that a blessing," he muttered. Well, maybe she was right. Maybe it was. At least he was still on his feet and hadn't had to go back to using crutches. That meant their next move wasn't as limited as he'd originally thought.

During the night, he'd decided they should revisit the scene of the attack as soon as possible. They needed to act before good old Buford was discharged from the hospital. Once the man was back on the street there was no telling how fast he'd be able to dispose of the canoe and any other evidence tying Jim to his property—including the young man's dead body.

Cody was about to ask for a ride up the hill to the camp store when he heard the ATV stop outside. Sailor was panting, wagging and eagerly looking at the closed door.

To Cody's delight his caller was Trudy Lynn instead of Will. "Hi! I was about to call you. I had an idea."

"Me, too."

She bent to greet Sailor with open arms and was almost bowled over by his exuberance. Ruffling his silky ears she smiled at Cody. "I found out more about Buford. Will says the guy owns hundreds of acres of forest land that he's never done anything with. Everybody assumed he was saving it for hunting, especially after he painted the perimeter trees with that lavender-colored paint they use for posting, and stuck up No Hunting signs on every corner. Most of the land is inaccessible except by water, which is why the ambulance had so much trouble finding their way."

"I wonder how the sheriff managed."

"He's an old-timer. Been here all his life. Will says Buford and the sheriff used to go fishing and hunting together when they were young. I imagine that's how he learned his way around."

"Interesting."

"I thought so." Trudy Lynn straightened. "I'm not saying the sheriff is crooked or anything. I doubt he is. But in view of that personal connection I think it might be wise to try to locate Jim's canoe again. Maybe take a few pictures. Our new buddy is still in the hospital. I checked. I'm heading downriver right now. Want to come along?"

Cody chuckled softly. "Gladly. They say great minds think alike. That's exactly what I was about to suggest."

"You're not going to beg off this time?"

"Not a chance, lady." Coming down the steps with the help of the hand-carved cane, he paused. "If I thought I could find that canoe by myself I'd leave you behind. Since that's probably impossible, I'm going to stick to you like glue. Buford may have friends we don't know about. I'm not letting you go out there alone."

"You think I can't take care of myself?"

"I know you can't. Remember?"

"How could I forget? You keep reminding me."

"I'll stop mentioning it as soon as you quit acting like you still think you're invincible," Cody said soberly. "I used to believe I was the best, that the Tuolumne couldn't touch me because I knew it so well. I was wrong. I was no more in charge in that situation than you are in this one."

"I know." Trudy Lynn reached to gently pat his cheek. "The difference is, I don't see my life as a series of random events. I may not have control in the way you meant but I trust God to bring me through. Somehow." She began to smile crookedly. "That said, I'd still swing an oar again if I felt I had to."

He stood, gazed into her eyes for a long moment, then nodded. "Good. Let me shut Sailor in the cabin and I'll be ready. The sooner we get going, the sooner we'll have the proof we need."

"Did you bring a camera?" Cody asked as they floated with the current, rowing mostly to guide their canoe into the deepest parts of the channel.

"In my jacket pocket." Trudy Lynn's nerves were definitely on edge. "We're getting close."

"Which side?"

"The left," she said. "I think it was... There! Over there. See it?"

"No." He shaded his eyes and squinted. "Where?"

"That way." She pointed. "A spot of red. In the bushes. It's only visible for a second in passing. I can't believe I saw it the first time."

"Neither can I." Cody worked with her as she expertly maneuvered their craft out of the main channel and into quieter water.

"This is it. The place I went ashore!" She vaulted over the side into hip-deep water and started to tow the canoe toward the bank.

"Slow down. Take your time. If the evidence is still there you don't have to strain."

"I want to! Don't you see? This vindicates me. I'm not imagining things and I'm not hysterical. The sheriff will have to believe me now. You'll see the canoe for yourself. And we'll have pictures, too."

"Okay." Cody nodded reluctantly. "Hold this thing steady while I get out, will you? I don't mind wet feet but I'd prefer to keep my clothes relatively dry. This time."

"I thought you weren't going to remind me anymore."

"Wrong." Cody swung his good leg out of the canoe first. "I said I'd stop when you began to act sensibly." One eyebrow arched as a lopsided smirk lifted the corners of his mouth. "That hasn't happened yet."

"It has so." Tugging the canoe up on the sandy bank, Trudy Lynn secured it to a hickory sapling with the mooring rope. "There. See? Safe and sensible. Can I take my life jacket off now or do I have to keep it on to satisfy your overblown ideas of proper precautions?"

"You can take it off," Cody said dryly. "Just don't go charging back into the water without it."

She saluted with mock sincerity. "Yes, sir, captain, sir. Whatever you say." Clearly, her companion was not amused. Well, too bad. She'd suffered enough. Having one less unknown to cope with was going to be a real relief. And maybe, just maybe, something in or near the canoe would lead them to clues about Jim's whereabouts.

"It's this way," she said, taking the lead. "Watch yourself. Some of those sticker vines are killers. I must have tripped a dozen times when I was here before."

"Is that where you got all those scratches?"

"Most of them. It's not usually a good idea to go into a thicket, especially not once the creepy-crawlies come out for the summer. Hopefully, we're early enough in the season to miss most of them."

"Hopefully."

Cody was keeping pace. Good. She didn't want to overtax him but she didn't want to have to slow down, either. The sooner they got the canoe uncovered and proved to themselves it truly was Jim's, the sooner she'd be rid of the churning feeling in her stomach and the throbbing in her temples.

Trudy pushed aside a clump of young cedars. "Here!" she shouted over her shoulder. "It's right here, like I said."

"Wait!"

She paused. "What for?"

"Suppose it's booby-trapped?"

"It can't be. I was already here once. Remember?"

"Yes." He stepped up beside her and spoke quietly. "But that was yesterday. Something could have changed since then. And I'd keep my voice down if I were you. Sound carries well out here. No telling who might overhear us."

"Buford's in the hospital."

"Who says he was out here alone?"

"Nobody else chased me."

"Which only means they didn't see you, not that they weren't here."

"Are you always this cynical?"

"I am when it's the wisest course to follow," Cody answered. "You're the kind of person who'd stand there and stare at the sky, looking for a flight of mallards, if somebody yelled, *duck*. I'd assume the worst and hit the dirt. If that's being cynical then I'm guilty as charged."

"I'd never thought of it quite that way."

"Well, try, at least while we're out here. Now start taking pictures. I'll stand guard."

"Okay. You're the boss. Whatever you say." She smiled. "There, does that make you happy?"

"Ecstatic." He was already scanning the surrounding woods. "Where were you when Buford jumped you?"

"Ten or fifteen yards to your left." Trudy Lynn

pointed. "He came from up there on that little bluff. The one with the poison ivy all over it."

The expression on Cody's face when his head snapped around was priceless. She giggled. "Just kidding."

He looked as though he was tempted to chastise her again. Instead, he mellowed. "All right. I'll cool it, too. Just take your pictures so we can get out of here. This place gives me the creeps."

Trudy Lynn silently shared his unsettling observation. There was a threatening feel to this place. It wasn't merely because she'd found the missing canoe or because she'd been accosted nearby. It was more. There was a sense of unnamed dread in the still, humid air, an aura of menace she couldn't ignore or explain away.

At first, she'd assumed her imagination was simply working overtime. Since Cody had had the same reaction, however, she was beginning to take her inner warnings a lot more seriously.

Her skin crawled. The fine hair on the back of her neck prickled. Cody was right. The sooner they got out of there, the better.

Trudy Lynn snapped a final picture. "Okay. That's enough. Let's go."

When she turned, she found Cody three-quarters of the way up the hill she'd teased him about. "What do you think you're doing?"

"Seeing what's up here." He paused to glance down at her. "I was curious."

"You shouldn't be doing that. Not with your sore knee."

"It's permanently attached to the rest of me. I couldn't leave it behind if I wanted to. I can make it. You coming?"

"No. I don't need to see any more. Neither do you."

"I'll be down in a sec. I'm almost to the top."

"Cody…"

"Nag, nag, nag. Has anybody ever told you that you talk too much?"

"Yes. You have. Often."

"That's because you do it so regularly."

"Flattery will get you nowhere, mister." She shivered. "I keep feeling like we're being watched."

"Maybe we are. Or were. That's one of the things I aim to find out."

She gave a nervous giggle. "You *aim* to? You've only been in Arkansas a couple of weeks and you're already starting to pick up native speech patterns. Next, you'll be saying you're *fixin'* to do something."

"I am. I'm fixin' to get to the top of this hill and have a look around as soon as you quit harassing me."

"Oh, for…" Trudy Lynn bit back the rest. "Go ahead. Wreck your leg if that's what you want. I'll be waiting in the canoe."

She saw Cody's shoulders shake with silent laughter as he resumed his climb. In seconds, he'd crested the rise and disappeared from sight.

Trudy Lynn's patience quickly wore thin. "Cody? You still there? What do you see?"

There was no answer. The forest was deathly silent, save for the hushed gurgle of the Spring River. Trudy Lynn had never felt more alone, not even when she'd been fleeing in fear for her life.

She cupped her hands around her mouth, set aside caution and called, "Cody! Answer me."

There was no reply. No sound to indicate he was even there, let alone confirm that he was all right.

Heart racing, Trudy Lynn visualized horrible catastrophes. Her breath shuddered, faltered, then resumed with urgency. Anxiety had placed a pillow of worry over her face and it was smothering her.

How could Cody do this to her? Didn't he know how frantic she'd be? Didn't he care?

Of course he cared. He'd proved that over and over. He wouldn't hide, not even to play a joke on her. Doing such a thing would be cruel and he was anything but that.

So where was he? Should she try to follow him or was it silly to fret? If he got the mistaken idea she thought he wasn't capable enough to make the climb by himself it would hurt his feelings. On the other hand, suppose he did need help and she wasn't there to offer it? Then what?

Clenching her fists and gritting her teeth she prayed simply, *Father! Help!*

No polished, perfect-sounding prayer had ever given her quicker peace. Taking a deep breath she began to regain a semblance of self-control. Everything would be fine. Cody had probably stepped away from the edge and hadn't heard her calling him, that was all. She'd go back to the canoe and wait, as promised. As soon as he was satisfied there was nothing sinister lurking at the top of the hill, he'd return. He was a big, strong guy. He didn't need her, or anybody else, to prop him up.

Speaking of propping, she thought, nearing the beached canoe, *he left the cane behind.* Maybe she should take it to him. That sounded like a plausible excuse, assuming she actually ended up needing to explain her actions. Then again, what was wrong with taking his advice and exercising a little patience?

She smiled. *Patience.* That was the key. All she had to do was ready the canoe and sit there till Cody got back. No sweat, no fuss, no problem.

Shading her eyes with her hand she was watching the last place she'd seen him when she heard someone—or something—crashing through the distant underbrush! This was no stealthy approach. It was a stampede. And the sound was getting closer. Fast!

Trudy Lynn hefted the cane and took a defensive stance, then thought better of it. She'd walked away from similar circumstances twice. There was no sense tempting the Lord and trying for a third victory when she could just as easily flee. Whatever was charging toward her could have the canoe and everything in it. But it couldn't have her. No siree. She was out of there. *Now.*

She fought her way through the knee-deep brush to the base of the incline and began to scamper higher. Brambles tore at her arms and caught in her hair. Pliable twigs snapped back and whipped against her cheeks, stinging like the horse nettle that grew wild in the meadows and along the fencerows.

Behind her, the noise had ceased, at least temporarily. Trudy Lynn wasn't about to stop long enough to sneak a peek and see if she could tell what was back there. Uh-uh. No way. She was almost to the crest. To Cody. Nothing could stop her now. Not even the unseen demons that had driven her to begin that haphazard climb.

One hand grasped at protruding tree roots while the other flattened, palm down, on a horizontal patch of soft moss. She threw herself over the top of the bank with more proficiency than she'd dreamed possible and landed with an "Oof", not twenty feet from Cody.

He was staring into the distance. He didn't do anything when she said, "Cody?", except put a finger to his lips.

"Shush."

Trudy Lynn tried to wipe the sticky red mud off her hands and knees as she clambered to her feet. The task was hopeless. "Why didn't you answer me? Huh? Do you know how worried I was?"

"Be quiet. Listen. Hear that?"

"No. I'll tell you what I *did* hear. A monster of some kind. It made enough noise for ten men. Sounded like an elephant was clomping around." She held out the cane. "I brought this along in case I needed to defend myself. Do you want it?"

"No." Scowling, Cody held up his hand. "Will you please be quiet? I thought I heard voices a minute ago. I was trying to decide which direction they were coming from when you showed up and started jabbering."

"I was just asking a simple question. You don't have to bite my head off." The stern look he sent her reminded Trudy Lynn of a similar expression she'd seen on her father's face, especially whenever her exuberance had become too overwhelming for him.

She grimaced. "Okay, okay. I'll be quiet."

Nervousness kept her from maintaining her silence for long. "Well? Do you hear anything? I don't. I sure heard plenty before I came up here after you. I don't know what it was. It kept getting closer and closer. I…"

Cody had faced her and stepped close. Very close. He grasped her upper arms firmly. Trudy Lynn gazed up at him just as he bent to place his lips on hers.

She'd closed her eyes to savor the moment until she realized this kiss was lacking the emotional wallop of their earlier efforts.

She blinked, confused. Cody was frowning and surreptitiously watching the woods. He wasn't being romantic. He was only kissing her to shut her up!

She pushed away. "Why you…you…"

Suddenly, a faint sound reached her. Cody *had* heard someone calling out. She held her breath. "I hear it, too," she said, straining to listen. "It's coming from over that way, I think."

"Can you recognize the voice?"

"I don't know. It…it sounds like…Jim!"

"Are you sure?" Cody asked.

"Positive! He's hollering for help."

"Okay. Then we'll…"

He clamped his jaw closed. Might as well save his breath. Trudy Lynn already had taken off. The cane lay at his feet. She was tearing recklessly through the woods toward who knows what, and she was totally defenseless.

Chapter Fourteen

Cody grabbed the cane and started after her. "Wait! Use your head."

She slowed. Whirled. Stared at him. "I am. Come on. We have to save Jim."

"Not if it gets us into hot water."

"Don't be silly. Listen. He sounds pitiful."

"He's also the one who stole from you."

"I know. But…"

"No buts," Cody said, joining her and taking her arm to keep her from running off before he'd had his say. "If that really is Jim, his voice is loud and strong. A few more minutes won't matter. We can't just barge in on whoever's holding him and expect them to hand him over because we ask politely. We need a plan."

"You mean we need to follow *your* plan, don't you? Well, it just so happens I have a few ideas of my own."

"Fine. What are they?"

Fidgeting, Trudy Lynn chewed her lower lip. "First, I'm going to find out exactly where Jim is."

"Okay. Then what?" When she stiffened and averted her gaze Cody knew she'd been bluffing.

"Then, I'll have enough information to make a sensible decision," she said.

"Fair enough. We'll reconnoiter together." He loosened his hold on her arm. "Agreed?"

"Okay. Agreed." She gestured toward the cane. "Are you going to be able to make it?"

"Unless I have to climb trees or leap canyons." It pleased him to see her start to smile.

"I thought you were going to say, 'leap tall buildings in a single bound.'"

"I'm good, but I'm not *that* good."

"Oh, I don't know. You were pretty impressive when Buford was trying to drown me."

Cody couldn't help noticing how pink her cheeks had grown. Embarrassment confirmed her candor. Coming from someone as stubborn and hardheaded as Trudy Lynn Brown, the compliment meant a lot. When he was around her he didn't feel defective or disabled. Not anymore. She didn't baby him, yet she wasn't cruel or off-putting, either. She might not always agree with him but she always accepted him.

That conclusion gave him pause. Perhaps he'd do well to give her the same consideration.

Up ahead, Trudy Lynn paused and raised her hand, then ducked behind the broad trunk of an oak.

Cody joined her. "What do you see?"

"Some kind of building. I think that's where the calls for help are coming from."

He leaned closer to her shoulder so he could peer past. The sweet, clean fragrance of her hair was so appealing, so distracting, he paused to take a deep breath before stepping back and saying, "I think so, too. Somebody's tacked plastic to a rough framework. Looks like a makeshift greenhouse."

"Out here? There isn't any electricity. Even if they had their own well they couldn't pump water without a generator."

"Maybe they have one." Cody's senses were still on overload from being so close to Trudy Lynn. That would never do. He needed to be vigilant. Ready for anything.

"Right, maybe they do," she whispered. "What now?"

"I don't know. You're supposed to be the one with the rescue plan." If he hadn't been trying to remain secretive he'd have laughed aloud at her look of consternation. "Okay. Tell you what. Let's circle around and check everything carefully before we stumble into an ambush. You go one way and I'll go the other. When we meet on the opposite side, we'll talk. How does that sound?"

"Logical," Trudy Lynn muttered.

"I thought so. Be careful. And stay out of sight."

"You, too."

Cody nodded. "I will."

Part of his heart kept insisting he shouldn't let her go by herself. Another part countered with the certainty that he'd be a lot more levelheaded once they were apart. Clear thinking was critical. Everything else was secondary, at least until they figured out what was going on.

Rocks the size of footballs, and smaller, lay hidden beneath the dead leaves littering the forest floor. Cody picked his way carefully. By peering through the trees he could catch reassuring glimpses of Trudy Lynn now and then. Every time he did, his heart responded by hammering harder.

Struggling to keep up a pace equal to hers, he lost sight of her until he rounded the far corner of the greenhouse. There she was! He raised the cane to signal and saw her wave back as he took a step.

Suddenly, something hit his ankle. Raked across it. Sent pain shooting up his leg.

Arms flailing wildly, Cody twisted his body to protect his injured knee and hit the ground on his side. Hard.

As he fell, the world around him exploded. Green leaves above were riddled and shredded. Bits of bark rained down like dusty hail. The blast echoed across the hills like the rumble of thunder.

Cody clung to the ground. The knifing pain across his ankle told him he must have stumbled over a trip wire that had set off a booby trap. Were there more? There *must* be.

He raised on one elbow before the dust had settled and shouted to Trudy Lynn. "Don't move. Stay where you are."

"What happened? Did somebody shoot at us?"

The quaver in her voice touched his heart. "No. I fell over a wire or something. Don't worry. I'm okay."

"You don't sound okay. Where are you?"

Cody could tell she was drawing nearer despite his warning. "Stand still!" he shouted. "I'll come to you."

In the confusion he'd lost the cane, so he worked himself up a hickory, hand over hand, till he could regain his balance. Gall rose in his throat. The trunk of an adjoining oak bore scars from the basketball-sized shotgun blast. It had struck at eye level. Right where his head should have been—would have been—if he hadn't fallen!

The urge to reach Trudy Lynn and protect her from the same unthinkable threat overpowered him. No pain registered. No rational thought reached his consciousness. All he cared about was getting to her. Before it was too late.

Trudy Lynn saw movement ahead, about where Cody should have been. Was he really all right or had he lied to keep her from coming to his aid?

The latter was most likely. That man was too brave

for his own good. And way too bossy. She wasn't helpless, nor was she foolish. These hills were her home. She could tell natural plants and rock formations from anything artificial. If there was a trap set in her path she'd be able to spot it early and avoid it. In that respect, she was probably safer moving around these woods than Cody was.

"No. *You* stay where *you* are. I'm coming," she shouted.

Dropping into a crouch she started to inch forward while carefully perusing the leaf-strewn forest floor. Every sense was heightened. Every muscle tense. Her temples throbbed in time with her rapid pulse and her stomach lurched, bringing bitterness to the back of her throat.

Ahead, she caught glimpses of Cody's blue T-shirt. He was moving, too! The thought of losing him tore at her heart. She didn't care if he wasn't as fond of her as she was of him, she wasn't going to let him continue to risk his life for her sake.

"I said, *stop,*" Trudy Lynn screeched angrily. "Freeze. I'm almost there."

Her skin prickled as if a thousand tiny insects were crawling on it. She lifted her foot to take another step. Hesitated. Pulled back. The leaves ahead didn't look quite right. The ridge piled across her path was too even.

Scanning the area she saw no easy way to bypass the strange formation without backtracking. That was out of the question. If she did manage to avoid the trap, assuming it was a trap, Cody would probably blunder into it before she could reach him.

Picking up a piece of a fallen limb she poked gingerly at the leaves. Nothing happened. She bent lower. Probed more forcefully. Still nothing. Oh, well. Sighing, she turned away as she tossed the broken branch aside.

Her eardrums popped. A shock wave knocked her off her feet and sent her sprawling, facedown, into the suspicious leaves. Intense sound followed a split second later. This blast was lower-pitched than the shot Cody had triggered. It reverberated like the growling of angry beasts, ready to devour anyone or anything in their path.

In the background, Trudy Lynn heard a bellow of pain that cut her all the way to the core. *Cody!*

"No!" she shouted, "No!"

Her heart ached. Tears filled her eyes. Cody had been hit. She'd failed him.

Cody yelled when he saw the flash of the ground blast, saw Trudy Lynn go down. Common sense abandoned him. Half hopping, half running, he raced toward her.

"Dear God," he prayed without reservation, "help her. Don't let anything happen to her. Please!"

In the deepest reaches of his soul he realized he did believe. Disillusionment and disappointment had clouded his faith but its basic tenets remained. He was the one who had given up. God hadn't.

He saw Trudy raise her head and look at him. Tears streaked her face. Her lips were quivering.

Cody closed the remaining distance and threw himself down beside her, gathering her into his arms. "Oh, honey." Unshed tears blurred his vision. He didn't try to hide his overwhelming relief. "I was afraid… Did it hurt you?"

She clung to him. "I don't think so. Are—are you okay?"

"I'm fine." He tightened his grip and stroked her hair, brushing away crushed leaves and other blast residue. "That was close. Why didn't you stop like I told you to?"

"Because I thought I'd be able to spot traps better than you would." She rested her forehead against his and sighed. "Guess not, huh?"

"No, I guess not."

"You can let go of me." She sounded unconvinced.

"I don't know if I'll ever let you go again."

He realized his confession had flustered her when she quipped, "We'd get awfully hungry and dirty if we stayed out here for the rest of our lives."

"Yeah. I suppose you're right." Slowly, reluctantly, he got to his feet and gave her a hand up. "All we have to do is figure out how to get ourselves out of this minefield in one piece."

"After we rescue Jim. Don't forget him."

"I'd like to," Cody said, grimacing and staring at the greenhouse. "He's quieted down. Probably figures whoever set off those traps is history."

"I suppose so." Her brow wrinkled. "If there was anyone else in there, don't you think they'd have come out to investigate? We didn't exactly sneak up on them."

"We sure didn't. Okay. You stay here and wait for me. I'll work my way over there and see who or what's in the greenhouse."

Trudy Lynn latched onto his hand. "Oh, no, you don't. You're not going anywhere without me."

"Yes, I am. I'll have enough to do keeping myself out of trouble. I don't need to be worrying about you, too."

"Fine. Don't worry. But don't think you're going to get away without me again. We split up once and look what happened."

"If we'd been together, one or both of us could have been killed. Use your head. What makes more sense, a small target or a big one?"

"I'm not real fond of becoming either."

Cody was about to continue arguing when he heard a disturbance in the distance. Leaves were rustling. Dry twigs were snapping. One quick glance at Trudy Lynn's widening eyes told him she'd heard it, too.

She tightened her grip on his fingers. "That's

the noise I heard down by the river. It's coming this way!"

"I know." Cody stepped forward and pushed her behind him. The forest was silent except for the approaching threat. Jim chose that moment to let out a howl that would have made a demented hyena proud.

An enormous ebony shape burst from the brush and charged at them.

Trudy Lynn started to scream, then choked it off when she recognized the beast.

Sailor gamboled up and shook himself, sending a shower of river water and forest refuse in all directions.

Jim cut loose with another heartrending wail.

Sailor's ears perked up. His big head swiveled, nose pointing to the greenhouse, hackles raised.

"Easy, boy," Cody said. "It's okay."

Sailor apparently disagreed because he sprang into action and made a beeline for the plastic-covered structure.

Cody shouted, "No!" in unison with Trudy Lynn.

The Newfoundland ignored them both. In seconds, he'd reached the side of the plastic-covered structure and made his own door by charging through the flimsy wall as if it were tissue paper.

"Follow that dog," Trudy Lynn said, tugging on Cody's hand. "If he made it safely, we can, too."

Trudy Lynn shinnied through the Newf-sized hole ahead of Cody. The sight that greeted her inside was so funny she couldn't help laughing in spite of the seriousness of the situation.

Jim was tied to a toppled chair and lying on his back, feet kicking in the air. Sailor stood over him, lapping his face, while he sputtered and cursed.

Green fronds on thick, segmented stalks were everywhere, some growing, some stacked in bundles after a recent harvest. The air was humid, cloying, with a pungent trace of wet dog.

"Come on, boy," Trudy Lynn said, tugging on Sailor's collar to ease him away. "That's clean enough. We'll let you wash him off again later if you want."

Jim was blubbering. "Get that monster off me."

"You don't want to be rescued?"

"Not by *that*." He spit. "Untie me."

Cody joined Trudy Lynn to look down on the captive youth. "Not so fast," he said. "Your cousin and I almost got ourselves killed out there. Before we let you loose I'd like to know just what we've stumbled into."

"Oh, like you don't know," Jim grumbled. "Give me a break, man. Everybody knows marijuana when they see it. What'd you think all this stuff was, okra?"

"The question is, who tied you up and why?"

"Never mind that. Just get me out of here before they come back."

"They, who? Buford's out of commission. Who else should we look out for?"

"What happened to him?" Jim was clearly frightened.

Cody chuckled and elbowed Trudy Lynn. "Some woman who doesn't know her own strength gave him a bad headache. He's stuck in the hospital for observation but he'll be released soon. I suggest you cut the macho act and start talking. Otherwise, we may decide to leave you right where you are."

"You wouldn't."

"Maybe. Maybe not," Cody drawled. "I don't think you want to take that chance, do you?"

"No." Jim's glare was hard, then softened as it settled on his cousin. "I really was trying to help you, Trudy Lynn. They said they'd hurt you if I didn't get you to sell or make you close down."

Incredulous, she shook her head slowly. "Why couldn't you have confided in me? I'd have helped you."

"Who says I wanted help? I had a sweet deal—" his glance shifted back to Cody "—till *he* showed up and ruined everything."

"In that case, we'll be going." Trudy Lynn took Cody's arm.

"No! Wait! I'm sorry. I didn't mean it." Tears filled the younger man's eyes. "Take me with you. Buford'll kill us all if he finds you here. This is his biggest crop yet. He'll do anything to protect it."

Cody's jaw muscles clenched. "I don't doubt that. He nearly blew us up out there."

"That's why you need me. I can guide you back to the river. I know all the safe trails. I can't believe you made it this far." Tears were streaming out the corners of his eyes and dripping into his ears. "Please? For Mamaw's sake?"

"That does it," Trudy Lynn told Cody. "Poor Earlene deserves to get him back in one piece, even if he isn't worth half as much as her little finger."

"If you say so." Cody found a pair of lopping shears and cut the ropes.

Jim stood stiffly, sniffled and rubbed his chafed wrists. Sailor had edged between him and the other two. Jim eyed the dog. "Is he gonna bite me?"

"Not as long as you behave yourself," Cody said soberly.

Trudy Lynn hid her face and stifled a snicker. That big moose was about as likely to bite as Widget was to become a cuddly lapdog. Of course, letting Jim believe Sailor might attack was advantageous, especially since they had no defensive weapons other than the dog's teeth.

Give me a canoe paddle anytime, Trudy Lynn mused. She was immediately penitent. *Sorry, Lord. I do love my neighbors. Honest, I do.*

Her thoughts broadened to include Cody Keringhoven. Now there was a neighbor she could easily learn to love.

Learn to? Hah! Who was she kidding? She was already so smitten with the man she could hardly think straight, let alone function when he was around. She cared so much for him it hurt to even think about it.

And that's not all, she added ruefully. *He's going to get well, just like I prayed he would, and then he's going to leave. He's much better already. It won't be long before he goes back to California.*

That thought was enough to bring a lump to her throat and threaten tears. She blinked them back and squared her shoulders. California was where Cody longed to be, where he should be. Running rapids was his life. Weeks ago he'd been ready to give up and now look at him! Resuming the career he loved was going to provide the incentive to make a full recovery and she wasn't going to do anything to ruin that. Not even confess that she was falling in love with him.

Chapter Fifteen

Cody used a piece of the rope from Jim's bindings as a makeshift leash. Sailor tolerated the restraint, though he plodded along looking thoroughly dejected. Jim was in the lead, followed by Trudy Lynn. Cody and his dog brought up the rear.

"Is Sailor sulking?" Trudy Lynn asked over her shoulder.

Cody chuckled. "I think so. He's used to being able to choose his own path. I couldn't let him do that here."

"No kidding." She lowered her voice and slowed to speak privately. "What are we going to do with you-know-who?"

"Now or later?"

"Either. I suppose he'll be safer if he's in jail."

"I'd say so. We know there'll be a raid on the greenhouse ASAP. Then the fur will really start to fly."

"That's true. How's your leg?"

"Not too bad. I know it's there."

"You seem to be doing a lot better."

Cody huffed. "Better than what?"

"Better than when you first came to Serenity. I'm amazed."

"I'm a little surprised, too. The doctors told me I might need arthroscopic surgery eventually. Right now, I'm just glad to be on my feet again."

"I'm happy for you," Trudy Lynn said, smiling back at him. "I was afraid you'd given up."

"On what?"

"Everything."

"Oh." Cody let his thoughts ramble as he kept pace. There was plenty of truth to her observation. Although his irrational anger had dissipated, he still nurtured a modicum of disillusionment. It was getting harder and harder, however, to pinpoint his problem, to give it a name and face. For one thing, he'd stopped blaming Stephanie for jilting him and was seeing their breakup in a new light. What if he'd married her? What a tragedy that would have been. He'd not only have taken sacred vows to honor her as his wife, he'd have been unable to freely enjoy Trudy Lynn's companionship.

That's what he and his sister's best friend were, Cody decided easily. Companions. They'd gone from being mere acquaintances to being good friends in

less time than it had taken him to convince Stephanie to accept their first date!

Which proves what? Cody asked himself. That he
really was meant to be there? Meant to meet Trudy
Lynn? Meant to come to her aid? Well, why not? How
else could he explain their harmony of thoughts and
feelings, the way they argued, yet always ended up
on the same side?

Cody smiled. He wasn't ready to call their meeting of the minds divinely inspired, but it certainly
had been interesting so far. He could hardly wait to
see what happened next.

Jim halted at the shore of a brackish green back-
water, just upstream from where Trudy Lynn and
Cody had beached their canoe. A beat-up bass boat
was moored to a stump. The only thing new about it
was its powerful outboard motor.

"We can take this," Jim said, grabbing the rope at
the boat's bow and tugging it closer. "It'll make good
time."

Trudy Lynn's brow furrowed. "Will we all fit?"

"Sure. No sweat," the younger man assured her.
"Buford and I haul…" He seemed to think better of
it. "Never mind. Just get in."

"Sailor, too," Trudy Lynn insisted. "I'm not going
anywhere without him."

Jim cursed under his breath. "Let him walk."

"He could swim the way he must have when he

followed us," Cody offered. "He's never been in a boat before. I'm not sure how he'll act."

"He'll be fine." She was adamant. "We'd still be stuck in the woods, wondering if we were going to be blown to bits with every step, if it hadn't been for him." She looked to Cody for confirmation, then stepped into the boat, sat to one side and patted the bench seat. "Come on, boy."

The Newfoundland shifted its feet in a nervous dance, acting unsure, until Cody said, "Okay," and released the tension on the improvised leash. Sailor leaped into the boat beside Trudy Lynn as if he'd been trained to do so.

The dog's momentum pushed the stern away from the bank and made the whole craft rock wildly. Trudy Lynn laughed and hugged the dog's neck. "Whoa! That was some jump. I thought you said he didn't know how to handle himself around boats."

"It must be a genetic talent," Cody answered. He waded knee deep to pull the port side of the craft parallel to the sandy shore. "You two stay where you are. Don't make any more waves. Jim and I'll get in the back by the motor."

Cody swung aboard and inched to the starboard side. "Okay, Jim. I'm set. Climb in."

The younger man shook his head, his eyes wide and frightened, his fists clenched. "No way. I ain't ridin' with that monster."

"You don't have a choice," Cody said. "You either ride with him or he has you for lunch. It's your call."

It was the tears welling in her cousin's eyes that spurred Trudy Lynn to suggest, "Maybe Jim could sit in our canoe and we could tow him behind."

"If we knew where it was," Cody said. "Got any idea?"

"Yes. I think it's right down there." She pointed. "Jim can walk along the bank to get it while we follow."

One of Cody's eyebrows arched quizzically. "You trust him that far?"

"Of course I do," she said sweetly. "If he tries to run you can always sic your man-eating beast on him." She had to turn away and bite her lower lip to keep from giggling. Now that the worst was over she was giddy with relief.

"That should work. I haven't fed him today."

His quip was almost too much for her. She pressed her fingertips to her mouth. Her shoulders shook. Laughter threatened to bubble out, as unstoppable as the Spring River emerging from Mammoth Spring.

Cody saved the situation by saying, "I know you're upset, Trudy Lynn, but don't cry. It'll be all right."

She kept her face averted and nodded silently. Cody was right about one thing. Tears were running down her cheeks. Only they weren't from sadness, they were from the pleasure of being there with him. Of sharing another private joke, a moment of joy meant only for them.

Nothing could ever steal the memories of this amazing encounter from her. Not even the passage of time.

Sniffling, she regained a shaky bit of self-control and began to lecture herself. She had a million things to be thankful for. It was wrong to brood. Wrong to borrow trouble. And wrong to anticipate missing Cody when he was still there.

His warning to not rock the boat took on a deeper meaning. She wouldn't make waves, wouldn't upset him when he was in such high spirits. And if—when—he left her, she'd wave goodbye and smile no matter how much her heart was breaking. He'd rescued her from her troubles. The least she could do was see that he triumphed over his, as well.

Becky and Logan were among the crowd gathered at the county line landing when Jim was finally taken into custody. Will was there with Jim's weeping grandmother, Earlene. A few straggling reporters had heard the police dispatch on their scanners and had shown up, too.

Becky hugged Trudy Lynn, then led her far from the newshounds who had begun to pester the sheriff for details.

Logan shook hands with Cody and thumped him on the back as they walked away. "Good job, man."

"Thanks." Cody was beginning to feel the strain. "I'm glad it's over." He felt a gentle nudge and reached down to pet Sailor.

"Did the kid explain where he was all this time?"

Cody nodded. "Yeah. He was skipping out on Trudy Lynn and me when he first disappeared. His cohorts decided he was too big a risk to have running around loose, so they tied him up till they could decide what to do with him."

"Sounds like Jim was lucky you found him."

"That's what the sheriff said." He looked back at the harried lawman. "I'm glad those reporters are leaving us alone. I've just about had it with their stupid questions."

"I imagine you have. How's Trudy Lynn doing?"

"Okay, I guess." Cody took a deep breath and released it as a sigh. "We almost got killed out there. I was never so scared in my life."

"But you made it through," Logan said quietly.

"I don't know how." Cody blinked back telltale moisture. "If Sailor hadn't shown up when he did we'd probably still be looking for a safe escape route."

Staring into the distance and focused on nothing in particular, Cody began to speak as if he were narrating a documentary. "I'd nearly had my head blown off by a booby trap. Trudy Lynn wouldn't listen to me. I told her to stop. To freeze. To let me make the next move. But she just kept coming. And then…" His voice cracked with emotion.

Logan rested a hand on his shoulder. "It's okay. Take your time."

"I heard this terrible explosion. I saw her fall. I thought…" A tear slid down Cody's cheek. He quickly wiped it away. "I thought I'd lost her."

"What did you do then?"

He shrugged. "I don't know, exactly. I remember running to her." His gaze shifted to Logan. "I think I was praying."

"And your prayers were answered."

"Before I asked. Sailor was already on his way. Guess I was wasting my time, huh?"

"Not at all." Logan smiled. "The important thing is that you proved you haven't lost your faith. If you had, you wouldn't have turned to God when the going got rough. Deep in your heart, you trusted Him to help you."

Cody was shaking his head. "I don't know why I should have. He didn't answer my prayers when my passenger and I were tossed into those rapids."

"Didn't He?"

"No. My client died. Drowned."

Logan was nodding. "I'd figured as much." He paused, then went on sympathetically. "We all tend to put the same limits on God that we experience as human beings. Because we can't look ahead and see what's in store, we forget that He knows our future, knows what's best for us. In spite of the fact we may disagree with God's answers to our prayers, they're still answers, even if we don't understand them at the time."

"I'll never understand why that kid had to drown. He was just starting to live."

"I don't have the answer to that, either," Logan said.

"So, I'm supposed to just trust? Blindly? Is that what you're saying?"

"Why not? You do it all the time." He gestured with a sweep of his arm. "Look around us. You breathe the air because you sense that it's here and you need it, yet you can't see it. You assume morning will come when you close your eyes to sleep because it always has."

"There's more to it than that."

"Of course there is. There's more to God and His universe than any mortal will ever be able to comprehend. We think we're geniuses when we supposedly figure out one tiny secret. Then, years later, somebody else comes along and contradicts what was once considered a brilliant discovery and proves it was wrong. All any of us can do is muddle through." Logan smiled. "I've chosen to do it by following the Lord's teachings as best I can."

Cody sighed again. "I used to feel the same way."

"Search your heart," the preacher said. "See what's in there now. Be honest with yourself. You may be surprised."

"Surprised? Hah! I've been astonished by just

about everything that's happened since I hit town. One more amazing thing will fall right in line with the rest."

"Around here, they call that being *bumfuzzled*. Becky tells me it means you're so bewildered and confused you're practically speechless."

Cody chuckled quietly and glanced across the parking lot to where Trudy Lynn and Becky stood. They were obviously rejoicing over the turn of the day's events and, as usual, Trudy's voice carried best.

"That's one thing my landlady doesn't have to worry about," Cody said wryly. "No matter how bumfuzzled she gets, she's never speechless."

Trudy Lynn pressed her fingertips to her temples. "What an adventure. I hope I never have one like it again." She gave Becky a smile of heartfelt appreciation. "I'm so glad you and Logan came to meet us. I need a friend, especially right now."

"I'm here for you, kiddo. Would you like to spend the night at our house? I know Logan wouldn't mind."

"Widget would," Trudy Lynn said. "He's probably been driving poor Anne crazy while I've been gone. Besides, he'll need me there tonight to let him out."

"You could just have Cody's dog take care of it for you," Becky joked. "He seems to love opening doors."

"Or running right through them. You should have

seen him go charging into that greenhouse after Jim hollered for help. He was a real hero."

"I thought Cody was your hero."

"Okay, him, too." She blushed. "I'm going to miss him."

"Why? Did he say he was leaving?"

"No, but…"

"Then stop borrowing trouble. He's made enormous progress since he's arrived. Maybe he'll decide to stay."

"Why should he?"

"I don't know. Can't you think of a good reason?" Becky grinned. One eyebrow arched. "I can."

"Don't look at me like that. There's nothing going on between your brother and me." The corners of her mouth twitched with a repressed smile. "Well, almost nothing."

"Aha! I knew it."

"Knew what? There's nothing to know. Cody and I are good friends, that's all."

"You're sure?"

"Yes."

"Positive?"

Trudy Lynn's voice rose. "Yes, already!"

"How many times has he kissed you?"

"Twice," she blurted, then began waving her hands like a kitten that had just accidentally stepped in a bowl of milk. "It's not like that. Once didn't even count. I was talking and he was only trying to shut me up." Her brow furrowed. "Wait. Maybe that was the third time. I don't remember exactly."

"You do so," Becky challenged.

"Okay. So he kissed me twice and I may have kissed him once, besides. It was my idea that time but it doesn't count either. I was only thanking him for saving my life."

"You could have done that by baking him some oatmeal raisin cookies," Becky countered.

Trudy Lynn quirked a smile and shook her head. "No, I couldn't have. I had to kiss him."

"Oh? Why is that?"

"Because I'm out of raisins. Used the last one on my cereal the other day."

Cody heard the pleasant sound of Trudy's Lynn's laughter and smiled in response.

"Sounds like our ladies are unwinding," Logan said.

"Yeah. I hope they're not laughing about us."

"Shall we join them and find out?"

"In a minute." Cody paused to clear his throat. "You counsel people, don't you?"

"Yes. If you want to talk more privately we can schedule an appointment in my office."

"I don't want to take up your time. I just had a couple of questions."

"About God?"

"No." Cody huffed and chuckled. "Something much harder to understand. Women."

Logan laughed with him and clapped him on the back. "Terrific. Why couldn't you have asked me to explain how long eternity lasts or why the world seems to be such a confusing mess these days? That, I could handle."

"That's too easy," Cody joked. "Why should I make this painless for you when I'm suffering."

"You want me to share your pain?"

"Something like that."

"Then I take it this isn't a rhetorical discussion. Remember, as Trudy Lynn's pastor I can't reveal anything told to me in confidence."

"Of course not. I wouldn't expect you to. I just wonder if you think it's possible to fall in love in a few weeks?"

"It was for Becky and me," Logan said. "Then again, people make mistakes about their feelings all the time."

"I know. I've done it. I guess what I'm asking is, do you think Trudy Lynn would settle for someone like me?" The question came out sounding too negative to suit Cody. He was about to rephrase it when Logan answered, "No."

Cody's heart fell. "I see."

"No, you don't," Logan said flatly. "She's not the type to settle for anything except what she really wants. That's why I think she'd *choose* a man like you." He began to grin. "And if you're planning to ask her how she feels, I suggest you phrase it more tactfully than you just did or she's liable to stomp off in a huff."

"That's her usual reaction to everything I say."

"This time it won't be," Logan advised.

"I don't want to rush her and scare her away. I've never met anyone half as wonderful as Trudy Lynn. I intend to stay right here and spend the rest of my life making her happy."

"Well, I'm sold," Logan gibed. "And judging by the way you two have been staring at each other ever since we got here, I'd say she is, too."

"I want it to be special for her when I propose. Really romantic. Women like that."

"If you're such an expert, why did you have to ask for my advice?"

"Maybe I wanted to humor you," Cody suggested. "After all, you are my brother-in-law. And the pastor of the woman I love. If she comes to you for guidance, I want to be sure you know my intentions are honorable."

"I never doubted that for a minute," Logan said. "Come on. Becky and I'll give you a lift back to camp. If you're planning on a romantic evening you're definitely going to need to shower and shave." He wrinkled up his nose. "It might be wise to wash that dog of yours, too. I'm not sure which one of you smells worse."

"Thanks for the confidence boost," Cody teased. "It was just what I needed."

"Hey, that's what spiritual advisors are for."

"So, how are you going to get us home?" Cody glanced down at his damp, muddy, canine companion. "In the backseat of your car?"

"I sincerely hope not. I think I saw Will in the crowd. He's probably driving the camp truck. Sailor can ride with him." Logan gave Cody the once-over. "Come to think of it, you might want to, too. So the dog doesn't worry, I mean."

Cody laughed heartily. "Smooth, Logan. Very smooth. We'll work something out." He gestured toward the women. "Let's go."

Falling into step beside him, Logan asked, "What's the hurry? Is your leg bothering you?"

"No worse than usual. I just want to get back to Trudy Lynn. We've been apart long enough."

"Oh, man, you do have it bad, don't you?" Logan was laughing softly and shaking his head. "I'll pray for you."

"While you're at it, you might want to pray for Trudy Lynn, too," Cody said. "The most important thing to me is that she be happy. Understand?"

"With or without you, you mean?"

Cody nodded soberly. "Exactly."

Buford scowled at the wall-mounted pay phone and squeezed the receiver till his knuckles whitened.

"No. I'm still in the county hospital. They're supposed to be lettin' me out soon."

"So, what's your problem?"

"The sheriff's been to see me. Twice. He and I go way back but I don't like the way he looked at me the last time he was here. Somethin's up. I can feel it."

"There better not be any glitches. I've got a bundle invested in your operation."

"Then you'd best have my bail ready."

"Think you'll need it?"

He snorted in disgust. "Who knows?"

"What about the kid? Is he going to keep his mouth shut?"

Buford cackled. "Oh, yeah. I've got that covered. Little Jimmy's not gonna be a bit of trouble. Matter of fact, if I don't get out of here soon he may start singin' with the heavenly choir."

A string of curses erupted on the other end of the line. "What do you mean? I told you to keep this operation clean."

"Except for the woman."

"Yeah. And that old man who works for her. I wouldn't mind if Will had an accident."

"What about her boyfriend?"

The cursing intensified. "If you have to get rough, start with him. Think you can handle it?"

"'Course I can."

"You sure? He put you in the hospital once."

"Did not!" Buford growled into the phone. "It was

that woman. She hit me from behind, when I wasn't lookin'. It won't happen again."

"Good. See that it doesn't. And if you do get arrested, call that bail-bondsman in Searcy, the one we used before. I'll leave word with him that I guarantee your bond."

"Hey, thanks, Mr.—"

"Shut up! I've told you never to use my name. Anybody could be listening."

"That's why I'm usin' the pay phone in the hall," Buford said, scowling. "Don't worry. Your secret's safe with me. I ain't told a soul who you are." He cackled. "Sure would like to, though. Give 'em a real surprise."

"No one who works with you knows who your backer is?"

"Nope. Nary a soul. 'Specially not Jimmy-boy."

"Good. See that it stays that way."

"Yes, sir."

"And Buford?"

"Yeah?"

"The kid stays alive. I don't know what you had in mind for him but forget it. Earlene's a nice old lady. She doesn't deserve to have to bury her grandson."

"I'll do my best."

"Do better than that."

"I don't know. If I go straight to jail from here it could put me in a bind. I left him…" There was a loud click on the line. "Hello? Hello?"

Buford held the receiver in front of his face and stared at it in disbelief. His benefactor had hung up on him! Just like that. As if he didn't matter any more than a cockroach crawling up a wall. Well, he'd see about that. When all this was over, Mister High-and-Mighty was gonna get his comeuppance. Yes, siree.

But first, he had a job to do. If Jimmy hadn't died of fright or thirst by now, he was going to let him go. If it was too late, then the kid would just disappear for keeps. Either way was fine with him.

Determined, he headed for the nearest room to look for some street clothes he could steal.

Chapter Sixteen

Will had escorted Earlene to the river landing so she could see for herself that Jim was alive and well. Trudy Lynn had felt she'd be intruding if she rode home with the older couple, so she'd asked Becky and Logan to give her a lift while Cody and Sailor hitched a chilly ride back to camp in the bed of Will's pickup.

Trudy Lynn had had to drag herself through evening chores. When she'd completed the absolute minimum she'd showered and collapsed into a deck chair on her porch.

Widget had been acting miffed ever since she'd returned. He started sniffing her shoes again, stiff-legged and hackles raised, when she finally took time to relax.

"Don't look at me like that," Trudy Lynn said with a smile. "I *had* to associate with Sailor. And I'm going to do it again, so you'd better get used to it."

The little terrier cocked its head and pricked its ears, obviously listening.

"You do understand, don't you? That's good. Because maybe you can explain everything to me."

She sighed. Deeply. Poignantly. Empathetic, the little dog jumped into her lap and rested his front paws on her shoulders, straining to lick her face.

Trudy Lynn held him away and smiled. "No kisses, baby. But thanks for forgiving me. I need a buddy like you right now. I'm really mixed-up."

Wiggling, Widget struggled to be let go.

"Okay, okay. I know you don't like to cuddle." She turned him sideways so he could sit comfortably in her lap and began to gently stroke his back to calm him. "Humor me and settle down, will you? Please? That's a good boy."

Another sigh whooshed out. "It's all over, Widget. Jim's safe in jail, where he belongs, and Will's commiserating with Earlene. If he doesn't waste this chance, he might actually have someone special to spend the rest of his life with, which is more than I have to look forward to at the moment."

The little dog shifted, wiggled, tried again to lick her and managed one quick swipe at the underside of her chin. She giggled. "Yes, I love you, too, even if you are too full of yourself to be endearing like a certain Newfie I could mention."

Thoughts of Sailor's easygoing temperament reminded her of his master. Some experts insisted that people chose dogs to complement their own personalities. In Cody's case, that might have been truer in the past. He had seemed laid-back and pretty carefree before he'd been injured. Now, it was hard to tell what he was feeling. Too bad she wasn't as intuitive about his thoughts as Widget was about hers.

Then again, she wasn't sure she wanted to know what Cody was really thinking. She might not like what she learned. She'd already tried to tell him how much she cared for him and he'd reacted like a bear trying to sidestep the jaws of a poacher's trap. Well, fine. She could wait a little longer to find out whether or not he was still planning to go back to California.

Or could she? Day after day of not knowing had left her so jittery she babbled incessantly every time she was near him. He'd made jokes about how much she talked but he had to be getting weary of it just the same.

"What would you do to get Cody to pay attention to you, Widget? Huh?" Trudy Lynn giggled. "Never mind. You'd probably growl at him or bite his ankle."

So, what was she going to do? *Nothing? Something? The wrong thing?* Probably the latter. When it came to Cody Keringhoven she seemed to stick her foot in her mouth on a regular basis.

"He'd say that's because my mouth is always open to talk," Trudy Lynn muttered. Well, when he was right, he was right. It was in her nature to express herself. Period. Even if she did manage to subdue the urge long enough to favorably impress him, she'd be creating an erroneous image of herself. That wouldn't be fair. If he liked her—even loved her—it should be because of her real self, not some pretend personality she'd created for his benefit.

She'd told Cody he'd be denying God's ultimate wisdom if he refused to accept himself. Now that she thought about it, that was good advice for her, too.

Her eyes closed. "Thank you, Father. I am glad to be me. And I'm glad You sent Cody into my life, even if he isn't going to stay."

She had so much more to be grateful for it was overwhelming. Memories of blessings cascaded through her mind like a raft racing down whitewater rapids. The Lord had taken care of her when her mother had died and her father had offered little emotional support. He'd sent her Will when she'd needed a good hand. He'd removed Ned to keep her from listening to the urging of friends and marrying the wrong man. And He'd revealed Jim's delinquency in time to not only save him from himself but to rescue her business.

Those things, and more, reinforced her optimism about the future. All she had to do was trust God as she had before, rely on His wisdom and get out of His way.

That notion brought a smile. She did trust the Lord. It was letting go and stepping back so He could work, unhindered, that had always been so hard for her.

"And keeping my mouth shut," she added, giving Widget a hug. "Think I can ever learn to do that?"

She giggled as the terrier jumped down and began circling her feet. "There's about as much chance of me being quiet as there is of you sitting still."

Widget was barking. Trudy Lynn opened heavy-lidded eyes. Lightning flashed in the distant night sky. The only other illumination was from red and blue lights atop a patrol car outside her window. How long had she been asleep? What time was it? And how long had it been raining?

She squinted at the illuminated digital clock by her bedside: 2:00 a.m. Terrific. If she ever got a good night's rest she wouldn't know what to do with all the extra energy.

Getting up, she pulled a terry cloth robe over her pajamas, fastened it, then bent to pick up her little dog. Widget was always on edge in stormy weather. The last thing she needed was for him to get overexcited and nip an innocent police officer.

Trudy Lynn unlocked the kitchen door, opened it a crack and peered out. She recognized the dripping deputy standing under the porch light and relaxed. "Hi, Nathan. Want to come in out of the rain? I can make some fresh coffee."

"Evening, Trudy Lynn." When he nodded and

touched the brim of his hat, the water poured off its plastic cover. "I'll have to take a rain check on that coffee. We're real busy tonight. Sheriff sent me over here to tell you Buford's on the loose. He walked out of the hospital. Nobody missed him till shift change."

"Surely, he won't come here."

"We don't think so, either, 'specially not if he's on foot. It's too far. Just being on the safe side. Take care and lock up, okay?" He touched his hat brim again. "Night."

"Good night. And thanks."

Widget growled menacingly as the deputy turned and headed for his car.

"Atta boy," Trudy Lynn said. "You protect me."

After watching the police cruiser roll out of camp she stepped back, closed and locked the door. Most of her cabins were empty after the mass exodus of reporters plus all the vacation cancellations. But Will was here. And Cody. They should be warned, too.

She put Widget down and hurriedly picked up the phone. There was no dial tone. "That figures. One little storm and everything quits working. As usual."

The little dog bristled. Concerned, Trudy Lynn watched him sniff the floor, then closely investigate the door she'd just locked. He was growling. His body stiffened, every muscle tense as if he were ready for an attack. When he pawed the door and whined she was positive something was wrong. Widget hated getting wet. He never asked to go out in bad weather. Never.

"That does it. Come on, boy."

Knowing he'd follow, she flipped off the kitchen lights, dashed down the hall to the rear of the camp store, and snatched up the phone there. *Dead as a doornail!*

Apprehensive, she ducked behind the sales counter. What now? She couldn't reach the panel controlling the overnight lighting in the store without passing the display windows. If she did that, anyone watching could spot her. But what else could she do? How else could she hide?

A silent prayer flickered through her subconscious. The bedroom! Her cell phone was in her purse in the bedroom! She stroked Widget. He was trembling as he always did during thunderstorms but he'd ceased growling. That was a good sign.

She got an extra jolt of energy when the electricity fluttered, then failed. Lunging toward the doorway, she would have fallen over her dog if he hadn't been so agile.

Together they tore down the dark hallway, Widget's claws scratching the bare floor like mice scrambling to escape a cat. At least the lights wouldn't give her away. If Buford was responsible for the power outage he'd made a big mistake. Darkness was to her advantage.

She caught her bare toes on the leading edge of a

crocheted rug and stumbled. Trying to regain her balance she reached for the doorjamb. All she grabbed was empty air! Her ankle wrenched. Her body jerked forward.

Widget yipped a warning at the last second. Trudy Lynn twisted to one side, barely missing him, and landed with a thud that echoed throughout the entire lodge building.

She lay still for a moment and took stock of the situation. Her head and arms were fine. Her back hurt but not terribly. So did her hip. When it came to her right ankle, however, there was no question that she had a problem. The slightest movement sent arrows of pain shooting up her leg.

She bit her lip to keep from crying out. Where, exactly, was she? How much farther to her purse? Had she put it in its usual place or had she gotten careless?

A tiny green light flashed three times near the floor. Then another answered. A couple of fireflies must have slipped inside when she'd opened the door to talk to Nathan! The little bugs weren't giving much light but their rhythmic flashes were enough to confirm that she was in the bedroom.

She held her breath and waited for the next series of green winks. There? Yes! Her purse! She must have knocked it to the floor when she'd been startled awake by the deputy.

Widget was crowding close. "It's okay, boy," she whispered. "Back off. Go on."

He refused to leave her side. Trudy Lynn gritted her teeth and pulled herself across the floor on her elbows. She had to reach her cell phone. It was her only lifeline.

Nausea forced her to pause three times before she reached her goal. Tears trickled down her cheeks, unnoticed till Widget tried to lick them off. His attempts at comfort helped her focus on something besides the knifing pain.

"It's okay, sweetie. We'll be fine. This is one time I wish you were a lot bigger and meaner, though."

It took several seconds, several more shuddering breaths, before she could steady her hands enough to retrieve the small cellular telephone and dial 911.

The dispatcher told her to stay on the line till help arrived. Trudy Lynn was far too preoccupied to comply. If all the landlines in camp were out she knew she couldn't warn Will, but there must be something she could do.

Her heart jumped like a grasshopper on a hot sidewalk. *Cody has a cell phone.* She wasn't helpless after all! Or was she? What was Cody's number? Had he written it down and given it to her? If so, where had she put it?

Frustration bred tears. She sniffled. *Stupid, stupid, stupid. Think. Better yet, pray.*

She desperately wanted to call out to God, yet it seemed there was nothing left inside her but pain. And fear.

Cheeks bathed in tears, she pulled the little dog into her arms, held him tight and counted the seconds.

Sailor was restless. So was Cody. He'd seen the police car leaving after Sailor had barked him awake. Local law enforcement had been keeping the place under pretty close surveillance ever since Jim's disappearance, so the visit wasn't unusual. Still, it was disquieting. Jim was in jail and Buford would be arrested soon, if he wasn't already in custody, so why continue the patrol?

Scowling, Cody paced to the window and peered through the drizzle at the lodge. Trudy Lynn was up there. Since there were no lights burning in her quarters he figured she must be sleeping, which was what he'd be doing if he had good sense.

Standing beside him, Sailor growled so deeply Cody felt the vibration of the dog's rib cage against his leg. That did it. He was going to get dressed and hike up the hill if it killed him. And if there was no sign Trudy Lynn was awake when he got there, he and Sailor would spend the rest of the night camped on her porch, standing guard. If she thought that was usurping too much control over her life, they could argue about it in the morning.

He pulled on jeans and a T-shirt, then grabbed his hooded jacket, thankful it was waterproof. His cell phone was in the pocket. He took it out, held it for a moment, then decided against calling ahead. No use giving her the opportunity to insist he wasn't needed.

Besides, he admitted, slipping his feet into running shoes, it wasn't Trudy Lynn he was really doing this for. He was the one who needed to see that she was safe, to place himself between her and any threat, real or imagined.

The second he reached for the doorknob Sailor was right there, waiting to poke his nose out first.

"Okay. Tonight you can go," Cody said. "But no barking and waking everybody up. I'll get your leash."

He'd no more than turned when he heard a horrendous splintering. He spun around. The door was hanging at an awkward angle, its lock free of the jamb. From the looks of the damage, Sailor had simply hurled himself against the old wood and taken off. Will's recent repairs hadn't stood a chance of withstanding so much concentrated force.

"Well, that tears it," Cody grumbled. "The whole camp will be awake in a few minutes."

He'd left the porch and was halfway up the hill when the phone in his pocket rang. Answering, he put his back to the wind and used the jacket's hood as a shield. The caller was so agitated he couldn't understand a word at first. "Slow down. Who is this?"

"It's me. Becky. Where are you?"

"In camp. Why?"

"The police were just here. They're looking everywhere for Buford. Somebody must have told him Jim had been arrested and he took off. They don't think he's had time to get as far as the Spring River but I thought I should warn you, anyway."

The back of Cody's neck bristled. "What's Trudy Lynn's number? Never mind. I'm almost to the lodge. Hang up and call the cops for me. Tell them to get out here in a hurry. Sailor's sure there's a prowler."

Blood was whooshing through the veins in Trudy's Lynn's head so fast it made a humming noise that hampered her hearing. Her temples were throbbing. Her ankle was, too, a quarter beat later. The skin felt drawn. Clearly, her foot and lower leg were starting to swell.

Widget stiffened, cocked his head. Moments later she thought she heard the tinkle of breaking glass. It wasn't loud, like a drinking glass shattering after being dropped onto the floor. It sounded more like one of the small panes in her back door was being tapped out.

She closed her eyes and clung tightly to her little dog. If anyone was searching the place they'd be found. Quickly.

A growl rumbled. Trudy Lynn closed her hand around Widget's pointy muzzle and whispered, "Shush."

Struggling to get loose, the little terrier continued sounding the warning.

She could hear soft footfalls now. A hesitant cadence. Someone had gotten inside! And they were coming closer.

Gritting her teeth she dragged herself farther behind the bed. Beads of perspiration glistened on her forehead and trickled down her spine. This would have to be good enough. She couldn't force herself to move one inch more.

"Easy, boy, easy," she whispered, hoping a soft tone and gentle petting would calm her anxious dog. Every muscle in his body was knotted, ready for action. If he got away from her and attacked the prowler the way he obviously wanted to, there was no telling how badly he'd be hurt. She couldn't let that happen.

A sudden jingling on the floor at the foot of the bed made Trudy Lynn jump. She bit back a gasp. The phone! She'd been so concerned for Widget she must have dropped it. Were the police calling her back? Were they almost there?

A sudden foreboding thought gave her chills. Suppose there had been confusion about who she was or where she was calling from? Had she mentioned the camp? She must have. Besides, the dispatcher had caller ID, right? But would it work with a portable number?

The little phone continued to play the tune she'd programmed into it instead of its normal ring. Music she'd once thought amusing was now mocking. Even if she could convince herself to crawl out of hiding to answer, the caller would probably have hung up by the time she got there. And then she'd be back in the open, a sitting duck.

Yeah. A duck with a broken wing and no way to defend myself, she added, grimacing. There was nothing to do but sit there and wait till the stupid thing finally shut up.

By the sixth repeat of the silly ditty she was ready to smash the phone with anything at hand. Only there wasn't anything at hand. Not even a canoe paddle. If she was so organized and perfectly prepared, why hadn't she put one in her bedroom? That question wasn't as ridiculous as it sounded.

"Because I didn't dream I was going to need a weapon," she whispered. "Not here. Not in Serenity."

The phone fell silent. Listening for footsteps in the background, Trudy Lynn thought she heard two sets, one slow and another faster, lighter. She held her breath. Strained to hear. She'd had to have been wearing earplugs to miss the ensuing groan and heavy thump.

Were the police here? If they were, if they'd captured her prowler, then why didn't somebody turn the electricity back on?

In her arms, Widget's growl intensified till his whole body shook. The beam from a flashlight swept through the door and around the room. It came to rest on the cell phone.

Someone laughed and said, "Well, well." Someone whose voice sounded familiar. Only it couldn't possibly be him.

Soft footfalls approached. The light blinded Trudy Lynn. She blinked and shaded her eyes, trying to see who was really there. Widget had ceased growling and was in full attack mode, barking so fervently he drowned out everything else.

"Still got the rat, I see," the voice said.

That was enough identification for Trudy. She didn't have to see his face to recognize his attitude. "Ned? What're you doing here?"

"Can't I stop by to see my ex-fiancée?"

In spite of the animosity evident in his tone she was glad he'd chosen this particular night to visit. "Listen. There's a prowler in the building. I heard him break in the back door. I think it's that Buford guy from downriver. He's been growing marijuana in the forest."

"Has he, now?"

"Yes. My cousin, Jim, was working for him."

"Who else?" Ned asked.

"Jim worked for me, too. He kept my books."

Ned snorted as if he thought she was the most dull-witted person on the planet. "I mean, who else was working with Buford and Jimmy?"

"How should I know?" Trudy Lynn was getting aggravated. "You'd better shut off that light before Buford sees it."

"He's not going to see anything. Not from where he is."

She brightened. "The noise in the hall? Was that you? Did you knock him out?"

"Something like that."

"Praise God. My prayers were answered!"

"Still on your soapbox, I see," Ned remarked. "That's probably for the best. At least you think you'll go to Heaven. That must be some comfort at a time like this."

Trudy Lynn instinctively started to inch away. Her ankle protested. "What are you talking about?"

"You couldn't leave well enough alone, could you? Had to go nosing into other people's business like you had a right. I've always hated that about you." He snorted. "Among other things."

"Then why did you ask me to marry you?"

"Haven't you figured that out by now? If you'd come to the city like you were supposed to, we wouldn't be having this discussion." He laughed menacingly. "You actually might have enjoyed being my wife for a while, at least until I got tired of you."

"You said you loved me!"

"I was good, wasn't I? Nobody suspected a thing. Not even your friends. Most of them were even on my side, trying to convince you to let go of this dump and move away. You should have listened to them. Why didn't you?"

Anger replaced astonishment, giving her courage.

"Because I knew something was wrong between us. In my heart, I knew."

"Women's intuition?"

She shook her head. "No. God must have been warning me all along. I'm just thankful I listened."

"Really?" Ned perched on the corner of the mattress, his feet mere inches from where she lay on the floor. "Did He also tell you why I wanted you to leave here?"

"No, of course not." Her thoughts spun. Her eyes widened. It was all starting to tie together and make sense—the vandalism, the other camps closing, the location of the illegal crop and the greenhouse... Ned's insistence that she had to leave Serenity for his sake.

Squinting, she could see only a shadowy form behind the light but she could tell when his head nodded.

"I see you've figured it out." He got to his feet and towered over her. "Too bad. I was hoping our friend Buford would take care of this for me." He gave a sardonic chuckle. "Oh, well, at least he's not alive to deny it. That'll do."

"You *killed* him?"

"In self-defense," Ned drawled. "Too bad I got here too late to prevent him from killing you, first."

Chapter Seventeen

Cody saw the beam of a flashlight moving through the lodge. Instead of burglar-like wandering, the light headed straight for Trudy Lynn's living quarters!

Rounding the corner of the store, Cody noticed a black sedan, parked where it couldn't be seen from the road. It was new. Clean. Expensive. If Buford had arrived in that, he'd sure come up in the world.

"Probably stole it," he muttered. Sailor loped up beside him, out of breath, tongue lolling. With his fur puffed out by aggression he looked even bigger than usual.

Cody grabbed the dog's collar. "Easy now. We'll do this together." He didn't want to endanger his best buddy but he figured Buford would be far more likely to back down if he saw he had a growling animal the size of a black bear to contend with.

The rear door stood ajar. Cody eased it open farther. Flashes of lightning glinted off shards of broken glass on the tile floor. He led Sailor around them to protect the dog's feet.

Muffled voices were drifting up the hall. The Newf heard them, too. It leaped ahead, almost jerked loose, and headed down the dark passageway at a gallop, dragging Cody along like a water skier following the wake of a speedboat.

A sharp turn at the doorway scraped him off. Sailor never slowed. He crossed the room and hit the person holding the flashlight at full gallop.

Trudy Lynn screamed. Instinct told her to throw herself backward and cover her face with her arms.

Widget scrambled away, bounced off the wall and dashed into the fray, yipping wildly.

Above and to one side, a terrible fight was taking place. Men were shouting. Animals were growling and snapping. Fabric tore. Furniture crashed into the walls. Glass shattered.

Trudy Lynn managed to slide her injured ankle far enough under the bed to protect it. The rest of her was hunkered down as close to the box spring as possible.

Something soggy and hairy bumped into her. That odor! Wet dog! It had to be Sailor. Nothing else was that big or smelled quite that doggy when it was damp. And if Sailor was here, Cody must be!

A man grunted. A punch connected. A body hit the wall and slid to the floor beyond the dresser.

Trudy Lynn held her breath and prayed that Cody was the one still on his feet.

Sailor's wagging tail began to slap her with a welcome cadence. He was no longer in attack mode! Someone was reaching for the discarded flashlight, picking it up. The beam once again swung in her direction.

"Cody?" she asked hopefully.

"I'm here," he answered. "Are you okay?"

"I am now."

"Thank God." It was definitely a prayerful statement.

"I'll second that," she said. "How did you know I was in trouble?"

"Sailor told me." Cody lowered himself to the edge of the bed and shined the flashlight on the crumpled attacker. "Whew! That was close. I thought..." The beam played over the man. "Hold it. That's not Buford."

"No," Trudy Lynn said sadly. "That's Ned."

"What's *he* doing here."

She shivered, suddenly chilled to the bone. "He just told me he killed Buford. He said he was going to kill me next and blame it on poor Buford."

Cody swung the light back to her face. "What?! Are you sure?"

"I'm afraid I am." Her lower lip began to quiver in spite of the immense relief of having Cody there. He

offered his hand to her. She shook her head. "Sorry.
I'd better sit tight till the paramedics arrive."

Cody leaned down beside her. "You said you were
fine. What's wrong?"

"I think my ankle's broken."

"Show me."

"Uh-uh. It's safe under the bed. I had to crawl to
get this far. I'm not moving one more inch on my
own."

She saw him shine the light around the room, then
return it to Ned. The other man was beginning to stir.

"Got any rope in here?" Cody asked.

"Will scarves do?"

"Belts would be better."

"In the closet. Hanging on a rack on the far right,"
Trudy Lynn said.

He returned and handed her the flashlight. "Hold
this for me while I tie him up."

"Okay." The throbbing in her foot was beginning
to keep her from thinking clearly. "I, um, I did call
the police," she said. "I'm not sure they got the right
information, though. Maybe you should call again."

"I already had Becky do that." Cody straightened.
"The one thing I'm not sure of is whether or not Ned
was alone."

"I did hear at least two sets of footsteps. I think
one of them was Buford, though, before Ned took
care of him." Her trembling had intensified so badly
she couldn't hold the light steady.

"You're going into shock," Cody said flatly. "I won't take the chance of getting trapped in here with another lunatic. Two's my limit." He again held out his hand. "Come on. Either you help or I'll have to carry you."

Pain colored her answer, turned it harsh. "Oh, yeah? How? You can hardly walk, yourself."

"I'll manage. Well, what'll it be?"

"I'll help, I'll help," she said quickly. "Let me do it slowly. It really hurts."

"I believe that. Where are those scarves you said you had?"

"In the dresser. Bottom drawer. Why?"

"I'm going to make a splint to keep you from damaging that ankle any worse." He paused. "Is that okay or are you planning to argue?"

"Not me." Trudy Lynn managed brief movements punctuated with gasps and gritted teeth. "Where's Widget?"

"Standing on Ned's chest, snarling at him."

"Good. Anybody who calls my darling little dog a rat deserves to be treated like the rotten person he is." She winced. "I hope he rots in jail for everything he's done. I can't believe I ever considered marrying that scumbag."

"Neither can I." Cody returned with two plastic hangers and bent down. "Can you hold one of these on each side of your ankle while I wrap it? I'll be as gentle as possible."

"I know you will." His hands were tender, his movements patient. She'd made up her mind not to cry out and she succeeded except for one little mew.

"Sorry," Cody said.

"It's okay. I'm a wimp."

"If you are, you're the bravest one I've ever known," he countered. "There. I'm done. Ready to get up?"

"As ready as I'll ever be. Are you sure this is necessary?"

"Not positive, no. But I think it's wise."

She let him hoist her into a standing position, gritting her teeth to keep from crying out. "That's good enough for me," she said. "I trust your judgment."

"You *do?*"

His incredulity was almost enough to make her laugh in spite of her suffering. "Yes, I do. Come on. Let's get out of here before I change my mind."

"Your ankle's broken," Cody told Trudy Lynn later.

"Surprise, surprise." She winced. "What about Ned? Did the sheriff arrest him? Was he alone?"

"Yes, and yes. Jimmy identified the other men involved in the operation and they've already been picked up. The Drug Task Force is raiding the greenhouse as we speak. It's all over."

"Thank God for that," she whispered prayerfully.

"Sounds like you can thank Him for a monetary reward, too. The DEA chief told me your share should provide enough money to pay your staff retroactive wages after all."

"Unbelievable!"

Trudy Lynn had been given an injection to help her temporarily cope with the pain and she was starting to feel its effects. She smiled and sighed.

Cody took her hand. "Are you feeling any better?"

"Some. I think my ankle's throbbing less. Now, I'm freezing."

"That's because they've put ice on your leg," he explained. "Shall I ask a nurse to bring you another blanket?"

"No. Don't leave. Stay and talk to me? Please?"

"Sure. I've been wanting to have a talk with you anyway."

"Really?" Trudy Lynn's ears were buzzing and her head felt funny, as if she were floating on a pillow of air instead of lying on a gurney in a hospital emergency room. "Me, too. Talk to you, I mean, not to myself."

"I figured as much." There was humor in his voice. "Maybe we'd better wait. You sound pretty out of it right now."

"Nonsense. I'm fine." She made a face. "I wasn't stupid. I know it must seem that way to you but I really wasn't. I mean, all my friends kept insisting Ned was the right man for me but I never bought it. He was too nice. Too perfect. Too…" She rolled her eyes. "I can't think of the right word. My brain's getting all fuzzy. Manipulative! That's it. Ned was always trying to get me to do things his way, only he was so sweet about it he made me sick."

"Trudy Lynn…"

"I should have known. I guess I did know. Like I told him when he was threatening to kill me, I think God was warning me all along. Does that make sense to you?"

"Yes." Cody stroked his thumb over the back of her hand as he held it and smiled at her. "I've been thinking…"

"Yeah, me, too. I didn't see it at first because I was too set in my ways, I guess. It wasn't that I wanted someone who never disagreed with me. I know I'm not perfect." She giggled. "Even if I am close to it."

Cody laughed softly. "Now, *that* we agree on."

"Oh, good, because I don't care if you're not—perfect, I mean. Forget the limp. It doesn't matter."

"I know that now."

"Hey! Maybe I'll limp, too!" She was grinning so widely her cheek muscles cramped. "Wouldn't that be wonderful!"

"No, it wouldn't. I don't want anything to hurt you. Ever."

"Why not? Just think, we could have his and hers canes or something. I could tie a pink bow on mine so we could tell them apart!" That struck her so funny she burst into a fit of giggling.

"I'm afraid the medicine they gave you is making you loopy, honey."

"Who, me?" Trudy Lynn couldn't stop laughing, even when tears began to stream down her cheeks.

"Yes, you." Cody gave her a lopsided smile and shook his head. "You've been talking so much I haven't been able to get a word in."

"You did so. You said—something. I heard you."

He waited for her laughter to wane. "I've been trying to tell you I love you."

"Oh, sure, but…" She gasped. "You do?"

"Uh-huh. I'm crazy about you."

"Am I hallucinating?"

"I sure hope not because I'm asking you to marry me, too."

"That's it. I am hallucinating. I knew it." She made a quirky face at him, then blinked rapidly as if trying to clear her vision. "Who are you?"

"I'm Cody. Remember?"

"Nope. You can't be." Her voice was beginning to slur. Her eyelids drooped "You're being nice. Cody always argues with me."

"That's because you're so stubborn." He stood, bent and placed a kiss on her forehead. "Get some rest, honey. We'll talk more when you wake up."

Her fingers tightened on his. "Don't go," she mouthed almost soundlessly.

"I'll stay as long as you want me. How about fifty or sixty years?"

Trudy Lynn heard him speaking but couldn't rouse herself enough to answer. She'd long dreamed of what she'd say when the right man proposed marriage. Being rendered speechless by medication and hearing his profession of undying love while lying in a hospital awaiting treatment was *not* the romantic scenario she'd pictured.

Lost in joyful thoughts, she smiled. Cody Keringhoven wasn't the kind of man she'd envisioned, either. He was better. Much better. And as soon as she could make her voice work again she was going to tell him so.

Trudy Lynn awoke with a start, surprised to find she'd been moved to a hospital room. Then, the details came flooding back. She could have died. And now she was about to start really living.

Metal rails on her bed made perfect handholds. She pulled herself into a sitting position and looked around the portion of the room that wasn't curtained off for her roommate's privacy. Cody was slumped, snoring, in the only visible chair. His light-colored hair was tousled, his chin shadowed by a beard so blond it probably wouldn't have been noticeable in brighter light. He looked absolutely dear. And so exhausted she hated to wake him.

Apparently, her intense concentration was enough to break through. He yawned, stretched and began to smile the moment he saw her sitting up. "Hi. How are you feeling?"

"Wonderful."

"Your ankle doesn't hurt?"

"It's killing me." She grinned. "Say it again."

"Your ankle doesn't hurt?"

"No, silly. Way before that. Did you or didn't you ask me to marry you?"

"I might have." He grinned and reached for her hand.

"Well, if you didn't, I've just had the best dream of my entire life."

"What was your answer in this dream?"

"I said yes."

"That wasn't because you were groggy from the medication?"

"My thinking might have been hazy but yours wasn't. Did you say you loved me, or not?"

"I did. I'm glad it registered. You didn't seem real sure who I even was, let alone what I was trying to say."

"My heart knew," Trudy Lynn said. "I think it always knew everything, even when you were depressed and being so hard on yourself." She twisted so she could place her opposite hand atop his and watch his expression as she asked, "What about California?"

"Maybe we'll go there on our honeymoon before we settle down here, if that's all right with you."

Her heart was filled to bursting. "It sounds wonderful. I love you, Cody. All of you. Just as you are." She chuckled softly. "I even love your dog."

One eyebrow arched. "Uh-oh. Does that mean I have to fall madly in love with Widget, too?"

"I'm not that picky. As long as you honestly like him that's good enough for me."

"What a relief," Cody teased. "I was afraid you'd want him to be in the wedding party."

"No," she said, her eyes meeting his with a mischievous twinkle, "I thought we'd let Sailor carry the basket of flowers down the aisle."

"You're joking!"

Trudy Lynn giggled. "I was. Now that I think about it, that idea doesn't sound half-bad."

"Honey," Cody said, looking at her with so much love it made her heart and soul sing, "if that's what you want, it's okay with me."

"I think you mean that."

"I do. This time. Just don't get in the habit of expecting me to do things your way every time."

"Perish the thought," Trudy Lynn quipped. "I wouldn't respect you if you changed too much. However, we do have other, more pressing decisions to make."

"The ring? Your dress? I know those things matter to women. I do want to have Logan perform the ceremony."

"Of course. And Becky will be my matron of honor. That wasn't what I was worried about."

"Then what? There's nothing you and I can't handle if we work it out together."

She pointed to the temporary cast on her swollen ankle. "I don't know how long it's going to take me to heal and I don't want to postpone our wedding for too long. Are you going to push me down the aisle in a wheelchair or shall we wait till I'm well enough to hobble?"

On the other side of the curtain between the beds, an elderly female patient tittered, then called, "Push her, son, push her. It'll probably be your last chance to be in charge for a good long time!"

Epilogue

❦

Becky had decorated Trudy Lynn's wheelchair with enough flowers and pastel ribbons to keep it from looking utilitarian and was preparing to escort her down the aisle of Serenity Chapel.

"I told you I could walk," Trudy Lynn whispered.

"I know you did. And I'm sure you'd manage. Except the doctor wants you to keep your weight off that leg for another four weeks."

"Maybe we should have put things off longer, made it a double wedding with Will and Earlene, now that he's finally gotten around to officially asking her to marry him."

Becky leaned over the bride's shoulder to whisper, "Not if you expected me to fit into this dress."

"I know." Trudy Lynn suppressed a giggle. "Have you told anybody else?"

"Besides you and Logan and Cody, no," Becky said. "The rumors will start to fly soon enough. I imagine it'll be like the whole church is expecting this baby."

"And I'll be an aunt!"

"Not till you marry my brother. He's waiting for you."

Trudy Lynn beamed. She'd never seen her beloved Cody look so handsome, so appealing. What a blessing to know that they shared not only their love, but also their faith. Suddenly, all she wanted was to go to him. To be near him.

She spoke aside to Becky. "I'm ready. Let's roll."

"You're supposed to wait for the organist to start playing 'The Wedding March.'"

"And if I don't? I'll still be married, won't I?"

"Of course, but…"

Trudy Lynn was laughing lightly at the astonishment on her friend's face as she laid her bouquet in her lap and reached for the large side wheels on her beribboned chrome chariot. One strong push forward sent the chair over the edge of the flat section of floor in the rear of the sanctuary and onto the sloping aisle that led to the altar. To Cody. To her future. As the old saying went, it was "downhill all the way."

Cody elbowed Logan. "Looks like my bride is in a hurry. Either that or she's out of control."

"Knowing Trudy Lynn she's probably both," the pastor said with admiration. "Brace yourself. Here she comes."

Cody was laughing as he helped his future wife

come to a full stop at the foot of the aisle. "Is that your last trick of the day or should I be ready for more?"

"I think I'm done." She was blushing. "I really didn't mean to go that fast."

"I know." Sobering, he lifted and supported her so she could stand beside him for the ceremony. "Don't worry. Whatever you do, I'll always be there to catch you," he promised quietly.

Trudy Lynn gazed at him through tears of thankfulness and incredible joy. "I wouldn't have it any other way."

* * * * *

Dear Reader,

In looking at the Scripture I chose for this book's theme, I was struck by how hard it sometimes is to accept the trials life brings us, whether they are only physical or go deeper as well, as Cody's did.

I don't pretend to have all the answers. Only in the realm of fiction can I make things work out the way I think they should. No one except God has the divine insight necessary to look ahead and see what the future holds for each of us, which is why I've decided to place my life in His hands, no matter what. Yes, I still slip and argue that my way is best from time to time, but in my heart I know that the Lord is patiently, lovingly watching over me—in the best and the worst of times.

If you don't have the assurance that you're God's child, I urge you to seek it. All you have to do is surrender your pride, ask Jesus to forgive and accept you right now, and He will. It's that easy.

I love to hear from readers. You can write to me at P.O. Box 13, Glencoe, AR 72539, contact me via my website, www.ValerieHansen.com, or send an email to Val@ValerieHansen.com.

Blessings,

Valerie Hansen

celebrating **15** YEARS

Love Inspired CLASSICS

Four sweet, heartfelt stories from fan-favorite
Love Inspired® Books authors!

The McKaslin clan returns with love and hope in

SWEET BLESSINGS and BLESSED VOWS

by Jillian Hart

And discover
another wonderful, heartfelt story of reconnection in

A SEASON FOR GRACE
and THE HEART OF GRACE

by Linda Goodnight

Get two happily-ever-afters for the price of one!

Available in July 2012 wherever books are sold.

www.LoveInspiredBooks.com

LIC65155

REQUEST YOUR FREE BOOKS!

2 FREE INSPIRATIONAL NOVELS
PLUS 2
FREE
MYSTERY GIFTS

YES! Please send me 2 FREE Love Inspired® novels and my 2 FREE mystery gifts (gifts are worth about $10). After receiving them, if I don't wish to receive any more books, I can return the shipping statement marked "cancel." If I don't cancel, I will receive 6 brand-new novels every month and be billed just $4.49 per book in the U.S. or $4.99 per book in Canada. That's a saving of at least 22% off the cover price. It's quite a bargain! Shipping and handling is just 50¢ per book in the U.S. and 75¢ per book in Canada.* I understand that accepting the 2 free books and gifts places me under no obligation to buy anything. I can always return a shipment and cancel at any time. Even if I never buy another book, the two free books and gifts are mine to keep forever.

105/305 IDN FEGR

Name   (PLEASE PRINT)

Address   Apt. #

City   State/Prov.   Zip/Postal Code

Signature (if under 18, a parent or guardian must sign)

Mail to the **Reader Service:**
IN U.S.A.: P.O. Box 1867, Buffalo, NY 14240-1867
IN CANADA: P.O. Box 609, Fort Erie, Ontario L2A 5X3

Not valid for current subscribers to Love Inspired books.

**Are you a subscriber to Love Inspired books
and want to receive the larger-print edition?
Call 1-800-873-8635 or visit www.ReaderService.com.**

* Terms and prices subject to change without notice. Prices do not include applicable taxes. Sales tax applicable in N.Y. Canadian residents will be charged applicable taxes. Offer not valid in Quebec. This offer is limited to one order per household. All orders subject to credit approval. Credit or debit balances in a customer's account(s) may be offset by any other outstanding balance owed by or to the customer. Please allow 4 to 6 weeks for delivery. Offer available while quantities last.

Your Privacy—The Reader Service is committed to protecting your privacy. Our Privacy Policy is available online at www.ReaderService.com or upon request from the Reader Service.

We make a portion of our mailing list available to reputable third parties that offer products we believe may interest you. If you prefer that we not exchange your name with third parties, or if you wish to clarify or modify your communication preferences, please visit us at www.ReaderService.com/consumerchoice or write to us at Reader Service Preference Service, P.O. Box 9062, Buffalo, NY 14269. Include your complete name and address.

LIREG11B

*For a sneak peek at Valerie Hansen's
heart-stopping inspirational romantic suspense
THREAT OF DARKNESS, read on!*

If Samantha Rochard hadn't already been so keyed up that she could barely think straight, she might have shrieked when she saw the cop's face. Her jaw did drop and she was pretty sure her gasp was audible. His light brown hair and eyes and his broad shoulders were all too familiar. It couldn't be him, of course. It simply couldn't be. She hadn't had one of these déjà vu moments for months. Maybe years.

Her pulse leaped as reality replaced imagination. She couldn't catch her breath. This was not another bad dream. John Waltham, the man who'd broken her heart so badly she'd wondered if she'd ever recover, was standing right in front of her, big as life.

Before she could decide how to greet him, he set the mood of their reunion. His "What did you think you were *doing?*" was delivered with such force it was practically a growl.

That attitude stiffened her spine and made it easy to answer, "My job."

"You're a nurse, not a cop."

"Oh, so I'm supposed to just stand there while you and your buddies waltz in here and start shooting?"

"If necessary, yes."

"Don't be silly. I knew Bobby Joe wasn't going to hurt me," she insisted, wishing she fully believed her own assertion. When an addict was under the influence, there was no way to predict what he or she might do.

Handling the pistol expertly, John unloaded it and passed

it to one of his fellow officers to bag as evidence before turning back to Samantha.

She noticed that his expression had softened some, but it was too little too late. "What are you doing back in town?" She eyed him from head to toe. "And why are you dressed like a member of our police force?"

"Because that's what I am. I've come home," he said flatly.

Samantha couldn't believe her ears. After all he'd put her through, all the tears she'd shed after he'd left her high and dry, he had the unmitigated gall to return and go back to work as if nothing had changed. How *dare* he!

Pick up THREAT OF DARKNESS
for the rest of Samantha and John's exciting, suspenseful
love story, available in June 2012, only from
Love Inspired® Suspense.

Love Inspired
SUSPENSE
RIVETING INSPIRATIONAL ROMANCE

FITZGERALD BAY

Law-enforcement siblings fight for justice and family.

Follow the men and women of Fitzgerald Bay as they unravel the mystery of their small town and find love in the process, with:

THE LAWMAN'S LEGACY by Shirlee McCoy
January 2012

THE ROOKIE'S ASSIGNMENT by Valerie Hansen
February 2012

THE DETECTIVE'S SECRET DAUGHTER
by Rachelle McCalla
March 2012

THE WIDOW'S PROTECTOR by Stephanie Newton
April 2012

THE BLACK SHEEP'S REDEMPTION by Lynette Eason
May 2012

THE DEPUTY'S DUTY by Terri Reed
June 2012